THE NOISE OF ZULU BATTLE

THE SOLDIER'S SON

BOOK I

MALCOLM ARCHIBALD

Published 2023 by Next Chapter

Edited by Graham (Fading Street Services)

Cover art by Lordan June Pinote

For Cathy

So, all day long the noise of battle rolled
Among the mountains by the winter sea.
Idylls of the King, by Alfred, Lord Tennyson

PART I

CHAPTER 1

ZULULAND, JUNE 1877

Jama halted and raised a hand. Obediently his small *amabutho* – regiment [1] - the Abanonya, stopped, crouched down and rested on the rustling grass of Zululand. Each man held an oval shield of stiffened cowhide, three foot six inches tall and two feet wide. The shields shared a pattern, with a black fringe around a white interior containing two black smudges. The warriors also held the *iKlwa,* the short stabbing spear the great King Shaka had introduced. With a shaft thirty inches long and an eighteen-inch long, one-and-a-half-inch wide blade, the *iKlwa* was lethal in the hands of a trained warrior, and each of Jama's men had been highly trained since youth.

As well as the stabbing *iKlwa*, the warriors held one or more throwing assegais- spears- and some carried knobkerries, heavy club-like weapons with a long shaft and a heavy knob used for braining the opponent. Only one carried a firearm, an ancient Brown Bess musket that had travelled a long way since its original owner, a British soldier, deserted from his regiment some forty years before.

"There is the king's *imuzi* – his homestead," Jama announced to his men.

Jama's *amabutho,* a mere hundred and twenty strong, looked and nodded solemnly. They were familiar with King Cetshswayo's royal *imuzi* of oNdini but paused to admire the spectacle before advancing.

oNdini, which the white people called Ulundi, was vast, far more extensive than the *imuzi* where they lived. Sitting on the quiet slopes easing from the valley of the White Umfolozi River, it was composed of thousands of *izindlu* – the local grass-built houses - behind a vast thornbush barrier, with an inner hedge enclosing a huge open space for cattle or ceremonies.

When he was satisfied his men had looked their fill, Jama led them down the slope to oNdini. He listened to the disciplined tramp of hard feet behind him and fought to contain his pride. These were his men, his warriors he was taking to meet Cetshwayo.

oNdini's gate was open, and the royal *amabuthos* of the Undi Corps lined the interior. Jama recognised each regiment by their shields, regalia, and the age of the warriors. He saw the uThulwane, 1,500 strong, and each man forty-four years old. He saw the Nkonkone, five hundred strong and two years younger than the uThulwane, with each man staring at his tiny *amabutho*. The Ndhlondhlo were there; the same age as the Nkonkone, they looked an impatient bunch of veterans. Beside them were the much younger inDluyengwe and finally the twenty-three-year-old inGobamakhosi, six thousand warriors all yearning for a chance to prove themselves in battle.

Jama studied each *amabutho*, comparing them to his Abanonya. The youngest regiments had all-black shields, and the most experienced carried all-white. Most regiments were in between, while mixed or married *amabuthos* carried red shields. Every warrior wore the *umuTsha,* a cord around the waist, with lengths of fur dangling in front and cowhide at the back. More senior regiments also wore extra fur and hide attached to the *umuTsha*. Decorative furs, feathers and hides augmented each warrior's basic clothing, each piece proudly worn, men proclaiming their allegiance and regiment.

Jama glanced back at his warriors as they trotted past the assembled Undi corps. They looked splendid with their leopard skin headbands, red cow tail necklaces and feathers that rustled beneath the knees. Each man of the Abanonya held himself proudly erect, ignored the jeers of their rival regiments and took their place in the assembly. Jama's oldest friend Ndleleni stood in the centre, with his necklace of *umzimbeet* seeds proving his bravery. Cetshwayo had granted Ndleleni the honour of wearing that badge of honour after the battle of Ndondakusuka over twenty years before.

After a few moments, Cetshwayo emerged from his *izindlu*; tall, broad-chested, and handsome with a neat beard, the king possessed the bearing of royalty and the powerful thighs common to his family. Every warrior in oNdini raised their spear and shouted the royal salute.

"*Bayete! Bayete!*"

Jama shouted with the rest, proud to be in the same *imuzi* as Cetshwayo, a descendant of Shaka, who was, in turn, a descendant of Zulu, the progenitor of the nation. As the name Zulu meant heaven, and all the clans and sub-clans within the Zulu empire adopted his name, they became the Children of Heaven.

King Cetshwayo was a proud man in a difficult situation. His kingdom bordered the Boers of the Transvaal on the northwest and the British colony of Natal on the southwest. To the north was Swaziland, while the Indian Ocean washed the western shore. Trouble could erupt across any of his borders.

"*Bayete*!" the warriors roared the royal salute. "*Bayete!*"

Cetshwayo knew his warriors wanted the opportunity to fight and were supremely confident of their ability to win against any enemy, yet the king did not want a war. His men carried assegais and shields, frighteningly lethal weapons at close quarters, but both British and Boers had firearms and fought at a distance. To defeat either, the Zulu warriors would have to endure concentrated rifle fire.

"*Bayete!*" the warriors shouted in a full-throated chorus. "*Bayete!*"

Cetshwayo acknowledged his people with an upraised hand.

Jama watched with awe as the king ordered the royal cattle herds to enter the vast central area. With cattle the mainspring of the Zulu economy, Cetshwayo was displaying his wealth.

The herds moved in unison, black cattle with black, white with white and red with red. They entered the *imuzi* in a ground-shaking rumble of thousands of hooves, with dust rising and the ground shaking. The assembled warriors stared in admiration. They knew their king was a powerful man and respected him even more for showing them his herds.

"*Bayete*!" an induna, the head of a regiment, shouted, and the others joined in, thrusting their spears to the sky. "*Bayete*!"

When all the warriors had witnessed the royal herds, Cetshwayo ordered the cattle away and addressed the *amabuthos*. Jama listened and watched as the king called the indunas to him and spoke to each man personally.

Eventually, Cetshwayo summoned Jama, who ran forward and prostrated himself on the ground.

"You, Jama, are induna of the Abanonya, the Vicious Ones."

Jama did not move, although he was proud that the king had recognised him, a minor induna of a small sub-clan.

"You are of the Quangebe clan." Cetshwayo displayed his impressive knowledge of his people and events in his kingdom. "Your chief Sihayo has his *imuzi* in the Batshe Valley, near the border with Natal."

Jama remained still, unsure whether to respond or not. As Cetshwayo continued, he knew it was better to stay silent.

"I want you and the Abanonya to keep watch on the Batshe Valley, Jama, and do not allow intruders into the land of the Zulus."

Jama allowed the words to burn into his soul. Serving the king was a warrior's duty; he had no other purpose in life.

"The white men in Natal, the British, are not to be trusted, Jama," Cetshwayo said. "Do not give them an excuse to start a war. Do not cross the Buffalo or the Tugela River into their lands."

Jama remained still until Cetshwayo dismissed him when he rose. The young woman behind the king smiled at him, and Jama recognised Thadie, one of Cetshwayo's relatives. He returned the smile, wishing he could make Thadie one of his wives, and trotted back to the Abanonya. He was proud his king had singled him out and knew his prestige and standing amongst the Abanonya had increased.

"THIS RIVER IS THE GREAT KEI." SERGEANT ASHANTI SMITH of the Frontier Armed and Mounted Police gestured with his right hand as his left held his horse's reins. "It is the boundary between British Kaffraria and Kaffirland, that is, the land of the free Kaffirs."

"What does Kaffir mean, Sergeant?" Andrew asked, looking across the river at a tangle of ochre and green hills scattered with trees. He could make out a small herd of cattle but no people.

Smith shrugged. "It's the name the Arabs give anybody who is not a Moslem, Constable Baird. I suppose it means unbeliever."

Andrew nodded. "We're Kaffirs too, then. It's not what the tribes call themselves, then?"

"No." Smith shook his head. "They might think of themselves as Xhosa, for they all speak that language. There are various tribes."

Andrew borrowed Smith's field glasses and stared across the river. "How many different tribes are there, Sergeant?"

"If you mean tribes, sub-tribes, and clans," Smith said, "There are probably hundreds. The main tribes are Galekas, Tambokies, Pondos, Bomvanas, Pondomise, and Fingoes." He paused for a moment. "To them, you may add the Gaikas under their chief Sandili, a drunken, dissipated old rogue who is waiting for somebody else to start trouble so he can raise his army. He hates us, of course."

"Do they all hate us?" Andrew asked.

Smith laughed, produced a pipe, and began to stuff tobacco into the bowl. "Probably," he said. "Kreli, the chief of the Galekas, certainly does. Gangeliswe of the Tambokies might do, and Moni of the Bomvanas. I'm not sure about Umquiqela of the Pondos. Umquiliso of the Pondomise is undoubtedly ready to attack."

Andrew stared across the Great Kei, wondering how many Xhosa warriors were watching him and whetting their assegais. "How about the Fingoes?"

Smith scratched a match and put it to his pipe. "They don't have a chief as such, but their head man is Veldtman, who is semi-educated. We can nearly trust the Fingoes on a good day." He puffed out aromatic blue smoke.

"It's reassuring that we have one friendly tribe in South Africa," Andrew said.

Smith smiled around the stem of his pipe. "Whatever they think of us, Baird, the tribes all have one thing in common. They all hate and fear the Zulus, the most powerful force in Black Africa."

"My knowledge of South African geography is vague, Sergeant," Andrew admitted. "Are the Zulus in Transkei as well?"

"No," Smith told him. "They are hundreds of miles north of here, bordering our Natal colony."

Andrew smiled. "I won't lose any sleep over them, then."

Smith removed his pipe and gave a gap-toothed smile. "Only a fool doesn't lose sleep over the Zulus."

"I'll bear that in mind," Andrew said. He watched others of the Frontier Armed and Mounted Police ride line up along the

Great Kei River. Most were in their twenties and thirties, and, to Andrew's eyes, their horses seemed overburdened for the duties they had to perform. In front of their leather saddle, they carried a waterproof coat, a valise, and an oversized blanket. These items of equipment reached nearly as high as their chin, impairing their vision. Behind the saddle, each rider carried two saddle bags, which banged against their flanks, while the troopers added personal equipment, such as a camp kettle, axe, or spare carbine.

"Are you all set, Baird?" Smith asked.

"As set as I'll ever be, Sergeant," Andrew replied.

Smith smiled. "The tribes are volatile at present," Smith told him. "I've knocked about across Africa for some years, Baird, and I've learned a thing or two. When the natives are insolent in the trading stores, and their witch doctors begin to doctor them, there is trouble in the wind."

"What do you mean, doctor them?" Andrew asked.

Smith removed the pipe from his mouth and added more tobacco, tamping it down with a calloused thumb. "When the witch doctors buy ox tails and skins from our stores or cut the tails from farmers' cattle, they are preparing some disgusting concoction to make their warriors invulnerable to our bullets." He replaced his pipe.

"Does it work, Sergeant?" Andrew asked.

"Not so far," Smith said, puffing blue smoke into the air. "But they're a superstitious bunch and believe in all sorts of charms and magic. They believe that wizards, *abaThakathis,* cause all illness and everything bad. These *abaThakathis* are like spirits that infest a plant, or a rock, an animal, or a human."

Smith removed the pipe from his mouth. "What's worse is that people don't know these spirits infest them. However, the witch doctors or witches can smell *abaThakathis.* As you may imagine, that gives the witches a special place in society."

"I can imagine," Andrew said. "A bit like our witch-finders in the seventeenth century."

"An apt analogy," Smith agreed. "As all the tribes fear the Zulus, even the bravest of Zulu warriors fear the witch doctors in case they smell an *abaThakathi* in them. Once the witch doctors condemn a warrior, his death is singularly unpleasant, so it's best to keep clear of those particular devils." He grinned. "You're a new chum here in Africa, Baird, but there's something about you I like. Stick with me, watch the skyline for movement and keep your carbine handy, and you'll be all right."

"Thank you; I'll do that," Andrew said. "I can't see any Xhosa here, though."

"Don't you?" Smith indicated a prominent hill beside the road. "This hill is Maunder's Kop," he said, guiding his horse with his knees and leaning back in the saddle. "Not long ago, a group of British officers rode to the top to view the countryside. It was a pleasure excursion, not a military expedition, but the local tribesmen took their chance."

"What happened, Sergeant?" Andrew asked.

"A horde of warriors scrambled up the side of the hill," Smith pointed to a nearly perpendicular track, "and attacked the officers. After a terrific struggle, the natives killed all the officers. Those they did not assegai, they grabbed and threw down the hill."

"Why?" Andrew asked.

Smith shrugged. "Ask the Xhosa, for I am sure I don't know. Presumably, because they were white men and vulnerable to attack. The moral of this story, young Baird, is never let your guard fall. However innocent the situation looks, danger could be lurking."

Andrew nodded. "I'll bear that in mind as well."

Smith lifted his Snider carbine. "This little beauty is your best friend out here, Baird. Its .577 cartridge is good; it's a man-stopper like the Martini-Henry and better than anything the enemy has. Keep it clean, oiled, and well-maintained, and it will repay you by saving your life."

Andrew nodded. "I know a little about guns," he said.

"You're fresh out from home," Smith said, more curtly than usual. "All your knowledge is theoretical. Until you've seen how your rifle acts in action, you know nothing about it and little about yourself. Did you shoot back home?"

"I did." Andrew did not want to give away his background.

"That's a start," Smith gave grudging praise. "Targets, clays or hunting?"

"All three," Andrew said with a faint smile.

"Even better." Smith seemed surprised. "Have you ever shot a man?"

"No, Sergeant." Andrew shook his head. "British law tends to frown on such things."

"It's one thing to fire and another to be fired at," Smith told him, "As you'll soon find out. The Galekas have attacked the Fingoes, who appealed to us for help." He tapped Andrew's shoulder with the stem of his pipe. "Why did you think we are on this patrol?"

"I wondered," Andrew said. "What happens now?"

"We help the friendly Fingoes, give the Galekas a bloody nose and hope the whole frontier does not explode." Smith puffed out smoke from his pipe. "You'll need a decent horse as well. Where did you get that beast?"

"The police supplied him." Andrew patted the neck of his raw-boned grey. "He's only temporary until I buy my own mount."

"Good." Smith nodded. "When you choose your horse, make sure he's salted. Distemper is rampant here, and you want one that's survived that disease." He removed the pipe from his mouth. "Do you know anything about horses, Baird?"

"A bit, Sergeant," Andrew replied cautiously. "I've been around horses all my life."

"Come on, Baird, you've been a frontier policeman for a month now. Time to earn your corn."

"THAT'S A RUM LOT OF BEASTS." ANDREW WALKED AROUND THE horses the dealer had brought to the barracks.

"You have two trials," Inspector Robert Fraser was a slender, straight-backed man with a florid face. "If you don't like either of the horses you choose, we'll allocate you a mount. Understood?"

Andrew, Hitchings, and Simpson, the three recruits, nodded.

"You have to pay for your horse," Fraser said, "so choose carefully."

Andrew circled the animals, inspecting each one. Most were in poor condition, underfed, undersized or nervous. When he asked about ages, the dealer shrugged and said, "Cape age," which meant anything from six to sixteen. Andrew stopped at one small, shaggy-looking animal of indeterminable age and looked into its eyes. "What's the provenance of this beast?"

The dealer, a thin-faced man with a loud checked suit and bowler hat, stepped closer. "A British officer brought that one from India," he said casually.

Andrew moved on as Hitchings and Simpson examined the taller, faster animals. He returned to the shaggy pony. "Has he been salted?"

"All my horses are salted," the dealer boasted.

"Let's see." Without bothering to saddle the horse, Andrew mounted and rode around the barrack square, whispering into the animal's ears. He returned within ten minutes, dismounted, and patted the horse's neck. "I'll take him," he said. "What happened to the previous owner?"

"He died of fever," the dealer said as Simpson and Hitchings laughed at Andrew's choice.

"That's not a horse," Simpson sneered. "It's only a pony! It's a girl's mount."

Hitchings spat on the ground. "Can't you manage a real horse, Baird?"

When Andrew said nothing, Inspector Fraser approached him. "Are you sure, Baird?"

"Yes, sir," Andrew replied. "He's a Kabul Pony, used to rough territory and with the heart of a lion. My father owned one."

Damn! Why did I say that? Andrew continued quickly to cover his wayward tongue.

"He's not the fastest horse in the world, but he'll ride through snow or heat in the worst conditions imaginable and keep going when thoroughbreds or Arabs give up." He patted the horse's neck. "I'll call him Lancelot."

"Lancelot, he is," Fraser said as Hitchings and Simpson looked on, sneering.

ON THE 18TH OF SEPTEMBER 1877, THE FRONTIER POLICE assembled at Ibeka, right on the border between the Fingoes and the Galekas. They fed the horses and erected their tents, ready to help the beleaguered Fingoes as they wondered what the future held.

There was nothing much to the tiny settlement and a potentially hostile nation on their doorstep, so for seven gruelling days, the men laboured to secure the camp. Using picks, spades, and a great deal of sweat, they dug trenches and threw up mud walls in case of a Galeka attack.

"There's nothing the Xhosa like less than attacking entrenchments or defended laagers," Inspector Fraser informed the toiling police. "The harder we work now, the easier life will be later."

Smith waited until Fraser was away before he grunted. "You'll notice the man giving the orders is not the man wielding the spade." He stopped to fill his pipe. "If you aim to make a career here, boys, don't stay at the bottom. Get a commission, and then you can give the orders rather than taking them."

Andrew said nothing, digging his spade into the stony ground and wondering why he was there. He looked across the narrow path that marked the boundary into the Galeka's territory and contemplated what sort of people lived there.

"Are you all right, Baird?" Fraser asked cheerfully, running a hand down his long face.

"Yes, sir," Baird said.

"You were looking pensive there. Cheer up; once we get the place more secure, we'll have a look into Fingoland. Tour a little, show the flag and eye up the opposition." He winked, raised a hand, and walked on with his hands behind his back. Andrew noticed the inspector had unbuttoned the flap of his pistol holster while the carbine across his back was ready to use. For all his flippant tone, Inspector Fraser was prepared if the Galekas attacked.

Andrew lifted another spadefuls of stony dust and piled it on the wall. He had not expected to be a navvy when he joined the Frontier Police. That thought raised the question: what had he expected?

Andrew shook his head. He had joined to escape his family heritage rather than search for a bright future. He did not dislike his family, but neither did he wish them to control his life. Andrew continued to dig, with the hot African sun bringing sweat to his body and a host of flies tormenting him.

"THAT'S LOOKING GOOD," ASHANTI SMITH APPROVED, studying the trenches and embrasures. "I doubt any Galekas would wish to rush us now."

Andrew estimated Smith to be in his late thirties or early forties, with a face that showed the years had not come easily to him. He walked warily, balancing on the soles of his feet, and his eyes were rarely static as he surveyed the surrounding terrain.

"Have you fought the Galekas before, Sergeant?" Andrew asked.

"No." Smith shook his head. "I've fought Ashantis in West

Africa and Paythans in India, but never Galekas. I reckon that will change soon."

Andrew brushed away a persistent fly. "How soon, Sergeant?"

"Very soon," Smith told him. "Top up your water bottle and make sure your carbine is oiled and clean. We're joining Number Five troop on patrol."

"Whither bound, Sergeant?" Andrew asked, glad of something to break the monotony of digging trenches and rifle pits.

"Ours not to reason why," Smith replied. "Ours but to bleed and die. In other words, young policeman, I have no idea. Pack up your bags and keep your powder dry."

"Yes, Sergeant," Andrew said. He felt an unusual mixture of apprehension and excitement. *I wonder if my father felt like this before he went on a campaign.* He shook his head. *No, he'd be calm and relaxed, looking for the opportunity to be a hero.*

At nine that morning, Andrew joined the little column of a hundred and forty men, a seven-pounder mountain gun and a handful of officers as they rode through the gate, around the newly completed entrenchments and into the brightness of the day. A handful of local Xhosa watched them, holding shields and assegais and saying nothing. Andrew eyed them, wondering if he might be fighting them soon.

"Me too," Smith murmured. "Keep your finger near the trigger, Bairdie, and watch your back."

Inspector Chalmers halted the column ten minutes march from the camp. "Gather round, gentlemen."

Andrew joined the others in crowding close to Chalmers while Smith kept a wary watch on the surroundings.

Chalmers gave them a few moments to settle down. "You may have heard that the Galekas attacked our friends, the Fingoes, on the government reserve near Guadana Hill. We are going to have a look and make peace if we can." He nodded to a bearded, sun-browned colonial. "Sergeant Duncan, you're a local man and know the tribes better than most. Take your section and ride in front. I don't want any surprises."

"Well, now we know," Smith said as they resumed their march along the main road, with the horses kicking up dust and the African sun beating on their heads and shoulders. Ochre-tinted or green hills surrounded them, with the occasional trees, small groups of round, thatched-roofed *izindlu,* and some grazing cattle. A woman, her face daubed in white clay and smoking a homemade pipe, stood outside one of the *izindlu*, watching them without responding to Andrew's wave.

"She's probably counting our numbers," Smith said.

"Or wondering who we are, passing her house." Andrew remembered the curiosity of people in rural Northumberland and Berwickshire. He tried again.

"*Molo*!" he shouted, using one of the few Xhosa words he knew. "Hello!"

"*Molo! Ujani*!" the woman replied, lifting her pipe in greeting. Her wide smile took Andrew by surprise. "Hello, how are you?"

"*Ndiphile enkosi unjani wena*," Andrew completed his Xhosa vocabulary. "I'm fine, thank you, how are you?"

When the woman replied with a long sentence Andrew could not grasp, he waved again.

Inspector Fraser gave Andrew an approving nod. "You've learned some Xhosa then, Baird."

"Only a few words, sir," Andrew said.

"More than most new chums learn in such a short time," Fraser said and rode on.

"While you've been sweet talking to the ladies," Smith said, "the natives have been gathering." He nodded to the skyline. "Somebody's watching us."

Andrew saw a small group of natives behind a clump of trees. As the police patrol drew near, two men broke away and sprinted to the north, with the sun glinting from the points of their assegais.

"They're off to warn Kreli," Smith said calmly, filling his pipe. "Don't be surprised if the whole Galeka army appears within the hour."

"Sergeant Smith," Inspector Fraser shouted. "Take two men and apprise Duncan of the situation. Scout ahead and be careful."

"Sir!" Smith responded. "You're with me, Bairdie, and you, Hitchings."

Hitchings was a tall, brown-haired, smooth-faced man to whom Andrew had taken an instant dislike. The three men kicked ahead of the column, with Andrew feeling suddenly vulnerable. The friendly locals of the morning had altered in his mind to predatory warriors waiting to attack him. He checked his carbine was secure in its bucket beside the saddle.

"Gunfire!" Smith held up his right hand. "Careful now, lads." He glanced around, quartering the ground with suddenly hard eyes.

Andrew became aware of the crackle ahead and shivered with a mixture of excitement and apprehension as he reached for his carbine.

"Is that gunfire, Sergeant?" Hitchings asked.

"It certainly is," Smith said tersely. He raised his voice. "Hitchings, you're rear guard. I'll go in front and, Baird, you're the meat in the sandwich. Watch the flanks and warn us if you see anything untoward."

They walked their horses forward, with Andrew's nerves jangling, expecting the Galekas to shoot him or charge with poised assegais at every step. He smelled smoke drifting in the faint breeze and heard what might have been the murmur of insects.

"There!" Smith said. "Half a mile ahead!" He halted his horse and motioned Andrew and Hitchings to join him. "Look!" He passed over his field glasses.

Andrew focussed the glasses and saw a confused mass of men, with sunlight flashing from the blades of assegais and smoke rising from burning *izindlu*.

"Here comes Duncan," Smith said as three horsemen thundered into view.

"Smith!" Duncan shouted. "There's trouble ahead! Don't go any further!"

"We've seen it," Smith said. "You two, Baird and Hitchings, ride back to Inspector Chalmers and tell him the Galekas are burning the kraals and killing the Fingoes," Smith said. "I'll wait here and observe."

Andrew hesitated for a moment, not wishing to leave Smith in danger.

"Go!" Smith snapped. "That's an order!"

Hitchings was already away, and Andrew followed, allowing Lancelot to stretch its legs on the dusty road. Duncan rode at his side, glancing behind him from time to time.

"I'll make the report, Baird," Duncan said.

"Yes, Sergeant," Andrew agreed.

The inspector considered for only a moment, then sent Hitchings two miles back towards Ibeka. "Find Mr Ayliff," Chalmers ordered. "He's there with a company of Fingos. Tell him to hurry along with his Fingo warriors."

"Now what, Sergeant?" Andrew asked.

"Now we wait," Sergeant Duncan said and winked. "Welcome to the Frontier Police, my boy, where we have ninety-nine hours of routine and waiting, followed by one hour of terror."

Andrew forced a lopsided grin and looked ahead, listening as the wind carried the faint popping of musketry.

CHAPTER 2

The police waited in the heat, listening to the distant crackle of gunfire.

"What's the to-do?" Smith cantered to Andrew with his forage hat pushed to the back of his head, puffing smoke from his pipe. "I thought Chalmers would bring the boys up."

"We're waiting for Ayliff's Fingoes, Sergeant," Andrew said.

"Are we, now?" Smith said. "By the time they arrive, the Galekas will have massacred half of Fingoland." He shrugged. "Not that it's any of my concern, but the women and children might feel a little miffed."

"Here they come now, Sergeant," Hitchings said.

The Fingoes marched or rode up the track, seemingly in no hurry to fight the invading Galekas. Some were dressed in cast-off European clothing, others in the traditional native blanket, while a few wore a mixture of both. While a few carried the usual assegais and shields, most had firearms, from ancient muskets that looked as if they would explode if fired to more modern Sniders as good as the carbine Andrew held.

"They're actually called Fengu, not Fingoes." A slender, gaunt-faced constable gestured to one warrior who wore

European clothes, a broad-brimmed hat and carried a long rifle. "And some of them are a damned sight better marksmen than we are."

"Is that so?" Andrew asked.

"It is so," the slender man said. "Walter Abernethy, by the way." He proffered his hand.

"Andrew Baird." Andrew shook the hand. Abernethy's grip was frank and powerful.

"The Xhosa tribes called them amaMfengu, which means "wanderers," and say that the Fengu, or Fingoes, came from the tribes the Zulu king Shaka shattered. They fled from the Zulu and settled here." Abernethy tamped a quarter inch of tobacco into the bowl of his pipe. "The Xhosa, particularly the Galekas, or Gcalakas to give them their proper name, called the Fengu their dogs and treated them abominably, as one would expect."

"Would one?" Andrew asked.

"The quality of mercy is not a recognised virtue in these parts," Abernethy said as he struck a match and began to puff smoke into the air. "Anyway, the Fengu came to the British for help and have proved valuable allies ever since."

"What's this current disturbance about?" Andrew asked.

"Drought, land and cattle," Abernethy told him. "Cattle is wealth for these people, and we've had years of drought here, leading to dry riverbeds and thirsty cattle." He looked up, holding his pipe between clenched teeth. "The trouble came to a head when some Fingoes brawled with a mob of Galekas at a wedding. So now you know."

"Now I know," Andrew agreed. "The usual reasons, clan warfare over resources and a drunken brawl. The same here as everywhere else." He sighed. "When will people learn to share what they have rather than grabbing everything for themselves?"

Abernethy raised his eyebrows. "That's a politician's question, not a policeman's," he said.

"Blame my father for that," Andrew said and quickly clamped his mouth shut.

"Hello, things are happening." Abernethy did not comment on Andrew's statement.

Inspector Chalmers and Ayliff conferred briefly, and Ayliff led his Fingo warriors up a nearby hill, where lone trees struggled up from the brown-ochre grass.

"That's Guadana Hill," Abernethy said. "The Fingoes are on this side and the Galekas on the other." He grinned. "Or rather, the Galekas have moved onto the Fingo side from the other."

Smith joined them. "It looks like the entire Galeka army has crossed into Fingo land," he said. "We have our work before us, however many Fingo warriors pretend to help."

"Come on, boys," Inspector Chalmers ordered. "Let's push the Galekas back where they belong." He posted the Fingoes onto the flanks, so they advanced along the hill slopes while the Mounted Police marched along on the road.

"Half a league, half a league, half a league onward
Into the valley of death rode the six hundred."[1]

No, this is not the place for Tennyson. Try something else.

Andrew changed Tennyson for *Blue Bonnets Over the Border* and closed his mouth.

"It's all right to be nervous," Smith told him. "We all are the first time. Just remember to aim low and watch your back." He winked. "You'll be all right, Bairdie. I'll keep my eye on you."

"Thanks, Sergeant," Andrew said. He felt some of his nerves ease at the thought of Smith looking out for him.

As the Fingoes began to shout and point ahead, the Mounted Police rounded a spur of the road, and Chalmers, leading from the front, held up a hand. The column halted, the dust slowly settled, and Andrew stared ahead.

"There they are, boys." Smith spoke as if offering a gift. Andrew stopped, taking a deep breath. He had grown up in a military family, hearing tales of military valour and bloody battles. His parents had met during the Indian Mutiny, and Andrew had watched his father's gradual rise through the officer's ranks. Now, he saw a hostile army for the first time.

Here we go. Welcome to the family business.

Andrew had expected the Galekas to be a formless mob carrying assegais. Instead, their commander had arranged them in three disciplined divisions, many carrying rifles. As soon as the Galekas saw the small force of police, they began to move forward.

"Now we'll have some sport," Abernethy said. He patted his horse's neck, added more tobacco to his pipe and checked his carbine was loaded.

"Sub-lieutenant Cochrane," Chalmers said softly to the artillery commander. "Does your seven-pounder have the range?"

"Yes, sir," Cochrane replied with a slight smile.

"Then fire," Chalmers ordered.

"Yes, sir," Cochrane said and gave a string of orders to his gunners. "Range! Elevation! Fire!"

Andrew started when Cochrane fired the mountain gun, with the report louder than he had expected. He saw the shell explode amongst the first division of the Galekas, knocking down a score of tribesmen and delaying their advance.

"Dismount!" Chalmers snapped. "Leave the horses and extend across the brow of the hill in skirmishing order!"

Andrew followed Smith's lead, waiting on the right of the gun as the Galekas continued their advance. The Fingoes were on the left, with their flank ending in an area of woodland known as the Guadana Forest.

Andrew felt a mixture of excitement and apprehension as the Galekas advanced, wavering every time a shell burst among them. He felt the sweat forming on his forehead, wiped it from his hands and gripped his carbine. His mouth felt dry, and he wondered how Smith and Fraser could look so calm.

"When we fought the Ashantis," Smith murmured, still holding his pipe between his teeth. "We hardly saw them. They hid in the forest and blasted us with their slug guns. These Galekas fight in the open, like men."

Andrew forced a grin and tried to make a joke, but the words caught in his throat.

"There's bloody thousands of them!" Hitchings' voice rose an octave.

"Which gives us more targets," Sergeant Duncan said. "Shut your mouth and fire low."

Andrew wriggled closer to the illusionary protection of a stunted thorn tree and pulled his carbine against his shoulder. A fly landed on a leaf beside his head, intent on its own world and unaware of the incipient violence humanity was about to create.

It is strange how humans and nature can co-exist side-by-side, yet each within its own orbit. Jesus, I am scared. Don't show it. Pretend you're as brave as Ashanti there, as immobile as Muckle Cheviot. Dear God, I hope I don't make a fool of myself. Concentrate on firing and forget what's coming your way, Andrew.

The three Galeka divisions gradually merged to form a single vast column, brandishing their weapons, and shouting to encourage each other. Cochrane's shells continued to pound them, tearing holes in their ranks, knocking warriors down and sending pieces of men high into the air.

How can they continue to attack through that? They must be brave men.

"They're nearly in range," Smith thundered. "Don't rush your shots, Bairdie; aim low and never mind their shooting. They always fire high and wild."

Andrew gave a weak smile. "There's a terrible lot of them."

"Every time the seven-pounder fires, there's less," Smith said.

Abernethy chewed on the stem of his pipe, puffed out smoke and hugged his Snider close to his cheek.

"Riflemen, fire!" Chalmers ordered.

Thank God! I can do something now rather than watch and wait.

Immediately Chalmers spoke, the police opened fire. Andrew took a deep breath, released it slowly, aimed into the mass of Galekas and fired. Without checking if he had hit his man, he ejected the spent round, thumbed in a brass cartridge, and fired again. He coughed as gun smoke caught at the back of his throat.

So, this is what it's like to be a soldier.

The combination of artillery and musketry stalled the Galekas' advance. They stopped, sought cover, and returned fire, with the muzzle flares stretching across the whole front. What sounded like a thousand bees buzzed and whined above the police's positions.

"Hold your ground," Chalmers ordered as the Fingoes also opened up. Gunsmoke wreathed the hillside, stinging Andrew's eyes and making him cough. He heard the whine of a bullet above his head and flinched when something scored the tree beside him. Splinters of bark and wood showered on his head.

"You couldn't hit a bull's arse with a banjo!" Hitchings sneered and laughed as he knocked back two tribesmen in two shots. "Keep bobbing up, boys, and I'll keep knocking you down!"

The mountain gun fired slowly, aiming for knots of the enemy to inflict more significant casualties, but the Galekas learned quickly, finding cover, and returning fire. For every shot the police and Fingoes fired, the Galekas fired four, adding to the noise with war cries, chants, and screams.

"Don't fire too fast," Smith warned Andrew. "Conserve your ammunition. We don't know how long this battle will last."

"The Xhosa don't like the seven-pounder," Abernethy said, still with the pipe between his teeth. "They don't understand where the explosions are coming from."

"Thank God for the guns," Hitchings said, thumbing in another cartridge. He ducked as a bullet whined overhead, gave a lopsided smile, and glanced behind him.

"The enemy is over there." Duncan jerked a thumb towards the Galeka. "Face your front, Hitchings, and earn your pay!"

Andrew saw Simpson lying close to the ground, firing without aiming and whimpering whenever a shot passed overhead.

When a Galeka warrior stood up and ran a few paces forward, Andrew aimed, traversed his carbine as if he were pheasant shooting in Berwickshire, and squeezed the trigger. He saw the warrior leap in the air as the bullet hit and felt a surge of satisfaction, instantly followed by regret.

That is a human being, not a game bird. A moment later, Andrew heard a loud curse from the artillerymen.

"Something's up," Abernethy sounded worried. "The gun's stopped firing."

Andrew looked round to see the artillerymen clustered around the seven-pounder, talking animatedly. The artillery sergeant ran to Chalmers, who nodded.

"The gun will retire under Mr Cochrane and the escort!" Chalmers ordered.

"The bloody thing's broken!" Hitchings shouted. "The Xhosas will run right over us!"

"Riflemen, hold the line!" Chalmers ordered as the seven-pounder began a slow withdrawal, with its escort keeping close to ensure the Galekas did not charge to capture the weapon.

"Keep firing, Bairdie!" Smith said, as calm as ever. "Hitchings is right. Once the enemy realises we've no artillery support, they'll advance again."

"There go the Fingoes," Inspector Fraser said as their allies fled in sudden panic. Some dropped their weapons, and others merely turned and ran, leaving the few dozen police to face thousands of Galeka warriors.

The Galekas raised a loud shout, encouraging each other to charge.

"Time to go, boys," Smith said, glancing hopefully at Inspector Chalmers. "We can't hold this lot on our own."

Realising the gun no longer tormented them, the Galekas grew bolder, creeping closer and firing more accurately. Hitchings swore when a bullet buried into the ground at his feet, and another whined dangerously close to his head.

"Let's get out of here!"

Andrew reloaded, checked his ammunition pouch, and realised he had only a dozen cartridges left. "What happens now, Sergeant?" He tried to sound nonchalant even though his heart was pounding madly.

Smith ducked as a Galeka bullet whistled close overhead. "Whatever the officers say, Bairdie, when the Galekas come close enough to throw their assegais, old Ashanti leaves." He grinned. "Duty is all very well, but self-preservation is a wonderful thing. I already have an Ashanti slug in my leg, and I don't want any more African souvenirs, thank you kindly."

"We'll have to wait for orders." Andrew glanced over his shoulder, where Inspector Chalmers was standing tall, sweeping the battlefield with his field glasses. Chalmers lowered his glasses to speak a few words to Fraser.

"Take some free advice, Bairdie," Smith said. "When it's a choice between saving your life and waiting for an officer to make up his mind, your life comes first every time."

A group of Galeka warriors rose and charged forward, screaming their battle cry. Andrew shot into them, saw one man fall and hastily reloaded, fumbling his cartridges as he controlled his nerves. Sergeant Duncan fired while Andrew closed the breech of his Snider. "Don't rush, Baird," Duncan said. "Treat a battle like a training exercise and follow the procedure we taught you."

"Yes, Sergeant," Andrew said.

"The Fingoes have scattered the horses," Hitchings yelled. "Look!"

Andrew glanced over his shoulder and saw several police horses had broken loose and were running in different directions. The retreating Fingoes were among them, with some grabbing mounts for themselves.

They'd better not take Lancelot.

"Get ready to run, boys," Smith said a second before Inspector Chalmers gave the order to retire.

"The Mounted Police will retire by numbers!"

"About bloody time," Smith said as Simpson turned and ran, losing his forage cap in the process.

Andrew heard a peculiar whizz and saw an assegai flick past him to thud into the tree at his side. The long blade embedded deeply into the trunk, with the shaft vibrating with the force of the throw.

"Come on, Bairdie!" Smith grabbed his arm. "This is no time to admire the view!"

The Galekas were advancing fast, encouraged by the diminished fire from the retreating allies. One warrior leapt in front of his comrades, carrying a traditional shield and a stabbing assegai and with a circlet of green feathers around his head. Smith turned and fired in the same movement, bringing the man down.

"And that's done for you, cully," Smith said. Dashing forward, he stooped, plucked two feathers from the warrior's head, and returned. Smiling, he attached the feathers to his forage cap. "I'll have these as souvenirs, my valiant Galeka friend."

"Form a firing line!" Chalmers ordered. "Inspector Fraser! Your troop will cover the retiral!"

"Yes, sir!" Fraser said. "Extended order, men. Fire at will, and don't let anybody fall behind."

"God help anybody the Galekas get hold of," Smith said.

Andrew rammed a cartridge into the breech of his Snider, knelt and aimed. The Galekas were about forty yards away, advancing at a run, with some firing and others throwing their assegais. Andrew fired and loaded without observing the effect of his shot. He heard the whizz-thud of another thrown assegai, fired again, and scrabbled for another cartridge in his ammunition pouch. "I'm running short," he said.

"We all are," Smith said.

"Mount and ride!" Fraser ordered. "Come on, lads. Time we were gone!"

Andrew saw that most of the police had already grabbed their horses and ridden down the slithering slope onto the road. He saw Lancelot running loose, seized the bridle and threw himself onto the saddle, thanking God that he was a good rider. When a Galeka warrior grabbed for the bridle, Andrew booted him away, glanced at a yelling face with wild eyes and kicked again, swearing. The tribesman fell back, and Andrew turned Lancelot and headed down the hill.

He heard somebody screaming and saw three Galekas repeatedly stabbing their assegais into the back of a dismounted policeman. He hesitated a second, saw the policeman lie still, decided he was already dead and thrust in his spurs.

More Galekas appeared, running alongside the retreating police. One warrior threw his assegai at Andrew, who ducked, swivelled in the saddle, and fired in the same movement. He did not see where the bullet landed but concentrated on controlling Lancelot.

"Rally here!" Inspector Chalmers stood in the middle of the road with a carbine in his hand and his forage cap missing. Half a dozen police rode to him, with Fraser on the road, counting his troop.

"Sergeant Duncan! Baird! Go to Inspector Chalmers!"

Andrew obeyed, panting, thankful for a return to disciplined normality. He noticed the seven-pounder was already half a mile away, with its escort ensuring no Galeka came close.

Smith reined up beside Andrew, panting, with sweat forming grooves through the dust on his sun-browned face. "That was a trifle hot," he said, loading his carbine. "I have three cartridges left."

Andrew nodded. "One less than me, Sergeant."

The Galekas hesitated when they saw a disciplined force waiting for them, but when they realised how few police there were, they began to work around the flanks.

"Pull back," Chalmers ordered. "One troop covering the other."

The police obeyed, keeping between the gun and the advancing Galekas until the tribesmen halted their pursuit and celebrated their victory with an impromptu dance.

"Listen to them celebrate," Hitchings said. "You'd think they'd won the Battle of Waterloo."

"Don't worry," Smith told him. "By the time they tell and retell the story of this little skirmish, they'll make it sound like they defeated the entire British Army rather than pushed back a handful of police."

Andrew said nothing; he was shaking with reaction after his first battle.

CHAPTER 3

"We lost six men and an officer," Smith said as they retired slowly towards Ibeka, "but I'd guess we accounted for at least two hundred of the enemy."

Andrew nodded and closed his eyes, seeing the sights and sounds of his first battle again.

I killed a man today, he thought. *Maybe more than one man. I do not know how many.*

Impressions of the battle returned to him. That unfortunate policeman, as the Galeka pounced on him, assegais stabbing. The tribesman he had shot and how the Snider bullet sent him spinning backwards. The spear that missed him by a couple of inches and thrummed into the tree.

"You're a veteran now." Smith broke into Andrew's thoughts.

"I don't feel like a veteran," Andrew said. He touched the gold signet ring on the index finger of his right hand, with his embossed initials intertwined. His mother had given him that on his seventeenth birthday as he left the family home for Sandhurst. "Do your best," she had said, with her white teeth gleaming in her dark face, "and remember who you are."

"I won't forget," Andrew had replied.

And now I am denying my identity every day. All I need is the crow of a cock, thrice repeated.

"Are you all right, Bairdie?" Abernethy asked, with his gaunt, haunted face a hint that he was also running from his past, and perhaps with more reason.

Everyone has a story.

"I am grand, thank you." Andrew mustered a smile.

"Who goes there?" Andrew heard the challenge when the weary police approached the Ibeka trenches.

"It's us, you stupid bugger!" Smith replied.

"Advance and be recognised." Andrew heard the tension in the sentry's voice. Two police rose from behind their entrenchments, with carbines ready to fire.

"Where did you lot come from?" a lanky corporal with a wispy beard asked. "We heard you were all dead!"

"Not yet, corporal," Smith snarled, "but if you don't take your finger off the trigger, we might soon be!"

"Sorry, Sergeant!" The corporal lifted the barrel of his carbine.

The garrison greeted the returning police as if they were heroes, more from relief than pleasure.

"We thought you were all dead." A dozen men repeated the sentry's statement.

"Not yet," Chalmers said tersely. "We'll have to get this place in condition to withstand an attack."

Andrew found the camp at Ibeka awash with rumours. A few frantic Fingoes had arrived with exaggerated reports of the skirmish, claiming the Galekas had massacred all the police and were advancing on the camp to finish the job. The police left in camp had heard the distant firing, believed the worst, and spent the night manning the defences and hourly expecting the entire Galeka army to arrive.

"How far behind you are the Fingoes?" a nervous constable asked.

"I have no idea," Abernethy replied coldly. "Why don't you

go and find out? I'll hold the fort for you."

"Fill your ammunition pouches," Chalmers ordered tersely. "We don't know if the Galekas will follow us. Fraser, find a fresh horse, grab a bite, and take a patrol out to see what's happening."

"As you know, gentlemen," Inspector Fraser reminded his men. "We are right on the border of Galekaland, with the nearest European settlement, Butterworth, only seven miles distant. We are also on the best road, so if the Galekas want to invade the Cape, they'll have to pass us first."

Andrew looked at the small garrison of police and the shaken Fingoes and wondered at Fraser's confident tone.

The inspector continued. "That means we'll have to hold them here. Conversely, we can expect no help. As you know, the Butterworth road is badly rutted and marred by large boulders." He grinned. "We're on our own, fellows!"

Andrew glanced at Smith, who winked and adjusted the two green feathers in his forage cap. "Do you regret joining the Frontier Police now, Bairdie?"

Andrew pondered the question. *What would my father do, damn him? He would fight.*

"No, I don't regret a thing," Andrew said, fighting his fear.

"Good man!" Fraser clapped Andrew on the shoulder.

Apart from the police camp, Ibeka had a single European house-cum-store-cum-stable, with a man named John Barnett as the owner.

"Are the Galekas coming, Sergeant?" Barnett asked Smith.

"I'd expect so," Smith replied. "They'll be buoyant at their victory and imagine they can push us back to Cape Town."

"Then we're leaving," Barnett decided.

Loading his family and personal possessions onto a wagon, Barnett left Ibeka and chanced the rocky road to Butterworth. Within a few hours of Barnett's departure, a new commandant, Charles Griffiths, arrived to take command of the camp. Scorning the tents of the garrison, Griffiths requisitioned Barnett's house.

"This will do me," he said. "We'll have the store as a hospital. Inspector Chalmers! Move all the spare ammunition into the shop." He stalked around his new command, issuing orders to strengthen the defences.

"The commandant expects trouble," Hitchings said, eying the road to Butterworth.

"So do I," Smith said as the police sweated with spades on the hard ground, creating more rifle trenches around the encampment and filling and carrying sandbags for bastions for the three artillery pieces.

"Join the police and work up a sweat," Hitchings said as he dropped a sandbag in front of the central seven-pounder. "All this for five shillings a day, less expenses, which amounts to about ninepence in my pocket."

Andrew said nothing as he looked at the nearby hills. He guessed the Galekas would be there, spying on everything the police did. He could nearly taste the apprehension in the camp. These men were police, not trained regular soldiers. They had not signed up for a last stand against overwhelming numbers of warriors.

"I'm looking for volunteers," Griffiths shouted. "I want a party to return to the battlefield and recover the bodies of our men."

Andrew stepped forward, remembering the constable he had seen die. "I'll go, sir," he said and realised most of the police had volunteered. He saw Fraser watching him through narrowed eyes.

Smith put a hand on Andrew's arm. "Don't volunteer," he said quietly. "Take my advice, Bairdie and don't volunteer for anything. Keep your head below the parapet if you want to live longer. It's fourteen miles from here to Guadana, and that means you are marching for fourteen miles in hostile territory, with the Galekas watching you every foot of the way. Only a fool puts his head in a lion's mouth and expects it not to bite."

"I saw the Galekas killing one of our men," Andrew

explained. "I wonder if I might have done more to help him."

"You couldn't," Smith told him. "It was every man for himself in that mad scramble down the hill."

"Baird," Chalmers said. "You come along too. Make sure you have ammunition and water."

"Yes, sir," Andrew said as Smith shook his head sorrowfully.

The patrol left half an hour later, with Chalmers leading twenty-five men towards the battlefield. Abernethy had also volunteered, riding alongside Andrew with his eyes dark and his mind evidently on something else.

"Back into your valley of death, eh, Baird?" Abernethy said. "Let's hope the Russians haven't loaded their cannon."

Andrew grinned, glad that Abernethy understood the literary associations.

Augmenting the police, a body of nervous Fingoes trotted at the side, carrying rifles and an assortment of assegais.

Chalmers nodded to Duncan. "Sergeant Duncan, take two experienced men and a dozen Fingoes as scouts. Watch for the Galekas."

Duncan nodded, selected a colonial and an ex-soldier and trotted ahead. The dust rose and slowly settled as Chalmers continued the slow advance. Riding three ranks back, Abernethy thrust an empty pipe into his mouth and hummed an unrecognisable tune.

Andrew felt as if he were venturing into hostile territory as the patrol advanced cautiously into Fingoland. Every man was on edge, with fingers curled around the triggers of their Sniders and their eyes constantly roving around the surrounding hills.

"I see two tribesmen," Abernethy said quietly. "They are beneath the crest of the hill, watching us."

Andrew stared without seeing anything.

"Don't look directly," Abernethy told him. "Look for things that don't belong, maybe a static shadow when others are moving or a solid block of one colour in a variegated bush. See that twisted tree beneath the skyline?"

"I see the tree," Andrew said.

"Good. Can you see the second tree close to the bole?"

Andrew nodded. "Yes."

"Well, that's a man watching us."

When Andrew concentrated, he could make out the figure of a man, partly concealed beneath a blanket. "I can barely see him," he admitted.

"You'll get your eye in," Abernethy reassured him.

"How do you know what to look for?" Andrew asked.

"I've knocked around a bit," Abernethy said.

About to ask more, Andrew saw the taut expression on Abernethy's face and closed his mouth. Some questions were best left unanswered.

The patrol continued, with Duncan and his scouts riding wide, inspecting isolated bushes, and swivelling to check the ground behind them. The watchers remained on the hill, following the police without descending.

"Here we are," Chalmers said when they reached the battle site. "Scouts, keep your eyes open."

"We will, sir," Duncan promised.

Andrew heard the buzz of flies before he realised they had been feasting on the bodies of the dead police. All the Galeka dead were gone, but the police remained beneath a black fur of insects.

"The Galeka have mutilated the bodies." Simpson sounded shocked.

"They always do," Abernethy told him. "It's their little way." He gave an entirely humourless smile. "Let's just pray the lads were dead before the Galeka began their butchery."

"Here's poor Evans." A man pointed to the man Andrew had seen killed. He stooped closer to inspect the body. "He's got seventeen assegai wounds, and the Galeka have ripped his stomach open."

"They rip open the stomach of everybody they kill," Abernethy said. "Such charming neighbours we have in this part of the world."

"Why?" Andrew asked. "Why tear the stomach open?"

"The Xhosa believe that if they don't, the ghost of those they kill will haunt them," Abernethy explained. "The Zulus do the same."

"Come on, lads," Chalmers ordered. "Sergeant Duncan, take twelve men and form a defensive perimeter. The rest of us will collect our dead."

Duncan selected the most experienced fighting men, leaving Andrew to help with the gruesome task of gathering the bodies.

The patrol recovered all the dead police, with men vowing vengeance when they saw the Galekas had stripped each man naked and mutilated the bodies. They had cut off one man's feet, scalped another and cut the fingers off two more.

"The witch doctors will use the knuckles for their potions," Abernethy said quietly as they rolled a man's remains into a blanket.

"These people live in the stone age." Andrew felt slightly sick at what he had witnessed.

"I think they've graduated to the iron age," Abernethy said grimly. "Certainly, no further."

"Gather them up, lads." Chalmers tied the ends of a blanket with his face taut. "Let's get back to camp and hope these bastards attack us at Ibeka."

Andrew could feel the alteration in the men's mood. In place of apprehension was a grimness. These men wanted to kill; they wanted vengeance for the mutilation of their friends and colleagues.

More Galeka warriors gathered to watch as the patrol returned to Ibeka. They moved parallel to the police, five hundred yards away on either flank, dodging in and out of cover with spears held horizontally above their heads. Occasionally they would shout a challenge, or a lone warrior ran towards the police but never approached sufficiently close to skirmish with the Fingoes.

"The Galekas seem confident," Andrew said.

Abernethy nodded. "They'll retell the story of the encounter at Guadana until they believe it's a major victory against us. By the time their grandchildren hear of it, they'll believe they conquered London and controlled the British Empire."

Andrew smiled. "A bit like our King Arthur conquering Rome," he said.

"Exactly so," Abernethy agreed. "Halloa! Something's happening!"

"What's that?" Andrew asked, lifting his carbine. He saw a swirl on the path a hundred yards away as some of the Fingoes ran back, shouting.

"It's the *IsiDawane*," one of the Fingoes said, immediately cowering behind Andrew.

"It's the what?"

"The *isiDawane,*" Abernethy explained. "I've heard of it in Zululand, but I didn't know it was also common in the Transkei. It's the Xhosa version of a werewolf or vampire, a mythical creature that hunts people to eat their brains."

"Whatever it is," Andrew said, staring ahead, "it's not alone. There are three of them."

Abernethy swore as the Fingo looked even more terrified. Three creatures emerged from behind a copse of thorn trees, with any remaining Fingoes taking one glance and running. "These things are worse than any *isiDawanes*," Abernethy said, altering the angle of his carbine so the muzzle pointed forward. "They're witch doctors."

"Witches?" Andrew remembered Smith's explanation of the power these people had and eyes them curiously. He lowered his carbine, despite seeing other police ready to fire.

The three women were of average height, very overweight and with animal entrails wrapped around their legs. What Andrew could see of their bodies was heavily tattooed and covered in what he hoped was red earth, while a variety of animal and human teeth and bones covered the short length of hide that passed for clothing around their waists.

"I was right," Andrew said. "These people are still in the stone age."

"Dear God," Simpson breathed.

"God's got little to do with these beauties," Abernethy said.

Simpson levelled his carbine, aiming at the women beside him. "I say we finish them off and do the world a favour."

Andrew shook his head, watching the nearest witch doctor with a snakeskin topping her matted hair. The snake's mouth gaped open, showing long teeth. For a second, Andrew thought the snake moved as if a spark of life still existed within the empty skin. He blinked, and the snake was static, although a necklace of human knucklebones rattled around the witch doctor's neck. She looked at him through dark, knowing eyes.

"Don't shoot them," Andrew said. "We don't understand their religion, but we should not interfere."

Andrew remembered his father taking him aside when they first discussed his proposed military career. "If you are ever at or beyond the fringes of Empire, my boy," Andrew's father had said. "The first and most important rules are never to interfere with the local women or religion. People will accept wars and a leadership change, but never that." He had given one of his rare smiles. "We are soldiers, and soldiers fight soldiers or warriors. We should always be merciful to women and children, whatever their station in life."

"They are terrible things," Simpson said, staring at the closest witch doctor. "They do horrible things."

"To our eyes, they are terrible," Andrew agreed. "Perhaps they are not terrible to the Xhosa. Let them go in peace."

Simpson lifted his carbine. "You can't tell me what to do!" He aimed directly at the closest woman until Andrew pushed down the barrel of his carbine.

"She's no threat to us," Andrew said.

Sergeant Duncan nodded. "Baird is right. Let them go in peace."

The witch doctor had not flinched when Simpson pointed his carbine. She stepped closer to Andrew and tapped him on the chest with a gnu's tail.

"You are not who you claim." Although she spoke in Xhosa, Andrew understood every word. "We shall meet twice more. The first time will be a disappointment, and by the second, you will know the truth." She bumped the gnu's tail off him twice more, with her dark eyes seeming to penetrate his soul.

"The truth, Mother?" Andrew asked in English. "What truth?"

"Beware of a foe who is a friend and take care of the friend who is a foe." The witch ignored Andrew's interruption. "Expect grief and loss. You have much blood in your future and a woman who will wait for you."

The witch tapped Andrew a final time with the gnu's tail and walked away unhurried. She spat on Simpson as she passed, and her two companions also touched Andrew. He found he was not afraid.

"What did she say? I didn't understand a word," Simpson said, wiping the spittle from his tunic with an expression of disgust.

"It was as clear as daylight," Andrew told him.

Sergeant Duncan shook his head. "Not to me; it wasn't." He looked curiously at Andrew. "You've hardly been in Africa long enough to get a suntan, yet you already understand Xhosa?"

"Only a few words," Andrew said and closed his mouth. He did not understand what had just happened, and it left him feeling unsettled. He did not look forward to the bloodshed in his future or the disappointment, sorrow, and loss, but the woman waiting for him was interesting.

"Beware of a foe who is a friend and take care of the friend who is a foe," Andrew repeated the witch's words to himself. *That makes no sense. "Expect grief and loss. You have much blood in your future and a*

woman who will wait for you." I'd expect grief and loss in a war, but which woman will wait for me? I don't know any women.

CHAPTER 4

The camp at Ibeka was on high alert when they returned, with the outlying picket challenging them behind a loaded rifle.

"Returning patrol," Chalmers replied and led his patrol in.

"You should have brought in your new friends," Simpson said as Andrew dismounted. "You could have shown them round the defences and made them a nice cup of tea."

"Maybe next time," Andrew replied. He felt Simpson's eyes on him and knew he had made an enemy.

Simpson hawked and spat on the ground. Of average height and wiry, he had a nearly permanent sneer on his face and a jaundiced look on life. Andrew watched as Simpson stepped to Hitchings and pushed the incident out of his mind.

I wonder who the woman is who waits for me.

He allowed himself a smile, imagining a tall blonde with bright blue eyes.

I have never had any success with women. The witch was talking nonsense, like the rest of their kind.

As the Galekas grew bolder, pushing small parties of warriors close to the pickets, the garrison of Ibeka tightened their procedures. Griffiths ordered regular mounted patrols, with men sleeping in their clothes, wearing their ammunition belts and with their Sniders constantly at their sides.

"We're on permanent watch," Abernethy said. "Kreli hates us, and pushing our patrol back will have increased his warrior's confidence. Once the witches have doctored the warriors, they'll come at us."

Andrew nodded. His first experience of battle had not been favourable, and he was desperate to prove himself.

I don't want to live in my father's shadow.

"Come on, Bairdie; we're on outlying picket duty this morning."

Andrew saddled and mounted Lancelot and joined Fraser. The inspector led them half a mile into Fingoland and stopped at a small group of thorn trees.

"This will do, lads," Fraser said. "Our Fingoes tell us that the Galekas have been extremely active these last two days, dancing and singing, with a few parties probing into Fingo territory."

"Do we expect trouble, sir?" Andrew asked.

"Always," Fraser replied with a slight smile. "When the Galekas dance and sing, they are preparing for war."

The morning passed slowly, with a breeze ruffling dust from the track and a small herd of deer running past the picket. Fraser led a short patrol around the area, returning after an uneventful hour.

"It's quiet as the proverbial grave," he said.

"I can feel that something's going to happen, sir," Abernethy replied. "There's something in the atmosphere."

Andrew nodded. The witch doctor's words still reverberated around his head. *Who is this woman who is waiting for me? I hope I meet her soon.*

"Dust, Bairdie!" Abernethy said tersely. "Over there!"

"Have a look, Baird," Fraser ordered.

Andrew rode Lancelot to a slight rise a hundred yards ahead and peered into Galekaland. He returned at a fast trot.

"Sir! The Galekas are coming. Horsemen!"

Inspector Fraser cantered to the rise and lifted his field glasses. "A powerful force of mounted tribesmen under a flag of truce," he said and raised his voice. "Retire to the camp, men. I don't trust them to meet a small group of police, truce or not. The temptation to attack might be too much for them. You're the rear guard, Sergeant Duncan."

"Come on, Bairdie," Abernethy said cheerfully. "Things are happening again."

The police withdrew to Ibeka, with Duncan's rear guard constantly turning to watch the advancing tribesmen. A bugle sounded the alert, and the police ran to the entrenchments, carbines ready. They threw themselves into position, stared outward and waited for the Galekas.

Andrew glanced upward, where the Union flag fluttered fitfully against a bright sky.

"Trust to God," Abernethy murmured, "and keep your powder dry."

Andrew checked his carbine was loaded and murmured Tennyson's words. "Theirs not to make reply, Theirs not to reason why, Theirs but to do and die."[1]

Abernethy grinned. "Let's hope it's more doing than dying," he said. "Here come the Galekas."

"Not once or twice in our fair island story, the path of duty was the way to glory," [2]Andrew replied.

"If you must quote Tennyson," Abernethy said, "wait until after the fighting's over." He looked across at Andrew. "And sometimes through the mirror blue,

The knights come riding two and two."[3]

Andrew grinned. "Imagine meeting an educated man out here in Africa."

"This madness has come on us for our sins," [4]Abernethy said. "Here they come, Bairdie!"

Andrew nodded, aware that Abernethy had opened a gate into his soul. *What did Abernethy mean by that last quote? What sins has he committed?*

When the Galekas approached within three hundred yards of the camp, Captain Robertson and an escort of two men rode to meet them.

"That's far enough!" Robertson snapped, in English and Xhosa.

While the bulk of the Galekas halted, their leader and half a dozen men rode forward under the white flag. The remainder, which Andrew estimated at five hundred men, remained in a hostile clump.

Abernethy held his carbine close to his cheek, aiming at the leading Galeka. "They're just waiting for their chance to attack. Thank God for the guns."

Andrew glanced back at the camp, where the artillerymen were rapidly loading the seven-pounders.

"We are honoured today," Abernethy said. "That's Sidgow under the flag, one of Kreli's sons, the crown prince if you like."

"Does he speak English?" Andrew asked.

"Quite probably," Abernethy replied. "Captain Robertson knows Xhosa, so I'll translate the gist for you."

Andrew nodded. "I'll have to learn the local languages," he said. "I only know enough to say hello."

Yet I understood every word the witches said.

Sidgow greeted Captain Robertson with a wide grin that fooled nobody. "My father, Kreli, sent me to apologise for killing the white policemen." His words carried clearly to the forward positions, and Abernethy translated for Andrew.

"Now Sidgow says the Galekas only wanted to fight the Fingoes, who are terrible cattle thieves." Abernethy nodded. "That's possibly true. I suspect Kreli's men were surprised to see us in Fingoland but attacked when they saw how few we were."

Andrew grunted. A bead of sweat rolled from his forehead down his face.

Abernethy continued. "Sidgow says his father likes the police and has no desire to fight them, so he is sending some oxen for us to eat."

"That's very kind of him," Andrew murmured.

Abernethy smiled. "Now Sidgow is asking Captain Robertson to kindly march away with his police and allow him to attack the Fingoes. If the captain refuses, Sidgow says he'd return with a larger force and hammer the Fingoes anyway, police or no police."

"I can believe that." Andrew shifted his hand. The steel barrel of the carbine was hot to the touch.

Captain Robertson shook his head and told Sidgow the police were not moving and asked why Sidgow had brought a five-hundred-man escort on a friendly visit.

"We're going into Fingoland," Sidgow replied with a wide smile.

"No, you're not," Robertson denied and jerked a thumb towards the three artillery pieces. While he had been talking, the gunners had dragged the guns outside the encampment and aimed them toward the Galekas. "I have ordered these guns to point toward your men. Each gun contains case shot. That means there are sixty-three bullets in each gun." Robertson waited for the inference to sink in before he continued.

"Now take your men back to your own land, Sidgow, and tell your father Kreli that if he crosses into Fingoland, we will stop him. That is my word and the word of the government."

Robertson's speech seemed to hang in the air as the two parties faced each other. A breeze ruffled the Union flag, with the red, white, and blue opening for a moment and then closing again, as if Queen Victoria had peered out from Windsor to observe the fringes of her empire.

"What happens now?" Andrew asked.

"Wait and see," Abernethy replied and gave a twisted smile. "Pray to God and keep your powder dry."

"Warty Cromwell could not have said it better," Andrew said.

Sidgow returned to his men, with the wind flapping the white flag, and a few moments later, the entire Galeka force turned around and rode back to Galekaland.

Abernethy let out his breath. "That was interesting," he said.

Andrew heard the strain in his voice.

"They'll be back," Smith gave his opinion. "And next time, they won't be under a flag of truce." He produced a short clasp knife and began to clean the bowl of his pipe. "Don't relax yet, boys."

Rather than wait for the Galekas to attack, Captain Robertson sent another patrol into Fingoland.

"Fraser, take a dozen men and see what's happening. Check the frontier," Robertson ordered. "Don't get involved in anything you can't handle, and for God's sake, don't leave any wounded behind."

"Yes, sir," Inspector Fraser agreed as Andrew joined the volunteers filing behind him.

"You're an observation patrol, not a fighting patrol," Robertson reminded. He frowned when he saw Andrew. "Were you not with the last incursion, Baird?"

"Yes, sir," Baird agreed.

Robertson nodded. "Don't take too many chances, son. The good Lord only grants us a certain amount of luck."

Baird smiled. "Yes, sir. Thank you." He saw Smith shaking a disapproving head, ignored Simpson's poisonous glare, and trotted outside the camp and into Fingoland.

Fraser advanced cautiously, marching with a screen of Fingo scouts and halting whenever they saw movement. Twice the Fingoes ran back to report activity, and Robertson had to order them back in front.

"The Fingoes are nervous," Andrew said.

"The Fingoes know what the Galekas are capable of," Abernethy replied, glancing over his shoulder. "I'm a bit nervous that the enemy will get behind us and cut us off from Ibeka."

They moved slowly, holding their Sniders in capable hands, each man studying the ground all around until the Fingo scouts ran back, talking rapidly.

"Sergeant Duncan," Fraser said. "Take fine men to see what's happening up there. I can't understand the Fingoes gabbling!"

"Come on, Bairdie," Abernethy said. "The Fingoes say there are thousands of Galeka warriors ahead." He grinned. "I'd estimate about fifty men herding cattle."

"Into the valley of death," Andrew said as they passed the Fingoes and pushed on. "Come on, Lancelot!"

They had not gone a quarter of a mile before Duncan held up his hand. "That's far enough, boys. We'd better warn the camp that the Fingoes were correct."

Kreli had formed up his Galekas on either side of the road, three solid columns of warriors in fighting formation. Some waved their weapons in defiance when they saw the police.

"Kreli knew we would send a patrol," Abernethy said as Inspector Fraser ordered a rapid withdrawal to Ibeka. "He's waiting to ambush us."

As the police trotted back down the road, their hoofbeats echoing from the surrounding hills, the Fingoes ran ahead, outpacing the horses in their eagerness to find safety.

"Don't look now, Bairdie, but somebody's following us," Abernethy said.

The Galekas tramped behind Fraser's patrol, remaining in their formation, and slowly creeping closer. The proximity of the tribesmen unnerved some of the police, who kicked their horses into a trot.

"Don't run, boys!" Fraser shouted. "Keep a steady pace and watch the flanks."

The Galekas closed to within three hundred yards, shouting, waving their weapons and challenging the police to stand and fight.

"They want us to fire at them," Abernethy said. "Keep moving, Bairdie."

"I will," Andrew promised.

"We'd better hurry up a little," Fraser decided as the Galekas closed the distance, chanting rhythmically. The police increased their speed, so their withdrawal nearly turned into an inglorious retreat. Andrew heard the crack of a rifle and turned around in his saddle.

"Don't look back, Bairdie," Abernethy warned. "Concentrate on your riding."

More musketry followed, with the whine of a bullet passing far overhead and then the patrol turned the final corner and saw the outlying picket.

"What's the to-do, boys?" a corporal sentry asked.

"About three thousand Galekas is the to-do!" Fraser reined up. "Get your men back to the camp, Corporal."

"Jesus! I mean, yes, sir!" the corporal replied. "Mount up, lads! You heard the inspector!"

The sentries at Ibeka camp were on full alert when the patrol returned.

"The Fingoes told us what happened," Smith said as Andrew dismounted. "I warned you not to volunteer for anything." He grinned. "Isn't life on the frontier interesting?"

"That's two victories the Galekas can boast about now," Abernethy said. "Kreli will claim he chased away a full British army, infantry, cavalry, and guns, and he'll want the full hat trick. If I were Commandant Griffiths, I'd expect the Galekas to attack Ibeka soon."

When Andrew stared back into Fingoland, the road was empty except for drifting dust. Kreli's Galekas had not followed the patrol to the British camp.

There was no valley of death then, and what did that witch mean that a woman would wait for me?

CAPTAIN ROBERTSON AND COMMANDANT GRIFFITHS increased the police patrols and ensured the vedettes were alert, watching for movement along the frontier. A stream of eager

Fingo spies informed them that the Galekas were gathering at Kreli's Great Kraal.

"That's the capital of Galekaland," Abernethy said. "Or the nearest thing Kreli can have as a capital." He chewed the end of his pipe. "I'd say Kreli is preparing some mischief on a larger scale than before."

Andrew cleaned his carbine for the fourth time that day. "Do you think he is preparing to attack us?"

"Kreli will either attack us or make a major incursion into Fingoland," Abernethy said. "Maybe both. If Kreli removes the British garrison at Ibeka – us - he can destroy the Fingoes and grab all their cattle."

Andrew looked along the barrel of his carbine. "We'll be fighting again, then."

"I'd say so," Abernethy agreed.

Andrew wondered if his father had felt so nervous before a battle. He glanced over the garrison, assessing the fighting capability of the men he was beginning to know. "How many men can Kreli field?"

Abernethy removed the pipe from his mouth. "Now that, Mr Baird, I could not tell you. Five thousand? Six thousand, maybe even seven thousand. A fair number against our little garrison."

Inspector Fraser joined them. "Discussing the situation, lads?"

"Yes, sir." Andrew scrambled to attention.

"Stand easy, Baird. If the Galekas come, we'll hold them," Fraser encouraged with a faint smile.

"Ibeka is not the best defensive site," Andrew said, looking around.

"Oh?" Fraser raised his eyebrows, semi-amused at such an observation from a junior constable. "What makes you say that Baird?"

"It's the position, sir," Andrew said. "We have a rising slope to the east, with a stony ridge at the top, so the Galekas can fire down on us, negating our protective wall."

Fraser nodded, checking Andrew's facts. "Carry on, Baird. Share your wisdom with us." He retained his tolerant smile.

Andrew pointed northwest and north. "Over there, the ground is level, with boulders and rocks to give cover to the Galekas. They can advance against us or snipe in safety. In the south, it's not too bad, a downward slope, but split by a stream and backed by a hill. The Galekas can use the bed of the stream for cover."

"We have artillery," Fraser said as his smile faded.

"The guns are only effective on the south side, sir," Andrew said. "Elsewhere, the low ground with plenty of cover favours the Galekas."

Fraser nodded. "Where did you get such tactical knowledge, Baird? You're fresh out of Britain, aren't you?"

"Yes, sir. A few months ago." Andrew hesitated for a moment. "I come from a military family, sir, and I must have picked it up somewhere."

I cannot tell the whole truth.

"A military family, eh?" Fraser said, with his eyes narrowed curiously. "You're from a long line of redcoats?"

"Something like that, sir," Baird said.

"Well, keep it up, and if you survive, you might make an officer someday," Fraser said. "How would you like that, eh, Baird? You could go home as a lieutenant or even a captain. Wouldn't that be a feather in your cap?"

"Yes, sir," Andrew agreed.

If only you knew!

"Aye." Smith hawked and spat on the ground when Fraser moved away. "All you have to do is survive, Bairdie-boy, and that might not be so easy if Kreli attacks."

Andrew nodded, wishing he had kept his mouth shut. He saw Fraser talking to Captain Robertson, both glancing in his direction. *I don't want them to ask too many questions about me.*

Three times that day, frightened Fingoes arrived at the camp with reports about Galekas appearing at various points on their border, and each time, Commandant Griffiths sent small parties of police to stiffen the Fingo defences.

"If Griffiths carries on as he's doing," Simpson said, "he'll leave us with three men and a one-legged dog to defend Ibeka."

"I'd rather have a one-legged dog than you, Simpson." Abernethy never concealed his dislike for Simpson. He lifted his tobacco pouch, realised it was empty and sighed. "You're right, though. We're already dangerously thin on the ground."

Augmenting the hundred and forty police, around two thousand Fingoes camped around and within the police base, with sub-inspector Allan Maclean, sub-inspector Veltman and a few local Europeans as officers.

"If I were Kreli," Abernethy said as they manned the trenches in the fading hour before dawn, "I'd attack now while we are undermanned."

"Kreli must agree with you," Smith said. "Look what's approaching."

A dozen terrified Fingoes ran toward Ibeka, keeping to their side of the narrow footpath that formed the boundary between Fingo and Galeka territory. The look on their faces was sufficient warning.

"Kreli is coming! Thousands of Galekas are coming!"

"From which direction?" Fraser stopped one of the refugees.

"That way!" The man pointed to the south, struggled free, and ran after his companions.

"Here we go," Hitchings said, smoothing a hand over the stock of his Snider. "This time tomorrow, we'll either be heroes or dead."

"Let's hope it's the former," Abernethy said. "I've always wanted to be a hero, feted by attractive women, drinking champagne and getting the best tables at London restaurants."

Smith shook his head. "It won't happen like that, Nethy. Nobody has heard of the Galekas, and I doubt one man in a hundred even knows where the Cape Frontier is, let alone that we're struggling to contain hostile tribes here. At the most, we'll get three lines in an inside page."

"Abernethy nodded. "You're probably right, Sergeant. The press is concentrating on the Russian-Turkish war or is over in Afghanistan. There's always trouble in Afghanistan. They'll send for General Roberts or Fighting Jack Windrush over there."

Andrew started at the name and quickly changed the subject. "Shall I ride forward and see if the Fingoes are exaggerating, sir?"

Fraser nodded. "Off you go, Baird. Take care."

Glad to be active, Andrew mounted Lancelot and pushed forward. Within half a mile, he realised the Fingoes were correct. Kreli had mustered the Galeka army on the hill south of Ibeka. He saw them form into columns of squares with a precision that told of long practice, halt and begin a deep sonorous chant. The bulk of the Galeka army was infantry, nearly equally divided between men with assegais and shields and others with rifles. The Galeka cavalry stood on the flanks, less disciplined than the infantry but still dangerous.

"Come on, boy," Andrew whispered to Lancelot. "Time we weren't here."

"They're coming," Andrew reported what he had seen.

"How many?" Fraser asked laconically.

"Between seven and eight thousand," Andrew estimated. "Riflemen, cavalry and spearmen."

"That must be the bulk of Kreli's army," Fraser said. "Sergeant Duncan, please inform the commandant that Kreli is coming with around seven thousand men, and we can expect him shortly."

"Very good, sir." Duncan saluted and headed for the main camp.

Simpson whistled and glanced over his shoulder. "We'll be hard-pressed to hold that lot off!"

Abernethy grunted. "At this moment, Kreli is telling his men that the witch doctors have made them invulnerable to our bullets. What a shock they'll get when we knock them down like skittles at a fairground."

Griffiths gave final orders to defend Ibeka. "Bring the horses inside the trenches," he said calmly. "Saddle and bridle them and secure them to the picket rope. Not you, Sergeant Duncan; I want you and three men to keep their mounts for scouting."

"Yes, sir," Duncan acknowledged.

The picket rope was in the house garden, stretched from tree to tree, with the confused horses attached. It would be the work of an instant to release them, ready for a hurried retreat or an equally rapid sally against the tribesmen.

Griffiths paced the defences, giving orders. "I want open ammunition boxes ready for use. Place them behind the walls and have water barrels nearby. Fighting is thirsty work."

The police ate a hasty breakfast, each man watching for the Galeka army approaching from the south. Andrew disguised his nervousness under false joviality that fooled nobody. The men shrugged off their coats, exchanged banter, lit their pipes, and readied themselves for the coming battle.

"Watch my back, Baird, and I'll watch yours," Abernethy said quietly.

"I'll do that," Andrew said. He watched a pair of vultures circling above, checked his rifle, counted his cartridges, and took a deep breath.

Here we go again.

CHAPTER 5

"Sergeant Duncan," Griffiths ordered. "Take three men and watch what Kreli does. Report back the minute he moves towards us."

Andrew watched Duncan canter forward into hostile territory. *They look very lonely out there.*

"Don't stray far from the horses," Hitchings advised. "If the day goes against us, we can grab a horse and bolt."

Andrew listened, unsure if Hitchings was serious.

"You saw what the Galekas did to our dead after our last encounter," Hitchings continued. "I'm not waiting for Kreli to chop me up like that."

"You're damned right, Hitch," Simpson said. "If they bastards get too close, you won't see old Simmy for dust and small pebbles." He grinned as if he had said something clever.

Abernethy whistled a tune which Andrew recognised as Rossini's *Largo al Factotum.*

"That's a little out of place here." Andrew forced a smile.

"Nonsense," Abernethy said. "One can sing opera anywhere. It brings a little culture to the midst of barbarity, and there's nothing more barbaric than a battlefield."

"That's true," Andrew agreed.

Come on, Kreli! The waiting is worse than the fighting.

At half past nine that morning, Sergeant Duncan appeared with his men at his side. He trotted past the outer pickets, looking dusty but relaxed.

"What's happening, Sergeant?" Abernethy asked.

"A couple of thousand horsemen have joined Kreli," Duncan reported laconically. "They're approaching the ridge on the south."

"That's all we need," Hitchings said, glancing at the horse lines.

Abernethy returned to whistling Rossini, puffing out blue smoke with every note. He winked at Andrew. "Shouldn't be long now, Bairdie. Trust in God and keep your powder dry." Andrew felt the vibration of thousands of feet on the ground before he heard the Galekas' war song rising from the ridge.

Smith peered ahead. "Here they come, boys. Look to your front."

Andrew took a deep breath, listening to the increasing chorus from ahead. He raised his carbine to his shoulder.

"Come on, Kreli," he said softly.

The Galekas emerged from a curtain of dust, with their mounted men concentrating on the ridge to the police left.

"There are thousands of them," Hitchings muttered.

"All the more targets, Hitchings," Fraser shouted with forced cheerfulness. "Even you can't miss."

Hitchings glared without replying. He had often boasted of his marksmanship.

The Galeka infantry advanced in three columns, shouting, and brandishing their weapons.

"They think they're bloody Frenchmen," Abernethy said. "And we're Wellington's army at Waterloo."

Andrew realised he was gripping his carbine so tightly his knuckles were white. He forced himself to relax.

The Galeka columns marched into a depression in the undulating ground, momentarily disappearing from view.

"Get ready, boys," Griffiths warned. "When they reappear, they'll only be twelve hundred yards away."

"Come, my Galeka friends," Andrew murmured and quoted Tennyson again. "It's not too late to seek a newer world." [1] He felt his heartbeat increase, wiped the sweat from his forehead, squinted down the barrel of his carbine and listened to Abernethy's singing.

When the Galekas reappeared, their skirmishers advanced to the front, moving with more discipline than Andrew expected, a whole host of lightly armed men trotting towards Ibeka.

Andrew aimed until Smith shook his head. "Don't waste your bullets, Bairdie. Let the Fingoes deal with the skirmishers."

Griffiths snapped an order, and Commander Veldtman led five hundred Fingoes outside the entrenchments on the British left flank. They faced the Galeka skirmishes in the rough, border-strewn ground beyond the British defences, exchanging taunts and bullets without causing many casualties. Allan Maclean did the same on the right, firing his revolver as he encouraged his hundreds of Fingo warriors to face the attackers.

"Advance, boys!" Griffiths ordered. "We're not waiting for Kreli to come to us. Extend into skirmishing order and meet them front and left."

Andrew took a deep breath and copied his colleagues. He held his Snider firmly and walked towards the Galeka mass. The noise was appalling as the Fingoes and Galeka skirmishers shouted, yelled, screamed, and fired at each other.

"Here comes the cavalry," Smith said, nodding towards the ridge, where the mounted Galekas began to pour towards Ibeka.

Griffiths raised his field glasses to study the Galeka cavalry. "Artillery!" He raised his voice. "Target the horsemen!"

Two of the seven-pounders swivelled towards the ridge and fired, with both shells screaming over the horsemen without exploding.

"That was pointless," Hitchings muttered. "What the hell are we doing?" He slowed down until Sergeant Duncan roared at him.

"Keep in line, Hitchings!"

The police tried a couple of rockets next, with greater success. The whoosh and fiery trail of the rockets terrified the Galeka horses, with some panicking and fleeing, carrying their riders to the rear.

"Artillery," Griffiths shouted. "Switch your targets. Hit these columns!"

The Galeka infantry was within a thousand yards of the entrenchment, a mass of warriors moving forward steadily as their skirmishers sparred with the Fingoes and the police readied their carbines.

"Can we fire, sir?" Simpson asked.

"Not yet. We might hit the Fingoes," Fraser replied.

"Bugger the Fingoes," Simpson muttered.

"Common shell!" Lieutenant Cochrane shouted, and all three seven-pounders fired at once. Only nine hundred yards away, the columns were easy targets, and the shells exploded in their midst, each killing and maiming a dozen men. The column shivered, and the police stepped closer.

"Wait!" Griffiths ordered as the Galeka skirmished merged with the main columns. Veldtman and Maclean pulled their Fingoes back, giving the police a clear field of fire.

"Now! Volleys!" Griffiths ordered, and the police opened fire. The sharp crack of the Sniders added to the ear-splitting bang of the mountain guns while the rockets hissed and flared among the Galeka cavalry.

Andrew aimed and fired, feeling the comfortable jerk as the carbine rammed against his shoulder. His nerves eased as soon as he knew he was hitting back. He loaded, aimed, and fired again on the word of command, tasting the now familiar gun smoke.

"They're firing at us!" Simpson howled, ducking.

"The dirty dogs! How dare they?" Smith mocked, laughing. "Keep firing, Simmy!"

Andrew saw men fall in the front line of the Galekas, toppling to the ground as bullets and shells hammered them.

"They're slowing," Smith shouted as the Galeka columns began to fragment.

"Fire!" Fraser ordered, and Andrew fired into the column, reloaded, and watched as the Galekas withdrew, still in good order despite their piled up dead and writhing wounded.

"One more volley!" Griffiths ordered, and the police fired again, reloaded, and waited for orders as gun smoke drifted in a grey-white haze.

The Galeka cavalry milled outside rifle range on the flanks, with the police rockets hissing amongst the horses, causing more panic than casualties.

"They're useless." Smith dismissed the mounted men in two words.

Andrew checked his Snider, counted his cartridges, and forced a smile. "We've pushed them back." He was no longer nervous.

"They'll return," Smith told him casually. "Say what you like about the Galekas, but they're not cowards."

Andrew looked ahead, where the Galeka dead lay individually, where the Sniders had got them, and in bloody heaps where the shells had landed. "No," he agreed. "No cowards would have run into musketry and artillery fire as they did."

"We showed them!" Hitchings shouted, suddenly brave. "I must have killed at least three."

"Did you see that last one I shot?" Simpson boasted. "I caught him right in the head. His skull exploded, with brains all over the place."

"Here they come again!" Abernethy shouted, slamming his Snider into his shoulder.

"Independent firing!" Griffiths ordered as the Galekas advanced a second time. No longer in mass columns, they had extended into skirmishing formation, presenting less of a target for the artillery.

"Case shot!" Cochrane decided, and each seven-pounder loaded with the canvas bags, each holding sixty-three bullets.

"Aim at the densest masses," Cochrane commanded. "Fire!"

The guns acted like giant shotguns, with each shot blasting a swathe into the advancing Galekas while the rocket men kept the enemy cavalry busy.

Andrew aimed, fired, and reloaded, feeling the acrid gun smoke nip his eyes and bite into his mouth and nostrils. He took a drink of smoke-tainted water and fired again, with the Galekas hardly seen through the smoke. It was impossible to target individual warriors, so Andrew fired where he hoped the enemy clustered most thickly.

"Keep firing, lads!" Fraser shouted. He walked the length of the police lines, firing and encouraging, exposing himself to the torrent of shots from the Galekas.

"They're firing high!" Andrew shouted as he heard a constant whine of bullets passing over his head.

"They always do," Smith told him. "And thank your God for that. We'll be in major trouble if the bastards ever learn to aim."

"They're slowing!" Fraser ordered, and Andrew realised he had been firing automatically. The steady firing of the police broke the Galeka attack, and they melted away, leaving their dead and wounded on the ground.

"Cease fire!" Fraser ordered. "Sergeants! Report any casualties to me!"

"Drink," Smith advised his section. "If you have anything to eat, take it now before the Galekas return. These lads won't give up yet."

Andrew realised he was ravenous and munched on a hard biscuit before drinking the smoke-tainted water.

"Check your ammunition," Fraser advised, pacing the ranks with encouragement and advice. He stopped at the newest members of his troop. "How are you doing, lads?"

"Killing them, sir." Simpson gave a greasy grin.

"Fine, sir," Hitchings said.

"Fine, sir," Andrew replied, replenishing his ammunition pouch from the chest. "Thank you."

"Good lads," Fraser continued his rounds.

"Here they come again," Abernethy shouted, his voice hoarse from smoke.

The Galekas had learned caution and advanced more slowly, hiding behind rocks and bushes and firing at the police, and Fingoes. They halted, rushed to the next piece of cover, and fired.

"When they get close," Smith advised. "Pick your man. Wait until he breaks cover and shoot him."

Andrew nodded, feeling the sweat trickling down his face. He blinked to clear his vision and sighted on a tall, athletic man who moved from rock to rock. For a moment, he was back on a Northumberland moor, shooting pheasants as a gentle rain cooled the sportsmen, and then his Galeka moved again, and Andree fired through instinct.

The warrior staggered but continued, still yelling. Andrew reloaded hastily, cursing as he nearly dropped the cartridge. He took a deep breath, slotted the cartridge home, and lifted the carbine to his shoulder.

The Galeka had found cover. Andrew swore softly and ducked when a bullet whined close above his head.

That fellow is a better shot than most.

He scanned the battlefield, ignoring the twitching wounded and the dead, searching for his man. Drifting smoke obscured his vision until Andrew saw the flash from a rifle muzzle, and something burrowed into the ground at his feet.

That fellow is aiming at me.

Andrew felt a peculiar sensation of vulnerability. He was no longer a cog in the official machinery fighting a faceless enemy but one man opposed to another. He instinctively knew that the

Galeka firing at him was the same man he was attempting to shoot.

Suddenly the battle took on a new intensity. Andrew was aware of the men to his left and right, the harsh bark of the artillery, the hoarse shouts of the men and the sharp crackle of musketry, but only his personal duel mattered.

You and me, my Galeka foe. One of us must die today.

Andrew knelt with his carbine pressed into his shoulder and the barrel hot from use. He waited, focussing on the last position he had seen his enemy.

The following bullet was high, but the Galeka had momentarily exposed his arm. Andrew fired, with his shot crashing into the man's elbow. He reloaded feverishly, hoping to catch his opponent as he jerked upright, but the Galeka disappeared.

Where are you, my worthy foe?

"They're retreating!" Abernethy shouted as the Galekas, hammered by artillery and musketry, pulled back.

"Help them on their way," Fraser ordered.

"It doesn't seem fair to shoot men running away," Andrew said, looking for his wounded opponent.

"The more we kill now, the less there'll be to kill us next time," Smith said, loading, aiming, and firing without pause.

Andrew saw the logic and reluctantly fired at the retreating warriors.

"That's eight!" Hitchings exulted, loaded, aimed, and fired again. "And another one winged!" He grinned across at Andrew. "How many have you bagged, Bairdie?"

"I haven't kept a score," Andrew replied. He suddenly felt drained.

"They'll come again," Fraser predicted. "Get ready, lads."

Andrew refilled his ammunition pouch, listened to his comrades boasting, waved away a cluster of questing flies and sunk to the ground.

"You're a learned man, Andrew." Abernethy scraped the bowl of his pipe. "Have you ever read Darwin's *The Descent of Man*?"

Andrew licked dry lips and shook his head. “No,” he said.

“You should,” Abernethy told him, blowing through the pipe stem to ensure it was clear. “Darwin thinks that Europeans are a civilised race and Africans are primitive.”

“Does he?” Andrew pretended interest.

“He does,” Abernethy said and thumbed a quarter inch of tobacco into his pipe. “I can’t quote directly, but Darwin says that what he calls the civilised races, us, will exterminate and replace what he calls the savage races.”

“Is that what you think we are doing now?” Andrew asked.

Abernethy shrugged, scratched a match, and puffed life into his pipe. “No; we’re fighting for our lives. I think Darwin equated civilisation with mechanical advances.” He tapped his rifle. “He thinks we are more civilised because we can kill more of them than they can kill of us.”

“Aren’t we more civilised?” Andrew asked.

“God knows,” Abernethy glanced at his watch. “It’s five o’clock.” He sounded surprised. “Doesn’t time fly when you’re having fun?” He raised his head. “I can hear them,” he said. “They’re coming again.”

The Galekas emerged from the dip, twelve hundred yards from the police entrenchments. They advanced at a run, seemingly undeterred by their previous losses and the shells and rockets that exploded among them.

“They’re not going to stop this time,” Simpson shouted, glancing behind him at the horse lines. “They’ll run right over us and kill us all!”

CHAPTER 6

Jama stood in the centre of his *imuzi* watching Yibanathi, his *iniKozikasi* - Great Wife - and Lerato, his second wife, preparing the mealies and milk curds – *amasi* – for the evening meal. Unlike most married Zulus, Jama's Great Wife was also his first wife, while prosperity had allowed him to afford three others. He was fortunate that all his wives got along well, with the younger women happy with their position. Yibanathi was his favourite, the companion of his youth and even now, she stirred a desire in him. Lerato was fifteen years younger, as shapely as a Zulu woman should be and obeyed Yibanathi's orders without demur.

Life was good, Jama thought as he walked around his *imuzi*, watching his people work and play with the elders sitting under the *umzimbeet* tree as the flowers splashed purple over the dark leaves. Two men were busy making assegai shafts from the hard wood, for the *umzimbeet* was the favoured tree for weapons.

Like many in Zululand, Jama's *imuzi* was east facing, built on sloping ground with easy access to a stream for fresh water, with woodland nearby for fuel, and only a short distance to grazing land for the cattle. In the centre of the *imuzi*, a circular fence of intertwined branches acted as a cattle pen. At midday, the herd boys escorted the cattle into the enclosure to be milked and again at night to keep them safe from wild animals.

It was a feature of Zulu culture that only males could tend the cattle. While women did most of the other work around the *imuzi*, including working with goats and lesser animals, dealing with cattle and fighting were left to the men.

Jama stopped at the cattle pen, wondering if the *amadlozi,* guardian ancestral spirits, were watching him. He knew they guarded the cattle pens and the winter grain reserve deep beneath the enclosure and hoped they approved of his actions.

Neat, bee-hive-shaped *izindlu* clustered around the cattle pen, where Jama's wives lived with their younger children. The *izindlu* were simple structures of a supple frame thatched with grass, with a central pole supporting the roof. The floor was of beaten clay and cow dung, with an open fire in a small hearth, over which earthenware pots hung for cooking. They were perfect for the climate, easy to build, provided shelter from the rain, cool on hot days and warm in winter. Jama knew the hazard of fire and ignored the cockroaches that infested the walls. They were as much part of life as road traffic was to city-dwelling Europeans.

Yibanathi lived in the central *izindlu,* where Jama ate his evening meal of *amasi* with boiled pumpkins and vegetables spiced with pumpkin leaves. The herd boys would drive the cattle to the central pen, and Jama would relax, watching the younger people dancing, telling stories, and playing board games by the light of reed torches. When he was ready, Jama would spend the night with whichever wife he fancied. They might make love, or not, as Jama decided, and slept on grass mats which hung on the wall during the day.

Life had always been thus and, in Jama's eyes, always would be. He did not consider changing his culture any more than he would consider flying to the moon.

Jama thought of his youth as a young warrior and the battles he had endured and enjoyed before the king had honoured his regiment by allowing them to marry. The *isicoco* [1] around his head proved his status as a married man. He smiled as he remembered fighting for his king, Cetshwayo, at the Battle of Ndondakusuka over twenty years ago. Cetshwayo's forces had defeated his rival, Mbuyazi, his brother, and gained the kingship.

Jama remembered hooking the edge of his shield under that of his opponent, thrusting his *iKlwa* into his body and shouting, "*Ngadla!* I have eaten!"

He had fought for the king since then, but that first kill was his favourite, and his *amabutho's* exploits had gained the king's favour and permission to take a wife. That was when he first met Yibanathi, the mother of two of his daughters and one of his sons. Jama caressed that memory and stopped to talk to the elders, enjoying their reminiscing and listening to their wisdom. He heard children's laughter from outside the circle of *izindlu* and smiled indulgently. If children were laughing, his *imuzi* was happy, and his world was complete.

Leaving the stout thorn barrier that protected the *imuzi* from prowling night-time predators, Jama trotted to the undulating grassy hills. Somebody had said that Zululand was the land of ten thousand hills, and Jama could not disagree. The land was the best in his knowledge of Africa, and under the benign rule of Cetshwayo, the people were healthy, free, and happy.

Within ten minutes, Jama was counting his cattle, talking to the youths who tended the herds, asking about predators and proving he had not forgotten them. Cattle were the pride and wealth of the Zulus, as of every tribe and people in southern Africa. Cattle formed the basis of the economy, with men measuring their wealth in the number of cattle they possessed. The animals were small by European standards, with long horns and only a vague regard for selective breeding. Jama had purchased all his wives with his cattle and was proud of the size of his herds.

Due to cattle's importance, herd boys had a vital place in Zulu society. In common with all Zulu males, Jama had spent his formative years with cattle and recognised each animal by its distinctive pattern, the shape of its horns or how it moved.

Two of the older boys were about to leave the herds and become warriors, so Jama sought them out.

"Funani and Kgabu. You will be leaving the cattle soon."

The boys looked at him, unsmiling. *No,* Jama thought, *they were youths now, no longer boys. Soon they would be men, carrying assegais and a shield with the Abanonya.*

"You will be taking your place with the men. Are you ready?"

The youths nodded. Both were as tall as men, with lithe, muscular bodies, hardened by spending years outdoors in all weathers.

"Good," Jama said. "Come to the *imuzi* in five days to start your training. Go now."

The youths left, running, and Jama watched them, hiding his pride, for both were his sons. Kgabu was his son by Yibanathi and Funani by Ulwazie.

A third boy approached Jama. Smaller and younger than Kgabu or Finani, he stretched himself to appear taller. "I want to be a warrior, too," he piped.

Jama tried to look stern. "You are too young, Jabulani," he said. "You'll have to wait for another year or two." He shook his head at Jabulani's disappointment. "The time will pass, Jabulani. Now get back to the cattle; that dun-and-black one with the twisted right horn was limping. Check its hooves." He watched as Jabulani, another of his sons, scampered away.

Smiling, Jama returned to the *imuzi*. His life had been a long succession of successes, and nothing should ever change.

"Keep firing, lads," Fraser stopped immediately behind Hitchings and fired his carbine a handbreadth from the constable's ear. "Push them back!"

The Galekas were yelling, firing as they ran, or brandishing their assegais and shields. The bravest of their cavalry had overcome their fear of the rockets and charged on the flanks, shaggy manes flying as the riders fired from the saddle. The infantry moved more slowly, with *indunas* in front and the warriors whooping and yelling as the rockets hissed among them.

Andrew looked for his wounded adversary, fired, aimed, and cursed as his carbine jammed. He hacked at the intractable cartridge with his clasp knife, cleared the jam, reloaded, and fired into the advancing mass.

"Here come the Fingoes!" Abernethy roared. "Come on, Maclean's boys!"

As the Galekas wavered, the Maclean brothers, Alan and John, led the Fingoes against the Galekas flanks, firing as they advanced. Caught in the crossfire, the Galekas lost their cohesion. They had hoped for a quick victory and believed the witch doctors had made them invulnerable. The truth lay around them in their colleagues screaming, shattered bodies.

"They're breaking!" Abernethy shouted.

Andrew nodded. That last charge had been the Galekas high tide. The concentrated fire of the police, plus the Fingoes' flank attack, had broken them. From a force of brave warriors intent on conquest, the Galekas became a mob of frightened men, scrambling to escape the bursting shells and vengeful assegais and firearms of the Fingoes.

Andrew suddenly felt exhausted as the day's excitement wore off. He slumped to the ground, watching as the artillery pumped shell after shell at the retreating Galekas and the Fingoes butchered the wounded.

"Well, Bairdie," Smith said, placing his pipe in his mouth, "you survived."

Andrew nodded, "I did," he agreed. All he wanted to do was close his eyes, but when he did, a thousand images of the battle returned. He looked upward as the rain began, destroying all hope of coffee or a hot meal.

"You did well, Baird," Fraser said. "I've got my eye on you.

Come with me." He took Andrew aside and lowered his voice. "Where are you from, Baird?"

"I arrived in South Africa a few months ago, sir," Andrew tried to avoid a direct answer.

"I know that," Fraser said. "And I know you put your home as Berwick-upon-Tweed. That's not what I mean. You're not an ordinary trooper, not with an accent and attitude like yours, and you've picked up the basics of military discipline like an old soldier."

"Thank you, sir," Andrew replied.

"You're an enigma, Baird," Fraser said. "A man of mystery."

Andrew did not reply.

"What's your story?" Fraser asked as the rain increased, hammering down on the exhausted men.

"I come from a military family," Andrew admitted some of his past.

Fraser nodded. "That would help. Infantry or cavalry?"

"Infantry," Andrew said.

"What rank?" Fraser asked.

Andrew hesitated before he replied. "My father holds a field rank," he said.

"He holds the queen's commission?" Fraser sounded surprised but was determined not to let Andrew off the hook.

"Yes, sir." Andrew was equally determined not to give too much away.

"Colonel Baird?" Fraser was smiling, ignoring the rain dripping from his face onto the sodden ground.

"I haven't heard from him for a while, sir," Andrew tried to alter the direction of the conversation. "I honestly don't know what rank he will currently hold."

"Ah!" Fraser nodded, thinking he understood. "That's the way the wind blows, is it? A family dispute?"

"I'd rather not talk about it, sir," Andrew said.

"I see. Well, Baird, you evidently come from good stock, and you have the attitude and bearing of a gentleman. If you continue behaving the way you have so far, I'll recommend you for a commission."

Andrew felt a leap of elation. He often regretted leaving Sandhurst without obtaining his commission, yet knew he wanted to advance by his merits, not because of an accident of birth.

Fraser smiled. "You may have something to boast about to your estranged father, and that might help patch up your disagreement."

"Thank you, sir."

THEY SAT OUTSIDE THEIR TENTS WITH THE CAMPFIRE throwing out a circle of heat and a million stars puncturing a sky of black velvet.

Smith stretched, took a long drink from a dark bottle, and passed it over to Andrew.

"Cape Smoke," he said. "It will either kill you or give you new life."

Andrew choked back a mouthful of the fiery spirits. "Thank you," he said, coughing.

"You know, Bairdie," Smith said, retrieving the brandy, "we're wasting our time here."

"What do you mean?" Andrew asked.

"I mean, we're risking our lives fighting a bunch of raggedy-arsed savages with no profit, but our pay, and that's little enough once they take off stoppages. Where's the benefit?"

"We're making the Frontier safer for farmers and settlers," Andrew gave the stock answer. "And advancing the flag and civilisation."

Smith grinned. "That's all very well if you believe that sort of thing, but what do we, you and I, benefit from it?"

"The knowledge that we're doing our duty, perhaps?" Andrew

was unsure where Smith was heading. He did not mention the possibility of a commission.

"That won't pay the rent," Smith told him. "You're still green behind the ears, young Baird. In this world, we must take the opportunities that present themselves, whatever they are. And if they don't present themselves, we must make them ourselves."

"What sort of opportunities, Sergeant?"

Smith took another mouthful of Cape Smoke, passed the bottle to Andrew, and raised his eyebrows when Andrew refused. "No? Well, suit yourself. I met a trader the other day; you may have seen me talking to him."

"I saw you were talking to somebody, Sergeant," Andrew agreed. "I didn't pay much attention, though."

"No? Well, there was no reason why you should," Smith said. "His name was Johann de Vries, and he wanders all over Southern Africa from the High Veldt, where the backcountry Boers are, to the Great Karoo. He probably knows Africa as well as anybody and picks up all sorts of interesting information."

"Yes, Sergeant," Andrew threw more wood on the fire and watched the flames and sparks rise. He waited to see where Smith was heading.

"Well, Johann is just back from Zululand, up beyond Natal, and told me things about the Zulus that I did not know."

Andrew reached for the brandy, realising that Smith was about to share his new knowledge. "What were they, Sergeant?"

"We're off duty, Bairdie. There's no need to call me sergeant. Smith will do, or Ashanti. Most people know me as Ashanti."

"Yes, Sergeant. Ashanti." Andrew choked down some of the Cape Smoke. The taste was quite pleasant when he accustomed himself to the burn.

Smith's gaze was level. "You might know that Zululand is extremely rich in minerals, with deposits scattered everywhere."

"I didn't know that, Ashanti."

"Well, it's true. The only drawback is that the deposits are in penny packets. You'll have heard of Shaka; I presume?"

"Yes," Andrew said. "He was the king that made the Zulu nation into an empire by attacking and conquering all his neighbours."

"Exactly so, young Andrew. You don't mind if I call you Andrew, do you?"

"Not at all, Ashanti." Andrew tried more of the brandy.

"One of the tribes Shake eradicated was the Lala, from the Tugela Valley," Smith continued. "The Lala were miners and metalworkers, with other tribes calling them *izinyanga zokukhanda*, which apparently meant doctors for beating. They beat out the iron ore to fashion hoes, farming tools, battle axes and spearheads."

"Such things would always be in demand," Andrew agreed cautiously.

"They would," Smith said, "but the Lala also mined copper, silver, and gold, and from these precious metals made jewellery, particularly armbands. Shaka decided he should hold the monopoly for such articles so that he could gift them to his favourites."

Andrew nodded. "Such is the way of royalty," he murmured.

Smith swallowed more brandy. "Despite Shaka's best intentions, his plan failed. Maybe there was an impurity in the metal, or perhaps Zulus have more delicate skin than other peoples, but when they wore these armbands, people developed an unpleasant skin complaint."

"Shaka would not be pleased," Andrew said.

"No. He called in his witch doctors to find out the cause, and they said the Lala miners had poisoned each piece of jewellery to avenge themselves on the Zulus." Smith shrugged. "Maybe they did. After all, the Zulus had grabbed their land and massacred most of their tribe."

"What did Shaka do?" Andrew asked, remembering the three witch doctors he had met.

"This is where opinions differ," Smith said, smiling. "The popular theory is that Shaka gathered every item of jewellery in

Zululand and sent it back to the Tugela Valley together with the Lala miners, smiths and all their relatives. The *indunas* – chiefs – threw the jewellery into one of the mines, and all the Lala people murdered and tossed on top of the jewellery so their spirits could stand guard."

"You said that was the popular theory," Andrew said. "What's the less popular one?"

Smith finished the brandy, casually tossed the bottle over his shoulder and grinned. "That's where things get interesting," he said. "According to Johann, Shaka did not send the jewellery to the Tugela Valley but kept it in a strong box bound with iron. He had the Lala people massacred and asked his witchdoctors to put a curse on the strongbox so nobody would touch it."

Andrew grinned. "That also sounds like the work of a king. I've never heard of a royal who willingly disposes of wealth."

Smith laughed. "I can't see it myself. Each successive king knows the secret of the treasure chest and carries it with them." He leaned forward, whispering confidentially. "Now all we have to do is wait for a war with Cetshwayo of the Zulus, get into his royal kraal of Ulundi and dig up the treasure."

Andrew nodded, half hoping the opportunity never arose and wondering if an officer could make his name fighting the ferocious Zulus. *That would make my father sit up and take notice.*

PART II

MEETING: JUNE 1878

CHAPTER 7

"We need you, Jama," Zuluhlenga, Chief Sihayo's brother, announced.

Zuluhlenga had summoned Jama to his *imuzi* and sat on a carved three-legged stool.

Jama stood before Zuluhlenga and his family in the centre of his *imuzi*. The people watched from a respectful distance, aware of what had happened and interested in how the chief's family would react.

"Yes, *inkosi*," Jama said. He noted that Mehlokazulu, Sihayo's eldest son was also present, looking restless as he shifted from foot to foot.

"Sihayo is absent at oNdini," Zuluhlenga reminded Jama. "While he is away, his Great Wife, Kaqwelebana and one of his lesser wives have been with other men."

Jama knew the story. The scandal of Kaqwelebana's adultery had spread around the area, with women speaking of it in hushed tones and men shaking their heads at the insult to Sihayo. Yibanathi had kept Jama fully informed as they sat together for their evening meal.

Jama remained mute until Zuluhlenga told him what his part

should be. Mehlokazulu looked embarrassed, he thought. Maybe even ashamed of his mother's actions.

Zuluhlenga continued. "The family held a meeting in the absence of Sihayo and decided we should kill Kaqwelabana."

Jama acknowledged the justice of the decision. Yibanathi had told him what Sihayo's family would decide, for she was a font of knowledge on such matters. Jama wondered if Mehlokazulu had contributed to the decision to execute his mother.

"We surrounded her *izindlu* and attacked them as they lay together," Zuluhlenga said, with anger strong in his voice. "We wounded Kaqwelabana, but she evaded us, as did the lesser wife, and they fled across the Buffalo River."

Jama gave a brief nod, although he scorned a raiding party that allowed their target to escape. He would have placed a double ring around the *imuzi* so that Kaqwelabana and her lover could never break free. He waited to see what Mehlokazulu and Zuluhlenga intended to do. Would they allow the offenders to evade justice or follow them across the frontier?

"I will take a strong party to pursue them," Mehlokazulu announced.

"That is the correct decision," Jama replied. "Did you ask the king's permission to enter the white man's country?

Jama thought Zuluhlenga and his compatriots had bungled the attack badly. What should have been a routine execution had turned into an ugly drama, and evidently, Zuluhlenga and Mehlokazulu had no choice but to chance Cetshwayo's wrath.

"Others have crossed the frontier on similar missions," Mehlokazulu reminded. "We shall bring Kaqwelabana back to Zululand for execution and hurt nobody on the Natal side of the river."

Jama gave another brief nod. "What do you want me to do?" he asked, although he had already guessed the answer.

"Bring your warriors," Mehlokazulu said. "Bring the Abanonya."

"We are at your command," Jama said. He would show Zuluhlenga how to manage such an affair.

LIEUTENANT ANDREW DAVID BAIRD OF THE CAPE MOUNTED Rifles reined up his horse and checked his men. He had a dozen riders behind him, all veterans of the Cape Frontier War with the Galekas, sun-browned, narrow-eyed, and dusty from hard campaigning and long hours in the saddle.

Andrew looked around the small settlement of Umtata with its handful of European houses and sprawl of African *izindlu.* "We'll outspan and camp here," he ordered. "Hitchings, go to the store and buy mealies for the horses."

"Yes, sir," Hitchings said.

"Kelly, attend to the horses. The rest of us will gather firewood and raise the tents, except Sinclair and Abernethy. You two are on picket duty."

Andrew watched for a moment as Kelly rung the horses. He fastened a *reim,* a length of rawhide, to the head collar of one horse, doubled it and secured it to the next until he had bound all the patrol's horses together. The horses were now in a circle, happy with each other's company and unable to stray, while a sentry ensured no wandering horse thief could take advantage of their position.

Once he was sure the horses were secure, Andrew rode to a nearby hillock to get a better view of his surroundings.

Brought up in the ancient towns of England and Scotland, Andrew had never been impressed with the settlements in South Africa, and Umtata was no exception. Twenty-five miles from the eastern coast, Umtata stood beside the Umtata River and looked raw. European settlers had recently founded the town, and the builders used galvanised iron as a building material. From his vantage point, Andrew could see the sun reflecting from the metal walls and the metal roof of the cathedral, although the Wesleyan chapel was brick-built, and the court-house was solid stone.

Trust the authorities to ensure the court will endure.

Between the European-style houses, the local Tembu, Bomvana, Pondo, Pondomise, and Hala people had built their homes and moved around the town beside the British and Boer population.

"Why are we here?" Hitchings asked, adding a reluctant "sir" when Andrew stared at him.

"I don't know yet," Andrew admitted. "Brigadier Simonds wants to see me tomorrow."

Hitchings grunted and walked away, grumbling.

With the men settled and pickets on watch, Andrew lay in his tent that night, wondering why the brigadier had summoned him.

My men have performed all their duties. We've obeyed orders and fought a dozen skirmishes. He sighed, decided worrying was pointless and lay down to sleep. *Let the morning take care of itself.*

The neat triple row of tents beside the village gleamed white under the morning sun as Andrew rode across. He took a deep breath of the crisp air, decided that life could be much worse and approached the main British encampment.

"I'm looking for Brigadier Simonds," he announced to the erect, moustached private of the 24th Foot who acted as sentry.

"Old Smoulder is in the central tent, mate." The sentry jerked a thumb towards the camp. "Over that way."

"You call me sir, private!" Andrew snapped.

"Sir?" the sentry repeated and stiffened to attention. "Sorry, sir. I didn't recognise the uniform. I thought you were one of the irregular horsemen."

"I am a lieutenant in the Cape Mounted Rifles," Andrew told him. "Be more careful in future." He pushed Lancelot into the tented lines. The army was already awake, with scarlet-uniformed men bustling around and hard-eyed sergeants barking orders.

A tall sentry eyed Andrew as he approached.

"Lieutenant Baird to see Brigadier Simonds," Andrew announced himself.

"Ah, Lieutenant Baird." Simonds was thin faced with a moustache that concealed most of his mouth and extended below his chin. He leaned back in his cane chair and stuffed tobacco into the bowl of his pipe. "You'll know why I sent for you."

"No, sir," Andrew said.

"No?" Simonds raised his eyebrows in disbelief. "Don't you read the newspapers?"

"I haven't had much chance recently, sir," Andrew admitted. "I've been a little preoccupied with the Galekas and Gaikas."

"Yes, I suppose you have," Simonds allowed. "You've been through the Xhosa campaign from the beginning, haven't you?"

"Yes, sir."

"You started as a trooper with the Frontier Armed and Mounted Police, gained quick promotion to commissioned rank and remained with them when the unit was transferred to the army and became the Cape Mounted Rifles."

"That's correct, sir," Andrew was surprised that Simonds should know his history.

Simonds lifted a newspaper, passed it over, clamped his pipe between his teeth, struck a match and ignited the tobacco. "Third column, the second article," he said, puffing blue smoke into the already stuffy tent.

Andrew ignored the piece about Fighting Jack Windrush's exploits in Afghanistan and focussed on the second article.

Local vessel comes aground on East Coast. Amelia was bound from Cape Town to D'Urban in Natal when an unexpected squall drove her ashore north of the Great Kei. Despite valiant efforts to refloat her, Amelia broke her back and sank. Two of the crew and three passengers were lost, although some of the cargo was saved. Amelia was fully insured, so the owners may not have suffered a financial loss.

"It's about a shipwreck, sir." Andrew did not hide his confusion.

"That's correct, Baird," Simonds said, puffing aromatic smoke. "I want you to take the survivors from Umtata to St John's at the Umzinvubu River. They'll catch a ship to D'Urban in Natal from St John's."

Andrew nodded. He had learned that life in the army meant obeying any order. One day he could be holding a small garrison against Xhosa attack and the next herding cattle to a missionary station. Escorting civilians across country was all part of the job.

"Yes, sir. When do we start?"

Simonds smiled, with his smouldering pipe clenched between his teeth. "As soon as you can, Lieutenant. Ships regularly put into St John's, and I might need you back here." He puffed out more smoke. "Between you, me and every other soldier in Southern Africa, Baird, we're expecting trouble from the Zulus next and might need every rifle. The Zulus are a fearsome people, not to be taken lightly."

"I thought we were at peace with Zululand," Andrew said.

Simonds removed his pipe. "Peace is an illusion out here, Baird. It's only a breathing space for the tribes to gather their strength." He pointed the stem of his pipe to Andrew. "Mark my words, young man, if the Zulus mean war, you'll see something that takes your mind off the Galekas."

"I have heard they are formidable, sir," Baird said.

"They are the most aggressive, best-disciplined fighting force in black Africa," Simonds said soberly. "And we'll need every good man we have to defeat them, so get these civilians to St John's and return as soon as possible."

"Yes, sir." Andrew saluted and left the tent. Only when he returned to his riflemen did he realise that Simonds had paid him a compliment by calling him a good man.

Thank you, Brigadier. Andrew patted Lancelot as he mounted. "We're getting there, Lance. We don't need a family name and influence to make our way in this world."

The local authorities had placed *Amelia's* survivors in half a dozen locations throughout the town, and Andrew set Abernethy the task of finding them.

"You're a gentleman, Abernethy," Andrew said, "and you are better with people than I am."

Abernethy nodded. "I'll bring them to our camp, sir."

"I want to make you an NCO at least, Abernethy. You're far too good to languish in the ranks."

Abernethy shook his head. "No, thank you, sir. I'm happy in the ranks."

Andrew nodded. "As you wish. Off you go, then, and round up *Amelia's* people."

While Abernethy combed Umtata for the survivors, Andrew tried to find transport for the journey to St John's. With the Frontier wars flickering to an untidy end and rumours of an impending struggle with the Zulus, wagons were hard to come by.

"Hire a wagon?" The Boer dragged a hand down his shaggy beard and looked at Andrew through narrow brown eyes. "Why?"

"To take the civilian shipwreck survivors to St John's," Andrew explained.

The Boer, sun-browned and slow of speech, stroked his beard again. "That's a bad road," he said. "You might damage my wagons."

In Andrew's experience, all the roads in South Africa had proved to be bad.

"Bad or not, we'll be travelling that road," Andrew said. "I've twenty-five civilians to take to St John's."

The Boer shook his head and turned away. "You'll be going without me," he said. "Or my boys. You'll have to look elsewhere, *rooineck*."

Andrew knew that *rooineck* meant redneck and was a derogatory term the Boers used for the often-sunburned British soldiers. Boers were descendants of Dutch settlers who had been in South Africa for centuries.

Andrew found the same response wherever he asked in Umtata. Nobody was willing to hire out their wagons for the journey to St John's.

Ashanti Smith approached Andrew, smiling. "You're still too polite, Bairdie." He shook his head. "You're a British officer now; you don't ask these people. You have to command them. That's the trouble with you home-grown men; you've too many scruples and insufficient drive."

"Sir," Andrew suggested helpfully, smiling.

"What?"

"You say sir to an officer. Even a home-grown one," Andrew reminded.

Smith stiffened. "I'm damned if I will."

"You'll be on a charge if you don't," Andrew hardened his tone.

Smith glanced around, where other Riflemen waited to see the outcome. He grinned. "Quite right," he said. "You're learning!"

"You're learning, sir," Andrew prompted.

"You're learning, sir." Smith emphasised the final word.

"And now, Smith." Andrew pressed home his point. "If us home-grown officers are too polite, you can utilise your colonial skills to requisition us some wagons. No stealing, mind. I want everything done legally with no shame attached to the Cape Mounted Rifles." He turned away before Smith could protest. If forcing more experienced men to call him sir was part of being an officer, so was delegating responsibility.

What was Tennyson's closing line in Ulysses, *"to strive, to seek, to find, and not to yield?" That suits an officer's learning process.*

While Ashanti Smith was seeking and finding transport, Andrew spoke to the civilians he was to escort to St John's. Most were serious-looking people; some were men and women who had immigrated to Africa hoping for a better life. Others were the children of settlers from the Cape Colony, men and women who had been born and lived in Africa all their lives. Work-worn men stood beside their worried wives, holding children close by them as they listened to Andrew's words of hope. A young, plain-faced woman stood at the back, with a younger version of herself nervously fingering her coat.

"We'll be leaving Umtata soon." Andrew forced himself to sound cheerful, minimising the difficulties of the journey ahead. "We'll travel overland to St John's, where a ship will carry you to D'Urban. I'll be in charge of the escort in case the native tribes cause any trouble."

"You look very young to command an escort," one bearded settler observed. He tapped the long rifle at his side. "I'll rely on this."

"Thank you for the compliment," Andrew replied. "I have one of my men gathering wagons at present. As soon as we are ready, I'll contact you all again, and we'll move the following day, so be ready."

"We're ready now," the bearded settler said. "We've been ready for the last week."

Andrew nodded, marking the man down as a troublemaker. "I am Lieutenant Andrew Baird. I'd like to know all your names."

"Martin Hancock," the bearded man said.

The others gave their names, some boldly, others quietly, as Andrew wrote them on a small notepad. The two women were last.

"Elaine Maxwell," the older said. "And this is my younger sister, Mariana." Elaine was plain-faced and steady-eyed, a practical woman who could probably turn her hand to anything.

"Well, people," Andrew said. "I'll contact you again when we have transport. In the meantime, please don't stray too far from the town."

Smith proved as good as his word, rounding up nine wagons within two days, while Brigadier Simonds provided army rations for the journey, plus a small herd of slaughter beef.

"Beef on the hoof," Smith said. "That's always a good idea, except it's also a temptation for hungry tribesmen."

"You'll have your Cape Riflemen," Simonds said with his pipe smouldering between his teeth. "I'll lend you a section of the 24th as well. You probably won't need them, but you never know. If the tribes see what they think is a vulnerable convoy, they might forget we're at peace and decide to grab what they can."

"Thank you, sir," Andrew said.

"Best of luck, Baird," Simonds told him and moved away to other things.

Andrew had two types of wagons in his convoy. Two were what the army called General Service Wagons, weighing eighteen hundredweight and nine feet long. The remaining four were colonial ox wagons, twelve feet long and much heavier at nearly thirty hundredweight and with a correspondingly greater span of oxen to tow them.

"We should have twenty oxen for these colonial wagons," Smith said. "I could only find fourteen to sixteen for each, and they are not all best quality."

"You did well to find any," Andrew gave grudging praise.

"We'll have to use what we can find. I've whistled up a few native drivers; they're the best in the world with ox-wagons, sir, as you'll know."

"You did well, Ashanti," Andrew said.

Smith smiled and tipped his forage cap over his left eye. The green feathers were still in place, a reminder of past battles. He looked up. "It's hot today," he said. "I sense a storm coming, so we might not get on the road tomorrow."

"That's unseasonal," Andrew said as he sniffed the air. "We don't usually get storms this early in the year. They normally arrive in September or October."

Smith nodded. "If only we could regulate the seasons, eh?"

"Will it be bad?" Andrew trusted Smith with all things African.

"Can you hear that thunder, sir?" Smith asked.

"I can," Andrew said.

"That's coming our way," Smith told him. "Batten down the hatches."

Dust devils foretold the onslaught, miniature whirlwinds that lifted the dust on the road, followed by a surprisingly chill wind and then lightning that ripped across the sky accompanied by thunder like heavy artillery.

"Welcome to Africa," Abernethy said as the first rail fell in heavy splashes. "Land of sunshine, adventure and," he looked upwards, "this."

Andrew smiled as the civilians took shelter under the canvas covers of the wagons. He moved to Lancelot, who was agitated by the thunder.

"It's all right, Lance," he whispered in its ear. "It's only thunder. It won't hurt." He held a handful of mealies for his horse to eat.

"Did you call him Lancelot?" The younger of the two sisters emerged from inside the General Service wagon. Blonde-haired, with her sister's grey eyes, Andrew could not remember her name.

"I did," Andrew admitted. The girl was around seventeen, he estimated, sun-browned, with a plain dress to match her homely features.

"Lancelot was one of King Arthur's knights." The girl ignored the rain that flattened her hat and soaked her long dress.

"One of Arthur's best knights," Andrew agreed.

"Do you know about King Arthur and the Round Table?" the girl asked.

"A little," Andrew said. He noticed the older sister emerging from the wagon, looking concerned. "You'd better get back under cover. It's very wet out here."

"I don't mind the rain," the girl said.

"I mind the rain," the elder sister said sternly. "Get back inside before you catch a fever. Stop annoying that poor soldier!"

"I'm not annoyed," Andrew said with a smile. "But you are right; it's a bit wet for a young lady."

"In you come," the elder sister insisted.

"I'm Mariana," the younger sister reminded before a firm sisterly hand pulled her back inside the wagon.

"Good night, Mariana," Andrew called.

"Good night, Lancelot," Mariana replied. "A bowshot from her bower-eaves,

He rode between the barley-sheaves,
The sun came dazzling thro' the leaves,
And flamed upon the brazen greaves
Of bold Sir Lancelot."[1]

"That's from the Lady of Shalott!" Andrew said, surprised that somebody should quote Tennyson to him, but both sisters were back inside their wagon. Elaine had laced the flap tightly shut against the rain, and thunder was grumbling in the sky.

Andrew ensured the horses were secure, checked the pickets and retired to his tent. He lay on his bed, listened to the rain hammering at the canvas and considered where he was.

Umtata had been a wild place, home to all the drifters, the lawless and unsettled who made the frontier their home. Boers, British, Xhosa and men of uncertain colour, race and provenance had graduated to Umtata, making the town devoid of pity but rife in crime, prostitution, and casual murder. The last few years had seen massive improvement, yet Andrew swore, rose, and posted a sentry on the sisters' wagon.

"Abernethy, you and Ramsay watch these two women."

"Yes, sir," Abernethy replied at once. "I've seen some unsavoury people hovering around. And not only the locals." He glanced meaningfully at Hitchings, cowering under the lashing rain.

Andrew thought it best not to comment on his men. "Ensure the women are safe, would you?"

"We will, sir." Ramsay was an older man in whom the fires of lust should have long burned out. He stamped his feet and grimaced at the teeming rain. "Although it would be a brave man who'd venture out in this."

Andrew nodded in agreement and stepped away. He had done all he could and intended to start the journey the following day, whatever the weather. Until then, the world would take its course.

CHAPTER 8

The rain hammered for another three hours and then stopped as if somebody had turned off a tap. The sudden silence woke Andrew. He rose, rechecked the pickets, retired to bed and woke when bugles in the British camp sounded reveille.

"I'll have to arrange a soldier-servant," he scolded himself as he dressed, shaving by candlelight, and nicking his chin in the process. He swore quietly, dabbed at the tiny spot of blood, and stooped out of the tent.

"Hello, Lancelot." Mariana was with the horse before Andrew arrived and greeted him with a broad smile. "Then answered Lancelot, the chief of knights, as Tennyson wrote. [1]Good morning, Lieutenant Baird."

"Good morning, Mariana," Andrew replied. "I'm afraid I need Lancelot," Andrew told her. "We have a busy day ahead of us."

"I know. We're heading for St John's." Mariana gave Lancelot a final pat and glanced at her wagon, where Elaine was making the final preparations.

"We'll be moving in an hour," Andrew said.

"We'll be ready." Andrew judged Elaine to be nineteen or

twenty, with the mannerisms of a woman of thirty. She raised her voice. "Come on, Mariana; I need a hand here!"

"Coming," Mariana said, with a final pat of Lancelot.

"You put a sentry on our wagon last night." Elaine sounded nearly accusing.

"I did," Andrew agreed.

"There was no need." Elaine patted the pistol at her belt. "But thank you." She gave a slight nod and began to check the fastenings of the wagon cover.

Andrew lifted his hat to Elaine and moved away, shouting to his men. He studied the map Brigadier Simonds had given him. The route to St John's seemed like a switchback, up and down a series of hills with little respite.

With the nine-wagon convoy lined up behind him, Andrew lifted his hand, patted Lancelot, and began the march. Although Brigadier Simonds had encouraged him to speed, he did not force the pace the first day, allowing the animals and drivers time to adjust to the conditions.

His riflemen, all veterans, rode as scouts a quarter of a mile from the wagons, with the infantry of the 24th Foot acting as close escort, ready to lend a hand when required. Andrew rode half a mile forward, checking the route, returning to supervise the wagons, and urging the men on.

Although Andrew had learned a lot about driving a wagon since he arrived in South Africa, he would not call himself an experienced driver. He watched the convoy struggle, noting the good drivers and the not-so-good. Some men required all their skill to drive up even the gentlest of the hills, while others worked with a nonchalance that spoke of hidden talents.

"Some of these lads are experts," Andrew said when Martin Hancock joined him.

"It depends on the team," Hancock told him. "If the oxen pull well together, this section of road isn't too bad." He removed his hat and scratched his tangled hair. "It's a lot worse further on."

Andrew viewed the road. Even the best sections were simply carved out of the side of the hills, with a rough, stony surface stretching forever and a steep drop to the left. The engineer, if there had been an engineer, had only left room for a single wagon, so the outside wheels were very close to the edge.

He watched as the infantrymen joked with the wagon drivers, black or white, and were always ready to lend a willing shoulder when the teams struggled. Private Miller, a cheerful Geordie, was constantly helping, with O'Donnell and Drummond close behind.

That first day they managed ten miles, and everybody was glad of the rest when Andrew called a halt. He posted three horsemen on mobile patrol as an outer line of pickets and three of the 24th as an inner defence pulled the wagons into a laager in case of attack and dismounted. Sitting on a fallen tree trunk, he lit his pipe, took off his forage cap and fanned his glowing face.

"Lieutenant Baird." Elaine approached him, smiling faintly. "You look exhausted."

Andrew lifted his head. "Good evening, Miss Maxwell," he said, standing up and taking the pipe from his mouth.

Elaine looked surprised at this small show of politeness. She bobbed in a brief curtsey. "Good evening, Lieutenant. I wondered if you would care to share our meal."

Andrew started. "That's very kind of you, but I have my duty to do."

"I'm sure you have, Lieutenant," Elaine replied quickly, "but even duty-bound officers must eat sometime."

Andrew could not stop his smile. "That is correct, Miss Maxwell."

"It's only stew," Elaine said, suddenly apprehensive in case Andrew did not like her cooking. "From the rations the army handed out, plus a few local vegetables I found."

"I haven't had anything except army cooking for over a year," Andrew admitted. "Stew would be most welcome." He smiled, blushed, and looked away. "My apologies, Miss Maxwell. I am unused to the company of a lady."

Elaine smiled. "I apologise if I seem forward," she said. "You were so kind to Mariana yesterday and this morning that I had to thank you." She pushed forward a bowl of steaming stew.

"Kind?" Andrew did not have to pretend confusion.

"When Mariana asked you about Lancelot and King Arthur."

Andrew shook his head. "I only spoke to her. It was nothing."

"It meant a lot to Mariana," Elaine said, looking away. "And to me."

Unsure what to say, Andrew tried the stew. "This is good," he told her. Andrew realised Elaine was not quite as plain-faced as he had thought. He studied her surreptitiously from the corner of his eyes, noting the firm line of her jaw, the high cheekbones, and the straight nose.

No, he told himself. *She is not plain at all. Elaine has a strong face.*

"Thank you." Elaine was watching him eat. She realised that Mariana was leaning out of the wagon, listening to everything she said. "We'd better get to work, Lieutenant, and you to your duty."

"We've finished work, Elaine," Mariana said, grinning.

"Come on, Mariana!" Elaine said. "Just leave the plate on the ground, Lieutenant," she said. "Mariana will wash it later."

Andrew began to protest, but Mariana had already lifted the plate. He walked away, aware that Elaine was watching every step he took.

They started before dawn the following day, with the road becoming progressively worse. As the hills grew steeper, Andrew took the advice of the experienced drivers and hooked one span of oxen onto another to haul one wagon at a time, yet they still made painfully slow progress.

"There should be a special kind of hell for the man who made these roads," Abernethy said. "They should have to lead a team of wagons up and down them for eternity."

"I feel that we're doing that already," Andrew said and raised his voice. "Get these beasts moving!" Brigadier Simond's instructions to hurry ran through his head. He rode beside each wagon, cajoling, threatening, and lending his strength by pushing at the back. "Get up this blasted road!"

"You'll hurt yourself." Elaine and Mariana had left their wagon to lighten it. "The oxen can only pull to their strength, Lieutenant Baird."

"Every little helps," Andrew said, hoping Elaine had not heard his strong language.

"We're making good time on these bad roads," Elaine told him.

"Maybe," Andrew conceded.

"Don't distress yourself so," Elaine said as Mariana nodded in agreement.

"You can't do the impossible, Lieutenant Baird," Mariana said and began to recite Tennyson.

"And up and down the people go,

Gazing where the lilies blow," [2]she smiled. "Except there are no lilies here."

"Not even one," Andrew agreed.

"Sorry to interrupt, sir, but somebody is watching us," Abernethy rode up. "If you look at the hill behind me and to the left, you'll see a body of natives."

Andrew was too experienced to look at once. The countryside was beautiful, with steep hills, fast-flowing rivers despite the recent drought, and well-wooded. It was also well populated, with the local tribe being the Amapondos.

"Who is the local chief?" Elaine asked, hushing Mariana with a raised hand.

"Umquiliso." Andrew had questioned the residents of Umtata about the local tribes. "He rules all the land between Umtata and the St John's River."

"Is he friendly, sir?" Abernethy asked, thumbing the lock of his Snider. "I don't know this area."

"I've been told that Umquiliso is friendly on the surface," Andrew said. "The Amapondos are not a warlike nation, but we'd be foolish to take chances." He warned the riflemen and infantry to stay alert and pushed on until the late afternoon. "Umquiliso pretends to be our friend, but we suspect he sent some warriors to help the Galekas. He's also attacked the Amsquesibes, who are undoubtedly friendly to us." Andrew realised he was talking too much. "Keep alert, boys."

"And girls," Elaine said, lifting her determined chin.

"And girls," Andrew amended with a smile.

They pushed on over hill country without a single level piece of ground. The distance to St John's was not great, but the road worsened hourly, with even the most experienced drivers muttering about the difficulties.

"We can usually carry nine thousand pounds weight in each wagon," one driver said. "I'm only carrying half that, and we're still struggling up these buggering inclines."

Andrew thought of the route ahead, Simond's warning about possible trouble with the Zulus, and studied the surrounding hills with his field glasses.

"Keep moving," he growled. "Use every trick you can but get these wagons to St John's."

"Yes, lieutenant," the driver said, hawked up phlegm from the back of his throat, saw Andrew glaring at him, and swallowed noisily. He stomped back to his wagon. Andrew watched him for a second, a weather-battered man in a broad-brimmed hat and faded brown corduroys, and turned away as Elaine pushed her wagon up the track with Mariana walking at the side. Elaine brushed a loose strand of hair from her face and spared a moment to smile at him before cracking her whip to encourage her oxen.

"Well done, Miss Maxwell," Andrew shouted.

The Amapondos followed the convoy, never coming close but always there as a potential threat. The male travellers carried their rifles and stayed close to their wives and families. With no men to look after them, the sisters looked more vulnerable, so Andrew frequently checked on them.

"Thank you for your concern, Lieutenant," Elaine said as Mariana smiled shyly and patted Lancelot.

"May I ask how you two ladies are alone?" Andrew asked.

"We lost our uncle in the shipwreck," Elaine said without visible emotion.

"Oh, I am sorry to hear that," Andrew was immediately contrite. "I didn't realise."

"We were in Cape Town on some legal business," Elaine said. "Settling the lease for more land for the farm." She smiled. "It's the first time we've been so far away from Natal."

"You are native to Natal?"

"Born and bred," Elaine told him with more than a hint of pride.

Andrew looked ahead, where the mountain of Quanyana presented a formidable obstacle. He knew the rest of the day would be challenging, and the Amapondos were still there, watching without approaching.

Andrew helped guide the leading oxen over a rough piece of track. "Is it not dangerous living close to Zululand?"

Elaine shook her head. "No more dangerous than anywhere else and less dangerous than the Cape frontier. From the stoep of our house, we can see across the Tugela into Zululand, and the herd boys water their cattle opposite our land. The Zulus have never given us any trouble."

Andrew raised his eyebrows. "People have told me the Zulus are Africa's most aggressive and dangerous nation."

When Elaine laughed, her hair bounced around her face, and the severe expression disappeared. "Their king, Cetshwayo, keeps them in order. I admit they have an interesting history, but they've never bothered us." She negotiated a turn with a skill any driver twice her age would have envied.

"What's your farm like?" Andrew asked as Mariana came

closer, walking beside the front wheel of the wagon. Her skirt snapped against her legs with every stride.

"It's called Inglenook, and it's not very big," Elaine said. "Only a few hundred acres or so, but having the Tugela close ensures it's well watered, which is very important in this part of the world." She smiled as she spoke, with her eyes warm as she described her home. "We have a huge mopane tree only fifty yards from the house, and Mariana and I made that our own. We've climbed every branch, despite Mother's attempts to make us ladylike."

Andrew could not picture Elaine climbing a tree.

Mariana laughed. "Poor Mother! You should have heard the things she called us!"

"I can imagine," Andrew said. He could see Mariana scampering to the top, with her hair flying wild and her laughter sounding. "Your mother would have her work cut out with you two!"

Elaine glanced at Mariana and smiled. "Do you know the mopane tree, Lieutenant Baird?" She continued before Andrew had time to reply. "It has butterfly-shaped leaves that change colours in the autumn. We call it the kaleidoscope tree because of the different colours."

Andrew laughed, enjoying the play of emotions on Elaine's face as much as her words.

"Our tree is home to the mopane worm, the caterpillar of the mopane moth. The local people eat it either fresh from the tree or dried, and sometimes the Zulu herd boys cross the Tugela to find the worms." Elaine smiled. "We don't mind." She looked up, cracked her whip, and pushed the wagon over another rough stretch of road.

Andrew realised he was neglecting his duty and touched a hand to his hat. "If you'll excuse me, ladies, I must see to the convoy."

"Of course, Lieutenant," Elaine said as Mariana gave Lancelot a farewell pat.

"We'll tell you more about Inglenook later," Mariana shouted as Andrew pushed back down the convoy.

The soldiers of the 24th Foot were busy pushing the more heavily laden wagons, joking with the drivers. Veterans of the Border War, Andrew knew they would never pass muster on a British parade ground. The men had stained their once-white sun helmets brown with a mixture of mud and cow dung and mud. Battered by hard service, their serge uniforms, brilliant scarlet when they left Britain, were sweat-stained and faded to a dozen shades of pink and white. Their blue trousers were discoloured by red dust, patched, and darned above mud-caked black boots and gaiters.

Andrew watched them for a moment, wondering what an Aldershot sergeant would say about their tarnished brass buttons and general demeanour as they spoke to the native drivers in a language of their own devising.

"Come on, Sammy!" Private Miller said in broad Geordie. "Get these beasts up the hill!"

"Push, you booger," Drummond encouraged in his Yorkshire accent. "Coom on, lad, you can do it!"

Andrew wondered if the soldiers had ever been happier as they toiled in this unfamiliar landscape so far from their home. No landowners expecting deference, no cramped back-to-back brick houses rife with rats and damp, no factory chimneys belching filth into the atmosphere. These men looked healthy and fit.

"Sir." Abernethy rode up, saluting. "These Amapondos are a bit closer now."

"Let's have a word with them," Andrew said. He raised his voice. "Sergeant McBain!"

"Sir!" McBain was the senior infantryman present. A scarred-faced veteran of medium height and villainous appearance, he spoke with a Welsh accent.

"Take charge of the convoy while I look at these Amapondos."

"Very good, sir!" McBain saluted.

"Smith!" Andrew shouted. "You're with me!" If there were to be trouble, he'd rather have the experienced Ashanti Smith at his back than anybody else. He knew he could trust Abernethy not to let him down, and the men of the 24th Foot were steady veterans, but Smith had guile as well as experience.

"Sir!" Smith joined them, riding towards the Amapondos.

"Wait!" Andrew shouted as the tribesmen began to withdraw. Smith lifted his carbine, pointed it to one of the men and repeated the command.

When the Amapondos stopped, Andrew raised a hand to show he was in peace.

"I am Lieutenant Andrew Baird of the Cape Mounted Rifles," he said in Xhosa. "We mean you no harm."

The Amapondos were tall, muscular men but wary as Smith held his carbine in the crook of his arm with the muzzle pointing towards their leader. Behind the small group, Andrew saw men gathering, most carrying assegais and shields.

"Why are you watching us?" Andrew asked.

"We want to know why you are in the land of the Amapondos," the spokesmen said. "Our chief did not give you permission to come here."

"We don't need your permission," Smith began until Andrew stopped him with an upraised hand.

"Do you think we are trespassing?" Andrew asked.

"You are on Amapondo land," the spokesman insisted.

Andrew considered for a moment. From where he stood, he could see his convoy straggling along the road, a succession of slow-moving, heavily laden wagons, each pulled by a dozen or more oxen. The small infantry escort looked very thin on the ground, while the mounted men were mere dots in a vast landscape.

"Times have been bad here lately," Andrew commented. "You've had drought and famine."

The Amapondo agreed, watching Andrew intently.

"We have no desire to journey where we are not wanted," Andrew said. "We only wish to cross your land. To show our friendship to the Amapondo, we will give you four of our slaughter cattle." He knew he might be setting a dangerous precedent, but his duty was to get the convoy safely to St John's.

The spokesman's smile told Andrew he had made the correct decision.

"I will have my men herd the cattle to you," Andrew said. He nodded to the warriors in the distance. "If you take your men away and grant us safe passage."

The spokesman rose. "You have safe passage," he said.

When Andrew returned to the convoy, he wondered if he was an army officer or a diplomat and decided he had to be both. He glanced at the surrounding hills, saw there no Amapondo warriors were watching and knew he could concentrate on pushing the wagons through.

Time to do my duty, he thought and smiled as Elaine waved to him.

CHAPTER 9

They sat inside the laagered wagons with three campfires sending flames and smoke toward the star-bright sky. Outside the laager, the oxen stood within a thornbush barrier, with bored sentries marching on slow boots while outer pickets waited with ready rifles.

Andrew placed another log on the fire and watched as a ribbon of sparks spiralled upward. He smiled across at Elaine, who held a mug in both hands while sitting on a handy boulder. Mariana pushed back her broad-brimmed hat and returned Andrew's smile.

"This is the best part of the day," Andrew said. "When we've done the day's work, and we can relax for a little while." He nodded beyond the laager. "Except for the sentries, but that's part of the soldier's bargain."

That was my father's phrase. I hope I am not copying him.

Elaine pounced on Andrew's words. "Part of the soldier's bargain? What does that mean, Lieutenant?"

"I mean, soldiers have to accept the rough with the smooth without complaints. They accepted the Queen's Shilling and must abide by the consequences."

"Soldiering is a hard life," Mariana said.

"So is farming," Andrew replied. "Or working down a coal mine, or in a fishing boat or a Cape Horn clipper ship." He lifted his tea to his lips. "I doubt soldiering is any worse, and we meet some interesting people."

"Oh?" Elaine said. "Have you met some interesting people?"

"From time to time," Andrew said. He wondered if Elaine was fishing for a compliment, decided she was not and turned the conversation around. "You promised to tell me about your home."

"So we did," Mariana said.

"We did." Elaine quietened her sister with a look that could crack glass. "In the morning, we can sit on the stoep at Inglenook and watch dawn rise over Zululand, tinting the Tugela pinky-red, and hear our cattle lowing to one another."

"Do you enjoy farming?" Andrew asked.

"It's the only thing to do," Elaine told him, with lights dancing behind her eyes.

Andrew nodded. "I can believe that." He listened as Elaine and Mariana took turns sharing their memories with him.

"We call it Inglenook," Elaine said. "The Zulus called it *Indawo Yokuthula* – the place of peace. Isn't that lovely? Zulu is the most beautiful language in the world. My grandfather came out with the Byrne Settlers in 1850 [1]and moved to our present land in 1858. We've carved a farm out of a wilderness."

"It sounds idyllic," Andrew said, watching the play of emotions on Elaine's face.

"Where do you come from, Lieutenant?" Mariana asked.

"A small town called Berwick-upon-Tweed, right on the Border between England and Scotland," Andrew said. "While you have the Tugela on your doorstep, I have the Tweed."

"Like Sir Walter Scott at Abbotsford," Mariana said.

"Yes, but without the towers and turrets," Andrew told her. "My house is a little more modest."

"Is it cold there?" Elaine asked.

"It can be cold in winter," Andrew admitted. "We get ice on

the Tweed sometimes, clinking under the bridge and against the harbour walls, where the swans cluster."

"Do you live on a farm?" Mariana wanted to know.

"No." Andrew shook his head. "I live in a townhouse built right on the town wall." He saw their confused expressions and explained. "Berwick was a fortress town when England and Scotland were enemies, and Queen Elizabeth of England built a great wall to keep the Scots out. I used to run around the walls in the morning, watching the dawn on the North Sea and dodging the seagulls."

"What's your house called?" Elaine added wood to the fire, moving closer as the night-time chill began to bite.

"I changed the name to Joyous Gard," Andrew said, glancing at Mariana.

"That was Lancelot's castle!" Mariana exclaimed. "He took it from a robber baron and altered the name!"

"That's right," Andrew said. "Some Arthurian legends have him living close to Berwick, at Bamburgh Castle, so I borrowed the name."

"Did he really live near Berwick?" Mariana asked as Elaine smiled at Andrew.

"I'd like to think so," Andrew said. He glanced at his watch. "Well, ladies, I am afraid duty calls, and I must check the sentries." He stood up. "I'd advise that you retire soon; there's another hard day ahead of us tomorrow."

"Yes, lieutenant," Elaine said as Andrew straightened his forage cap and walked to the perimeter of the laager. When he glanced behind him, Andrew saw that the firelight was highlighting Elaine's face and reflecting from her fine grey eyes. He turned away before she saw him looking and did not see Mariana peering out from the half-closed wagon flap.

They crossed the Tugela in the darkness before dawn, with Mehlokazulu leading thirty mounted men and Jama with fifty of his Abanonya as insurance against any outside interference.

Jama heard the steady tramp of feet behind him. He knew Ndleleni and Bangizwe were at his back. They had been his constant companions since they were herd boys together, men he would trust to the death. Bhekizizwe and Bafana were nearly as close, veteran warriors, while his sons, Funani and Kgabu, were on the fringe. Jama expected Cetshwayo would soon call up his sons to place them in another *amabutho* of their age group but wanted to lead them on their first expedition himself.

Mehlokazulu stopped immediately after they crossed the Tugela, with moonlight reflected on the shifting water and the cry of a jackal eerie in the night. Jama hefted his shield, grinned across to Ndleleni and looked forward to the night's excitement. He was content with his wives and cattle but missed the excitement of fighting with his men.

"We have executed one of the errant women," Mehlokazulu told them. "And have found Kaqwelebana."

The warriors nodded their satisfaction.

"She is hurt and hiding in Maziyana's *imuzi*. Mazinyana is a border guard, paid by the British to stop any Zulus from crossing the Tugela into Natal." Mehlokazulu led the laughter.

"Cetshwayo does not want us to hurt anybody on the Natal side of the river." Mehlokazulu reminded. "Be careful with your assegais, for we don't want to anger the king."

Jama and the other warriors nodded. "We will take Kaqwelebana back to Zululand without killing anybody in Natal," Mehlokazulu ordered, mounted his horse, and led them into Natal.

Maziyana's *imuzi* was a short distance from the river and slept in the security that no Zulu would cross the Tugela. Jama's impi formed a guard around the *imuzi*, with half facing inwards and the remainder outwards. They held their assegais ready in case any of Maziyana's people resisted, but nobody did.

Mehlokazulu took only three men inside the *imuzi* and demanded his mother's return. Maziyana objected, knowing what the outcome would be. He ran outside his *indlu*, shouting for his warriors.

Jama saw Maziyana emerge and stepped inside the *imuzi*, holding his assegai ready to strike. Maziyana halted, hesitated, looked at the Abanonya warriors surrounding the *imuzi* and returned. He watched as Mehlokazulu grabbed Kaqwelebana and hauled the terrified woman away. Jama's Abanonya followed the mounted men across the drift to the Zulu side of the Tugela.

"Don't kill me!" Kaqwelebana pleaded. "I am your mother!"

"You shamed our family," Mehlokazulu replied. "Kill her."

The Zulus were merciful, shooting Kaqwelebana rather than subjecting her to a more lingering death.

The woman died immediately, and, according to Mehlokazulu, her demise closed the incident. Justice had been done, the Zulus had hurt nobody on the Natal side of the river, and life continued as before.

Jama returned to his *imuzi*, his wives, and his cattle. In his mind, Mehlokazulu had managed the whole affair poorly, but the outcome was satisfactory, although he hoped Cetshwayo did not object to the impi crossing the Tugela. Yibanathi was waiting for him with a meal, and after he had eaten, he trotted out to his cattle. One cow was due to calve, and Jama wanted to ensure the birth was trouble-free.

THE MOUNTAIN OF QUANYANA WAS THE FIRST MAJOR OBSTACLE in the day's journey. The upward road was tricky but manageable, with a steady three-mile-long climb, while the downward slope swooped down at a fifty-degree angle for three-quarters of a mile.

Andrew noticed that the Amapondos had returned, with a handful of warriors standing on a neighbouring hill, silently watching.

"We might have to unload before we try this road," Hancock said, tugging at his beard. He spat on the ground and glared at Andrew as if he had created the mountain himself.

"Maybe so," Andrew glanced at his watch, "but I'd like to reach the bottom before dark, and it's already two in the afternoon."

"We can try it," a Hottentot driver known as Saul said with a sudden reckless smile. "I'll take the first wagon down."

"Take care," Andrew warned. He watched as Saul jumped onto his perch, released the brake, and cracked his whip. The wagon picked up speed, forcing the oxen to gallop down the hill, with Saul losing control before they were halfway to the bottom. The wagon lurched to the side, bounced on a protruding rock, balanced on two wheels, and turned over with a terrible crash, spilling the contents over the road.

"I warned you," Hancock said smugly.

Andrew swore softly. The journey was bad enough without careless delays. "Ramsay, ride down and check on Saul."

"Yes, sir." Before Ramsay was halfway, Saul appeared beside the wagon, limping but unhurt. He raised a hand in cheerful acknowledgement.

"It looks like we're not going much further today," Smith said, winking at Elaine.

"We'll get the wagons to the bottom of the hill," Andrew told him. He raised his voice. "Take the horses down with whatever loads they can carry. Abernethy, you and Sinclair are horse guards; watch for the Amapondos."

"They're watching us." Abernethy pointed to the warriors on the opposite hill.

"That's why you're on guard," Andrew told him. "Off-saddle the horses and let them graze. The rest of us will right the wagon and gather the goods." He was surprised when the Maxwell sisters joined the men at the stricken vehicle.

"We know how to work," Elaine explained as she lent her slight weight in attempting to right the heavy wagon. Fortunately, the accident had only superficially damaged the sturdy wagon, but it took half an hour to reload the contents.

"Right, Saul, on you get," Andrew ordered, and the chastened driver took his place in the driving seat.

"Drive slowly, Saul," Andrew ordered. "We can't afford to lose the wagon or the oxen." He paused for a significant second. "And we don't want to lose you."

He pretended not to notice Elaine's approving nod.

With the wagon and its contents safely at the bottom of the hill, Andrew wondered how to get the other wagons down safely. He called together the drivers for a conference.

"We need a more efficient brake," Andrew said. "Something to slow the wagons down without unbalancing them."

"I have an idea," Elaine said from outside the circle.

Nobody listened to her as they debated various plans. Andrew and Hancock were discussing locking the rear wheels together when he saw Elaine pulling Mariana to her side.

"Come on, Mariana," Elaine said, "we know what to do." Ten minutes later, Andrew saw Elaine take the reins of her wagon and head for the downward slope.

"Miss Maxwell," Andrew shouted, but Elaine was already on the move. As the wagon passed him, Andrew saw that the sisters had hacked down a couple of small trees and attached them to the back to act as drag. He could only hold his breath and watch as the wagon negotiated the slope, with Mariana leaning out of the back, laughing, and reached the bottom in perfect safety.

Andrew shook his head as Elaine leapt from her perch and gave him a cheerful wave. He lifted a hand in rueful acknowledgement.

"The rest of you, do the same," Andrew shouted. "Miss Maxwell has shown us the way!"

Grumbling that they should not have to copy a woman, the other drivers cut small trees from the surrounding countryside and tied them to the back of their wagons.

"This won't work," Hancock said. "It's a waste of time."

"Cut a second tree," Andrew told him. "You have a heavy wagon." He watched as the ever-helpful Miller hacked down a bush and fastened it to Hancock's wagon.

"There you go, chum," Miller said. "That should help." He stepped back, retrieved his Martini-Henry from O'Donnell, and stuck a stubby pipe between his teeth.

Andrew nodded to Hancock. "If you're scared, I'll ask Miss Maxwell to drive your wagon. I'm sure she'll oblige." He smiled at the expression on Hancock's face as he cracked his whip and guided the wagon down the hill.

Using the sister's braking technique, the wagons all reached the foot of the hill, but by then, the sun had set. Andrew ordered them to outspan for the night, set sentries and wondered what the next day would bring. The Amapondos were still watching without making any move to interfere.

"Watch for night-time raiders," Andrew warned the sentries. "They might try to sneak past you in the dark."

"Yes, sir." Miller patted his Martini. "We'll look for them."

"That was daring of you," Andrew said when Elaine was making her evening meal.

Elaine looked up and brushed the hair from her eyes. "I knew what I was doing."

"I noticed," Andrew said dryly. "How long have you been driving?"

"Since I was old enough to walk," Elaine told him.

Andrew nodded slowly. "You do it very well," he replied, stepped away and turned around. "Very well indeed." He took another step. "You do everything very well, Miss Maxwell."

"Elaine," she said without a smile. "My name is Elaine."

"Elaine," Andrew turned back to see her standing with a

spoon in her hand, watching him with her head tilted to one side. She brushed another loose strand of hair from her face.

"Thank you for the compliment, Lieutenant Baird."

"Andrew."

"Andrew," Elaine repeated.

"Andrew," Mariana whispered from inside the wagon as Andrew walked away.

THE FOLLOWING DAY'S TERRAIN WAS THE WORST YET, WITH slopes so steep that not even a double team of oxen could pull a loaded wagon.

"That must be a sixty, even sixty-two-degree slope," Smith said, pushing back his forage cap. "We'll never get up that with a full wagon." He shook his head. "I reckon we'll have to unload them and try that way."

Andrew sighed and glanced at Elaine, who nodded in agreement and made his decision.

"We'll lighten the loads," he said. "Try with half a load." He ignored Smith's headshaking and Elaine's raised eyebrows and gave the orders.

Even with a double team, the oxen failed to haul a half-loaded wagon up the incline. Exasperated, Andrew ordered the rest of the contents piled up beside the road.

"Sergeant McBain," Andrew snapped. "Set a guard on these goods. They'll be a temptation for the Amapondos."

"Very good, sir," McBain said.

It took the entire day for Andrew to ease the convoy up that single hill, with half the mounted men watching for the Amapondos and the rest helping the wagons. The infantry continued to mount close guard and toiled uphill with the contents.

"What is all this stuff for anyway, sir?" McBain asked.

"Most of it is material for the army garrison at St John's,"

Andrew explained. "The remainder is what the settlers salvaged from *Emilia's* shipwreck."

McBain nodded. "I see, sir." He raised his voice to a bellow. "Bancroft! Be careful with that chest! It could be the young lady's best china, damn your clumsiness!"

Andrew smiled and moved on. By the evening, he could look down on the steep slope, with his wagons formed into a laager and the sweet smoke of a campfire drifting over Amapondoland. He looked ahead, where a panorama of endless hills stretched before them.

"We'll be another week at least," Andrew said.

CHAPTER 10

While part of him was frustrated at the length of time the journey was taking, Andrew also felt his gaze settling on Elaine and hoped for more of her company.

"It will take us at least a week to reach St John's, sir," Smith agreed. "Unless we find some help." He indicated the riflemen and infantry slouched against the wagons. "The men are about out on their feet."

"Where will we get help?" Andrew asked.

"Dragoon the tribesmen," Smith replied at once.

"What do you mean?" Andrew guessed the answer.

"Round them up at gunpoint and force them to drag the wagons," Smith said. "Use them as forced labour."

Andrew did not have to consider. "No," he said. "We'll struggle on."

"Brigadier Simonds is waiting," Smith reminded.

"He'll have to wait," Andrew said.

"It was just an idea, sir," Smith said, grinning. He touched a finger to his hat and walked away, leaving Andrew wondering.

"I don't like that man." Elaine checked her oxen, removed a tick, and squashed it underfoot.

Andrew smiled. "He's all right," he told her. "He looked after me when I first arrived in Africa."

"Maybe there's some good in him," Elaine grudgingly acceded. "I still don't like him."

"He's one of the best soldiers I've ever met," Andrew said, "and we have a long journey ahead of us."

Elaine smiled.

"The way was long; the wind was cold,
The Minstrel was infirm and old."

Andrew joined in with the following lines.

"His wither'd cheek, and tresses grey,
Seem'd to have known a better day;
The harp, his sole remaining joy,
Was carried by an orphan boy.
The last of all the Bards was he,
Who sung of Border chivalry."[1]

Elaine laughed. "You know that poem, then?" She stepped away from the oxen.

"*The Lay of the Last Minstrel*, by Sir Walter Scott," Andrew replied. "My mother can quote it by heart. She loves Scott."

"She must be a very cultured lady," Elaine said. "You never talk about your family."

"No," Andrew said. "I never do."

"Why is that?"

Andrew looked away without replying.

"Come now, lieutenant," Elaine teased him. "You can't evade me with silence forever."

Andrew had resolved never to mention his family background. "I don't like to talk about it," he said.

"I sense a family squabble," Elaine said as Mariana edged closer.

Andrew shook his head.

Elaine raised her eyebrows and brushed a non-existent strand of hair from her face. "I see you don't trust me, Lieutenant Baird." Her voice was suddenly cold.

"Of course, I trust you," Andrew said, but Elaine was already walking away.

"Go after her, old man." Abernethy had been a silent witness. "Go on!" Forgetting their respective ranks, he gave Andrew a gentle push.

"Miss Maxwell! Elaine!" Andrew followed as Elaine stormed away, her skirt swaying and her head held high.

The sentries on picket duty looked, grinned, and sensibly said nothing as Andrew chased after Elaine. She did not look behind her, striding on until she was a quarter of a mile clear of the laager.

"Have you seen anything like this before?" Elaine spoke as if nothing had happened, catching Andrew entirely off balance.

"Like what?" Andrew wondered if Elaine was proffering an olive branch or asking an honest question.

"These." Elaine pointed to several paintings on the rocky side of the hill.

"No," Andrew said. "What are they?"

"Bushmen art." Elaine traced one with a stubby, work-hardened finger. "I don't know how long they've been here, but many years, I think."

"I've heard that Bushmen are dangerous," Andrew warned.

"Everybody's dangerous when somebody pushes them into a corner," Elaine said. "The Bantu, Xhosa, Zulu and all the rest have been hunting the Bushmen like animals for generations, maybe hundreds of years. The Bushmen hide in the mountains and deserts."

"Have they? How do you know that?" Andrew showed he was willing to be friendly.

"My Zulu friends told me," Elaine said.

"Do the Zulus speak English?"

"Not as well as I speak Zulu," Elaine said, saying a few Zulu phrases.

"You're a truly impressive lady," Andrew told her. "I've never met anybody like you."

"You must have a sweetheart back home in Berwick," Elaine probed hopefully. "Somebody you trust."

"No." Andrew shook his head, ignoring the barb. "I have no sweetheart," he told her.

"Oh, that's a shame. You must have somebody to go back for." Elaine probed again.

"Maybe," Andrew said, "but no sweetheart."

Elaine brushed another imaginary strand of hair from her face. "You don't say much about yourself."

"No, I don't," Andrew agreed. He knew they would reach St John's in a few days but did not want the journey to end, whatever Brigadier Simonds wished. Andrew did not want to say farewell to Elaine. Or to Mariana, who he was also beginning to like.

"Will you ever be posted to Natal?" Elaine asked.

"I don't think so. I am a Cape Mounted Rifleman, so my unit only operates on the Cape frontier."

"Oh." Elaine did not hide her disappointment. "If you ever are, would you like to come and visit us at Inglenook?"

"Yes," Andrew said and regretted his impulsive answer. He was afraid to reveal his feelings for this girl. *No*, he told himself, *she is not a girl; she's a full-grown woman.*

Is this the girl who will wait for me? Oh, God, I hope so.

That realisation brought a rush of blood to Andrew's face as he looked at Elaine from a new perspective. She was shapely, with finely curved hips and breasts that pushed against her top. He realised that she had lured him here so she could talk to him alone, without an audience of grinning soldiery or a curious sister.

I am a soldier; Elaine is my responsibility.

"Andrew?" Elaine noticed his discomfort. "Will you visit us

even if the army doesn't post you to Natal?"

"I will," Andrew wondered why his voice had become a few octaves lower. "I'd like that." Why did he feel like a young boy rather than an experienced army officer?

Get a hold of yourself, Andrew. Take control.

"I'd like that, too," Elaine said quietly. "You can talk about King Arthur with Mariana and discuss horses with my father."

Andrew took a deep breath. "I'd rather talk with you," he said. "Unless you have your sweetheart with you."

"I don't have a sweetheart either," Elaine said quickly.

"That's good," Andrew said, feeling his heartbeat race, knowing what he wanted to do yet unsure what to say.

They were silent for a moment as the peace of the ancient Bushmen site washed over them. A pair of birds called, and a soft breeze carried cooled them.

"I like Tennyson and Scott," Elaine said. "*The Lady of Shalott* is my favourite, even though it's a sad story." She smiled and quoted the final stanza.

"They cross'd themselves, their stars they blest,
Knight, minstrel, abbot, squire, and guest.
There lay a parchment on her breast,
That puzzled more than all the rest,
The well fed wits at Camelot.
'The web was woven curiously,
The charm is broken utterly,
Draw near and fear not,—this is I,
The Lady of Shalott."

Andrew listened to her voice, knowing he would never forget this moment.

"I'm named Elaine after the Lady," Elaine said, suddenly eager to speak. "You'll like Inglenook." She stepped so close that Andrew could smell the perfume of her hair.

She's worn that, especially for me.

Andrew stretched his hand, brushed against Elaine's arm, and daringly slid down his hand until he gripped her fingers. Elaine gasped.

"Sorry!" Andrew said, immediately releasing her.

"No," Elaine felt for his hand. "It's all right. It's very all right."

Her hands were warm and hard as they gripped Andrew's fingers. He felt a thrill run through him and heard himself breathing. "Tell me about Inglenook."

Elaine squeezed his fingers. "In the morning, we can have a silver mist rising from the Tugela, so our cattle are like ethereal animals floating above the ground. I ride around them, checking the numbers while Father tends to the fences. Mornings are always the best times of day when the world is waking up, and the land is still."

"I like the mornings too." Andrew guided her to a couple of handy boulders, and both sat down. "I am up before dawn and walk around Berwick Walls, looking down on the town or out to sea, where the surf splinters silver on the beach, and the seagulls follow, hoping for food."

"Kiss me, Andrew," Elaine said.

Andrew hesitated. "I won't be very good, Elaine. I've never kissed anybody before."

"I've never been kissed," Elaine countered.

Suddenly, Andrew did not care. He was no longer nervous with Elaine. "We'll share a first time," he said and bent closer.

"The dark is falling," Elaine said a few moments later.

"Yes. I'd better get you back to the laager." Andrew did not want to leave this place. The Bushmen paintings seemed to glow as if the long-gone artists had left something of their spirit behind.

"Yes," Elaine said, clutching his sleeve. "Mariana will be worried."

"Elaine, take my signet ring." Andrew slipped it from his finger, held it for a second and pressed it into her hand. "It's the only thing of any value that I possess." He smiled, knowing she would take care of it. "Think of me every time you look at it."

Elaine closed her hand over the ring. "It will be like having you with me all the time," she said.

"That's the idea," Andrew agreed.

The ring was too large to fit on any of Elaine's fingers, so Andrew slid it onto the thumb of her left hand. "Wear this until I can buy a proper engagement ring."

"I will," Elaine promised. "Was that a proposal?"

Andrew was confused for a moment. "Yes," he said. "I thought," he hesitated. "It seems so obvious that we should be together; I didn't need to ask."

"I knew before you did," Elaine said, smiling. "When will you come for me?"

"As soon as I can," Andrew promised.

Elaine examined the ring. "These initials are not yours," she said. "It says ADW, and you are Andrew David Baird. Why is that?" She raised her eyebrows quizzically, with a slight smile on her face. "If you think you can trust me."

Andrew closed his eyes. "I don't tell anybody that," he said.

"Not even your fiancé?" Elaine teased. "Please? Unless it's some terrible scandal in which you were involved that you are scared to tell me? A passionate affair with an older woman, or a robbery that went wrong, and you had to shoot the burglar, and you are hiding from the police." She smiled with her mouth slightly open. "Mariana reads the most awful books, you see, but truly, you can tell me anything, but it's all right if you don't want to."

"There's no scandal," Andrew assured her. "But you might think I am silly when you hear my reason."

"You don't have to tell me," Elaine said, putting a finger to Andrew's lips. "It's quite all right."

"Have you heard of Major Jack Windrush?" Andrew asked.

"Fighting Jack Windrush? The soldier who tamed the Northwest Frontier and fought the Ashantis?" Elaine said. "Everybody's heard of him."

"The W on my ring stands for Windrush," Andrew said. "Major Jack Windrush is my father."

Elaine looked at him for a moment, evidently puzzled. "I don't understand," she said. "Why change your name?"

"If you lived in the shadow of a hero, you'd understand," Andrew told her. "Everywhere I went, I was Fighting Jack's son. I was never me, and people expected me to be like my father."

"Aren't you?" Elaine asked.

"I want people to recognise me as myself," Andrew said. "I want to make my own way in life, rather than people praising me or helping me because of what my father did."

"Ah, I see," Elaine nodded. "Well, I didn't know anything about your family until five minutes ago." She smiled. "Although I knew Mariana likes you because you called your horse Lancelot and know about King Arthur!"

Andrew smiled. "Thank you, Elaine."

"Good. You can forget all that nonsense about your family with me." Elaine said sternly. "I notice you still joined the army, though, like your father."

Andrew shook his head. "I joined the police. I was at Sandhurst, the officer's training school, and every few minutes, somebody mentioned my father's exploits and told me how lucky I was to be a hero's son. When I realised, they all expected me to be my father, I walked out of Sandhurst and left the country."

"That was a bit drastic, wasn't it?" Elaine asked. "You must have felt very strongly about your name."

"I do," Andrew said. "I joined the Frontier Armed and Mounted Police as there was nothing else I could do; I mean, I have no other skills. A year or so later, the powers that be decided to transform the Armed and Mounted into an army unit, the Cape Mounted Rifles." [2]He shrugged. "So, my attempts to avoid the army came to nothing, and I ended up a soldier after all."

"But why did you choose South Africa?" Elaine asked, with a quizzical smile on her face.

"It was either South Africa, China, New Zealand or Australia," Andrew replied. "They're the only places my dear papa has never soldiered."

Elaine laughed. "Well, that's as good a reason as any, I suppose." She smiled at him. "I don't have such an interesting story. I was born in Natal, lived in Inglenook, and I'll probably die there." Her smile broadened. "I've been to Cape Town once, and the ship coming home ran aground."

"By the sound of Inglenook, you have made the right choice." Andrew did not mention his fear of war with the Zulus. He glanced at the sky. "I think we'd better be on our way, you'll need your sleep, and I have a convoy to get to St John's."

"Your men will think the Amapondos have got us," Elaine said.

Andrew saw the flicker of movement from the corner of his eye, decided it must have been an animal and guided Elaine away from the Bushmen's paintings. Strange, he thought, he had imagined a flicker of blue, like the uniform he wore, but he must have been mistaken.

CHAPTER 11

"And they came unto Camelot," Mariana said as they looked down on the small settlement of St John's.

"I didn't want that journey to end," Andrew admitted.

"Nor did I," Elaine said.

Mariana watched them, smiling. Although she petted Lancelot, her gaze never strayed from Andrew.

Andrew watched as the infantrymen of the 24th helped the civilians unload the wagons. As always, Miller was at the forefront, his voice loud and cheerful, with O'Donnell and Drummond at his back.

Andrew and Abernethy helped the Maxwell sisters, while Hitchings and Simpson managed to avoid manual labour.

"What are you doing now?" Elaine asked.

"Returning to Umtata," Andrew told her. "I'm taking the wagons back empty, which will make the journey easier. I'm afraid you'll have to wait for a boat to take you to D'Urban."

"We'll wait," Elaine said. She looked at the signet ring on her thumb. "I'll return your ring when you come to see us."

Andrew smiled, feeling sick at the thought of leaving her. "I have to go," he said.

"I know." Elaine put a small hand on his arm. "It's your duty. Take care until we meet again."

"I will," Andrew said. He saw Mariana watching from the opposite side of Lancelot. "You take care as well, Mariana, and we'll discuss Mallory and Tennyson's *Morte d'Arthur* in Inglenook."

Mariana smiled and intoned,

"To him replied the bold Sir Bedivere:

"It is not meet, Sir King, to leave thee thus."[1]

Andrew saw something shadow Mariana's eyes. "You know your Tennyson as well as I do, Mariana."

"Yes, Andrew," Mariana agreed and mouthed, "I love you," as Andrew turned away. She watched him march to the empty wagons, ignoring the single tear that seeped from her left eye.

The return journey to Umtata was faster than their outward trip, with the oxen pulling empty wagons and no civilians to nurse. Yet Andrew was unhappy, for every mile carried him further away from Elaine. He attended to his duties, driving the men harder than before and snarling at small matters he would have ignored a few days earlier.

"The men are noticing, sir," Abernethy said as they sat around a campfire in the evening of the third day.

"What are the men noticing?" Andrew asked, ramming tobacco into the bowl of his pipe.

"They're noticing your change of mood since we left Miss Maxwell."

"Nonsense!" Andrew snapped, grabbed a smouldering twig from the fire and thrust it onto his pipe.

"Sorry old boy," Abernethy drawled, throwing a log on the flames. "There's nothing nonsense about it. You were an efficient soldier before, and then you met the delightful Miss Maxwell. Now she's gone, and you're pining for her company." He stared into the distance. "You're turning into a bear without her, a veritable bear."

"I am nothing of the sort," Andrew said. "And you call me sir!"

"Yes, sir," Abernethy replied smoothly. "What's that in your hand?"

Andrew glared at him. "My pipe," he replied.

"Your other hand, sir," Abernethy said. "No, let me tell you. It's a button off Miss Maxwell's coat. You found it on the ground at the last campsite, where she must have lost it. You deliberately camped on the ground where she parked her wagon." Abernethy laughed. "Don't glare at me, sir. You're smitten, and the only cure is to scratch the itch."

Andrew opened his hand to look at the button. "How the devil can I do that if she's in Natal and I'm here?"

"Either find another woman," Abernethy said blandly, "or go to Miss Maxwell, depending on whether the itch is purely physical or something more serious." He stood up, humming opera music. "Plenty of women are willing to share their bodies with a British officer, sir. It's the uniform, you see, and the thrill of mating with a man of violence, a trained killer, added to the allure of position and money."

"I have no money except my wages, and I'm only a subaltern," Andrew reminded.

"I know that sir," Abernethy said. "But that sort of women see what they want to see and believe what their empty-headed little friends tell them. Take your opportunities when they arise, young sir, because you don't know if they'll ever come again."

Andrew lit his pipe and puffed furiously as Abernethy walked away, still humming.

Find another woman or go to Elaine.

Andrew considered his options. He thought of the women out here on the frontier, from the hardy wives of the settlers to their equally sturdy daughters or the gaudy drifters who haunted the bars. He discarded the wives out of hand. He had been brought up a gentleman and would never break the code; married women were sacrosanct. The daughters? If he used them in the way Abernethy hinted, he believed he would ruin them for life. That left the prostitutes, and Andrew had heard sufficient tales of the diseases they carried to give them a wide berth.

Neither of these options is viable to scratch this particular itch,

That left one option. Standing up, Andrew began to pace around the camp, nodding when men saluted him and looking outward as if watching for prowling tribesmen.

Damn it. I know what I am going to do. When I return to Umtata, I'll resign my commission and travel to Natal. I don't know what I can offer Elaine, but I want her. Maybe her father can employ me at Inglenook. I can ride, am strong and fit, and I've been around farms most of my life.

"We'll move before dawn tomorrow," Andrew decided. "I want everybody up, fed and ready to move before first light."

"Yes, sir." Sergeant Smith saluted, eyeing Andrew cynically.

With the decision made, Andrew relaxed a little, although he pushed his men as hard to return to Umtata. When small groups of Amapondo tribesmen watched their progress without attempting to hinder or communicate, Andrew ordered his mounted men to keep an eye on them.

"Get these blasted wagons moving! Double teams up the incline, damn it!"

"You're in a hurry, sir," Abernethy commented.

"Yes, Abernethy. I am in a hurry," Andrew agreed. The thought of seeing Elaine again spurred him, and the words of *Lady of Shalott* filled his head.

"DID YOU HEAR THE NEWS?" NEWLY PROMOTED CAPTAIN Fraser asked when they rode into the camp at Umtata. He ushered Andrew into his tent.

"What news, sir? We've been pushing wagons up and down hills for weeks," Andrew said. "The only news we've heard is what the Amapondos tell us, which was about crop failures and raiders on their borders."

Fraser shook his head. "It's a bit more serious than poor crops or border raiders, Baird. There is trouble brewing with the Zulus."

"What sort of trouble?" Andrew immediately thought of Elaine, with her farm so close to the Zulu border. He calmed down, telling himself that the frontiers between the European colonies and the native kingdoms were always rife with rumours of trouble and possible wars. Even the Boers, who had been in Africa for centuries, quarrelled with their neighbours.

"When Shepstone crowned Cetshwayo king of the Zulus, he warned him not to murder too many of his people," Fraser said, pouring them both a glass of brandy. "Here, Baird. You'll need this after your travels."

Andrew sipped the brandy, allowing the fire to spread through his body. He knew that Theophilus Shepstone, the Secretary for Native Affairs in Natal, had been alarmed when Cetshwayo succeeded to the Zulu throne in 1873. While a hostile Zulu nation would directly threaten the colony of Natal, Shepstone was more concerned that the Zulus might form an alliance with the Boers of the Transvaal and the Orange Free State. Such an alliance would allow the Boers, never pro-British, access to the sea, which Britain did not want. Accordingly, Shepstone made overtures of friendship to Cetshwayo, recognising him as king and crowning him with a gaudy tinsel crown in Queen Victoria's name.

However, British recognition came at a high price. Shepstone demanded that Cetshwayo obey certain British-orientated laws, including not killing his subjects at will and forbidding his warriors to pass into British territory.

"Do we have any right to tell the Zulu king how to reign in his country?" Andrew asked.

"Probably not," Fraser said with a grin, "no more than we

have to tell the Czar of Russia how to reign, but that's not the point."

Andrew nodded, hoping Fraser could finish quickly so he could inform him of his decision to resign.

Fraser finished his brandy, looked at the bottle, and regretfully put it away. "When Shepstone warned the Zulus about their behaviour, Cetshwayo announced he would rule according to his laws, Zulu laws."

Andrew nodded again. "That's understandable."

As long as he doesn't bother Elaine.

"Perhaps so," Fraser did not argue. "In July, when you were pushing your convoy to St John's, matters deteriorated. A couple of chief Sihayo's wives fled from Zululand into Natal with their lovers."

"Love is like that," Andrew thought of Elaine.

"That was the beginning of the trouble. Some Zulus pursued the women into Natal, dragged them back to Zululand and executed them."

"That's a bit harsh," Andrew said.

Hurry up, Fraser. I have important news for you.

"Sir Henry Bulwer, the Lieutenant-governor of Natal, contacted Cetshwayo, demanding the men who crossed the border should be extradited for trial. Cetshwayo said he'd punish them for venturing onto Natal soil, but as the women had broken the law and the warriors had not killed them in Natal, he would not send them to Natal for trial."

Andrew nodded. "Cetshwayo has a point," he agreed. "As long as they don't attack people in Natal." He thought of Elaine again and shifted his feet in agitation.

"Bulwer was inclined to agree with Cetshwayo and let things go, but Sir Bartle Frere, the High Commissioner for Southern Africa and Bulwer's superior, disagreed." Fraser grinned. "If any of the accounts I heard were correct, he was spitting blood and feathers."

Andrew curbed his impatience until Fraser had finished. "What happened next, sir?"

"Frere stated that this border incident demonstrated the Zulus' savagery and thinks that Natal is in danger of a Zulu invasion."

Andrew shuddered, thinking again how close Inglenook was to the Zulu border. "God forbid that happens, sir." He took a deep breath. "That would mean war."

"You're damned right, it would," Fraser agreed, "but politics are behind our protests, of course. Sir Bartle plans to join all the scattered southern African colonies to create a confederation of South Africa. You know we are gradually reducing the danger by annexing the native tribes and civilising them with missionaries, schools, roads, hospitals and so on, and Zululand is on the list."

"Sir Bartle is merely looking for an excuse to start a war?" Andrew asked.

"I imagine so," Fraser agreed. "We've already annexed the Transvaal, and now we'll defeat the Zulus and later add Zululand to Natal."

"Is that fair on the Zulus, sir?" Andrew asked. "And how about the British settlers on the borders of Zululand?"

"It's for the Zulus' own good," Fraser said, "and to ensure the security of the settlers on the Zululand borders. Now, I'm not sure how things stand at present, but the Brigadier has cancelled all leave, and Frere has requested reinforcements from Great Britain."

"Yes, sir," Andrew said. He felt his heartbeat increase. *What does war with the Zulus mean to Elaine?*

Fraser fixed Andrew with a steady smile. "I know you've just returned from a rather arduous journey, Baird, but our company of the Mounted Rifles is moving to Natal soon, so get your men ready."

"Yes, sir." Andrew wondered what he should do.

We're moving to Natal to fight the Zulus! If I hand in my papers with war imminent, people will brand me a coward. If I remain, we'll be in Natal anyway, closer to Elaine.

Fraser smiled. "Now, we're the only company of the Cape Mounted Rifles moving to Natal. The others are remaining to guard Cape Colony. We're expecting trouble with the Basutos as well as the Zulus." He held Andrew's arm. "We're the chosen men, Baird, veterans of the Frontier War, and we'll show the redcoats how to defeat the Zulus!"

"Yes, sir," Andrew said, more confused than ever.

"Now, Baird, give your report to Brigadier Simonds, get some rest for you and your men, and prepare to face the Zulus." Fraser's eyes were bright. "We all knew we'd have to fight them, and the Cape Mounted Rifles, the CMR, will be in the forefront!"

As he marched away, Andrew told himself he could not resign on the eve of war. If he was bound for Natal, he would be closer to Elaine and could surely find an excuse to visit Inglenook.

I'm off to Natal at the government's expense. Once we defeat the Zulus, nobody can complain when I resign. He raised his head, with his life's path clear before him and Elaine waiting at the golden door of the future.

"Lieutenant Baird!" Fraser thrust a head through the open flap of Andrew's tent.

"Yes, sir?"

"I have some important news for our company," Fraser said without entering the tent.

"What's that, sir?"

"The powers-that-be have decided to issue our company with Martini-Henry rifles rather than Sniders. That way, we'll be in line with the rest of the army and have no trouble with ammunition." Fraser was smiling.

"That's good, sir," Andrew said. "I've heard the Martini is a more powerful rifle."

"Here you are, Baird," Fraser said, handing over a Martini-Henry and a training manual. "I expect you to be conversant with the Martini by tomorrow."

"Yes, sir."

"You'd better be," Fraser said, "because you're teaching the men how to use it immediately after the morning parade." He grinned and raised a hand. "Aren't you glad you're a commissioned officer now, Andrew, with all these responsibilities to earn your extra two shillings and sixpence a day?"

"I wouldn't swap it for the world, sir," Andrew said as Fraser withdrew.

Andrew had a busy evening. After penning a short but heartfelt note to Elaine, he opened the Martini manual, sighed, and began to read. He had not gone beyond the first three pages when somebody scratched on the outside of his tent.

"Come in!" Andrew said.

"Sir!" Abernethy poked his head into the tent. "I'm sorry to bother you, sir, but we have some men missing."

Andrew sighed again. "I'm coming. Who's missing?"

"Sergeant Smith, sir, and Riflemen Simpson and Hitchings."

"Ashanti Smith?" Andrew shook his head. "That's unexpected." He left his tent. "Sergeant Duncan!"

Duncan was in his late thirties, a red-faced, stocky man with a fine display of whiskers and eyes that had seen all the world's troubles. "Yes, sir."

"Sergeant Smith, Simpson and Hitchings appear to have mislaid themselves," Andrew said. "Do you have any idea where they might be?"

"Have you tried the local brothels, sir?" Duncan replied immediately. "Smith fancies himself as a lady's man, whether willing or not."

"I haven't tried anywhere yet," Andrew said. "That's your job, Sergeant."

"Yes, sir." Duncan mused for a moment. "I'll take half a dozen men, sir, with your permission."

"Granted," Andrew said, thought of the manual lying beside his bed and swore. "Damn the men. I'll come with you, Sergeant."

"Yes, sir." Duncan saluted and stepped back.

There was one recognised brothel in Umtata and a handful of lesser-known houses where willing ladies entertained sex-starved British soldiers. Sergeant Duncan knew them all and introduced Andrew to the gentle art of brothel raiding. Duncan's technique was to hide his men around the nearest corner, tap politely on the door and charge in when the inhabitants answered.

The evening taught Andrew a lot about the depravity of human nature and confirmed his belief that he'd avoid brothels in future. The search also failed to find Smith, Simpson, or Hitchings, although it confirmed that four horses were missing.

"They've gone," Andrew said. "Deserted."

"We'll miss Smith's experience," Duncan said. "Hitchings was a decent shot, but Simpson is no loss at all."

When Andrew reported the desertions, Captain Fraser sighed and leaned back in his cane chair. "I'm surprised about Ashanti Smith. I had him in mind for a commission once, but he is certainly no gentleman. The other two?" He shrugged. "Well, Baird, it's better we lose the dross now than when the fighting starts. The men must be able to rely on their comrades. Have you read that manual yet?"

"Not yet, sir," Andrew admitted.

"Best get down to it, then," Fraser advised, leaned back, set his hat over his face, and closed his eyes.

ANDREW RUBBED THE SLEEP FROM HIS EYES, STIFLED A YAWN and faced the assembled riflemen.

"All right, gentlemen," he said. "You'll have heard that

Sergeant Smith and Riflemen Simpson and Hitchings deserted last night. If anybody has any information, let me or Sergeant Duncan know."

Andrew did not expect an immediate flood of volunteers, but faced with utter silence, he moved quickly on.

"Today, we are looking at our new rifle, the Martini-Henry. We were promised a carbine, but unfortunately, we have the full-length rifle, but perhaps somebody will see fit to issue us with the carbine later."

Andrew waited until Sergeant Duncan handed out the Martini-Henry rifle to every man and gave them a few moments to get used to the length and weight.

"As you can see," Andrew said, "the Martini is forty-nine inches long, five inches shorter than the Snider, and weighs eight pounds twelve ounces, so it's lighter as well."

The men murmured their appreciation of the shorter, lighter rifle. Some pulled it into their shoulder, others held it at arm's length.

Andrew spoke again. "The Martini is sighted up to thirteen hundred yards, about three hundred longer than the Snider, and both are single-shot breech loaders."

The men grunted, with some hoping for a repeating rifle.

"The Martini is more powerful and more accurate at a longer distance," Andrew said. "You'll all have noticed the underlever. Pull it down to eject the spent cartridge and open the breech. Push in the cartridge and push up the underlever to close the breech, and you are ready to fire."

The men all tried the lever, nodding at the ease of loading.

"That little device will increase your rate of fire from ten to twelve rounds a minute," Andrew said. "And you'll see the calibre is different, a .45 bullet as opposed to the Snider's .577."

The men exchanged comments, with some nodding in appreciation.

"It's a man-stopper," Andrew said. "Most of you will have fought alongside regulars in the last war, so you'll have heard them praising and cursing the Martini. Now it's our chance to see how good it is. Sergeant Duncan has made up a rifle range specifically for the Martini, so we can spend all morning learning about our new friend." He grinned at the ironic cheer.

Andrew and the Cape Mounted Riflemen spent the next five hours with the Martini-Henry. They learned that the rifle had a powerful kick that surprised even experienced soldiers, so after a dozen shots, men were holding the weapon away from their shoulders. They also found the Martini overheated faster than the Snider, but the worst fault was the cartridge's dangerous tendency to stick in the breech when the soldier operated the underlever.

"We'll have to watch for jams," Andrew warned. "If your rifle jams in action, inform your NCO or officer, step out of the firing line, clear the jam and return. Don't panic."

The men nodded. The veterans of the Cape Frontier knew a cool head was essential when facing a thousand rampaging warriors.

Andrew liked the Martini. It felt like a soldier's rifle, robust and accurate. His men also liked it, yet at the back of Andrew's mind was the worry about losing three experienced men to desertion. Fraser brushed the affair aside, reminding Andrew that desertion was always a possibility, especially on the eve of a new campaign.

"It's not your fault, Baird," Fraser consoled him. "Desertion is a constant problem, especially in the colonies. Men look for adventure and find tedium and danger, or they cannot cope with the discipline, or they realise they can jump ship and carve out a better life for themselves here, away from the restrictions of Britain." He shrugged. "We might miss Smith and maybe Hitchings, but Simpson was a bad lot."

"Yes, sir," Andrew said. "Thank you, sir."

"Put them out of your mind, Baird, and concentrate on getting your men ready. We leave for D'Urban in two days."

"Yes, sir," Andrew threw a quick salute, turned, and left the tent. While part of him was unsure whether war with the Zulus was justified, another part sang with the prospect of seeing Elaine again.

When we beat the Zulus, we'll make it safer at Inglenook. That's sufficient motivation for anybody.

The riflemen saw Andrew's new enthusiasm as he organised them.

"God, Sandy, our Andy is keen to fight the Zulus," Kelly said.

"You'd think he had enough facing the bloody Galekas and Gaikas, but no, he wants more," Sinclair replied as he rubbed a cloth along the barrel of his rifle.

Kelly bit on a hunk of tobacco and ejected brown spittle onto the ground. "He's mustard keen, is Andy, a right firebrand. God help the Zulus when he gets at them."

"Aye," Sinclair said. "Afghanistan has Bobs Roberts and Fighting Jack Windrush. We have Gentleman Freddy Chelmsford and Up-and-at-em-Andy." He shook his head. "We don't have to go, Pat, Up-and-at-em, and the Gentleman will clear it up without our help."

Kelly laughed. "Oh, don't deprive me of all the fun, Sandy. I want my share of Cetshwayo's treasure."

Andrew walked away, smiling. When men gave him a nickname and unknowingly compared him to his father, he was making progress. Elaine would be proud of him.

CHAPTER 12

Natal was not what Andrew had expected. D'Urban impressed him as a growing, bustling port town with a mixed population and more positive energy than he had expected. The hinterland was green, fertile, and hot, with a beauty that surprised him.

I am not surprised people immigrate here.

When the troopship *Aberdare* landed the company of Cape Mounted Riflemen at Port D'Urban, Andrew hoped to visit Inglenook. He was disappointed when Captain Fraser marched them inland, past a mixture of settlers' farms and native kraals.

"The captain's pushing us hard," Sinclair grumbled.

Ramsay took off his forage hat to wipe the sweat from his forehead. "It's even hotter here than in Cape Colony." He took a swig from his water bottle. "He's pushing us hard because we're off to the Zulu frontier to make sure the Zulus don't invade."

"There are fifty of us," Sinclair said. "How many warriors does Cetshwayo have?"

Abernethy whistled his opera song, looking around at the scenery. "About forty thousand," he said cheerfully.

"Aye, but we've got Up-and-at- 'em Andy," Kelly reminded. "He's enough to scare anybody."

"He bloody scares me," Ramsay said gloomily.

"How good are these Zulus?" Sinclair asked. "They must be pretty ferocious if the Xhosa are all terrified of them."

"The Zulus are better than good," Abernethy assured them. "They are the bravest and best-disciplined soldiers in Africa."

"How the hell do you know?" Ramsay glared at Abernethy. "Have you met them?"

"I've seen them," Abernethy said and returned to whistling his opera airs.

After days of hard marching, the Cape Mounted Rifles camped on rising ground with a view northward over a broad river to rolling hills. Captain Fraser called the riflemen together, stood on a prominent rock and lifted a hand for silence.

"Right gentlemen, Riflemen and others," he said, smiling. "I've heard some of you wondering what the Zulus are like and what we might expect to face when and if we fight them."

The men nodded, with some voicing their opinion of the Zulus and others silent, content to listen. Andrew sat at the front, scanning the land with his newly purchased field glasses, wondering if any of the farms he saw was Inglenook.

"Well, light your pipes and pay attention," Fraser said. "Because I am going to educate you."

The men settled into silence as a pall of blue smoke rose above them.

"The Zulus have dominated this part of Africa for half a century, ever since their great king Shaka founded an empire by destroying all the other tribes and clans between the Drakensberg Mountains and the Indian Ocean. They are the most ferocious, bravest, and best disciplined native army in Africa, and we'd be foolish to think anything else."

Andrew realised that Fraser had captured the men's attention as he had intended. He saw Abernethy nod in agreement as Fraser continued.

"These Zulus are trained as warriors from early childhood and fight like fiends," Fraser said. "They are warriors from their teenage years until they are too old to carry weapons, which means that every man in Zululand is a trained fighter, able and willing to kill on his king's orders." He paused to allow his words to sink in.

"How many warriors does Cetshwayo have?" Ramsay's worried voice broke the silence.

"I am not sure," Fraser admitted. "Maybe forty thousand, maybe fifty thousand and maybe more. They are organised into regiments, each with its unique traditions, and, like our British regiments, some are antagonistic to others. Fights between regiments can be bloody and often fatal."

Sinclair laughed. "We were like that in the Cameronians,[1] sir," he said. "We were a Lowland Scottish infantry regiment and hated the Cameron Highlanders! We preferred to fight them than the enemy!"

"Exactly so," Fraser agreed. "Regiments with the darker shields are younger, those with lighter shields older and more experienced. Either will kill without compulsion. The Zulus have no idea of mercy or compassion. They kill the enemy wounded, and they expect us to treat them the same way."

When some of the men stirred restlessly, Andrew wondered if Fraser was lowering their morale by praising the Zulus to such an extent.

"I've lived in this continent all my life," Fraser said and hardened his voice, "as have many of you. We have lived alongside the native tribes and know their capabilities. We've fought and defeated them before, and we'll do it again."

Andrew noted the change in tone and direction and watched the men's reaction. They were paying close attention, some cradling their still new Martini-Henrys, others looking concerned.

Fraser lit his pipe, taking his time to heighten the tension. He shook the flame from his match, puffed blue smoke into the air and grinned. "You lads look scared," he said. "And with cause. The Zulus are a frightening enemy. They fight in a recognised formation, with a chest that hits their enemy head-on and two flanking attacks to surround them, the chest, and horns of the buffalo, as they call it, with a reserve they call the loins."

"Do they always attack, sir?" Andrew asked.

"They do," Fraser said. "They know nothing about defensive formations. They attack with shields and assegais. They know little about firearms and despise them, probably because the traders only sell them Brummagem rubbish or worn-out Tower muskets that Marlborough would have discarded."

The small piece of humour lightened the mood, and Abernethy led the laughter. Andrew saw some of the men looking puzzled, perhaps wondering who Marlborough was. He did not expect Frontier farmers to have a deep knowledge of eighteenth-century military history.

Andrew waited for a moment and asked the question that filled the men's heads. "How do we defeat such ferocious warriors, sir?"

"I was hoping somebody would ask that," Fraser said. He stepped to Abernethy. "May I borrow your rifle?"

"Of course, sir," Abernethy said.

"Thank you." Fraser lifted the Martini-Henry. "We stop them with this little lady," he said. "The British army is small, but it's one of the most professional in the world. We have fought in every climate and latitude, from Canadian snows to tropical jungles, from Egyptian sands to the bitter plains of Crimea." He grinned. "The Zulus may be good in their chosen environment, but we are good everywhere."

Andrew saw the men's mood lift as Fraser praised them.

"How do we defeat the Zulus? We keep our discipline, gentlemen; fire twelve rounds a minute and stop them before they get close."

Some of the men laughed nervously.

Fraser turned around. "Face that direction, Riflemen," he said. "Can you all see the river?"

The men nodded.

"That is the Tugela. On this side, we stand in Natal and across the river is Zululand."

While the men stared at the misty land of their potential enemy, Andrew swept his field glasses across the Natal side of the Tugela, wondering if Elaine had seen the same view.

"She'll wait for you," Abernethy whispered as the meeting broke up. "Have faith. Women, or most women, are more loyal than men."

"Is it that obvious?" Andrew asked.

Abernethy nodded. "I think it was Joseph Joubert who said a man should choose for a wife only a woman he would choose for a friend if she were a man."

"It is that obvious, then," Andrew said.

"Scratch the itch, sir," Abernethy advised. "Inglenook is only five miles to the southeast."

"How the hell do you know that?" Andrew asked.

"I used to be a trader in Zululand," Abernethy told him and nodded as Fraser dismissed his company, leaving Andrew alone. The Tugela slithered past, with the hills of Zululand beyond.

As a pre-dawn mist slithered over the Tugela, Andrew fitted his saddle to Lancelot and left the camp. He was not orderly officer and had no duties until ten that day, so he rode away with a clear conscience.

"Keep a good lookout, boys," he shouted to the sentry, who lifted a hand in farewell.

"Give her our best, sir," the trooper replied, grinning.

Damn! Does everybody know my business?

Remembering Elaine's description of Inglenook, he rode towards the Tugela.

"Excuse me," Andrew tried his Xhosa on a group of men. "I'm looking for a farm called Inglenook." When the men looked blank, Andrew remembered the Zulu name. "You might know it as *Indawo Yokuthula*."

The men became animated, pointing southward, pleased that they were able to help.

"How far?" Andrew asked.

The men shook their heads. "Not far," the oldest told him at last.

Within fifteen minutes, Andrew saw the mopane tree thrusting skyward a spear cast from the river. He smiled, imagining Elaine and Mariana perched on the branches. Elaine would attempt the climb in deadly earnest, chiding Mariana for laughing and taking too many risks.

A hundred yards from the tree, Inglenook farmhouse was low and long, with a stoep facing the Tugela and a small fence defending a wrap-around garden from wildlife. Andrew lingered for a few minutes, enjoying his thoughts before he pushed Lancelot to the front gate. He dismounted, knee-hobbled the horse, straightened his uniform in a sudden bout of nervousness and walked to the front door.

"You took your time!" Mariana opened the door before he knocked. "We've been watching you dallying for the past seven minutes!"

"Seven minutes!" Andrew could not restrain his smile. "That's very precise!"

"Come in!" Mariana stepped aside, grinning. "Elaine is waiting for you." She lowered her voice. "She's pretending to be calm."

"Mariana!" That was Elaine's voice from an inner room as an older man and woman stepped behind Mariana.

"You must be Lieutenant Baird." The man was broad-shouldered, clean-shaven, and deeply tanned. "I am John Maxwell, and my wife is Linda."

Andrew took off his hat. "I am Andrew Baird," he said.

"My girls have told me all about you," Mrs Maxwell told him, with her shrewd eyes examining him from the cut of his hair to the scuffed toes of his boots. "In you come. Elaine is waiting for you."

Andrew felt something churning inside him at the words. *The witch told me a woman would wait for me.*

Elaine met him at the living room door, smiling nervously as she brushed a non-existent strand of hair from her face.

"Hello," Elaine said.

"I told you I'd come."

They looked at each other for a moment, unsure what to say.

"How long do you have?" Elaine asked.

Andrew glanced at his watch. "About an hour," he said. "I'm on duty at ten."

"So short a time!"

Andrew put out his hand. "It's good to see you."

Solid, serviceable, handmade furniture filled the room, while a packed bookcase occupied one wall.

"You, too," Elaine said.

They relapsed into silence, broken only by the ticking of a wall clock.

"Andrew!" Mariana burst into the room, laughing. "You must stay for dinner!"

"Mariana!" Mrs Maxwell cajoled. "Give them time alone together!" She poked her head through the open door. "Did you say only an hour, Lieutenant Baird?"

"Yes, Mrs Maxwell," Andrew replied. *She's been listening at the door.*

"We'll leave you alone, then," Mrs Maxwell said.

"No." Elaine shook her head. "I want you all to meet each other."

Andrew knew Elaine was correct, although he wanted her all to himself. He took a deep breath and prepared for an hour of dutiful self-sacrifice.

"Come on, Andrew." Mariana slipped a small arm inside his, smiling.

PART III
WAR

CHAPTER 13

DECEMBER 1878

The summons to oNdini took Jama by surprise. He had nearly forgotten about the incident with Sihayo's wives and travelled to the royal *imuzi* with as much curiosity as trepidation. His warriors trotted behind him, with each man aware he could face execution if Cetshwayo decided they had transgressed.

On his previous visit to oNdini, Jama had been excited to see the royal herds. Now only his meeting with the king mattered, and he led his Abanonya through the gate without hesitation. Ordering them to squat in the central space, where the king could see them, Jama approached Cetshwayo's *imuzi*.

Cetshwayo waited for him in the semi-darkness, an imposing presence with three or four veteran *indunas* inside the *isiGodlo* – the king's private enclosure.

"This man is Jama of the Abanonya," Ntshingwayo, one of the warriors announced in a deep voice.

Jama lay on the ground, hiding his fear.

Cetshwayo sat on a carved wooden stool, saying nothing as he contemplated Jama for what seemed like a long time. Jama remained still, knowing he would accept whatever judgement the king announced. The warrior who had spoken carried an axe and a knobkerry and watched Jama through dispassionate eyes.

"When you were last here," Cetshwayo said without preamble, "I ordered you never to cross the river into Natal. Why did you disobey my order?"

"My *inkosi* ordered me to," Jama knew he could never lie to the king.

"Jama's *inkosi* is Sihayo of the Quangebe," Ntshingwayo reminded.

"You disobeyed my order." Cetshwayo ignored the interruption.

"I did," Jama agreed.

"I could kill you, as you helped kill the disobedient wife," Cetshwayo mused without any apparent malice. He contemplated Jama for a few moments before arriving at a decision. "Sir Bartle Frere of the British has given me an ultimatum that includes disbanding the Zulu Army and accepting a British resident in our country to force us to live as they wish."

Jama lay still, awaiting the order for his execution.

"I will not agree to terms that mean we change our way of life to be under British control," Cetshwayo said. "There will be war between the British and us, and we will need every warrior we have to fight them."

Jama realised Cetshwayo was not going to order his execution that day. He felt a wave of relief.

"When the war comes," Cetshwayo said. "You and the Abanonya will be in the forefront. You will lead your warriors into every battle and wash your spears in British blood. If you survive the war or if you die, you will have atoned for your transgression against my orders. That is my judgement."

"Yes, *inkosi*," Jama said. He knew that Cetshwayo was treating him with leniency, for every warrior in the Zulu army would wish to be at the forefront of battle. He stood up and shouted the royal salute. "*Bayete*!"

"*Bayete*!" the men in the king's *indlu* echoed, and Jama trotted outside to give the news to his *amabutho*.

"Gentlemen, we're about to go to war," Captain Fraser told the Cape Mounted Riflemen. "We gave Cetshwayo an ultimatum, he'll refuse to agree to our terms, and then we'll be at war with the Zulus."

"The largest Empire in the world facing the most potent army in Black Africa," Abernethy said. He whistled a bar of Handel's *Hallelujah*. "This will be interesting."

"What was the ultimatum, sir?" Andrew asked.

"The ultimatum was a long, detailed document," Fraser said, "perhaps purposefully so, for Sir Bartle Frere intends to quell the Zulu threat. I can only paraphrase it. To the north of Cetshwayo's domain, a Swazi renegade called Mbilini has been raiding the Boers in Transvaal and the Swazis. Frere demanded that Cetshwayo hand Mbilini over to British justice."

Andrew nodded. "I see."

"Also, an induna called Sihayo had an unfaithful wife who fled into Natal. Sihayo's sons led a small impi across the Tugela and dragged her back to Zululand, where they executed her, according to Zulu law."

Andrew nodded again, glad that Elaine was not involved.

"Our ultimatum demanded that Cetshwayo hand over the Sihayo's sons and pay a fine of five hundred cattle." Fraser looked up. "I think these terms are pretty insulting to the ruler of a sovereign nation."

"Yes, sir," Andrew said.

"There was more. Frere demanded that Cetshwayo institute fair trials in Zululand, with only the king having the power to sentence anybody to death. He also ordered Cetshwayo to abandon his military system, disband the army, allow men to marry when they wished and accept a British resident to supervise these alterations. Finally, he must accept missionaries and only muster the army when Britain permits him."

"Dear God and all his angels," Andrew said. "How long did Cetshwayo have to comply?"

"He had thirty days," Fraser replied, tight-lipped.

"That's tantamount to a declaration of war," Andrew said. "No ruler, anywhere, would accept these terms."

"I agree with you," Fraser said. "We're pushing Cetshwayo into a war so we can smash him and annex Zululand."

Andrew sighed. He had imagined soldiering to be a noble profession of defending his country from foreign aggression, not being a pawn of deceitful politicians.

"Do you think there will be a peaceful resolution, sir?"

Fraser shook his head. "No," he said. "Prepare your men for war, Baird." He gave a crooked. "General Lord Chelmsford said he only hopes the Zulus fight. Oh, his Lordship defeated the Gakelas handily enough, but the lads over the river," he nodded to the Tugela, "are on a different level. Now is your chance to win your spurs, Baird, and impress your girl."

ANDREW WAS UNSURE WHICH OF TENNYSON'S QUOTES WAS more relevant. Was it the last line of *Ulysses*, "to strive, to seek, to find, and not to yield", or "Theirs not to reason why, theirs but to do and die" from *The Charge of the Light Brigade?*

Both probably, Andrew decided, as he prepared his men for the forthcoming war. They all knew of the power and bravery of the Zulu army, which terrorised all its neighbours.

"Don't drop your guard," Andrew ordered. "Keep alert at all times, shoot low and ride hard."

As the thirty days of grace passed, Andrew knew he would be leading his men to war. He thought of Elaine, perched on the lip of the Zulu lion, wrote her a dozen letters advising her to leave before the war started and trained his men.

When the ultimatum expired, Lord Chelmsford allowed his invasion plans to filter to the junior officers, and Andrew gathered his men.

"We'll soon be crossing the Buffalo River into Zululand," Andrew informed the stern, weathered faces. "It is a land of rolling hills and red earth, dotted with kraals, as we call the *imizi*. I have spoken to traders and hunters, who tell me the countryside is not as open as it appears."

Andrew's troop listened.

"Have any of you ever been to Zululand?" Andrew asked, looking directly at Abernethy.

Abernethy lifted his hand. "I lived there for years," he admitted.

Andrew nodded. "Tell us what you know, Abernethy," Andrew said. "The more intelligence we have, the better."

"I was a hunter in Zululand," Abernethy said. "From a distance, the land may look like English parkland, but the ground is uneven, with rock-strewn *koppies* – hills – small streams that twist and turn, hidden gullies, isolated rocks and antbear hills."

The more intelligent of the men listened, realising that any scrap of information may save their lives.

"There are no roads in Zululand, just tracks connecting the kraals of beehive-shaped *izindlu* and the few hunting trails we left behind." Abernethy's face changed as if he were reliving his days of hunting beyond the Tugela.

"The coastal strip is low-lying, and the ground rises to the west, with two rivers, the Black Umfolozi and White Umfolozi, dissecting the land. In the north, the Zulus and the Boers dispute where the border should be." Abernethy stopped for a moment. "The king rules from oNdini, that you'll know better as Ulundi and the people are hardy, honest, loyal and bound by rules and laws as strict as any you'll find in Europe."

"Did you like them?" Andrew asked.

"I did, sir," Abernethy said. "They're a straightforward people, with a lot to admire."

Andrew listened to Abernethy's words, then unfolded a map from his saddlebag and spread it on his camp table, weighing down the corners with rocks.

"Here we are, gentlemen," Andrew said. "Our target is the royal kraal at Ulundi." He decided to use the more commonly understood names to avoid confusion. "We cannot defend two hundred miles of border with the small number of troops we have. We'd stretch ourselves too thin, and the Zulus, with their highly mobile impis, could punch through our defences at will. Therefore, we must invade, bring the Zulu army to battle, defeat it in the open, burn Ulundi and show all Africa that we are the masters."

Do I believe all that? Or am I merely saying what I have to say to justify our invasion of a nation that has not threatened us? We are going to war, and I am a British soldier; therefore, it is my duty to fight to the best of my ability.

"Ulundi is around seventy miles from the frontier," Andrew continued. "General Chelmsford has decided on a multi-pronged invasion; Colonel Pearson will lead Number One Column crossing the Lower Drift of the Tugela. Lieutenant-Colonel Durnford will lead Number Two Column at the Middle Drift. Number Three Column under Colonel Glyn will cross at Rorke's Drift, and Colonel Wood will lead Number Four Column in the north at Bemba's Kop."

The men listened, wondering which column they would join.

"There will be a fifth column held in reserve at Luneburg in the Transvaal to ensure the Boers don't take advantage when we're embroiled with the Zulus." Andrew had met a few Boers and found them resentful of British interference. He would not be surprised if they took the opportunity to rebel when the British troops were fighting in Zululand.

"We are with Number Three, or Central Column," Andrew said. "We'll be travelling with N Battery, Royal Field Artillery, plus the Royal Engineers, most of the 24th Regiment, a squadron each of the Imperial Mounted Infantry, Natal Mounted Police and Colonial Mounted Volunteers, the third regiment Natal Native Contingent and a company of Natal Native Pioneers."

The men gave their opinions of each unit, with everybody happy that the 24th Foot was with them.

"We fought with the 24th in Galekaland," Andrew said. "They're steady men with experience in Africa. The last thing we want is a regiment of raw *rooinecks* straight out from Britain."

The men laughed, with some making comments under their breath. After over a year in Africa, Andrew felt himself to be a veteran, an old soldier fit to stand alongside his peers.

"Right, men," Andrew was satisfied his men were ready to fight, and their morale was high. "Dismissed!"

"Sir." Andrew approached Captain Fraser, who was talking to the regimental farrier. "Could I have permission to leave the column for a day?"

"Why?" Fraser asked.

"To see a lady, sir," Andrew said. "Her farm is only a few miles away."

Fraser shook his head. "Sorry, Baird, Miss Maxwell will have to do without your amorous advances. We need all hands on deck, and there's too much to do to afford leave."

"Yes, sir," Andrew was too young to hide his disappointment.

"Cheer up, Baird," Fraser said. "It will be all the sweeter when you meet her again, and you can impress her with tales of your adventures in Zululand." He grinned. "Now you might have another opportunity to prove your nickname; Up-and-at- 'em Andy." He laughed at the expression on Andrew's face.

"Yes, sir," Andrew said, although Fraser's words were little consolation. *Is nothing secret in this army?*

Andrew wrote a long letter that afternoon, telling Elaine what he had been doing and how much he thought about her. He pondered over the final paragraph, started it three times, scratched out the words and sighed deeply before saying. "When we meet again, we can arrange a date for our wedding. Until then, please think of me fondly and be assured that I love you."

Andrew read and reread the final passage, afraid that he had said too much. Finally, he shook his head, decided he was only telling her what she already knew, folded the letter, and placed it inside an envelope.

Scribbling Elaine's address, *Elaine Maxwell, Inglenook, Tugela River*, on the front, he handed it over to be posted and walked away quickly before he lost his nerve.

Well, Elaine, now I've told you what I think. All I have to do is defeat the Zulus, survive the war, and return to you.

"It is war," Jama said solemnly, brandishing his knobkerrie. "The British have ordered the Zulus to give up our cattle, disband our army and allow the British to rule our lives. King Cetshwayo replied that the Zulus do not tell the British how to live and they have no right to tell us."

The Abanonya listened, nodding their agreement. One or two commented, with Bangizwe drumming the shaft of his assegai off his shield.

Ndleleni touched his *umzimbeet* necklace and took a pinch of snuff. "When do we march, Jama?"

"We have never fought the British," Jama spoke so even the least intelligent of his men understood. "They have soldiers in red uniforms who carry guns and obey a queen who lives across the ocean."

The Abanonya listened without comment. The warriors were mature married men with families and responsibilities rather than hot-headed young *amaqhawe* - untried warriors eager to prove their manhood.

"The British are known as fierce soldiers," Jama said, "but we are Zulus, and this is our land. Cetshwayo has ordered us to defeat the British and not to invade Natal."

Bhekizizwe led the Abanonya in drumming the shafts of their spears on their shields in response.

"*Usuthu!*" Kgabu shouted the war cry, and the others followed. "*Usuthu*!"

"I want larger shields to protect us," Jama said. "In the days of Shaka, we carried a war shield, the *isiHlangu*. I want every man of the Abanonya to carry such a shield."

The warriors drummed again.

"Although a shield will not stop a bullet," Jama said, "It will help conceal us until we are close and will give protection against a bayonet."

The warriors listened without drumming.

Jama continued. "We will also carry an extra throwing assegai. The red soldiers kill at a distance, and we will do the same. We'll break up their formations with the throwing spears, then close with the *iKlwa* or the knobkerry."

Nobody argued with their induna. They understood Jama's strategy.

"We have few guns," Jama said. "I want the men who have them to practise. When we meet the enemy, they will stand together and fire into the British ranks."

Jama stood up, saw Kgabu and Funani in the front rank and hid his pride. "Before our time, Shaka made the Zulus great, and we will not dishonour his memory." Raising his voice, he sang the first line of one of Shaka's favourite songs, with his men joining in, so the words rose to the free sky of Zululand.

"Thou hast finished off the tribes.
Where wilt thou wage war?
Yes, where wilt thou wage war?
Thou hast conquered the kings.
Where wilt thou wage war?
Thou hast finished off the tribes.
Where wilt thou wage war?
Yes, yes, yes! Where wilt thou wage war?

The Abanonya danced as they sang, preparing for the contest with the greatest colonial power the world had ever known.

THE DELICATE TRUMPET NOTES SOUNDED OVER THE WHITE ranks of British tents. Andrew woke from a fitful sleep, glanced at his watch, saw it was two in the morning and struggled from his camp bed. He shaved in cold water, scraping the razor across his chin and wincing as he nicked the skin.

Damn it. I always do that before a busy day.

He dressed, fastened the revolver around his waist, adjusted his forage cap and stooped out of his tent to greet the day. The camp was awake, with flaring torches giving a near-mediaeval atmosphere to the hurrying infantry, labouring bullocks and creaking carts.

"Ready, Baird?" Fraser appeared as fresh as if he'd been awake for hours.

"Ready, sir," Andrew replied.

"Check the horses and men are fed, strike the tents and let's be on our way," Fraser said. "We have a country to invade and a king to break."

"Yes, sir." Andrew saluted, glanced towards Zululand, and got to work, thinking that none of the books he had read as a boy prepared him for the hundreds of hours of administration and organisation that any military procedure demanded. In books, it was all battle and glory.

"I don't mind the killing part," Sinclair said as he stifled a yawn and buckled his equipment. "That's easy. It's just that on campaign, I'm so bloody tired all the time."

Andrew nodded. Tiredness, irritability, and hunger go hand-in-hand with war. Add dirt, boredom, and fear, and that was the life of a soldier. *Part of the soldier's bargain, as my father would say. I wonder what he's doing now in Afghanistan.* He grunted, *probably winning fresh laurels.*

A chilling mist sat heavily on the Buffalo River that morning of the 11th of January 1879. The river was fast flowing, a hundred yards wide and churned frothy brown around an islet in the centre.

"This crossing is known as Rorke's Drift," Andrew told his men. "The infantry will cross here. Our ford is five minutes ride upstream."

The Cape Riflemen watched as Colonel Harness unlimbered a battery of six seven-pounder guns on a rocky piece of rising ground to cover the landing.

"That's the stuff to give them!" Sinclair said.

"That's the give to stuff them," Napier agreed and laughed at his supposed cleverness.

Andrew said nothing as he wondered how many soldiers had cracked the same joke over the past thousand years. He could imagine the Roman legionnaires using similar humour as they prepared their catapults at the siege of Jerusalem.

"Come on, lads!" For some obscure reason, Lord Chelmsford had decided the mounted men should load their carbines onto the ponts at Rorke's Drift, ride upstream, plough through the ford and return for the weapons. Upstream of the ford, the Buffalo seethed white over dangerous rocks, negating any possibility of an easy passage. Andrew watched Lieutenant Chard of the Royal Engineers working on a pair of flat-bottomed iron ponts, ready to ferry the scarlet-coated 24th Foot to Zululand.

"Come on, Riflemen!" Andrew encouraged as the mounted men hesitated at the edge of the river. For a moment, he remembered the Common Ridings in the Scottish Borders, when scores of energetic riders forded the bright, shallow rivers in front of enthusiastic crowds. The Buffalo was neither bright nor shallow, and the only crowds here carried rifles or spears as the warriors of the Natal Native Contingent watched the horsemen test the water.

"Follow me, lads!" Andrew shouted, kicked in his heels, and plunged Lancelot into the river.

The water was colder than Andrew expected as the current pushed against him, but he was a skilled horseman and crossed without difficulty. His riflemen followed, with only one man struggling until Andrew rode back into the river to help him over the final few yards.

"Come on, Sinclair," Andrew said. "We can't lose an old Cameronian in an African river when we've fighting to do."

"Thank you, sir," Sinclair said, spitting out a mouthful of Buffalo water. "I think my horse slipped."

"That must be what happened," Andrew agreed.

"Push inland," Fraser ordered. "Hold the high ground and watch for any Zulu impis. I am sure Cetshwayo has men watching everything we do."

"Yes, sir." Andrew nodded and rode on, disturbing a lone bushbuck, which thundered through the long grass. He rode to a slight ridge, from where he could see into Zululand and over the river. The Royal Artillery battery still covered the crossing at Rorke's Drift, six guns eager for a target, while a battalion of the Natal Native Contingent waited to cross the Buffalo.

"They're a rum lot, sir," Abernethy said.

"I think they're from a mixture of tribes," Andrew said. "I wonder how many volunteered and how many we coerced." Most of the NNC carried assegais and shields, with only one in ten carrying a firearm.

"I doubt many volunteered," Abernethy said. "Hobson's Choice." He shook his head. "I didn't mean the men were a rum lot, sir; I meant the European officers and NCOs."

Andrew nodded. "You could be right, Abernethy. I think we scraped the bottom of a murky barrel for that lot."

Urged by their mounted officers, the NNC linked arms and rushed into the river, hoping to use the force of numbers to defeat the current. In mid-stream, the water reached their necks, and a few lost their grip, with the current sweeping them away. None of the NCOs or officers tried to help.

"Poor buggers," Abernethy said.

"Why don't they use the ponts like the 24th?" Andrew asked.

Abernethy whistled a few bars of Tchaikovsky's *1812 Overture*. "The army doesn't value the NNC," he said.

Andrew frowned without commenting. He understood.

Once across the river, the NNC lined the ridge to guard the crossing while the British infantry marched stoically onto the ponts. Each pont held eighty men, standing shoulder to shoulder with moisture beading on their bright scarlet uniforms.

The 24th, stoic and tanned, crossed without comment. Veteran soldiers, they would follow orders to invade Zululand, Afghanistan, or Russia. Some looked over to the opposite side of the river; others watched their allies, the Natal Native Contingent, the beleaguered NNC.

"Baird." Fraser joined them on the ridge. "Take a patrol inland and see what's happening. Don't get involved in any fighting."

"Yes, sir."

With the bulk of the NNC on the Zulu side of the river and the engineers gradually taking the 24th across, Andrew pushed further into Zululand. Although he expected an immediate Zulu counterattack, the only Zulus he saw was a group of herd boys with a small herd of cattle.

"It's as peaceful as a Sunday afternoon in Hyde Park," Abernethy said.

The rising sun burned away the mist, and then the heat grew, bringing sweat to Andrew's face and under his arms. He rode in increasing circles, learning the lie of the land, and feeling as if every eye in Zululand was fixed on him. He followed the track deeper into Zululand and found it plunged into a stretch of marshland.

Andrew dismounted and probed the mud while a flight of pigeons exploded from a nearby tree. "The engineers will have to strengthen the track here." He noted the area. "The wagons will sink axle deep into this filth."

"The Zulus are keeping out of our way," Abernethy said quietly.

"I wonder why?" Andrew replied. He stopped on a small hill and scanned the interior of Zululand with his field glasses. "I can see something over there beside that rocky hill. A native kraal." He consulted his map, ignoring the drops of sweat that fell from his face. "According to this map, that's Sihayo's kraal."

"Siyaho's the man who caused all the problems, sir," Abernethy said. "It was his wife who absconded and who his son killed."

"That's right," Andrew said. "More importantly, his kraal commands the track Lord Chelmsford must use to reach Ulundi, and he could give us all sorts of trouble." He raised his field glasses again, noting the *imuzi* was situated on a steep *kranz* above a deep valley. "The Zulus have a good eye for a strategic position."

"They are natural warriors," Abernethy said. "And Sihayo is one of Cetshwayo's favourites."

"I'll report the marsh and Siyaho's kraal to General Chelmsford," Andrew was satisfied with the reconnaissance.

When Andrew's patrol returned to the bridgehead, the British had completed crossing the Buffalo. Their camp spread along the bank in neat rows of white tents, with the cooks already busy preparing the next meal and the horses in neat lines.

"Haven't these men learned anything?" Andrew asked as he entered the camp. "The general's instructions were for every camp to be laagered, with the wagons drawn into a defensive circle."

"Relax, Lieutenant," Fraser said. "We haven't seen a sign of a hostile Zulu."

"That doesn't mean they haven't seen a sign of us, sir," Andrew said.

"Lord Chelmsford knows what he's doing." Fraser shook his head.

Chelmsford smiled benignly as he listened to Andrew's

report. "Thank you, Lieutenant Baird," he said, speaking in short, crisp sentences. "I'll send Hamilton-Browne's battalion of the NNC to capture Sihayo's kraal."

Andrew had met George Hamilton-Browne, an articulate Ulsterman with much experience in the Maori Wars in New Zealand. Although Andrew was not impressed, he decided to reserve judgement until he had seen him in action.

"I'd better send you Cape Mounted Riflemen chaps with the cavalry, Baird. Captain Fraser can support the NNC," Chelmsford said casually. "You fought the Galekas, so you know how to handle these fellows."

"Yes, sir," Andrew said. He felt a leap of elation that he would be involved in the opening action of the Zulu War, with General Chelmsford as a witness.

The quicker we finish this war, the sooner I will see Elaine again, and when we defeat Cetshwayo's Zulus, Inglenook will be safe.

CHAPTER 14

Lieutenant-Colonel Russell commanded the cavalry that scouted ahead of the NNC. They rode well, as British cavalry always did, with the morning sun burning off Zululand's morning mist and the men tall in the saddle. The Cape Mounted Rifles were in the centre, with Lord Chelmsford and his gorgeously attired staff officers accompanying the striking force to Sihayo's kraal but remaining in the rear.

"Don't hurt any women or children," Chelmsford ordered. "And don't shoot unless the Zulus fire first."

"Yes, sir," Fraser agreed, winking at Andrew.

"We're at war with Cetshwayo," Chelmsford reminded. "Not with the Zulu people."

The riflemen listened, cast a jaundiced eye over the NNC with their heterogeneous collection of NCOs and wondered how they would fare against Zulu warriors.

Chelmsford smiled at Andrew. "How do you find Africa, Baird?"

Not used to a general addressing him, Andrew hesitated before replying. "I like it well enough, sir," he said at last.

Chelmsford beamed from under his low white helmet. With

his long nose and black, bushy eyebrows, he looked like a professor rather than a victorious general.

"You've done rather well, Baird," Chelmsford said, "gaining a commission within a year. But you were at Sandhurst, I believe."

Andrew started. *How the devil did you know that?* "Yes, sir," he said, feeling Fraser's gaze fixed on him.

"You have the right background then," Chelmsford said, pleased he had surprised his most junior officer. "Good. Carry on, Baird."

Andrew could understand why everybody, officers and men, liked Lord Chelmsford. He cared for his men and treated his officers like individuals. "Remember, gentlemen," Chelmsford said, "don't hurt the women and children. We are only here to fight the Zulu army."

"We won't forget, sir," Fraser said, turning away.

Andrew felt his heartbeat increase as they advanced toward Sihayo's kraal. The Martini was a comforting weight beside the saddle, and his revolver was reassuring in its holster, yet he knew the Zulus were more formidable than the Galekas had been.

"Extended formation, lads," Fraser ordered calmly. "Watch the flanks."

The riflemen spread out, each man two yards from his neighbour and the horses trotting over the uneven ground. A deer broke cover in front of them, jinking madly this way and that to escape the horsemen. A pair of white-backed vultures circled above.

"Trust the vultures to be here," Sinclair said. "I hate these bastards."

Andrew agreed. Vultures seemed to have a sixth sense where they could find fresh meat. They were a harbinger of death.

"There's the *kranz*, the rocky overhang." Andrew motioned ahead. "Sihayo's kraal is on the lower slope."

He spoke for the sake of talking, for Captain Fraser knew the location. *I'm showing my nerves,* he thought. *A good officer should be laconic and never reveal any weakness.*

When the riflemen came close, they heard cattle from the deep valley beside the *kranz*, and Andrew saw busy youngsters driving a herd before them. He lifted his voice.

"Sinclair and Kelly, check that valley in case there's an impi waiting to ambush us."

The two riflemen peeled away as Lord Chelmsford halted his staff, allowing the cavalry, NNC and Cape Mounted Rifles to advance.

Hamilton-Browne's NNC jogged behind the riflemen, easily keeping pace with the horses. Andrew watched them, wondering what they felt moving against the Zulus, warriors who had terrorised the local tribes for decades. The NNC looked no different from African civilians except for the strip of red rag tied around their foreheads. Although some waved their firearms threateningly, most seemed reluctant to advance, with the European NCOs and officers encouraging them with threats and kicks.

"That company seems better than the others." Andrew indicated one formation of the NNC.

"Number Eight Company is of Zulu stock." Abernethy was always a font of information. "Captain Duncombe leads them, and he chose the best men."

Andrew had never met Duncombe but respected his foresight. "Zulus fighting against their king?"

"They are the remains of a young regiment that defeated Cetshwayo's royal regiment in a stick fight," Abernethy explained. "The king was annoyed and had a fully armed regiment against them, spears against sticks. The survivors escaped to Natal and are back for revenge." Abernethy grinned. "Sihayo was the induna of the inGobamakhosi regiment who destroyed the youngsters, sir."

Andrew grunted. "Nothing is ever set in stone, is it, Abernethy?"

My father spoke of the Guides on India's northwest frontier, where

Pashtun tribesmen were amongst the best soldiers Britain had. It seems that I am mirroring his experience in Zululand.

Sinclair and Kelly returned. "The Zulus hold the valley, sir! They've rolled boulders across the entrance and posted riflemen on the slopes."

"Thank you," Andrew said and reported the information to Fraser, who told Colonel Richard Glyn of the 24th Foot, commanding the assaulting party.

"Damned cheek," Glyn, a white-bearded, pipe-smoking veteran with dancing eyes, replied. "Shooting at British soldiers, eh? We can't allow that," he said and ordered Hamilton-Browne's NNC to make a flanking attack.

"Four companies of the 24th will support the NNC," Glyn ordered.

The NNC moved forward, shaking their weapons and shouting. Immediately they were in range, Zulu riflemen on the rocky slopes opened fire, with puffs of grey-white smoke revealing their position. Andrew heard the angry buzz as bullets passed overhead.

"They're firing high again," he said without ducking.

"Long may that continue, sir," Abernethy replied as they approached the gorge.

Sihayo's *imuzi* was on top of a steep hill, with the cattle in the gorge at the bottom and a profusion of rocks and thorn bushes littering the lower slopes. Fraser split the riflemen to the left and right while Hamilton-Browne charged forward with his infantry. The NNC had been shouting their war cries and brandishing their assegais while the riflemen were close, but when they realised they faced a Zulu *imuzi* alone, they fell silent.

"They know how dangerous the Zulus are," Abernethy said.

The NNC at the rear slowed down when they realised the British infantry were not accompanying them. They began to hang back, with one or two trying to retreat or hiding behind convenient rocks until the sergeants encouraged them with mighty kicks.

"Get up there, you cowardly bastards!"

"Fight! The Zulus are your enemies; now's your chance to get even!"

Abernethy watched, shaking his head. "The NNC volunteers don't seem eager to fight, sir."

"No, they're in a blue funk," Andrew agreed.

"No firing!" Hamilton-Brown ordered his men. Unlike many of his NCOs, he led from the front, with the Zulu-speaking Duncombe prominent. "Only use the assegai!"

As they approached the kraal, a man stepped in front of them. Tall, powerfully built and dignified, he wore the *isicoco,* the head-ring of a married man and carried a long shield, three assegais and a knobkerry. Andrew noted the leopard skin band around his head, the feathers around his knees and the pattern of his shield. While most of the cowhide was white, the outer border was black, and three black smudges sat in the lower half.

"Now there's a Zulu warrior," Abernethy said. "That's Jama, *induna* of the Abanonya."

Andrew reined up to study the first enemy warrior he had seen. "He looks very confident."

"He should be, sir," Abernethy told him. "He is one of the Children of Heaven."

The lone Zulu warrior seemed to paralyze the NNC, who hesitated despite the brutal urgings of their non-commissioned officers.

"By whose orders do you enter the land of the Zulus?" Jama demanded, facing the entire NNC without a flicker of fear.

Captain Duncombe answered after a slight pause. "By the orders of the Great White Queen!"

At Duncombe's words, the warrior withdrew, and a ragged volley of musketry sounded from the rocky slopes and Sihayo's kraal.

"They're sheltering in caves," Sinclair shouted. "Sir, can we shoot back?"

"Not until Colonel Glyn gives the order," Fraser replied.

Most of the shots were high, but a couple landed in the NNC ranks, which, combined with the challenge, was enough. The majority of the NNC either wavered or turned to flee, with only Dunscomb's Number Eight Company following Hamilton-Browne and the officers.

The firing continued for a few moments, joined by a rolling avalanche of boulders. One rock crashed into the backside of a Scottish officer, who swore loudly and long in Gaelic.

"Somebody's unhappy," Abernethy said, grinning. "When will Fraser let us play?"

"I don't know," Andrew said, fingering his rifle.

As they watched, the defending Zulus abandoned their firearms and resorted to more traditional weapons. They charged out of the kraal in a disciplined formation carrying long shields and stabbing assegais to crash into Number Eight Company with loud yells. Number Eight responded in kind, and Andrew saw the two Zulu forces fighting in the old, traditional manner with no holds barred and no quarter asked or expected.

Andrew looked for Jama and saw him leading a small *amabutho* into the NNC flank, scattering them in moments and striking with his knobkerry.

"I want to fight that man," Andrew said, glancing at Fraser.

"There he goes again," Kelly growled. "Go-get- 'em Andy, desperate to fight."

"Keep back, lads," Fraser ordered. "Let the Zulus deal with the Zulus. We'll remain out of this fight and mop up any who break through."

Despite his experiences against the Galeka, Andrew had never seen such ferocity as when the two rival Zulu regiments fought.

He heard the Zulu war cry "*Usuthu!*" and the oft-repeated, hissing "*ngadla*," – "I have eaten," - as a warrior thrust home with his assegai. Andrew saw the technique, the way the warrior used his shield to hook away that of his adversary, exposing his left side, then stabbed underhand with the short, broad-bladed assegai. The victor would thrust the assegai into the midriff and rip sideways with the same movement as he shouted the triumphant "*ngadla!*"

Andrew saw Jama carve a bloody path through Number Eight company, only to find more warriors opposing him. "It's a bloody business," Andrew said, controlling Lancelot as the noise and smell of raw blood unsettled him.

"No bloodier than the charge of case shot at close quarters or the battle of Flodden or Bannockburn," Abernethy replied. "We are just as bloody as the Zulus."

Andrew nodded. "That's for sure."

Jama's determined warriors broke through Number Eight Company, leaving a trail of dead and wounded men. They halted, panting and with blood dripping from their spears as they saw the riflemen waiting for them.

"Get ready, boys!" Andrew lifted his Martini-Henry, feeling a surge of apprehension and regret. Apprehension in case the Zulus should prove too much for him, and regret that he would have to kill such brave men defending their territory.

A dozen warriors grouped together, each man with a similar pattern on his shield, the black fringe around white cowhide. More Zulus joined them until twenty warriors faced the riflemen.

"Sihayo must have asked for help," Abernethy mused. "Jama's Abanonya are from the Batshe valley, but not this kraal. You'll notice their shields are different, sir."

Andrew nodded. Jama's men had more white on their shields, denoting an older, more experienced regiment. Jama lifted his spear, pointed to the Riflemen, and shouted, "*Usuthu!*"

His followers drummed the hafts of their spears on their shields, chanting, "*Usuthu*!" as they squared up to the Cape Mounted Rifles.

"Get ready, boys!" Fraser shouted. "Be careful if you fire in case you shoot our own men!"

The Zulus charged, with their shields held in their left hands and assegais in their right. They covered the ground faster than any human Andrew had ever seen, so he could only fire one shot before they reached him. Discarding the Martini, he drew his revolver and fired again, seeing his bullet slam into a shield. The Zulu staggered and continued, still shouting his war cry.

"Usuthu!"

"Usuthu!"

The Zulus crashed into the Riflemen, leapt into the air, and thrust with their assegais. Andrew heard a Rifleman scream as Jama stabbed him in the chest, and then he was too busy defending himself to notice anything else.

Two warriors leapt at him. He shot the first through the head, then swore as the second smashed his shield against Lancelot, nearly unbalancing horse and rider. Andrew fired, missed, and gasped as the assegai ripped through the leg of his trousers and opened a stinging wound in his calf. He swung his revolver sideways, felt the thrill of contact and fired again, with the bullet knocking the warrior backwards.

For a second, Andrew saw the man clearly. He was young, still a teenager, with a handsome face and his mouth wide open in surprise. *That could be me,* Andrew thought as the Zulu fell, and then he shot at the next man, hitting him in the leg. The warrior spun round, recovered, and threw his assegai. Developed for thrusting rather than throwing, the assegai was clumsy in flight, and Andrew dodged sideways, thankful for his years of training on the Scottish Border rugby pitches.

The assegai whistled past, with the staff skiffing Andrew's back, and he lifted his revolver and fired again. The bullet hit the warrior in the chest, stopping him dead, and then Number Eight Company smashed into the Zulu flank, with a company of the 24th in close support.

Andrew saw Jama stop beside the men he had shot. The Zulu stooped over the young man with an expression of utter anguish on his face, and in a flash of insight, Andrew knew they were father and son.

"Oh, dear God," Andrew breathed. For the first time, he saw the enemy not as ferocious warriors but as people with wives and children, hopes and dreams. With two bullets, he had ruined that man's life.

Sorry, my Zulu enemy, but if I had not killed your son, he would have killed me.

Jama stood still amid the battlefield, and Andrew saw the pain in his eyes. Ignoring the battle that raged around him, the warrior lifted his assegai and pointed it directly at Andrew.

He's marked me down, Andrew said to himself. *He's telling me he's going to kill me for killing his son. No, his sons. Both these men I killed were his sons.*

Two men of Number Eight Company approached Jama, shouting. Andrew watched as Jama casually hooked away the leading man's shield and thrust his assegai into his chest, ducked the swing of the second man, smashed his shield into the man's face and killed him.

"That one's mine!" Sinclair yelled, aiming his Martini.

"No." Andrew pushed the barrel of the rifle down. "There's been enough killing for one day."

Lifting his bloody spear towards Andrew, Jama called on the remnants of his men and trotted away.

CHAPTER 15

"That was a success," Fraser said as the British set fire to Sihayo's *imuzi*, rounded up hundreds of cattle and counted the casualties.

"We lost two men," Andrew reminded, "and another was wounded." He did not mention the minor injury to his calf.

Fraser nodded. "I know about our casualties, Baird, but we captured a Zulu kraal and delivered a bloody nose to the induna who started the war by breaking the law. Now Cetshwayo knows we are in earnest he might agree to our terms."

"Maybe," Andrew said, although privately, he doubted Cetshwayo would back down.

"Now, Baird, while the engineers improve the track and move the transport forward, the infantry will consolidate our victory." Fraser smiled. "Colonel Russell wants us to scout forward into Zululand."

"Yes, sir," Andrew said.

"That means you, Up-and-at-em, Andy," Fraser said. He lowered his voice. "Be careful out there, Baird. We've won a border skirmish, that's all. I expect Cetshwayo is gathering his impis to send against us even as we speak."

"I expect he is, sir," Andrew replied. "If they are all as fierce as the men who defended Siyaho's kraal, we won't find this an easy campaign."

Fraser tapped his rifle. "Not even the fiercest and bravest warrior is proof against a Martini-Henry bullet."

"Yes, sir. You're right, of course. I'll get my men ready."

"Get your leg seen to first, Baird," Fraser said. "The surgeon will give you a couple of stitches."

"Yes, sir," Andrew agreed.

Lieutenant-Colonel John Cecil Russell of the 12th Lancers commanded Number Three Column's mounted men and sent forward strong patrols to explore the route towards Ulundi.

"Find us a credible route and camping places," Russell ordered. "And watch for any impis."

Andrew led his troop of Riflemen into Zululand, constantly wary in case of an ambush. He knew the establishment thought highly of Russell, who was a friend of Chelmsford, the Prince of Wales and General Wolseley, Britain's most notable soldier. However, although he had served in the Ashanti War, Russell had never led mounted men in action, and his promotion over the heads of veteran colonial troops did not enhance his popularity.

Andrew glanced over the other colonial mounted forces, for there was no British cavalry in the invading army. He saw the Natal Carabineers, the Natal Hussars, and the Buffalo Border Guard with the Natal Mounted Police. All were colonials, excellent on horseback and good shots, and many were experienced in frontier warfare.

This conflict is a colonial war as much as a British war. With all these mounted troops and the NNC, only the infantry, engineers and artillery are home-grown.

Despite the skirmish at Sihayo's kraal, Cetshwayo had not despatched an impi to deal with the straggling British column, and Chelmsford was free to consolidate his position on the Zulu side of the Buffalo River.

"Cetshwayo's dallying a bit," Fraser mused. "He's giving us time to settle in."

"That's kind of him," Andrew said. "By the time he acts, His Lordship will have us tucked up nice and snug behind a wagon laager with half a dozen guns, and Cetshwayo can whistle for his supper."

Fraser laughed. "Let's hope so, Baird. One decent battle should finish this war. We want the Zulu impis to smash themselves against a wall of our rifles."

Russell's mounted patrols pushed deeper into Zululand, probing towards the distinctive Isipezi Hill without molestation.

"Maybe they won't fight," Sergeant Duncan said, chewing his moustache as he peered into the misty distance. "Maybe Cetshwayo will prove a paper tiger."

"He'll fight," Abernethy said quietly. "Even if Cetshwayo doesn't want to fight, his indunas and young warriors will force the issue."

"Will they?" Andrew lifted his field glasses and scanned the land ahead, where a strangely shaped hill pushed out from a terminal spur of the Nqutu Range. "That looks like a suitable place for an initial camping ground. We're only ten miles from Rorke's Drift, an easy day's march for the infantry and wagons."

"Yes, sir," Abernethy agreed.

"That hill isn't named on my map," Andrew said and smiled. "It looks a bit like a crouching sphinx."

Abernethy looked more nervous than the other Riflemen, with his eyes constantly roving around the countryside. "The Zulus call it Isandhlwana," he said, "which is their word for a cow's second stomach."

"How evocative," Andrew said with a smile. "Trust the Zulus to involve cattle."

"This will do," Russell agreed with Andrew's location. "There is water for man and beast, fuel for fires and adequate grazing. Report to General Chelmsford, Baird, and tell him what we've found."

"Yes, sir," Andrew wheeled Lancelot around and returned to the camp at Rorke's Drift.

Chelmsford accepted Russell's recommendation with his habitual polite smile. "We'll form an advanced base at Isandhlwana," he said and ordered the army to begin its ponderous march.

Andrew helped guide the column to Isandlwana, pointing out the boggy areas of the track and watching for ambushes. The weather had been wet, making the ground soft, unsuitable for the heavy wagons, which rolled ponderously onward while the infantry marched like a scarlet snake.

"They're watching us," Abernethy warned.

"Where?" Andrew was too experienced to look around.

"A small group of Zulus are standing on the hill beyond your left shoulder," Abernethy said. "Five of them, from the Abanonya."

"That's the regiment that attacked us at Sihayo's kraal," Andrew said. "Jama's warriors."

"Yes, sir," Abernethy agreed.

"They were a handy bunch," Andrew turned casually, removed his forage cap, and looked around. "I see them."

"Maybe we'd best warn the captain, sir," Abernethy suggested.

"Do that," Andrew said. "Give Captain Fraser my compliments and tell him what you've seen." He watched as Abernethy trotted away, had a last glance at the Zulus and returned to his task of guiding the convoy along the track.

When they reached the campsite beneath the rocky hill, Fraser set out pickets.

Andrew found a small knoll on the slopes of Isandhlwana, dismounted and swept the landscape with his field glasses when a corporal and two privates of the 24th joined him.

"Here we go again, sir." Private Miller gave Andrew a gap-toothed grin. "You'll be missing your sweetheart."

Andrew was unsure how to respond to that. "Yes, Miller," he said. "I am."

Miller laughed, although he continued to watch his surroundings. "We used to leave you alone as much as possible, sir," he said. "Sergeant McBain sent us on picket duty to ensure nobody bothered Miss Maxwell's wagon when you were courting her."

Andrew had learned to accept his relationship with Elaine was common knowledge. "I'll have to thank the sergeant." The mention of Elaine made him smile and think of her mopane tree at Inglenook, and he jerked his mind back to the present.

The sooner we win this war, the sooner I will see her again. And her sister with that cheeky sense of humour.

Andrew lowered his field glasses for a moment and watched the infantrymen work in the camp. Sun-browned, with bristling moustaches or beards, they looked formidable in their single-breasted scarlet tunics and stained white, canvas-covered cork sun helmets. Dust and mud smeared their blue trousers, and their heavy ammunition boots thumped securely on the ground, although they were ponderous compared to the lightly clad Zulu warrior.

Fully equipped, each soldier suffered under fifty-seven pounds weight, including their Martini and bayonet, with great-coat, mess-tin, seventy rounds of ammunition and a haversack. The infantry carried the Martini-Henry rifles and the triangular bayonet, which many soldiers called the lung or lunge bayonet. Unfortunately, not all the bayonets were well-made, and the cheap steel could bend or twist on contact.

Behind the infantry came the wagons, each pulled by an immense team of oxen with a driver managing them with the aid of a long whip. One by one, they rolled to the campsite in what seemed like ordered confusion.

"There are two hundred and twenty wagons in the column," Fraser said when Andrew returned to the camp, "each one with eight or nine pairs of oxen. No wonder the road's in such a mess." He looked up as thunder grumbled across the sky. "And that won't help any."

"A bloke in a pub told me that Africa was always warm and sunny," O'Donnell mumbled as he slouched past. "Wait till I meet him again! I'll tell him he's a bloody liar!"

Andrew looked up as the first of the fat raindrops wept from low, bruised clouds. "You're right, sir. The rain will make the roads even worse," he said.

"I'll be glad when this lot is safely laagered," Fraser said. "Half the wagons are still on the road to Rorke's Drift, with penny packets of infantry to guard them. If I were Cetshwayo, I'd send an impi to strike at the road and mop up the wagons when they're strung out."

Andrew nodded. "Yes, sir. Cetshwayo's missing a golden opportunity."

Fraser nodded. "Thank God. I know we haven't seen many Zulus yet, but that's when they're at their most dangerous."

"I agree, sir." Andrew lifted his collar as a meagre defence against the rain. "The Galekas were hard enough to defeat, and they were terrified of the Zulus."

"Everybody's scared of the Zulus," Fraser said. "That's why we're invading. We have to negate their threat."

Behind the campsite, the rocky hill of Isandhlwana reared skyward like a Southern African sphynx. It rose for hundreds of feet, dropped abruptly, and rose in a spur of the Nqutu plateau.

After an hour, the rain transformed every dry *spruit* – riverbed - on Isandhlwana into a waterfall, with rivulets cutting into the ground where the British camped.

"You look wet, Baird, and you're going to get wetter," Fraser said. "Check the Nqutu plateau. We don't want any more Zulus spying on us while we make camp."

Always hating to be idle, Andrew obeyed willingly. He rode Lancelot as far up the hill as he thought safe, dismounted, and scrambled to the summit on foot, holding his rifle but leaving his sword behind. When he reached the plateau, he found the rain had stopped, leaving everything clear and fresh. The tableland stretched into the hazy distance north and eastward, lovely under the watery sun. Andrew scanned the plain with his field glasses, checking every crevasse and bush for possible Zulus.

Empty, he told himself. *It's as if Cetshwayo doesn't care that we've invaded his land. What game is that man playing? We saw Jama's Abanonya, so the Zulus know we're here.*

Along the southern edge of the plateau, the ground dropped abruptly in an escarpment, broken here and there by *dongas*, wide ditches through which new streams gushed. From the head of the precipice, Andrew could see the four-mile-wide plateau east of Isandlwana, bisected by the rough track that eventually led to the royal kraal of oNdini. South of the plain were ranges of hills, blue in the distance, reminding Andrew of the Cheviot Hills along the English-Scottish border.

With his year of experience in Africa, Andrew scanned the position with a military eye. If the British kept Isandlwana behind them and formed a proper wagon laager, they would have a solid defensive position, should the Zulus choose to attack. They had an excellent field of fire to the east, as any attacking force must advance over the open, although they could use the *dongas* and a scattering of boulders. The only weakness Andrew could see was where he stood, where the northern spur linked to the plateau. A daring Zulu commander could descend from the spur and take the British in the rear.

Chelmsford's no fool. He'll post a strong picket on the spur to watch the plateau. If I can see the weakness, that vastly experienced man will have it covered. As long as we have a laager and decent defences, we can hold out against any number of Zulus.

"No sign of any Zulus, sir," Andrew reported when he returned.

"His Lordship is posting a picket on the spur," Fraser said. "You'd better get some rest, Baird. You've had a busy day."

"What do you mean, treasure?" Andrew paused as he overheard the conversation outside his tent early the following morning.

"In Cetshwayo's palace," Miller said. "I'm telling you, man, Cetshwayo's been gathering gold for years, and he's got all the treasure from previous Zulu kings as well, from Shaka onward."

"What sort of treasure, Dusty?" Drummond was sceptical. "How would they get it?"

"All sorts," Miller said. "The Zulus robbed the shipwrecks and took everything from the Boers they killed, mined for gold, and taxed the ivory hunters for decades. I'm telling you, man, there's a whole kraal full of treasure at Ulundi."

Andrew listened for a moment, remembering Ashanti Smith's tales of treasure in Cetshwayo's kraal. These rumours, or shaves as the army called them, would be prevalent in any campaign and were usually without foundation.

Andrew dressed, buckled on his revolver, and left the tent. He was not interested in Cetshwayo's treasure. He only wanted to finish the war, escape from Zululand with its changeable weather and ferocious warriors and return to Inglenook. He smiled, quoting poetry as he walked.

"Elaine the fair, Elaine the loveable,
Elaine, the lily maid of Astolat."[1]

Jama smelled the smoke before he reached his *imuzi*. He increased his speed to a run, with his men following. They crested the final ridge and stopped as the flames and smoke rose in a funeral pyre over their homes.

"The British have been here," Ndleleni said quietly. He

looked over the Batshe Valley, where smoke rose from the other *imizi*. "They have burned all our homes."

Jama grunted. "Spread out." Although his *imuzi* was in flames, Jama did not lose his warrior instinct or forget his training. He ordered scouts to check the neighbourhood for British patrols and advanced cautiously, ready for a trap, ready to fight and kill.

There were no traps. The raiders had struck the undefended *imuzi* and departed, leaving destruction in their wake.

Jama leapt over the burning thorn barricade and ran through the smoke to his *izindlu*. "Yibanathi! Lerate!"

Yibanathi's home was on fire, with the roof already collapsed and flames licking up the walls. Jama saw two bodies inside, one smouldering and the other ablaze. Jumping into the *izindlu*, he pulled both out, knowing he was too late to save them.

Both were dead, with Yibanathi nearly unrecognisable and Lerate's lower half on fire. Jama doused the flames with his hands, uncaring of the pain. He stared at both, momentarily unable to comprehend the magnitude of his loss. Lerate looked upwards with her fine brown eyes wide and a gash on her forehead where somebody had struck her.

"Jama." Ndleleni touched his shoulder. "You cannot help them, now." His voice was gruff with shared sorrow.

Jama stood up, hiding his emotions. "No," he said. "I cannot bring back the dead."

He knew the reality of war; the victor killed the vanquished without sympathy or mercy. Yet he would avenge the death of his wives and the destruction of his *imuzi*.

"They have taken all the cattle," Ndleleni reported, "and trampled or burned the crops. Our people will be hungry this winter."

Jama listened without expression. He could see his wives lying dead in their burning home. This war had barely started, and already it had taken everything except his life. Ndleleni guided Jama outside the *imuzi,* so they stood amid the swirling smoke.

"They killed all of the herd boys except two." Ndleleni waited for Jama to react.

"Where are they?" Jama asked.

"Here." Ndleleni pointed to a pair of young boys, the youngest barely nine years old, who stood a few yards away, staring at the burning *imuzi*. The older boy was Jabulani, Jama's youngest and sole surviving son.

"Bring them to me," Jama ordered, feeling sick relief that one member of his family survived.

The boys stood with their heads down until Jama spoke. "Lift your chin, Jabulani, and don't be afraid. You are a Zulu!"

Both boys obeyed, defiance sparking alongside the horror and fear in their eyes as he faced Jama.

"Tell me what happened," Jama ordered.

"The horse soldiers came," Jabulani said. "They surrounded the *imuzi*, killed everybody and set it alight. Then they trampled and burned the crops while others hunted for the cattle."

"How many horse soldiers?" Jama asked.

Jabulani did not know how many. "They were everywhere. White soldiers and black soldiers."

"Who led them?" Jama put a hand on Jabulani's shoulder.

"A white man with two green feathers in his hat," Jabulani said.

"Was he wearing a uniform?" Jama asked.

"No," Jabulani replied at once. "He wore dark clothes and boots, with a wide hat."

"A white man in dark clothes with two green feathers in his wide hat," Jama repeated. "I will find him. We are going to war, and I do not want you both with us."

"*Ubaba!* Father!" Jabulani said and closed his mouth.

"You." Jama touched the younger boy. "Go eastward and find an *imuzi* the white soldiers have not burned. Tell them who you are, and say I sent you. Go now." He watched as the boy trotted away.

"You must be a man now, Jabulani," Jama said. "You will come with us and carry our spears, fetch water and do as we tell you."

"Yes, *Ubaba,"* Jabulani agreed, happy to be with his father and the warriors.

"What will we do, Jama?" Ndleleni asked.

"Fight the invaders," Jama said. "Find the man with the green feathers and kill him, too." He lifted his assegais and knobkerrie and headed towards Lord Chelmsford's army.

CHAPTER 16

As the mounted men gradually extended their patrols to search for the elusive Zulu army, the central Number Three column settled in at Isandhlwana.

Rather than form a laager, the British set up their tents in a line from north to south, with the NNC on the north and the mounted men and the First Battalion of the 24th Foot on the extreme south. Even after his experience in the Frontier War, Andrew was surprised at the number of tents. As well as the bell tents, which held sixteen private soldiers each, there were hospital tents, headquarter tents, tents for officers and sergeants, mess tents and the adjutant's administration tent.

"We need scores of tents for even a simple camp," Andrew said. "How many do the Zulus need?"

"None, sir," Abernethy said. "They travel light."

Andrew grunted. "No wonder they can cover so much ground."

Andrew had read the orders for setting up the bell tents, although he had never seen an entire regiment erect them. He knew the men slept in a circle, with their heads on the outside and feet nearly touching the single central pole. With the guy ropes stretched outside the tents, even the most rigid sergeant major could not squeeze in more than thirty to the acre, so an entire regiment occupied a large area.

Andrew watched from a safe distance as officers supervised and sergeants shouted hoarse orders to the sweating privates.

Each NCO will be extended sixteen paces from the left by Officers Commanding, the instructions read.

Andrew had learned the theory at Sandhurst. *The senior Major will dress the NCOs of the first row of tents, along the front of the column, so that they will stand exactly on the line marked out as the front of the camp and the Captain of each Company will, from them, dress the NCOs of his squads who whilst being so dressed will stand to attention. After being dressed, No 7 of each squad will drive a peg in-between the heels of his NCO, who will, after turning about, take eighteen paces to the front where another peg will be driven in a similar manner.*

Andrew watched as the veteran 24th followed the procedure to the letter, and the tents rose like a row of giant white mushrooms in minutes.

These men know their job, Andrew thought. *The instructions sound cumbersome, but with good NCOs, they work.*

Dwarfed by the bulk of Isandhlwana, the regimental transport sat behind each regiment while Chelmsford placed the main wagon lines to the rear of the mounted camp and north of the tents of the 24th Foot.

"Why are the wagons not in a laager, sir?" Andrew asked when he reported to Captain Fraser.

"Ask His Lordship," Fraser replied. "Colonel Glyn, our esteemed column commander of the splendid beard, asked Lord Chelmsford for permission to form a laager, but our even more esteemed Lordship refused."

"It was Lord Chelmsford who gave standing orders for every camp to be within a laager!" Andrew reminded. He took a deep breath, remembering the tales of Zulu ferocity.

Fraser nodded. "I am aware of that, Baird. Many senior officers have raised similar objections, but his Lordship replied that forming a laager would take too long." Fraser poured two glasses of port and handed one to Andrew. "Especially with many of the wagons due to return to Rorke's Drift."

"Thank you, sir." Andrew sipped the port. "We could at least entrench the camp." He remembered his father's words about always building sangars – stone defences – along the Northwest Frontier. Zululand could prove equally perilous. *Damn! I am trying to escape the old man's influence, and here I am, looking for his advice.*

Fraser jerked a thumb outside the tent. "There are more stones than dirt here, Baird. It would take far too much effort for minimal reward." His grin was more crooked than Andrew liked. "We'll have to depend on the good old British infantry and volleys of musketry."

Andrew nodded. He wanted to put trust in Lord Chelmsford but remembered his father's tales of service on the fringes of the Empire. Not all British officers treated the opposition with respect. "We're trusting to luck," he said.

"We're trusting to the Martini-Henry," Fraser corrected, and Andrew thought it better not to argue with his superior officer.

Andrew kept two of his men on watch that night and was up before dawn to check the perimeter. He saw no sign of Zulus, and the men grumbled they had wasted their night.

"Better tired than assegaid." Andrew silenced their complaints and ordered his troop to build a breastwork around their section of the camp.

"More wasted effort!" Ramsay grumbled as a group of the 24th jeered at the sweating Riflemen.

"The Zulus know what's good for them," one heavily bearded Natal Hussar commented. "They won't attack a camp full of British regulars."

"I hope they do attack," his companion said. He was a teenage farmer with a sun-browned face and a bandolier of ammunition crossing his chest. "We'll give them pepper, won't we just?" He tapped his rifle, a long-barrelled German weapon that looked about thirty years old.

Andrew hoped the Hussars were correct and he was being

overly cautious. He looked up at the great sphinx of Isandhlwana, wondering if any of the Abanonya was observing the lack of defences.

"Keep it up, lads," Andrew encouraged.

"Something's happening, sir." Abernethy looked up from his digging. "His Lordship looks agitated."

"He does," Andrew agreed as Lord Chelmsford rode past without his customary smile.

"He's concerned our supplies won't last," Abernethy said, "so he's going to push us on a bit toward Ulundi."

"How the devil do you know that?" Andrew asked.

"His soldier-servant told me," Abernethy replied with a casual shrug.

Andrew smiled. The rankers had diverse methods of discovering what was happening in the army. He resolved never to discount the intelligence of the other ranks.

"THE ENEMY HAS CAMPED AT ISANDHLWANA, NTSHINGWAYO," Jama reported. He stood erect with his assegais and knobkerrie in his hand and his face immobile. He did not mention the pain that tore him apart or the images that ran through his head, hour after hour.

"How many?" Ntshingwayo kaMahole was one of Cetshwayo's senior commanders, a serious-faced man who dressed simply and held his staff of office in his left hand. He listened to Jama's report silently, with his quiet, intelligent eyes never straying from Jama's face.

"They have two *amabuthos* of red-coated infantry, some artillery and mounted men," Jama said. "The mounted men are all colonials, and they also have *amabuthos* of Africans."

Ntshingwayo kaMahole pondered the information. "Are the British behind entrenchments, Jama?"

"No," Jama said. "They have not dug themselves in like ant bears."

Ntshingwayo digested the information for a few moments before asking the next question.

"Have they formed their wagons into a fortification as the Boers do?"

"No," Jama said again. "Their tents are spread across the hillside, and their wagons are behind them. Many of the wagons go back and forward to *kwaJimu*.[1]"

Ntshingwayo contemplated Jama's answer before deciding what to do. "We'll split the British and defeat them in detail," he decided. "Without fortifications, they are vulnerable to our impis. I want you to lure some of them away from the camp, Jama, and we'll attack."

"Yes, *induna*," Jama agreed.

Jama knew that with his wives and two of his sons dead, war was the only thing left to him, and if he died in battle, he would see Yibanathi again and all his ancestors. He trotted away; his mind busy on the task Ntshingwayo had set him. He did not care about the possibility of death.

"We have work to do, Abanonya," he told his men. "We'll show ourselves to the enemy and lure some away from their camp."

"Then what?" Ndleleni asked.

Jama smiled and ran a finger up the blade of his *iKlwa*.

RUMOURS OF A ZULU IMPI RAN AROUND THE BRITISH CAMP, with the sentries reporting bodies of warriors in the distance, trotting purposefully in different directions.

"They're planning something," Captain Fraser said.

"It looks like it, sir," Andrew agreed.

On the 20th of January 1879, Lord Chelmsford and a strong

escort patrolled to the east of the British camp and returned without sighting any Zulus.

"What the devil is Cetshwayo playing at?" Fraser asked. "I wonder if he's going to fight at all."

Andrew caught Abernethy raising his eyebrows. "I think he will, sir."

"So do I," Fraser said, frowning. "I don't like doing nothing." He packed tobacco into his pipe. "This war is too quiet for my liking. I don't believe Cetshwayo is just sitting on his thumb waiting for us to pay him a visit or sending small impis to run around without reason." He stood up. "No, Baird. Cetshwayo is planning something. Take your men back to the Nqutu plateau. Keep out of trouble; there's a good chap."

Andrew had studied the track and found an easier route for his Riflemen. With a dozen men at his back, he rode on the windy plateau for an hour before he saw a flicker of movement.

"Over there, lads." Andrew indicated with his chin. "Extended order and take care."

Veterans all, the Riflemen did not need the extra orders and rode carefully with rifles placed across their saddles.

"I see them," Abernethy said quietly. "To our right and ahead, behind that stunted thorn tree."

"How many?" Andrew asked.

"Not sure, sir," Abernethy replied. "I'd estimate a dozen at least."

"Halt." Andrew lifted a hand, feeling the tension rise inside him. He rode to a slight knoll, took out his field glasses and swore when he saw half a dozen shields with the distinct black edging around the mainly white centre.

"Those are the Abanonya we fought at Sihayo's kraal," Andrew said. "Walk wide, lads. If there are some, there will likely be more."

"There are!" Sergeant Duncan said as a line of warriors emerged from a gulley to their right. They moved silently, with their shields on their left arms and assegais held ready to throw.

"Retire, boys," Andrew said and waited until the last of his men had turned before joining them in withdrawing across the plateau.

That's another of my father's maxims: an officer should be first in and last out of danger. Damn it! That man is with me everywhere.

The Zulus followed, running easily over the rocky ground as they carried their tall shields and spears. They kept pace with the horsemen, neither closing the gap nor falling behind. A brisk wind ruffled the feathers around their knees but carried no sound of their silent passage to Andrew.

"What will we do, sir?" Abernethy asked.

"Return to camp," Andrew decided. "We'll report their presence to the captain."

When the Riflemen descended to the camp, the Zulus lined the edge of the plateau, with their shields linked together and their assegais pointing upwards.

"Well, Cetshwayo knows where we are," Abernethy said.

"He does," Andrew agreed. "Now we'll see how he reacts."

While Andrew had been on the plateau, Chelmsford had sent Major John Dartnell of the Natal Mounted Police with most of the mounted men and a considerable number of the NNC in an extended patrol to the southeast. When he was ten miles from the camp, Dartnell encountered Zulus. Andrew heard the staccato rattle of musketry as darkness closed the day.

"Feed the horses, lads, and grab some food yourselves. Ensure your water bottles are full and snatch some sleep while you can. It sounds like Dartnell's found trouble."

"About time the Zulus fought," Sinclair said. "When they come, we can smash them and go home. This place is too wet for me."

Abernethy glanced at Sinclair, raised his eyebrows, and said nothing.

"Come on, lads, tend to the horses," Andrew ordered.

The Riflemen readied themselves and threw themselves into their tents with their rifles to hand. Within half an hour, those who were awake heard the drumbeat of hooves and the sentry's hoarse challenge.

"Halt! Identify yourself, or I'll fire! Who are you, you bastard?"

"Friend!" a lone horseman shouted breathlessly. "From Major Dartnell with a message for Lord Chelmsford!"

"Pass, friend!" The sentry lowered the rifle from his shoulder.

In common with half the officers present, Andrew walked to Lord Chelmsford's tent to discover what was happening, limping as his calf wound began to nip.

"Dartnell's brushed with two thousand Zulus near Isipezi Hill." The word spread around the camp. "He wants infantry reinforcements so he can attack them tomorrow."

"Dartnell's found the Zulu army!"

"Cetshwayo's main impi is at Isipezi Hill!"

"Thousands of Zulus have attacked Dartnell, and he needs help urgently!"

The rumours circulated, each one more impressive than the last. Andrew ensured the sentries were alert and lay in his tent, hoping to sleep.

Find the Zulus, defeat them, end the war, leave the army, and marry Elaine. Andrew planned his life. He closed his eyes, wished he had written to Elaine and woke to the sound of the bugle.

"Come on, lads! Let's be having you!" Barking sergeants roused the men with a mixture of threats and black humour; messengers ran around the camp, cooks worked feverishly at the fires, and farriers banged nails in horseshoes.

Andrew emerged, trying to appear calm as Fraser returned from a meeting with the staff officers.

"Dartnell's made contact with what he thinks is the main Zulu army," Fraser told him quickly. "His Lordship is marching out with Colonel Glyn, most of the second battalion 24th, the Mounted Infantry, four artillery pieces and the Natal Pioneers."

"Us?" Andrew asked hopefully.

Fraser shook his head. "Don't get excited, Baird. We're not required."

"Chelmsford has left the camp dangerously short of men," Andrew said. "We have a large perimeter to defend, and we know there are Zulus around."

Fraser watched as the second battalion of the 24th formed up. They were younger and less experienced than the first battalion, eager men with youthful faces. "Don't worry, Baird. His Lordship has ordered Colonel Durnford at Rorke's Drift to march here with every spare man he has. He'll leave a skeleton garrison at the drift, and until he arrives, Colonel Pulleine commands the camp."

Andrew nodded. He knew Henry Pulleine slightly, a forty-year-old brevet Lieutenant-Colonel who had no experience of active service but a talent for administration. He had only seen Anthony Durnford from a distance. One of the many able Irish officers in the British Army, Durnford was a Royal Engineer of thirty years' service. He had fought in one of the minor frontier wars, where his Natal Carbineers had abandoned him at a crucial juncture, but his Basuto horsemen remained by his side.

"Pulleine was on the staff during the last Galeka war without firing a shot or seeing an angry warrior," Fraser confirmed Andrew's thoughts.

"Let's hope Lord Chelmsford engages the Zulu Impi before it reaches us." Andrew did not hide his concerns as he looked around the camp. "We've got about eight hundred Europeans and about four hundred and thirty ill-armed Africans to guard two hundred wagons, fifteen hundred draught animals and nine hundred yards of tents."

"And no laager, entrenchments or defences," Fraser added. "Still, we do have the first battalion, 24th Foot, Praise the Lord, and thank God for a battalion of British infantry."

Andrew forced a smile, although he felt a terrible sense of foreboding. He watched General Chelmsford march his army eastward, ordered his men to build up their scanty defences and sniffed the wind.

"What are you doing, sir?" Abernethy asked curiously.

"It was something my father said," Andrew said unguardedly. "He told me you could smell the enemy if the wind's in the right quarter. You can smell fear, sweat and cooking."

"I can't smell anything, sir," Abernethy said.

Andrew grinned. "Nor can I, and long may that continue."

Why did I mention my father? And why am I so apprehensive? I've fought in a dozen skirmishes and battles already. Are the Zulus so ferocious? They are only a tribal army armed with primitive weapons, while we have trained professional soldiers with the most modern weapons man's ingenuity can devise.

Pulleine sent out strong infantry pickets, with Lieutenant Pope and G Company of the second battalion 24th fifteen hundred yards in front of the camp. The young soldiers stood in groups of fours along the crest of a rocky donga, looking very exposed against the vastness of Africa.

"We need more men or a laager," Abernethy said. "Maybe we can't smell anything, but we know something's going to happen."

Pulleine may have thought the same, for he extended two companies of the 24th and a nearly equal number of the NNC in an arc around the right front and the flank of the camp. A vedette of mounted men stood lonely guard further out on the high ground while one company of the 24th were busy improving the track.

"Listen to them." Fraser tamped tobacco into the bowl of his pipe. "Cursing and blinding like true British soldiers." He scratched a match and lit the tobacco, speaking between puffs of smoke. "If ever British soldiers stop grousing, then I'll begin to worry."

"There's nothing to worry about," a bearded Natal Hussar said. "It's not a good day for the Zulus to fight. It's the time of the dead moon, and the Zulus never fight then."

Andrew did not argue, knowing the Natal men understood

the Zulus better than he did. He remembered the warriors on the plateau, the impi Dartnell had seen and wondered if the Zulu commander was forcing Chelmsford to split his army and said nothing.

My father always said to put oneself in the enemy's camp and think as he does. If the Zulu commander saw us from above, he may well wish to divide our forces and defeat us piecemeal.

"Even less cause to worry now," Fraser said as he saw dust rising on the road. "That's Durnford coming with our reinforcements."

CHAPTER 17

Andrew watched with relief as Lieutenant-Colonel Durnford of the Royal Engineers arrived from Rorke's Drift. One-armed and with an impressive moustache that drooped well below his chin, Durnford brought five troops of Natal Native Horse to reinforce the garrison. More men followed; two companies of the NNC and a rocket battery.

"I'd prefer more British infantry," Fraser admitted his apprehension. "Now that Colonel Durnford is here, I wonder if Pulleine is still in charge of the camp. Durnford has three years' seniority and more experience of actual battle."

Durnford made an immediate impact, sending Captain Shepstone and Lieutenant Raw's Sikali Native Horse to the plateau. These horsemen were from the local tribes and carried throwing spears and knobkerries as well as carbines.

"I heard there were groups of Zulus up there," Durnford informed Shepstone as the Sikali Horse mounted up. "A Lieutenant Baird found them yesterday. Clear them up."

"Yes, sir." Shepstone saluted and led his men up to the plateau. Some of the horsemen sang psalms as they ascended the path, and Andrew killed his envy.

Good luck, lads.

When the last of the Sikali Horse disappeared, Pulleine and Durnford sat down to lunch and called for a magnum of champagne.

"A toast, Pulleine." Durnford lifted his glass. "To a bloody war and a quick victory."

"I'll agree to the victory," Pulleine said and looked up in irritation as a gasping messenger arrived in a haze of dust.

"What is it, man?" Durnford asked, with the sun glittering from his crystal glass.

The messenger reigned up and caught his breath as the dust settled around him. "Five hundred Zulus to the northeast, sir," he reported. "They might be hoping to intercept Lord Chelmsford."

"Thank you," Durnford replied at once. He stood up and finished his champagne. "Call up my Basutos, will you, somebody? I'll take them and the Edendale men with the Rocket Battery. We'll stop these Zulu chaps from bothering His Lordship. He'll have quite enough to do as it is." He put down his glass. "I'll press you for a couple of companies of the 24th, Pulleine."

"I'll need all my infantry to guard the camp, Durnford," Pulleine said, visibly upset at the request.

Durnford pulled at his moustache. "Oh, come now, Pulleine. The 24th is sitting around doing nothing!"

"If I weaken the garrison any further," Pulleine said, "we'll be wide open to a Zulu attack."

"You'll still have the NNC," Durnford reminded.

"How reliable are they?"

"That depends on how well you've trained them," Durnford retorted.

Andrew was not the only officer listening as Pulleine capitulated until his adjutant, Lieutenant Teignmouth Melville, intervened, saying they had a large perimeter and a relatively weak garrison. "We'll need all the infantry, sir," he said firmly.

Durnford agreed reluctantly. "If I get into difficulties," he growled, "I'll expect you to support me!"

Andrew and the CMR watched Durnford ride away, leaving a rising ribbon of dust. A battalion of the NNC followed while a string of mules pulled the rocket tubes, bouncing over the rocky ground. When they departed, the camp seemed quiet, with an NCO bawling out a file of offenders, a few men guarding the spur and the last of the Sikali Horse vanishing on the plateau.

The dust settled, the NCO sent the offenders to double march around the camp perimeter, and Andrew spent a leisurely hour inspecting the horses until he saw a heliograph winking from the plateau.

A signaller read the flashing lights and reported to Colonel Pulleine, who immediately jumped to his feet.

"Captain Fraser!" Pulleine shouted. "Take your Riflemen to the plateau. Lieutenant Raw of the Sikali Horse reports some scattered bands of Zulus up there. Help him scatter them further."

"Yes, sir," Fraser saluted. "You heard the colonel, lads! Check your ammunition! Mount up! Come on, Baird, you young firebrand; you lead us; you know the way best!"

"Yes, sir!" Andrew responded, glad to be doing something. "Come on, men. Sergeant Duncan, you bring up the rear."

After his two previous trips, Andrew knew the route well and led his troop to the plateau with hardly a pause, with Fraser only a few yards behind. The final few steps were a scramble of loose stones and swearing troopers, and then the Cape Mounted Rifles were on top of the plateau with the vast dome of the sky above, and half of Zululand stretched before them.

Andrew lifted his field glasses and watched Raw leading his Native Horse to the east. He saw them disappearing behind the scattered boulders and then appearing again as they searched for the Zulus until one of the riders whooped.

"He's seen something, Baird!" Fraser said.

"Yes, sir," Andrew agreed and shouted for his men to get ready.

"What's that, sir?" Sergeant Duncan pointed ahead. "I saw movement!"

"Push forward," Fraser ordered. "Extended order."

Andrew allowed Lancelot to pick his way across the rough ground as he watched for Zulus. The wound in his calf throbbed, perhaps in anticipation of violence to come, and Andrew grunted, pushing away the irritation. Clouds gathered above, hazing the once-bright sky, and he heard nothing except the chink of equipment and the soft padding of horses' hooves.

"You were imagining things, Sergeant," Kelly grumbled.

Andrew glanced at Abernethy, who shook his head, holding his rifle ready.

"There!" a man shouted as a small herd of cattle broke cover in front of the Riflemen, twenty animals crashing over the undergrowth and around the rocks.

"Beef on the hoof!" Kelly shouted, pulling his horse to follow them.

"No." Andrew grabbed Kelly's bridle. "Cattle don't suddenly run without reason. Somebody's driving them."

"Round up these cattle, Baird," Fraser ordered. "The cooks will always welcome fresh meat."

"Yes, sir." Andrew raised his voice. "After me, lads! Keep your eyes open for the Zulus!" He kicked Lancelot forward with his men in extended order behind him. He heard the clatter of hooves on loose stones, a grunt as a horse stumbled, and the mutter as its rider regained control, and then they were ahead of the main body and heading off the small herd.

"There's a ravine ahead, sir," Abernethy shouted. "Be careful."

"I see it," Andrew said, thankful that Lancelot was sure-footed as he headed off a panicking cow. When he reached the edge of a ravine, Andrew pulled Lancelot up in disbelief. Below him, covering the foot of the gorge, extending up the sides and stretching as far as he could see, were Zulu warriors.

"Dear God in heaven!" Andrew shouted. "Zulus!" He hauled Lancelot back from the rim. "Halt, lads!" He signalled to Fraser and gestured urgently downwards.

Fraser hurried up, glanced over the edge, and made an instant decision.

"Bugler, sound the alert!"

"It's the entire Zulu army," Kelly yelled. "Thousands and thousands of the buggers."

"That's the uMcijo regiment." Abernethy halted on the lip of the ravine and looked down. He pointed to the massed warriors, speaking as calmly as if he were reading from a book, "with the uNokhenke and the uNodwengu on the right."

Andrew listened to the names without much interest as he counted his men.

"And the iNgobamakhosi and uMbonambi on the left," Abernethy continued as he scanned the static warriors. "This is the bulk of the Zulu army."

"Dismount!" Fraser ordered, and the Riflemen obeyed with a rustle of uniforms and a few muttered curses. Andrew saw Lieutenant Raw and the Sikali Horse line up beside the Cape Riflemen, stare into the ravine and load their carbines.

Raw looked to his Sikali Horse. "We'll try and thin them a little, boys!"

"Aim!" Fraser sounded surprisingly calm. Andrew looked at the mass of Zulu warriors, lifted his rifle and aimed at a stalwart man who stared up at the line of threatening horsemen.

"They're coming, boys!" Sinclair called as the uMcijo rose, humming like angry bees and began to climb from the ravine. Most of the other *amabuthos* followed, holding their shields in front of them and their assegais in their right hands.

"They'll form the horns of a bull," Abernethy said, aiming at a broad-shouldered induna. "The chest will come straight for us, with the horns overlapping to take us in the rear and flanks."

Andrew noticed two Zulu units, the uNdi and uDloko waiting in reserve. "How about them?"

"They're the loins," Abernethy said, still calm despite the vast array climbing towards him. "They'll reinforce wherever they're required."

"Fire!" Fraser ordered, with Raw echoing the command a second later.

Andrew fired, worked the underlever to eject the spent cartridge, inserted a bullet, closed the lever, aimed, and fired. He saw the Riflemen and the Sikali Horse firing into the advancing warriors, some snarling, others scared, yet all standing their ground.

Although warriors fell, dead or injured, the Zulus continued to push forward, with their losses not slowing their advance. When one warrior fell, more took their place, humming as they moved and with some rattling the butts of their spears on their shields.

"Keep firing, lads!" Andrew shouted. "Kelly, lower your muzzle! You're aiming too high."

Andrew was unsure how many rounds he had fired. He only saw the Zulus advancing, warriors with shields and spears, some with knobkerries and a few with rifles. He blinked away the gun smoke that nipped his eyes, reloaded, and fired again.

"They're getting close! Back, boys!" Fraser ordered. "Bugler! Sound the retire!" The Sikali Horse was already withdrawing, the men running to their horses without panic. The Riflemen fired a final volley, mounted, and retired, with the Zulus following, shouting, and rattling the butts of their assegais on their shields.

Andrew barely glanced up as tall Captain Shepstone assumed command of the Sikali Horse. He took in the situation at a glance. "Conduct a fighting retreat," he ordered.

"We are," Fraser said quietly and raised his voice. "Listen for the bugle calls, men!"

The Riflemen and Sikali Horse halted on a slight rise, loaded, and waited for the order to fire.

Andrew checked his watch. It was 11.45 AM. He glanced over his shoulder, where a company of the NNC had marched in support of the mounted men. The NNC took a single look at the thousands of Zulus spilling over the edge of the ravine, turned and ran without firing a shot or throwing a single spear.

The Sikali Horse watched them run, shouted abuse, and remained in the firing line.

"So much for our infantry support," Abernethy said cynically.

"Fire!" Fraser ordered.

The Riflemen fired, with more warriors falling. A small body of Zulus rushed ahead of the rest, ignoring the bullets that zipped and bounced around them. They stopped, threw their long assegais, and dropped into cover. One spear slammed into the ground a yard from Andrew and stuck there, vibrating.

"They're getting close," Sinclair shouted.

"Fire and withdraw!" Fraser ordered.

"There are warriors behind us!" Kelly yelled.

Are they friendly NNC or hostile Zulu? Andrew asked himself as he fired into the mass of advancing tribesmen. He loaded, feeling the Martini already hot in his hands.

The mounted troops, around a hundred strong, fired, reloaded, withdrew a hundred yards, and fired again, hitting their targets, bowling men over yet without delaying the Zulu advance in the slightest.

Andrew gaped at the approaching warriors, suddenly realising why all the other tribes in Southern Africa were afraid of the Zulus. They seemed unstoppable, a force of nature equipped with stabbing spears, incredible bravery, and a merciless desire to kill.

"They're pushing us off the plateau," Abernethy warned, glancing over his shoulder. "I hope the 24th are prepared to meet them."

As the horsemen withdrew, they merged with the infantry pickets, but even their combined firepower did not slow the Zulu impi. Andrew fired, reloaded, fired, and reloaded, seeing

Zulu warriors fall, for their comrades to step over the bodies and continue. He blinked away the sweat from his forehead, felt the Martini-Henry grow hotter in his hands and wondered how many cartridges he had left. Reaching a rise, he glanced down at the plain and swore.

"The Zulus are everywhere!"

Out on the plain, Durnford was also in contact with a Zulu impi while more warriors surged over the escarpment to attack the scattered camp. The latter Zulu force could easily cut off Durnford, leaving him surrounded and hopelessly outnumbered.

"The Zulus have timed it well." Captain Fraser immediately took in the overall position. "We're spread out in penny packets, with no concentration of force anywhere."

Andrew nodded, loaded, fired, and ducked as a stray bullet whined overhead.

"Even our main camp is spread out," Fraser said. "Pulleine should pull everybody back and form a cohesive defence. Without a laager, he should form a square."

Andrew agreed. Masses of Zulus attacked each separate British force, with the individual companies of the 24th scarlet islands inside a Zulu sea. He saw the British artillery fire, with the smoke jetting out a couple of seconds before the sound reached him, and then the Zulus on the plateau charged again, and he had no time for anything except looking after his men.

"Sergeant Duncan! Watch your flank!" Andrew shouted and swore as a group of warriors broke ahead of the mass to close on the Riflemen.

The leading men of the group carried different shields from the others, and Andrew recognised the white shields within a black fringe.

"The Abanonya!" He aimed and squeezed the trigger, but his overheating Martini jammed. Swearing, Andrew opened the breech and worked at the offending cartridge with the ramrod. Old soldiers had warned him that the rifling in the Martini's barrel was cut deep and square, so they quickly fouled while the heat softened the thin brass case of the cartridges.

The Abanonya were frighteningly close, and Andrew could discern individual faces among the mass. The jammed cartridge seemed immobile, and in desperation, he resorted to his clasp knife, hacking at the brass and swearing in a long monotone.

Andrew heard the cries, "*Usuthu! Usuthu*!" as the Zulus advanced, a sea of leopard-skin headdresses, tossing feathers, broad shields and raised assegais.

"Thank God!" Andrew said when he finally yanked out the damaged cartridge, thumbed in another and closed the breech. As he raised the Martini to his shoulder, he saw Jama and another tall warrior approaching.

Kelly rose slightly from his saddle, aimed, and fired, with the bullet crashing into the second warrior's shield. The Zulu staggered, righted himself, poised an assegai and threw it from fifty yards distance. Andrew looked up and shouted another warning, but Kelly was too slow in responding. Andrew saw the spear hiss towards him with the tall Zulu still in the throwing posture. The point took Kelly in the side, burying itself deep between his third and fourth ribs. Kelly looked down in puzzlement as he saw the weapon protruding from his body.

Kelly stared at Andrew. "The bastards got me!" he screamed, dropped his rifle, and attempted to pluck out the spear. "Take it out! For God's sake, somebody take it out!"

"Get out of the firing line!" Andrew ordered, aimed, fired, and missed as his target ducked down. "Kelly!" He glanced up to see the Zulus only thirty yards away and Jama drumming the butt of his stabbing assegai on his shield.

Pushing Lancelot in front of Kelly, Andrew tried to shield him. He thumbed another cartridge into the breech of his rifle, lifted it to his shoulder, and searched for the Zulu who had thrown the spear.

The man was gone. Andrew fired into the mass, felt the thump as the Martini recoiled and saw the Zulu right beneath him. He shouted, swung his rifle in a clumsy attempt to knock the man down and swore again when the warrior easily deflected the blow with his shield.

The Zulu jumped at Kelly, thrust in his iKlwa, shouted "*Ngadla!*" and dragged the assegai clear.

Kelly crumpled in the saddle with his eyes wide. His Martini clattered at his horse's feet.

The victorious warrior looked around at Andrew, shouted something, and plunged his assegai into Kelly again. Kelly slumped over the neck of his horse which bolted, carrying his rider's body away from the battle.

"Pull back towards the camp!" Shepstone roared. "For God's sake, pull back! They're all around us!"

Momentarily stunned by the death of Kelly, Andrew realised that Shepstone was correct. If the Sikali Horse and Cape Mounted Riflemen remained where they were, the Zulus would encircle and destroy them.

"Bugler! Sound the recall!" Fraser shouted. He had lost his hat somewhere, and his fair hair was tousled. "Get your men away, Baird!"

The horsemen's withdrawal became a hurried retreat. They fired when they could and avoided the more forward parties of Zulus.

Andrew tried to organise his men, saw Jama leap into the air and swing his knobkerrie at one of the Sikali Horse, heard another Native Horseman shout that he had no ammunition and then turn to flee.

"Keep together," Andrew shouted as some of the men began to panic. "Napier, don't dash ahead! Form up around me!" He fired, feeling the heat of his Martini-Henry, saw half a dozen warriors bounding up from the left and thumbed a cartridge into the breech.

Please, God, don't jam again!

Fraser was a hundred yards away with the bulk of the Cape Mounted Rifles. Andrew fired, reloaded, and called on his men.

"Don't scatter, lads! Stay together." He saw one man panic, spur his horse, and run towards Fraser's unit.

"On me, lads!" Andrew shouted.

About half the men joined him; others dug in their spurs and ran. Andrew saw a strong force of Zulus break away and chase after them, throwing assegais and leaping over the rough terrain. He saw Ramsay struggling with a jammed rifle and Sinclair covering him. Sinclair shouted something obscene, fired, fumbled for another cartridge, and pushed closer to Ramsay.

Andrew swore again and concentrated on the men at his side.

"Fire and ride!" Andrew ordered. "If we stay together, we can form a more cohesive defence!"

"Here come the uNdi and uDloko," Abernethy sounded as calm as ever, although his eyes were wild, and blood seeped from a cut on his forehead. "The Zulu reserves have joined in the fun."

Andrew nodded. *Never panic,* his father had said. *Keep your men together, for ten rifles are better than one, and if the enemy is chasing you, they'll look for an easy target and avoid men who can fight back.*

Andrew grinned ruefully and entirely without humour. He wanted to avoid his father, and Fighting Jack was already inside him, giving advice. He checked his men; nine had remained with him. "Three men to fire," he ordered, "three to load and the rest as scouts. We'll move and fire together. Guard each other's backs!"

It was the best advice he could give. He ushed his men away, heading back towards the camp from where he could hear the regular volley fire of infantry augmenting the crash of artillery.

The Zulus have reached the camp then. It sounds as if they're not getting much change out of the 24th.

"If we get back to camp, we'll be fine, boys!" Andrew shouted. "Keep your nerve and hold together!"

Zulus surrounded them, running across the plateau, drumming their assegais on their shields, and shouting. Andrew saw one of his runaway men lying screaming on the ground with a

Zulu ripping his belly open, turned and shot the warrior. The Zulu crumpled, and Andrew reloaded.

"Sir!" Ramsay pointed to a body of Zulus on their flank, running to head them off.

That's Jama's Abanonya again. These lads are good.

"Don't let them get in front of us!" Andrew shouted. "Volley fire, boys, on my word!" He waited a moment, took a deep breath, and aimed. "Fire!"

The Riflemen obeyed, with the crash of musketry nearly unheard among the triumphant shouts of the Zulus. Andrew saw his old adversaries' familiar, black-edged shields alongside, with Jama lifting another throwing spear.

"Sir!" Abernethy shouted, pointing.

"I see them!" Andrew said. He aimed at Jama, but more Zulus intervened. Sinclair yelled as a throwing spear sliced into his thigh.

"Take it out!" Sinclair screamed, and Ramsay leaned forward to help.

"Sir!" Abernethy roared and fired as a mass of Zulus erupted from behind a rock. He felled one and tried to pull away, swearing when two Zulus plunged assegais into his horse.

"Abernethy!" Andrew turned Lancelot towards Abernethy, who threw himself off the dying horse.

Abernethy rolled on the ground and lifted a hand to Andrew. "For God's sake, don't leave me!"

Andrew reined up and extended a hand. "Get behind me! Come on!"

Abernethy grabbed Andrew's hand, but before he climbed on Lancelot, a Zulu thrust an assegai into his kidneys. Abernethy screamed, twisting. Andrew saw his face contort in agony and shot the Zulu. Abernethy crumpled, writhing, and another warrior leapt on his body, stabbing downward into his back.

Andrew reloaded, aimed, and fired at the Zulu, knowing he was too late to save Abernethy. Another rush of warriors arrived, stabbing downwards at Abernethy's lifeless body before confronting Andrew. He saw the leopard skin headdresses, the tall shields, and upraised assegais, with Jama at the front. Without time to reload, Andrew jabbed in his spurs. In the short time he had spared to try and save Abernethy, his men had raced on, leaving him isolated.

The Zulus seemed to be everywhere, racing after the retreating British horsemen. Andrew paused to reload, pressed in his spurs, and headed for the track. He saw a trail of dead horsemen, European and Sikali, and a mass of Zulus in his path, running down towards the camp.

Where are my men? Where are the Cape Mounted Riflemen?

A spear whizzed past him, to thud into the ground at his side. Another followed, and a body of warriors charged at him. Without thinking, Andrew turned Lancelot and dug in his spurs. The horse responded, bounding away as Andrew leaned over its neck, aiming his rifle one-handed.

Ten Zulus were following, with their shields prominent and stabbing assegais ready.

This is where I die, in a pointless skirmish against an iron-age tribe in an obscure corner of Africa.

Andrew looked ahead, where a sea of warriors raced down to join the fight around the camp, and behind, where his pursuers were slowly gaining ground.

Damn it! I'm a good horseman; let's do what they don't expect.

"Come on, Lancelot! Come on, boy, let's show these Zulu lads what we can do!"

Spurring, Andrew pushed forward over the rough ground with a sudden spurt of devil-may-care bravado. He remembered a race he participated in on the Malvern Hills a few years previously when he took foolish chances, and now he was in a more important ride.

"Make way!" Andrew shouted and charged into the back of the Zulus. Lancelot's momentum and weight knocked aside the surprised warriors; Andrew parried a wildly swung assegai, smashed the barrel of his rifle against a warrior's head and powered through, shouting. He had already given himself up as dead, so he felt no fear. After a few moments of confused struggle, he powered clear, realised he was laughing hysterically and saw the camp at the foot of Isandhlwana.

The infantry was still formed in isolated companies, rather than a cohesive whole, with a mass of warriors attacking each unit. Gunsmoke wreathed the battlefield without concealing the piled-up Zulu dead as the 24th's volleys hammered into them.

This is a full-scale battle. I thought I knew war after the Galeka campaigns, but anything I experienced there was only a border skirmish compared to this.

Andrew guided Lancelot into a gulley, ducked as a spear whizzed past his head and heard the volley firing suddenly diminish. He pushed on with high rocks obscuring his view and emerged to see a terrible sight. The Zulus had overrun most of the 24th, with scarlet-uniformed bodies lying in neat lines and the survivors retreating to the wagons, firing all the way.

Dear God, the Zulus have defeated Chelmsford's army.

Andrew looked for the Cape Mounted Rifles and saw them at their old campsite, holding the line of trenches they had complained about creating.

Hold them off, boys! I'll be with you in a few moments.

Andrew saw the Zulus chasing after the remnants of the British infantry, with the 24th forming small groups and fighting back-to-back with bayonet and rifle-butt. He saw horsemen spurring to escape and a sergeant gathering men around him for a gallant stand. Mounted officers fled to safety, ignoring the frantic pleas of wounded men and the NNC.

Andrew guided Lancelot to the head of the path, avoiding the scattering of bodies as he rode down. He could hear nothing except the triumphant cries of the Zulus, the shouts of "*usuthu*!" and the sinister "*ngadla*!" as a warrior thrust his iKlwa into a cringing body.

Andrew spurred as a group of warriors emerged from the shelter of a rock and guided Lancelot down the path in a slither of loose stones and dust. Lancelot stumbled, recovered, and continued.

Thank God I chose a Kabul pony.

Andrew loaded desperately and fired at the foremost of his pursuers. He saw the man stagger, sawed at the reins, and pushed on, gasping.

The battlefield spread below him, with Zulus charging through the camp and knots of British soldiers continuing a hopeless defence.

"So, all day long the noise of Zulu battle rolled," Andrew gasped, misquoting Tennyson.

Two of the wagons were already ablaze, with flames and smoke obscuring what Andrew knew would be scenes of horror. Andrew saw Miller and Drummond standing back-to-back, parrying Zulu assegais with their bayonets, and then a warrior threw his assegai; Miller staggered, and the Zulus swarmed forward.

Andrew swore when he saw an impi leave the battlefield and run purposefully toward the Buffalo River and the Natal Border. The warriors were in a long column with the induna at its head.

They're going to invade Natal. Elaine's out there on Inglenook, and the Zulus have smashed our army. Cetshwayo will send his impis into Natal to kill and destroy, and we've nothing left to defend the Border.

CHAPTER 18

As Andrew descended the final hundred yards of the path, the Zulus overran the last organised resistance in the British camp. Andrew saw the First Battalion of the 24th Foot die, swamped by the sheer number of Zulus. He saw a thin trickle of men running for safety and knew he could not help; one rifle could not stem the Zulu flood.

The Cape Mounted Rifles were gone. Fraser and his men had died fighting, with a pile of Zulu bodies before them. Fraser lay in the forefront with two assegai wounds in his stomach and his head crushed. His company lay around him, most facing their front and only three where they had tried to run.

Andrew pulled Lancelot into the wagon park, watching the Zulus destroy what they could not loot and kill everybody they found. South African tribes did not take prisoners. He saw a group of Zulus surround a young drummer boy, who stood with his fists raised in an attitude of defiance. The Zulus closed in, lifted the boy, suspended him head down and ripped open his stomach.

Andrew fought nausea that rose in his throat. He could do no good here but must warn Elaine about that impi heading towards Natal. Deliberately aiming at the warrior who had sliced open the drummer boy, Andrew shot him in the back, reloaded without haste and joined the stream of refugees. A few moments before, he had not thought of survival. Now he had a purpose; he had to warn Elaine and get her away from Inglenook before the Zulus arrived. Saving Elaine was all that mattered. The death of the young drummer was an example of what the Zulus could do to Elaine and Mariana.

Andrew noticed that most of the fugitives ran in panic without looking right or left. He felt curiously detached, as if he were not here, not part of this massacre but a member of a theatre audience observing some play. Andrew was aware of the noise; he heard the screams of men and beasts, the war cries, and yells of triumph, yet they did not affect him. He rode with his rifle loaded, avoided any large groups of Zulus, and shot any who seemed threatening, immediately stopped to reload and rode on.

While others galloped, Andrew moved at a steady canter, aware that Lancelot must be tiring now. He saw warriors staring at him, but when they realised he was prepared to fight, they moved on to easier victims. A small impi jogged past, each man wearing bobbing plumes and green monkey caps.

A trail of dead men led to the drift across the Buffalo River, with men on foot pleading for help and small parties forming for self-defence. Andrew ignored them all, concentrating on survival to warn Elaine. After that, he knew it did not matter.

Andrew hardly noticed the others as he arrived at the drift. He heard the noise and saw Zulus, British and NNC, but they could be a thousand miles away for the little difference it made to him. Andrew slid his rifle into its holster and rode Lancelot into the river, where corpses and stray items of equipment bobbed, and bullets zipped and splashed in the water.

"*Usuthu!*" the warriors chanted.

A blue-coated officer stood on the bank, firing his revolver at a party of Zulus. He glanced at Andrew and lifted a hand.

"Get away, youngster," he said calmly. "I'm already dead." He pointed to the blood that bubbled from the gaping wound in his chest, reloaded and continued to fire.

When a Zulu spear hissed past, Andrew shrugged without any notion of danger and allowed the current to carry him downstream. By Andrew's reckoning, the greatest danger was at the drift, where both fugitives and Zulus gathered. The further he was from the main body, the safer he would be, and as Inglenook was also downstream, every hundred yards carried him closer to Elaine.

The river was rough, foaming past ragged rocks, and Andrew needed all his skill to keep Lancelot safe. He whispered encouragement into the horse's ear, prayed for Elaine and waited for an opportunity to get ashore on the Natal bank of the river.

A party of Zulus ran alongside on the Zulu bank of the river, but after a few moments, they lost interest and returned upstream to the main body. Andrew ignored them, patting Lancelot to keep him calm until the current eased and the river became smoother, although deep and fast flowing.

Get to Elaine, Andrew ordered himself as a strange lethargy set in. *I must warn Elaine.*

Everything seemed so peaceful that it was hard to believe thousands of men had died in great violence only a few miles away. There was no sound here except the soothing rush of the river, and Andrew barely looked when the body of a British soldier floated past, with an assegai protruding from his neck and his eyes wide with horror.

After another ten minutes, Andrew began to push Lancelot toward the Natal bank, gradually crossing the river and watching for rocks. He grunted when another body floated past, recognised a soldier of the NNC and pushed on.

Lancelot was flagging when Andrew saw a suitably low bank and eased onto dry land. He dismounted, dried his rifle, allowed Lancelot a precious half hour to rest and graze and remounted.

"I'm sorry, Lance. You'll get a decent rest when we reach

Inglenook," Andrew promised. "Until then, we'll have to keep moving."

The sun beat down on them as Andrew pushed south, looking for familiar landmarks, hoping to meet anybody who could tell him how Elaine was. He saw no sign of any Zulus, only a few small farms and peaceful native kraals.

"Halloa!" Andrew stood outside a low, thatched farmhouse. The door was locked, and shutters covered the windows. "Is anybody there?"

"Who's that?" a suspicious voice called, and a rifle barrel poked through a hole in the shutters. "What do you want?"

"I'm Lieutenant Andrew Baird of the Cape Mounted Riflemen," Andrew replied. "I'm looking for Inglenook."

"This is Greenyards!" the reply came. "Don't you know there are Zulus about?"

"I know," Andrew said. "How far is Inglenook?"

"Three miles away. Follow the river!" The rifle barrel followed Andrew as he rode away. He sniffed the air, smelling smoke.

"Sorry, Lance," he said. "Just a little longer, and you can rest." Lancelot was slowing when Andrew recognised Inglenook's mopane tree nodding above a slight ridge. He smiled at the memories of Elaine's stories and patted the horse's neck. "Nearly there, Lance."

It was not how he had envisaged coming to Inglenook. Rather than arriving in triumph, he was a bedraggled fugitive running from defeat. For weeks he had imagined riding to the front door after a successful campaign, laden with honours and glory, to find Elaine waiting at the door.

The acrid smell of smoke alerted Andrew that all was not well. He raised his head and kicked Lancelot to one final effort. "Come on, Lance." He pushed the horse to the top of the ridge and stopped.

Inglenook was a smoking ruin, with the thatched roof collapsed onto the interior and the outbuildings still aflame.

Oh, dear God in heaven.

Dismounting in a rush, Andrew ran inside the house, shouting, "Elaine!"

He nearly tripped over the first body, an elderly servant who lay spreadeagled on the stoep with a gaping hole in her head and her stomach ripped open. He swore and pushed into the house. "Elaine! Mariana!"

Mr Maxwell was next, sitting against the wall with a bullet hole between his eyes. He was naked, with his entrails piled around him.

Andrew ran past. "Elaine!" he shouted, knowing he was wasting his time. "Elaine! For God's sake, where are you?"

Another servant lay on the ground, spreadeagled and obscene in death. Andrew covered her with a scorched blanket as his search became frantic. "Elaine! Mariana! Where are you?"

Flies rose in ugly clusters as Andrew ran from room to room. Mrs Maxwell's body lay under the kitchen table, with blood stains on the floor showing the family had put up a fight. Andrew glanced at Mrs Maxwell and looked away quickly.

"Dear God. What sort of creatures treat people like that? Elaine! Mariana!" He shouted the names, gagging at the sights in the house.

Andrew heard a slight movement in the next room and dashed in with his hopes rising, only to see a lizard scuttle across the floor and escape outside. "Elaine!" He pushed open her bedroom door and stopped.

Elaine lay on the bed with her eyes wide open, her skirt rucked up to her waist, and her throat cut from side to side. The killer had also slit her stomach, and a host of buzzing flies rose from the corpse.

"Oh, dear God." Andrew could only stare for a moment, and then he stepped forward, lowered her skirt, and closed her eyes. "Why? Why kill Elaine?" He stood still, too numb to react, unable to absorb the enormity of his loss.

"I'm sorry, Elaine," Andrew murmured. "I saw the impi move to the frontier. I should have come then."

Where is Mariana?

"Mariana!" Andrew shouted, knowing it was hopeless. When Mariana's room was empty, Andrew felt a slight lift of hope that she had hidden somewhere. He opened every cupboard and looked in all the corners as he searched the rest of the house without success. She was not in the dairy, barns, outhouses, or the surrounding fields.

Either Mariana escaped and is hiding somewhere, or the Zulus took her with them.

Andrew shuddered at the thought. He called Lancelot over, removed his rifle and held it tight, hoping for a Zulu raiding party.

Come now, you murdering bastards! Come here so I can kill you. Andrew felt himself shaking with silent sobs.

I'll have to find Mariana. I cannot leave her in Zululand with the savages that murdered Elaine and her family. Andrew raised his head to the sky and roared a wordless, formless cry of grief and anger.

He buried the dead underneath the mopane tree, hacking into the stony ground with garden tools and taking satisfaction from the physical work. He laid the bodies down and piled stones on the graves to protect them from wild beasts, all the time mouthing a combination of prayers and obscenities.

Andrew stood beside the grave, unable to stem the tears that slid from his eyes. He said a few words, choked and realised his mind was blank.

"I don't know what to say, Elaine," he admitted. "I hardly got to know you." He took a deep breath to control himself and intoned the final verse of *Lady of Shalott*.

"Who is this? And what is here?
And in the lighted palace near
Died the sound of royal cheer;
And they crossed themselves for fear,
All the knights at Camelot:
But Lancelot mused a little space;

He said, "She has a lovely face;
God in his mercy lend her grace,
The Lady of Shalott."

He stood, uncaring of the rain that suited his mood.

"Goodbye, Elaine," he said. "I'll finish this war, smash the Zulus and return to bury you properly," Andrew said. "And when I find Mariana, I'll look after her. I promise."

When he looked up at the mopane tree, he seemed to hear children's voices and see smiling faces among the branches.

CHAPTER 19

As Andrew approached the town of Helpmakaar, he saw the glow of campfires and the reflection on white sun helmets. The inhabitants had raised a wagon barricade around the settlement, and what was probably most of the male population waited nervously for a Zulu attack.

"Halloa!" Andrew shouted as he approached.

"Who's there?" a voice sounded from the dark, and somebody held up a flaming torch, the orange flame casting bouncing shadows across the ground.

"Lieutenant Andrew Baird of the Cape Mounted Riflemen," Andrew said.

"Come closer so I can identify you!" the voice ordered, and Andrew stepped into the circle of light. A line of men stared at him, some in ragged uniforms, others in civilian attire but all with rifles. "Where have you come from?"

"Isandlwana," Andrew replied curtly. "Who's in charge of the defences here?"

"I am." The speaker was a middle-aged sergeant with grey hair and a worried expression on his face. Torchlight reflected from his eyes and the barrel of his Martini. "Did you see any Zulus out there?"

"Thousands of them," Andrew said, "but none around this area. "Who's in charge of the town?"

"Nobody," the sergeant replied and added. "Maybe Lieutenant Smith-Dorrien or Spalding." His lips curled in a revealing sneer. "Smith-Dorrien returned from Isandhlwana, but Spalding fled from Rorke's Drift."

Andrew did not know either man. "What happened at Rorke's Drift?"

The sergeant shook his head. "I dunno, sir. Last I heard, the Zulus was attacking the mission station, so it's probably gone by now. Major Spalding led his men away when he heard the battle."

"Spalding ran from a fight?" Andrew asked without disguising his contempt. "Where's Smith-Dorrien?"

"In that house over there." The sergeant nodded to a simple house. "The one with the sentries outside. He's been awake for the last thirty-six hours."

Andrew grunted. He had lost count of time.

"Are any Zulus close by?" the sergeant asked.

"I hope so," Andrew said.

"You hope so?" the sergeant repeated. "Why?"

"So I can kill them," Andrew said and pushed past to Smith-Dorrien's house, where a pair of red-coated soldiers watched him approach.

"Is the lieutenant awake?" Andrew asked.

"I don't know, sir. You can't go in." The nearest sentry barred the door with his rifle.

"Don't try to stop me," Andrew advised, pushed the rifle aside and stepped inside.

Smith-Dorrien was sleeping on a camp bed when Andrew entered. He looked up and grabbed his revolver when Andrew lit the lantern on a side table.

"It's all right," Andrew said. "I'm not a Zulu."

Smith-Dorrien looked exhausted and unshaven, and his uniform was dirty and torn.

"Who are you, and what the devil do you want?"

"Lieutenant Andrew Baird of the Cape Mounted Rifles," Andrew said curtly. "Did any of the Cape Mounted Rifles make it back? We were separated on the plateau above Isandhlwana."

"What?" Smith-Dorrien put down his revolver. "I don't rightly know, Lieutenant."

Andrew looked around when a second man entered the room with his braces hanging over his hips. The man glowered at Andrew. "You have no right to barge in here disturbing our rest."

"Who are you?" Andrew already guessed the answer.

"Major Henry Spalding, and you call me sir!"

"Do I? You have no right resting after hundreds of good men died, and the Zulus are rampaging around the colony, murdering at will!" The words left Andrew's mouth before he considered them. "Do we have any men still in Zululand, Lieutenant Smith-Dorrien?"

"What?" Smith-Dorrien was still only half awake.

"In Zululand," Andrew persisted. "Are there any troops still fighting?" He leaned over the bed, glaring into Smith-Dorrien's eyes. He ignored Spalding, who stood beside the door.

Smith-Dorrien gathered his wits. "Yes, of course. Colonel Pearson crossed by the Lower Drift, and Brigadier Evelyn Wood is up north."

"Brigadier Wood!" Andrew repeated with satisfaction. "Unless I have orders to the contrary, sir, I'm heading north to join Brigadier Wood." Andrew knew Wood by reputation. He was a resolute soldier who had fought in the Crimea aged sixteen, won his Victoria Cross before his twentieth birthday and served in the Ashanti Campaign.

"The devil you will," Spalding blustered.

"If any Mounted Riflemen arrive, send them up to me," Andrew said. "I'll draw some stores and ammunition and grab a couple of hours' sleep before I leave."

"Good luck, lieutenant," Smith-Dorrien said.

Ignoring Spalding's protests, Andrew left the tent. Although Helpmakaar was not a garrison town, Andrew managed to scrounge seventy rounds of ammunition, and nobody objected when he helped himself to bread, cheese and salt pork from a mobile cookhouse. A private stable provided him with fodder and water for Lancelot, who ate with relish. Rather than enter one of the military tents, Andrew bedded down beneath a wagon with Lancelot knee-hobbled at his side.

"Enjoy the rest, Lancelot," Andrew said. "We're on our travels again tomorrow."

Images of Isandhlwana and Inglenook disturbed his dreams. He saw Abernethy dying again, a horde of yelling Zulu faces, that unknown, badly wounded officer in the Buffalo calmly firing at the Zulus and then Elaine's torn, ravaged body. Andrew woke with a start, mouthing Elaine's name, found he was damp with sweat and checked his rifle. The night was dark, with stars faint through a clouded sky and the sentries' muttered voices tense in the silence.

I'll find you, Mariana, Andrew promised and lay back down.

Andrew left before dawn the following day, acknowledging the sentries' greetings with a curt "good morning" and riding north before the day's heat became too oppressive. Andrew knew his behaviour could lead to serious disciplinary issues, including losing his commission, but he did not care. He had buried his girl, and the Zulus had kidnapped her young sister; nothing else mattered.

Where would the Zulus take Mariana? If Cetshwayo had sanctioned the raid, the attackers would carry her to oNdini. Therefore, Andrew would go there by the quickest route possible. With the central column shattered, that meant joining either the southern or northern invasion force, and Colonel Wood was the more dynamic of the two commanders.

What the army did to him after the war did not matter. With the decision made, Andrew settled his mind and rode north.

❄

"I'M LOOKING FOR BRIGADIER WOOD." ANDREW ANNOUNCED his arrival at the British camp.

"Over there." A morose-faced major jerked a thumb towards a man in the uniform and insignia of a colonel of the 90th Foot, the Perthshire Light Infantry. Wood was a balding man with a fierce moustache that contrasted with his mild eyes.

"Sir!" Andrew thought it best not to reveal too much. "Lieutenant Andrew Baird of the Cape Mounted Riflemen. I've come to join your column, sir."

"Are you alone, lieutenant?" Wood seemed amused.

"Yes, sir."

"Where are your men?"

"At Isandhlwana, sir," Andrew replied. "Dead."

Wood raised an inquisitive eyebrow. "You got away from that slaughterhouse?"

"Yes, sir."

"Well, Colonel Buller can always use an extra horseman. Do you have any battle experience apart from Isandhlwana, Baird?"

"I fought through the Galeka campaign, sir."

Wood frowned, searching Andrew's face.

He is wondering how I escaped, and my men died. I don't blame him.

"I see," Wood said at length. "Do you have a message for me, Baird?"

"The Zulus have murdered a family and kidnapped a white woman, sir," Andrew said.

"What?" Wood nearly stuttered. "Who and where?"

"They've massacred the Maxwell family and kidnapped the younger daughter." Andrew gave limited details without explaining how he happened to be at Inglenook.

"The current swept you far downstream." Wood was too experienced not to read between the lines.

"Yes, sir," Andrew gave a safe answer.

"We'll look for them," Wood said. "I'll give orders to Lieutenant-Colonel Buller."

Andrew knew Redvers Buller by name, as he had served with

his father in the Ashanti War of 1873 and 1874. Buller had also fought in the late Galeka War, although Andrew had never met him. He was a big bluff man with a reputation for daring and one of General Garnet Wolseley's favourites.

"Do I know you?" Buller asked when Andrew made his introductions.

"No, sir. We've never met."

"You look familiar," Buller said and shrugged. "I know you served against the Galekas but never near me. The Ashanti campaign, perhaps?" He shook his head. "No, I must be mistaken; you're too young to have served in West Africa."

"I was fifteen at the time, sir." Andrew forced a smile. "Did you hear about the kidnapped woman, sir?"

"Brigadier Wood informed me," Buller said. "I've passed the news down the line, and all our patrols will be on the lookout."

"Do we have any spies among the Zulus, sir? People who could give us information?"

Buller frowned. "We may have," he said. "Can you speak Zulu?"

"A few words, sir. I learned some Xhosa during the Galeka war so I can make myself understood. I'll learn more Zulu during this campaign."

"I'm sure you will," Buller said. "I'll be sending out patrols to gather information about the Zulu movements, Baird, and we'll ask about this woman as well. Between you and me, if Cetshwayo sanctioned the raid, the woman will be in Ulundi. If he didn't, then she's already dead, if she's lucky."

Andrew said nothing. His hatred had partially masked his grief at Abernethy and then Elaine's death, but he hoped to salvage something by rescuing Mariana. If she were also dead, he would have nothing in his life.

"Sir, permission to take a fighting patrol to Ulundi to rescue the woman?"

"Denied," Buller said. "That would be suicide for you and cost me good men." He touched Andrew's shoulder. "Why the concern over a civilian, Baird?" He peered closer. "You know her, don't you?"

"Yes, sir," Andrew replied.

"I'm sorry to hear that." Buller sounded genuinely sympathetic. "We'll do our best to find her, Baird, and you can command one of the search parties, but riding directly to Cetshwayo is not on, you know."

"Yes, sir."

Buller pulled at his moustache and looked sideways at Andrew. "Are you sure we haven't met, Baird? There's something very familiar about you."

"Quite sure, sir."

"I know what the men called you," Buller said with a wry smile. "Up-and-at- 'em Andy. Well, Baird, I hope to give you the opportunity to earn your name."

How does Buller know that? The British Army is like a bunch of old women gossiping at a village well.

ANDREW LIFTED HIS FIELD GLASSES FOR THE FIFTH TIME IN half an hour and surveyed the land. Today was his fourth patrol in a week, and he was weary, with sweat blurring his vision as it seeped into his eyes. He coughed, trying to clear the dust of their passage from grating the back of his throat.

Andrew's initial hatred of everything Zulu after Abernethy's death and Elaine's murder had abated into a dull, ever-present ache and a desire to find Mariana.

The quicker we destroy Cetshwayo's empire, the sooner I can find Mariana. Now I've seen what the Zulus are like, I've no sympathy for them.

This northern section of Zululand was further from Cetshwayo's oNdini, and the chiefs were more independent than those further south. The terrain consisted of ranges of flat-topped mountains, where local indunas had held their warriors back to defend the locality rather than joining the royal army.

Andrew lowered his field glasses and considered the current situation in Zululand. When Wood's Number Four Column had crossed the Blood River, he made camp on the East -Zulu - side at a place named Bemba's Kop. Chelmsford ordered him to throw his weight about and ensure the local tribes did not reinforce Chelmsford's main invasion.

"We're only a diversion," Second Lieutenant Fletcher had groaned to Andrew. "While the Central Column grabbed the glory, we were forgotten away up here in the north."

Andrew grunted. "There was no glory at Isandhlwana," he said.

"What was it like, sir?" Fletcher asked with all the curiosity of an unblooded soldier. He was a young, freckle-faced youth with wide blue eyes.

Andrew swept his field glasses over the hill they were about to climb. "Confusion, chaos and slaughter," he replied at length.

"Why, sir?"

"Why?" Andrew lowered his field glasses and stared at Fletcher's red, peeling face. Although only a couple of years older, Andrew felt like an old man compared to this newly arrived subaltern. He considered the question. "Why were we defeated? It was a combination of bad generalship, poor organisation, laziness, and a refusal to treat the Zulus with the respect they deserved. They out-generalled us, Fletcher."

Fletcher looked shocked at the expression on Andrew's face. "Do you think we can defeat them?"

"Yes," Andrew said shortly. He hid his doubts, remembering how the Zulus had lured away half of Chelmsford's force before attacking the poorly organised camp. They had primitive weapons but used sophisticated tactics.

"They're good soldiers," Andrew said.

He remembered the superb discipline of the impis as they

withstood the massed volleys of veteran British infantry, and he remembered Abernethy's dying scream.

"Are they as good as us?" Fletcher asked.

Andrew saw the nervousness in Fletcher's eyes. "No," he said. "We're better than them."

"That's a relief." Fletcher gave a weak smile.

"It all depends on the officers," Andrew said. "As far as I can see, we need to keep the infantry in a close formation. The Zulus are fast-moving, aggressive, and very dangerous at close quarters. If we want to defeat them, we'll have to use our best advantage, which is musketry and artillery."

"Yes, sir," Fletcher said.

Andrew looked at the hill ahead, searching for Zulus. His hand curled around the stock of his Martini as he imagined squeezing the trigger and the bullet smashing into a warrior's head.

I'll get them for you, Elaine, and I'll find Mariana.

After days of pouring rain, the sun had broken through to bake the mounted patrols Wood sent out. In command of the mounted men, Redvers Buller had demonstrated his skill by leading the Frontier Light Horse in recent South African campaigns. Not many British officers could lead the independently minded colonials, but Buller had the requisite combination of tact, strength, skill, and endurance. He won their trust and even admiration.

By the time Andrew joined Number Four Column, Wood had left his original base to establish a laagered camp at Tinta's kraal. A few days after Andrew arrived, Wood marched his force north-westward to a stronger position at Khambula Hill.

"What do you think, sir?" Fletcher asked as Andrew surveyed the camp.

Andrew nodded. "It's a good site," he approved. "We're between the settlement of Utrecht and the strongholds of the abaQulusi tribe. They can't attack Natal without passing us."

"Baird!" Wood called Andrew over as they stood on Khambula Ridge. "How did His Lordship fortify the camp at Isandlwana? How did the Zulus manage to overcome the defences?"

Wood listened to Andrew's description of the battle without commenting on what Andrew saw as Chelmsford's failures.

"There was no wagon laager, sir," Andrew explained. "The wagons were constantly moving between Isandhlwana and Rorke's Drift, so Lord Chelmsford did not think it possible to laager them."

"Did Pulleine have the infantry in a square?"

"No, sir. Each company acted as an individual unit."

"Entrenched?" Wood asked.

Andrew shook his head. "No, sir."

Wood's mouth tautened. "Thank you, Baird. How did the Zulus attack? Describe their tactics." He listened to Andrew's reply, nodding at the right places. The brigadier was not as unfailingly polite as Chelmsford but still treated his junior officers with respect. "You can return to your patrolling work with Colonel Buller. Let me know if you have any success tracking this missing girl."

The tone of Wood's voice and the shadows in his eyes told Andrew the brigadier had already given up hope of finding Mariana alive.

"I will, sir," Andrew said. *I've not given up.*

While Andrew perfected the art of patrolling under Buller's expert guidance, Wood ensured the Zulus would not take his camp by surprise. He had two battalions of good quality infantry, the first battalion of the 13th Foot and the 90th Perthshire Light Infantry and used both to strengthen the camp.

Every time Andrew returned to Khambula from patrol, Khambula Hill was better prepared. Wood positioned his wagons in a hexagonal laager, with the boom of each wagon running under the body of the next. He ordered the pioneers to cut thorn bushes, and swearing infantry jammed them beneath the wagons to prevent any Zulus from ducking through to attack the defenders.

"I don't know about the Zulus," one ginger-haired private said, sucking blood from his hand. "But these wait-a-bit thorns would stop me."

"I haven't ordered you to stop, Sanderson," Corporal Peters growled. "So, no waiting a bit until I say so!"

Two hundred yards away, Wood ordered a second fortification for the beef cattle, with the toiling infantry hacking trenches from the stony ground and building stone barricades on the outside.

"Sangers, my father would call them," Andrew said in an unguarded moment.

"Would he indeed?" Brigadier Wood asked. "An old Indian hand, was he?"

"Yes, sir," Andrew confessed, cursing his wayward tongue.

Wood nodded. "I might have bumped into him," he said, "although I can't remember an officer named Baird."

Andrew kept quiet as the Brigadier continued.

"As you see, we also have a redoubt on that rise a little beyond the cattle kraal, with a palisade joining both. We've positioned four seven-pounders to cover the gap between the main laager and the redoubt, and a further two seven-pounders in the redoubt, facing north-east."

"Yes, sir."

"You're the only man here who's seen a Zulu attack, Baird." Wood revealed his professionalism by continuing to ask for advice. "Can you think of anything else that might assist in repelling them?"

"Maybe, sir." A few weeks back, Andrew would have hesitated to offer his opinion to a senior officer, but since Isandhlwana, he was less concerned with rank. "I'd put trip wires in front of the defences to slow the Zulus down."

Wood nodded. "I'll order that, Baird."

"And when the men have drunk their beer, sir, we can smash the empty bottles and strew them on the dead ground. I know the Zulus have hard feet, but nobody will enjoy treading on broken glass."

Wood narrowed his eyes. "You could be an asset, Baird. Now report to Colonel Buller and get back on patrol."

"Yes, sir." Andrew raised his chin. "Permission to take a patrol towards Ulundi, sir? If I get nearer to Cetshwayo's capital, I might learn about Miss Maxwell."

"You have already asked that Lieutenant Baird and Colonel Buller denied you permission," Wood said. "The AbaQulusi has been active these last few days. Buller has created a pattern of patrols without tempting the AbaQulusi to wipe one out. You're more useful here than lying dead with your men outside Ulundi."

Andrew swallowed his frustration. "Yes, sir."

I haven't forgotten you, Mariana. If you're still alive, I'll find you.

CHAPTER 20

"What do you see, sir?" Second Lieutenant Fletcher asked.

Andrew wiped the sweat from the eyepiece of his field glasses and raised them to the long ridge of Hlobane. He knew that Buller had already skirmished with the Zulus on the hill, and everybody expected another encounter. Even before Chelmsford's disaster at Isandlwana, Buller had led a patrol to this range of flat-topped mountains ten miles north of Tinta's Kraal in northern Zululand. The hills were named Zunguin. Hlobane and Ityentika, and Andrew winced as he remembered Elaine saying she thought the Zulu language was the most beautiful in the world. At that moment, he could not agree but ran the names over his tongue, savouring each syllable, and wishing Elaine was still here to speak them.

A thousand Zulus of the abaQulusi had chased Buller's small force away, but when Wood had returned the following day with infantry, the Zulus had withdrawn. British observers saw thousands of Zulus on top of Hlobane, and Wood had prepared for a full-scale attack when a messenger brought news of Isandhlwana.

Rather than hazarding one of the two remaining British forces in Zululand, Wood altered his plans and withdrew. Now, securely based at Khambula Hill, Wood sent mounted patrols to watch the Zulus at Hlobane and monitor the roads to the European settlements at Luneburg and Utrecht.

"What do you see, sir?" Fletcher repeated.

Andrew continued to survey the hills, looking for evidence of Zulu activity while always hoping to find some clue as to Mariana's whereabouts.

"I can see movement on Hlobane," he said. "Cattle and men." He glanced over his patrol of twenty-five men, a mixture of colonials and British Mounted Infantry. "We'll go closer." Ordering two colonials to ride wide on each flank, he told Fletcher to take command while he scouted towards the hills.

"Be careful, sir!" Fletcher advised while Andrew pushed Lancelot ahead.

Holding his Martini across the front of his saddle, Andrew headed for a small *imuzi* on the lower edge of Hlobane. He approached cautiously, ignoring the boys who ushered a small herd of cattle away at his approach. Women worked in the fields, backs bowed as they toiled with simple tools. One looked up when Andrew rode up and shouted a warning to her companions. The other women joined her, with all running back to the *imuzi*.

"You're in no danger from me," Andrew shouted.

A simple thorn barrier shielded a dozen neat beehive *izindlu*, with one slightly larger than the others.

The man here is not wealthy, Andrew told himself. *He has two or three wives and about twenty cattle.*

"You lads, wait here," Andrew ordered. "Allow any women or children to enter and keep watch for warriors."

"Yes, sir," Fletcher said as Andrew rode through the open gate.

"Who is the headman here?" He spoke in Xhosa, hoping the people understood him.

The interior of the *imuzi* was similar to a score of others Andrew had visited over the past year. He remained on horseback with his Martini-Henry across his saddle, ready for instant use, and his revolver loose in its holster.

The *izindlu* were neat, with women working outside or peering at him through the doorways while small children played happily or stared at Andrew in wonder. As was the custom in Zululand, the young, unmarried women wore nothing except a belt of woven grass around their waists. They looked at this stranger in their midst through wide eyes, some smiling and one, evidently the village flirt, thrusting a hip towards Andrew. Dogs lazed in the dirt, with a couple of thin goats wandering in their perennial search for food.

An old man rested in the shade of a tree and eventually lifted a frail arm to point in the direction of the slightly larger *indlu*. He gave a gummy smile and settled back down, watching Andrew with unafraid curiosity.

"Thank you," Andrew said to the old man. He shook away the image of Elaine's bloody, violated body, dismounted, and stepped to the larger *indlu*. It was unlikely that anybody from this far north had participated in Elaine's murder, yet Andrew still had to force away his twist of dislike.

"Come out!" Andrew ordered, pushing aside the door with the barrel of his rifle.

An elderly man emerged, with the *isicoco* only emphasising the silver hair on his head. He stood proudly in the sunlight, holding Andrew's gaze without fear.

"My name is Lieutenant Andrew Baird," Andrew said. "I am searching for a white woman."

The headman frowned as he translated Andrew's Xhosa into Zulu. "There is no white woman here," he said in a surprisingly deep voice.

"Have you heard of a white woman held captive in Zululand?" Andrew asked.

The headman frowned again. "If Cetshwayo ordered a white woman captured, he would have her in oNdini," the headman confirmed Andrew's suspicions.

"Have you heard of any white women in Zululand?" Andrew asked.

The headman denied any knowledge of white women. Andrew heard movement behind him and guessed the women and children were gathering their courage to inspect this strange white man.

"We are at war with King Cetshwayo," Andrew reminded. "Yet we have no quarrel with the people in this part of the country."

The headman eyed Andrew's Martini and said nothing.

"My chief, Brigadier Wood, wants to make an alliance with Uhamu, who rules this area of Zululand so that we can have peace with the Zulus. Do you know where Uhamu is?"

The headman denied any knowledge of Uhamu. Most of the population of the *imuzi* were now surrounding Andrew, keeping a respectful distance as they stared at him.

"If you hear of Uhamu or the white woman, let us know," Andrew said. "We will reward you with gifts of cattle."

Andrew hoped that bribery would prove more effective than threats to such a warlike people. Realising that the headman either knew nothing or would say nothing, Andrew withdrew from the *imuzi* with the crowd parting before him.

"Any luck, sir?" Fletcher asked.

"Not this time," Andrew replied.

"They won't tell you anything," Giles, one of the colonials, a heavily bearded man with bright blue eyes, said. "You'll have to force it out of them."

Kerr, his companion, younger and with a mobile face and well-groomed side whiskers, listened without speaking.

"Come on, lads," Andrew said as a gaggle of children followed, pointing at these strangers as their mothers called them back.

Andrew led his patrol around the area, asking about Mariana and Uhamu, for Brigadier Wood hoped to tear the northern region from Cetshwayo's authority, either by force or persuasion.

Apart from differences in size, the *imizi* were all similar, with the same barrier, the same circular *izindlu* and women performing much of the work except on the cattle. Very few contained adult males, which Andrew thought ominous, and nobody had heard of a white woman prisoner or Uhamu.

"You are too gentle, Baird," Buller echoed Giles' words when Andrew returned. "Force is the only thing these people understand."

"Yes, sir," Andrew said. "Are we not trying to teach them about civilisation?"

Buller's eyes narrowed as he looked at Andrew. "You say we haven't met before, Baird, yet you remind me of somebody. I am damned if I know who, but it will come to me."

As the infantry strengthened Khambula's defences, Buller's mounted men spent all of February patrolling in an ever-increasing radius. They raided any *imuzi* that seemed hostile, rounded up the cattle and penned them in the kraal at Khambula. They asked about the missing white woman, sought Uhamu and had an occasional skirmish with small parties of Zulu warriors. Andrew's patrol had one minor encounter when an impi of young abaQulusi warriors, eager to prove their manhood, ambushed them.

The abaQulusi exploded from a patch of woodland, drumming their assegais on their shields as they ran.

"Fire and withdraw," Andrew said, with bloodlust hot on him as he thought of Elaine.

The Zulus charged forward on a broad front, holding the shields in their left hand and assegais in their right. Andrew waited until they closed to a hundred yards, with the hatred washing over him.

"Fire!"

He selected a warrior in the central front, aimed and fired.

"Withdraw a hundred yards and reload."

His men obeyed, reining up to find the Zulus had nearly kept pace with the horses. "Fire!" Andrew ordered again, watched as more young warriors fell, and withdrew two hundred yards. The ground was uneven, broken by rocks and isolated trees, and he chose a slight rise to halt his men.

"Two volleys, lads," he ordered and picked his target.

The rifles cracked out, more warriors fell, and the Zulus stopped and retreated. Andrew watched them go.

"We could follow them and kill more," Giles suggested.

"No," Andrew said. "The Zulus led Chelmsford into an ambush and destroyed his camp. I am not falling for their wiles."

Giles grunted. "We're better to kill as many as we can," he said.

When he heard of Zulus raiding into the recently annexed Transvaal, Buller led a strong patrol of mounted men to scatter them. The patrol returned the next day with a couple of wounded men, and Andrew asked if they had heard anything about Mariana.

"Not a dicky bird, Baird," Buller reported. "Sorry, old man."

Lieutenant Peterson of the Mounted Infantry climbed down from his horse, shaking the dust from his clothes. "We bagged a few Zulus, but others are joining the fun now."

"Galekas?" Andrew asked.

"Swazis, ruffians, and God knows what else," Peterson said. "Some band of border renegades taking the opportunity to raid and despoil amidst the general chaos. I heard a shave there are white men amongst them, too."

Andrew nodded, remembering his father's tales of trouble along the Northwest Frontier when a minor incident would escalate, and half the tribes would rise. "Let's hope we end this war soon."

Peterson began to rub down his horse. "The way it's heading now, Cetshwayo will be the victor."

Andrew looked over the countryside, where the heat haze shimmered across the arid plain, and the distant hills were misty-blue. "No, he won't," he said softly. "We won't let that happen."

Peterson paused for a moment. "You were at Isandhlwana,

Baird. You saw what the Zulus did to our men. Maybe this is a fight we can't win."

"I don't believe that," Andrew said. "The Zulus defeated us at Isandhlwana, but we often lose the first battle and win the war."

"I've heard a shave that we're going to make a negotiated peace with Cetshwayo," Peterson said. "We'll withdraw our army, and he'll pay the cattle fine. We'll let him keep his impis as long as he agrees not to invade Natal."

"No." Andrew shook his head. "That won't do."

Peterson stopped grooming. "Look at it this way, Baird, we're already embroiled in a major war in Afghanistan, and the Russians and Turks are still growling at each other. We can't afford to be diverted into a prolonged war with a backward native kingdom here as well."

Andrew looked away. If the British left Zululand, he would have virtually no chance of discovering what happened to Mariana. "I won't leave Zululand," he said.

"Oh, that missing woman," Peterson remembered.

"That missing woman," Andrew agreed.

"I forgot you were obsessed with finding her." Peterson shrugged. "You're wasting your time, Baird; the Zulus will have killed her weeks ago, or worse."

Andrew raised his chin. "If she's alive, I'll find her," he said. "And if she's dead, I'll give her a decent Christian burial."

"Maybe Chelmsford will include her in the peace settlement," Peterson said.

Andrew nodded. "Maybe so," he agreed, but he had already reached his decision. Whatever happened, he would continue his search for Mariana.

JAMA CROUCHED BENEATH THE SKYLINE OF A LONG RIDGE, ignoring the rain that cascaded from low clouds as he surveyed the Intombi River half a mile away. He took a pinch of snuff as the clumsy British convoy splashed and jolted along the road.

"They won't cross the drift," Jama said.

"No," Ndleleni agreed, touching his *umzimbeet* seed necklace.

Jama looked over his shoulder, knowing his Abanonya were on the opposite side of the ridge, crouched out of sight and waiting for his command. They had been there for half a day in perfect silence and would remain for another day without complaint.

"Stay with the Abanonya," Jama ordered. "I'll follow the wagons."

Ndleleni moved at once, and Jama trotted down the slope. The small British convoy had outriders scouting for Zulus and infantry of the 80th Foot marching beside the wagons, but Jama knew he could avoid them without difficulty. The infantry slogged with heads bowed before the persistent rain, their heavy boots dragging and splashing through the mud.

Jama knew there was already a long wagon convoy stranded at a drift over the Intombi River, with the flooded river making crossing impossible. Now a second British convoy trudged over the muddy track, carrying planks, ropes, and other materials to build a raft. Jama followed at a distance, calculating the number of British soldiers in the escort, and planning how best to attack. He noted that the main convoy had split, with half a dozen wagons slogging ahead and the others a few miles away.

Didn't they learn from Ntshingwayo's victory? They are asking us to defeat them again.

Jama watched as the small convoy arrived at the drift, with hectoring sergeants supervising most of the infantry to build a raft to pass the wagons over the river.

"What shall we do?" Ndleleni asked.

Jama smiled. "Wagons without oxen are useless," he said and told the Abanonya his plan.

The British concentrated on driving the wagons, so their defences were down when Jama led the Abanonya in a sudden rush. The scattered infantry shouted a surprised challenge and fired a few shots as the Zulus drummed their assegais from their shields and shouted their war cry.

"Usuthu! Usuthu!"

Jama led from the front, thrust his *iKlwa* into the ribs of the first guard, shouted "*Ngadla*!" and finished his victim with a savage blow of his knobkerrie. He heard other warriors shouting behind him and pushed on. There were more soldiers and drivers, but today was not about killing.

As half the Abanonya fought the escort, Ndleleni led the others to cut the traces and drive the oxen away. The Zulus were accustomed to cattle since early childhood and captured the animals without difficulty, running through and past the convoy before the escort had time to gather their senses.

"How many oxen did we get?" Jama asked as he cleaned his *iKlwa*.

"Forty-six," Ndleleni replied, touching his necklace.

"That will bring more British," Jama said.

"Then what?" Ndleleni asked.

Jama's expression altered as he thought of Yibanathi, Lerato and his sons. "Then we kill them," he said.

Even Ndleleni turned away at the expression in Jama's eyes.

The following day, the scouts reported that another band of Zulus was approaching, and an hour later, they arrived.

"I am Mbilini." The leader was spare and intelligent. "More warriors are coming."

Jama eyed him sourly. "We don't need you," he said.

Mbilini touched his *iKlwa*. "Cetshwayo has appointed me to take command."

"As the king commands." Jama accepted the inevitable. He faced Mbilini. "Don't get in my way, Mbilini."

Mbilini saw Ndleleni slowly nod and guessed the temper of the Abanonya.

"You look after the Abanonya," Mbilini said. "I'll take the rest."

Jama agreed. "Together, we'll destroy them." He began to whet his *iKlwa* blade smoothing the stone in the same direction with intense concentration.

Ndleleni turned away to raise more reinforcements.

THE ABANONYA WATCHED AS THE BRITISH INFANTRY OFFICER located the stranded convoy. Jama noticed the officer was large, overweight, and slow-moving.

"We could kill them all now," Bafana said, raising his iKlwa.

"Wait," Jama ordered.

"One rush, and they'd be ours," Bangizwe insisted, whetting his assegai and humming Shaka's war song.

"Wait!" Jama repeated.

The British used their remaining oxen with more skill than Jama expected, with the officer in charge hitching the same animals to the wagons, one at a time. Despite the soft ground, the British dragged the wagons to the banks of the Intombi and formed them in a vee shape, with the open end closer to the river.

"We can kill them now," Bhekizizwe, always impatient, urged. "They'll cross the river and move to the British garrison at Luneburg."

"Wait!" Jama said, placing a hand on Bhekizizwe's bicep. He glanced upward. "The rain is coming."

Jama's prediction was correct. The rain began again, hammering down for two days, raising the river level and stranding the redcoats on the north bank. They pulled their helmets down, raised the collars of their tunics, and cursed the rain, the war, the Zulus, their NCOs, and everything else.

"Now?" Bhekizizwe urged.

"Wait," Jama replied and conferred with Mbilini. He continued to watch the British. The wagons remained in their Vee-shape, not close together and based at the river, with tents inside. Although dense bush covered the ground, the commanding officer in charge only posted a single sentry at each side of the laager and no outlying or mobile pickets.

"Why is he separate from his men?" Bhekizizwe asked as the commanding officer pitched his tent outside the laager.

"He's making it easy to kill him," Ndleleni told him.

"The rain will stop," Jama said, "and the river will fall. There will be a gap between the end wagons and the river."

That evening, more warriors joined Mbilini and Jama's Abanonya, so eight hundred Zulus waited within a short distance of the 80th Foot's laager. Mbilini sent another two hundred further up the river to attack the small British detachment on the south bank.

"Now?" Bhekizizwe asked.

"At dawn," Jama told him.

Jama gave orders to the assembled warriors, who circled the laager, moving silently into the familiar horns of the buffalo formation.

In the early morning, the rain began again, and the expected dense mist drifted across the river. Jama ordered his men to creep forward until a nervous young warrior fired his captured British rifle by mistake.

"Halt!" Jama commanded, and the attackers stopped and slid to the ground. They lay there, expecting the British to stand to their arms.

Nothing happened. Mbilini and Jama waited for an hour and gave the order for the slow advance to continue. The Zulus moved forward, inch by inch. They formed a vast horseshoe with the ends on the bank of the Intombi River. As the mist began to clear, a sentry with the small British detachment on the opposite side of the river spotted movement, shouted a warning, and fired.

"Zulus! Zulus attacking the laager!"

The sentries on the north bank, belatedly aware of the threat, also fired.

"Turn out! For God's sake, get up! The Zulus are all around us!"

Immediately the shots rang out; Jama stood up and charged forward, drumming his assegai on his shield.

"Come on, men! *Usuthu! Usuthu!*"

The Abanonya followed at once, with the other warriors joining them in a dense wave of shouting men, broad shields and stabbing *iKlwas*. Jama leapt through the gap between two wagons and thrust his *iKlwa* into a shouting sentry.

"Ngadla!"

Jama ripped the blade sideways, watched the light fade from the soldier's eyes and ran on. The Zulus were clambering over the wagons, disposing of the stumbling sentries as more soldiers emerged from the bell tents within the laager. Some of the 80th wore scarlet tunics, others wore shirt sleeves and blue trousers, with braces hanging loose over their hips. One man wore only a shirt, but all carried their rifles and attempted to repel these invaders.

The commanding officer emerged from his tent outside the laager, and rather than attempt to run, he climbed over a wagon to help his men. Jama ran forward, shield and assegai held ready.

"Captain Moriarty!" a young man shouted a second before Bhekizizwe attacked the officer.

Captain Moriarty stood on top of the wagon, firing a revolver. He shot Bafana and two more warriors before Jama launched his throwing assegai, catching the officer high in the chest.

"I'm done for!" Moriarty yelled, staggering back. "Fire away, boys! Death or glory!"

Leaping on the wagon, Jama thrust his *iKlwa* into Moriarty's stomach and finished him with the knobkerrie. As the captain fell, Jama turned to view the fight. The Zulus had won the battle with that single rush. Scores of British soldiers lay dead, with a scattering of Zulus, while another dozen British had jumped into the fast-flowing river to escape. The whole affair had taken only a few minutes.

Jama stood on the wagon beside Moriarty and watched as the rest of his plan unfolded. The two hundred men Mbilini had sent across the river descended on the British detachment on the opposite bank in a yelling rush of spears, feathers, and raw courage. Almost immediately, a British officer mounted his horse and galloped to safety while a tall, severe-faced NCO gathered a handful of survivors and made a fighting retreat.

Jama nodded with satisfaction, lifted his bloodied *iKlwa* and sang.

"Thou hast finished off the tribes.
Where wilt thou wage war?
Yes, where wilt thou wage war?
Thou hast conquered the kings.
Where wilt thou wage war?
Thou hast finished off the tribes.
Where wilt thou wage war?
Yes, yes, yes! Where wilt thou wage war?"

Yet even as he sang and the victorious Abanonya ripped open the stomachs of the dead and looted the wagons, Jama could only see Yibanathi. He knew he would swap all this triumph to have her back in his *imuzi*. He saw Jabulani watching him and felt a warm glow. Jabulani was all he had left of Yibanathi; as long as the boy was with him, he retained a part of his Great Wife.

CHAPTER 21

February eased into March, with Wood still pressing Buller and the mounted men into extended patrols. After a brief lull to lick their Isandhlwana wounds, the Zulus were also active. Small bands roamed the countryside, occasionally clashing with the British patrols and harassing the supply convoys.

"This period feels like the lull before the storm, sir," Fletcher said as they walked across the interior of the laager at Khambula.

"I agree, Fletcher," Andrew watched the 13th Foot pickets change, with the men hurrying under the driving rain, each footstep bringing a muddy splash.

The weather had deteriorated again, throwing down heavy rain that saturated the tents and turned roads into quagmires and every drift into a flood. The flooded roads delayed the supplies to Khambula, worried the quartermaster, and caused Wood to send extended patrols westward to escort the struggling wagons.

Andrew walked to a field forge to check on a shirt-sleeved farrier who was shoeing Lancelot when a sentry spied an urgent messenger panting towards the camp.

"Why don't people use the heliograph?" Andrew asked. "It's a damned good invention."

"Maybe they don't work in the rain," Fletcher suggested.

Andrew grunted and checked the farrier's work. "Make sure these nails are secure, farrier. I don't want Lancelot to shed a shoe when a hundred baying Zulus are chasing me across Africa."

"She won't, sir," the farrier said, double-checking his work to make sure, for Andrew already had a reputation as a firebrand.

"Sergeant Meek!" Andrew shouted. "Find out what that messenger said."

"Yes, sir." Sergeant Meek was a hard-headed, bitter-eyed veteran of the Mutiny and the Border Wars. He strode away, straight-backed, as Andrew continued to watch the farrier. He depended on Lancelot, and any message was less important than his horse.

"Sir!" Sergeant Meek returned a few moments later as the farrier was finishing the fourth shoe. "Another disaster, sir! The Zulus have wiped out a detachment of the 80th!"

Andrew felt the sudden chill as men looked around. All work stopped as one man crossed himself and muttered a prayer, and another checked his rifle was nearby.

"H Company of the 80th were camped beside the Intombi." The sergeant had to stop to take a deep breath. "Captain Moriarty didn't form a proper laager, only a vee-shaped defence, with no trenches and gaps between the wagons."

"Bloody idiot!" Andrew growled. He was aware it was bad form for one officer to criticise another in front of the men, but since the death of Elaine, he had little time for observing the niceties. "How many men did we lose, Meek?"

The sergeant paused for a moment and looked around as if expecting a Zulu impi to crash over the laager and assegai everybody inside. "Captain Moriarty posted a couple of sentries outside the laager and retired to bed."

"Did he have pickets?" Andrew asked sharply.

"No, sir," Meek replied crisply.

"What was the terrain like?"

"Thick bush, sir."

"Dear God," Andrew said. "Continue, Sergeant."

"There was a small detachment on the opposite side of the river, sir, under Lieutenant Harward and Colour Sergeant Booth. About five in the morning, with the usual morning mist clearing, the sentry there saw a Zulu impi around the laager. He fired at them and raised the alarm. The sentries at the laager also fired, and the men turned out of the tents." The sergeant took another breath. "The Zulus killed them all, sir. Everybody in the laager. Eighty men gone, just like that."

Andrew could picture the scene, with the Zulus' sudden rush and the sleepy, half-dressed soldiers staggering from the tents in shirt sleeves. He saw men grabbing for unloaded rifles and trying to fix bayonets in the dark and the bounding warriors stabbing and shouting and stabbing again.

"Captain Moriarty died well," the sergeant said. "He was in a tent outside the wagon laager and tried to get back inside when the Zulus speared him as he climbed over a wagon. He shouted, "I'm done for. Fire away, boys! Death or glory!"

He was a brave man but a poor officer not to take every precaution. Glory is no good when it gets good men killed.

"Did anybody survive?" Andrew asked.

"Some," the sergeant replied. "Eleven or twelve jumped into the river and managed to reach the other side, but the Zulus were there as well."

"They arranged an excellent ambush," Andrew gave grudging professional approval.

"Yes, sir. Lieutenant Harward ordered Colour Sergeant Booth to retreat to a farmhouse while he galloped away to get help."

An officer fled, leaving his men in danger? What is the army coming to? God, Harward was lucky my father was not there.

"Colour Sergeant Booth got the men to safety, sir, and Lieutenant Harward brought reinforcements."

Andrew nodded. "Thank you, Sergeant."

Another Zulu victory! If we don't show some success soon, the men will begin to doubt themselves. We'll need to do a lot better.

"SO FAR," COLONEL WOOD SAID AS HE GATHERED HIS OFFICERS together, "Cetshwayo is winning this war. He's wiped out our central column, stopped the southern invasion in its tracks and destroyed eighty men of a good-quality regiment. Oh, I know the press and politicians will emphasise the defence of Rorke's Drift as an example of British pluck and all that, but that was merely a border skirmish. Colour Sergeant Booth did well at the Intombi, but his actions do not counteract the disaster. Or disasters, rather."

Although Wood did not elaborate, Andrew knew he was referring to Harward's desertion of his men. A few officers stirred uncomfortably as they listened, with Buller shaking his head in disbelief.

"Now, we must strive to overcome these difficulties by defeating Cetshwayo's army," Wood said. "You all know that we have been searching for Uhamu; some of you may not know he came into camp with some seven hundred of his people and a request for us to escort the others to safety. That's the first piece of good news we've had, gentlemen. It shows we have created a crack in Cetshwayo's kingdom."

Andrew wondered if Wood was attempting to raise morale after the recent reverse on the Intombi.

"Colonel Buller," Wood said, "I am sending you and a strong mounted force, together with two hundred of Uhamu's warriors, to the headwaters of the Black Umfolozi River. Bring back as many refugees as possible."

"Yes, sir," Buller said.

"In the meantime, I want the local patrols stepped up. Lieutenant Baird, I want you to guard the supply routes."

"Yes, sir," Andrew said.

"I know you won't find Miss Maxwell there, but you might help win this unfortunate war."

Some of the assembled officers murmured their sympathy, for all knew of Andrew's attachment to Mariana.

Andrew watched Buller ride away and concentrated on his routine patrols. After the disaster on the Intombi, the men were more alert, with some nervous but most angry, hoping for revenge on the Zulus.

"They've all gone," Fletcher said two days later as the patrol returned, weary, wet and without sighting a single enemy warrior.

"It seems so," Andrew agreed shortly.

The following day Buller returned after another successful mission that brought back a long column of refugees. Peterson approached Andrew as he checked his men's rifles.

"I might have something for you, Lieutenant Baird. Good news and bad, I'm afraid."

"What's that, Peterson?"

"A village headman told me about a white woman in a kraal three day's ride away to the east. Siyanda's Kraal, it's called. It might be nothing, just a crazy rumour, but the fellow said the villagers regarded her highly because she had magical properties."

"Where?"

Peterson gave the most accurate directions he could.

"I hope the magic properties help keep her safe," Andrew said, noting the details as he felt a flicker of hope for Mariana.

"That's the bad news," Peterson said. "Witch doctors and such like also think white women may have magic properties. My informant only heard about the white woman because a couple of witch doctors want to steal her and cut her up."

"Do they, by God?" Andrew felt his heartbeat increase. "Thank you, Peterson." He was on his feet in a second and ran to Brigadier Wood with the news.

"A white woman?" Wood looked up from behind his desk. "Are you sure it's her?"

"No, sir," Andrew said. "But how many white women will there be in Zululand? Whoever she is, we'll have to try and rescue her."

Wood grunted, nodding his head. "I suppose you'll want to lead the rescue mission?"

"Yes, sir," Andrew responded.

"I imagined you would. How many men do you want?"

"Twenty, sir," Andrew said after a moment's consideration. "Any more would be cumbersome, and twenty could fight off a small Zulu impi."

"Find twenty volunteers," Wood said. "Good luck, Baird."

"Thank you, sir." Andrew saluted and hurried from Wood's tent, full of conflicting emotions. Hope battled with sick dread as he thought of Mariana in the hands of a Zulu warrior and the horror of witch doctors using her for their medicine.

Andrew was surprised when more than forty men volunteered for what could be a dangerous mission, and he picked a score of experienced men, mostly older than him. He selected a mixture of colonials with knowledge of African conditions and steady regulars who could be relied on to obey orders and not panic in a crisis.

"Could I come, sir?" Kerr asked, stepping forward. "I speak Zulu and know the people."

"Do you know this part of the country?" Andrew asked.

"No, sir," Kerr said. "I know the south and east of Zululand better."

Andrew mused for a moment. "Yes, come along, Kerr."

Not wishing to waste time, Andrew left that same day, following Peterson's directions and the rough location of Siyanda's Kraal Peterson had marked on his map.

He made good time, pushing his men towards the east, so it was after dark when they camped on a piece of rising ground, with a group of Buffalo thorn threes offering shelter.

"No fire tonight, boys." Andrew consulted his map. "The Zulus probably already knew we are here, but we don't want to advertise the fact."

The men nodded, accepting Andrew's orders.

"I want five men on picket duty," Andrew said and spent half the night touring the sentries. Twice they heard animals prowling outside the camp, and all were glad to leave before dawn the following day. Despite his desire for speed, Andrew kept alert, with scouts out constantly.

"No Zulu warriors so far," Kerr said as they perused the terrain. "I've never seen the land so quiet. Even the last two *imizi* were empty of men."

"Not even a whisper of an impi," Andrew agreed. "It's as if a giant brush has swept them up, or they are gathering elsewhere for some major attack."

"Yes," Kerr agreed. "It's a bit worrying. The Zulus are not a people to cross with impunity. They're planning something."

"Maybe they're going to attack our camp at Khambula," Andrew guessed. "I think Brigadier Wood commands the only active British force left in Zululand." Andrew knew the southern invasion had bogged down, with the Zulus besieging the British in a fort at Eshowe. Only Wood's force was making aggressive moves against the Zulus.

"We'll have to return and inform the brigadier," Kerr said.

"Inform him of what?" Andrew asked. "Inform him we haven't seen anything? Keep moving."

They found spoor the following morning, beaten earth and the marks of humanity. Kerr crouched, inspecting the ground. "About thirty men," he said, "moving slowly to the east, with some women in the middle."

Andrew remained on horseback with his eyes never still as he surveyed the surrounding land. "Not warriors, then?"

"I'm not sure what they are, sir," Kerr admitted. "They're moving too slowly for an impi, yet if they were a family, they'd have livestock with them."

"Are they heading towards Siyanda's Kraal?"

"They may be, sir," Kerr said. "Or in that direction, at least."

"When will we overtake them?" Andrew asked.

Kerr screwed up his face, making calculations based on the relative speed and the difficulties of the terrain. "Maybe this evening, sir," he said at last.

"Before or after we reach the kraal?"

"About the same time, sir." Kerr sounded more confident.

Andrew raised his voice. "Increase the speed, boys!"

Rather than send out a scout, he left Sergeant Meek in charge and pushed in front, following the trail. With his rifle held ready and his hat shading him from the sun and the sudden showers, he moved quickly.

"They're making no effort to hide their spoor," Kerr said.

"All the better for us," Andrew replied.

In the early afternoon, Andrew pushed Lancelot to the summit of a rise and saw a straggling group of people a mile ahead. Glancing behind to check his men, he increased speed, so Lancelot cantered over the rough ground.

I see you, you bastards. You're not taking Mariana away for your filthy practices.

With a mixture of excitement and trepidation, Andrew moved in a wide arc around his quarry, not caring if any stray party of warriors tried to ambush him. When he overtook the column, he rode to them and reined up.

"Stop there!" he ordered.

The column halted immediately, thirty men carrying hunting spears and three women in the centre.

The witches.

"Lieutenant Baird." The leading witch recognised Andrew. "I told you we would meet three times."

"This is the second time." Andrew put his rifle in its sheath. "Where are you heading?"

"Siyanda's *imuzi*." The witch glowered at Andrew, flicking the gnu's tail in her right hand.

"Why?" Andrew's hand hovered over the butt of his rifle. His men arrived and surrounded the column with rifles ready to fire.

"We have somebody to see," the leading witch replied.

"We'll travel together," Andrew told her.

The witch flicked the gnu's tail, rattled the bones on her clothes and walked on with Andrew's men forming around the column of Zulus.

"Who do you have to see?" Andrew had resolved to be polite to the witches, although his insides were churning with apprehension.

"A woman," the leading witch replied.

"Is she a white woman?" Andrew asked.

"She is a woman without colour," the witch replied.

"Kerr!" Andrew snapped. "Scout ahead."

"Yes, sir." Kerr bounded forward, returning within fifteen minutes. "This way, sir." He led Andrew to a slight ridge.

"That's Siyanda's *imuzi*." Kerr pointed to the usual circle of *izindlu* within a protective screen of thorn bushes.

Andrew lifted his field glasses and peered ahead. Siyanda's *imuzi* looked similar to a hundred others he had seen. Smoke from cooking fires rose into the still air, and women moved around purposefully as children played and young boys herded scrawny cattle outside fields of mealies.

Is Mariana in there, waiting for me?

"Take over, Fletcher," Andrew ordered and spurred through the open gate and into the kraal. Hauling out his rifle, he dismounted and looked around.

"Mariana!"

The inhabitants of the *imuzi* stared at him, women, children, and old men. Nobody made a threatening move.

"I'm looking for a white woman," Andrew said in Xhosa. "Her name is Mariana Maxwell. Is she here?"

An elderly man approached, walking erect and proud despite his white hair and lined face. "The woman without colour died yesterday," he said. "The witches are coming to take her away."

Andrew felt despair grip him. "Mariana died?" he said and then shook his head. "Let me see her. I'll be damned if I allow the witches to take her!" When he realised he was speaking English, he took a deep breath and switched to Xhosa. "Where is she?"

The elderly man indicated the largest *indlu*, and Andrew stooped through the door. The interior was dark and smoky, with a group of women around a sleeping mat on the floor. Andrew stepped forward.

"Let me see, please," he said.

The woman lay nearly naked on the mat, with her arms crossed in front of her and her eyes closed. Andrew leaned closer and sighed with relief.

"That's not Mariana," he said. "Thank God, oh, thank you, God."

"Africans don't like albinos," Kerr explained when he stepped to Andrew's side. "They fear what they don't understand and call them *inkawu* – white baboons – or *isishawa*, people who are cursed."

"Poor woman," Andrew said. "I doubt she had a very happy life."

"Outsiders rarely do," Kerr murmured.

"I said you would be disappointed when we met again," the leading witch said as she stood behind Andrew. She looked down at the albino woman. "This *isishawa* has no colour, but she is not the one you seek."

"No, she is not," Andrew agreed. He stood back as four men from the witches' column entered the *indlu* and lifted the body.

"Should we stop them?" Kerr asked.

Andrew shook his head. "One thing my father imprinted on my mind was never to interfere with local religions. I'd say that these witches are part of Zulu religious life."

"They are," Kerr agreed.

"We might disapprove," Andrew said, "but I don't think we have any right to interfere." He watched as the witches' male assistants gently lifted the dead woman and carried her out of the *imuzi*. The horsemen stood back, some with expressions of disgust, others of concern or apprehension.

"Sir?" Kerr asked as Andrew stood in the *indlu*. "Orders, sir?"

"Orders?" Andrew repeated as he struggled with his feelings, relief mingling with disappointment. "We'll return to Khambula," he decided.

Maybe I am overly optimistic, and Mariana is already dead.

WHEN ANDREW RETURNED FROM HIS ABORTIVE EXPEDITION, he found that reinforcements had reached Brigadier Wood. Lieutenant-Colonel Russell had ridden in with a squadron of Mounted Infantry plus the Edendale troop of Natal Native Horse. A few hours later, Commandant Pieter Raaf arrived with his professional-looking Transvaal Rangers, and then the Border Horse trotted in, bridles jingling, and horses lathered with sweat.

Andrew knew Raaf was a Boer and an experienced fighting man, while his Rangers included European and African riders.

"These Transvaal lads look quite a formidable force, sir," Andrew commented.

Buller nodded. "I'm not sure how far we can trust the Boers," he said. "I'll keep my eyes on Mister Pieter Raaf." He lit a cigarette and blew out a thin ribbon of smoke. "We seem to be collecting characters in this war. Commandant Weatherley of the Border Horse is also well known. He's a Canadian, a veteran of the Crimea and the Mutiny and a divorcee."

Andrew looked for the notorious Weatherley, for anybody who had gone through a divorce was subject to scandal.

"The frontiers attract the footloose and those who don't fit in elsewhere," Andrew said, remembering his father had told him the same thing.

Buller nodded. "The unconventional, the loners, the unwanted and the wild." He drew on his cigarette. "We also have a bunch of German settlers in the Kaffrarian Vanguard and, more importantly, five companies of the 80th Foot. They're at Luneburg."

"With that lot and Brigadier Wood in command, Cetshwayo can whistle for his supper," Andrew said.

Buller smiled, watching the Border Horse through critical eyes. "I hope you're right, Baird."

"Now we know the capabilities of the Zulus," Andrew said, "I doubt any semi-competent British officer will allow the Zulus to take his men by surprise. They'll laager in every camp and dig entrenchments every night."

Buller nodded. "Aye, Isandhlwana and the Intombi taught us a lesson, all right." He glanced at Andrew. "You didn't find your girl, then?"

"No, sir." Andrew shook his head. "All I found was a dead albino."

"Hard luck, Baird." Buller finished his cigarette, dropped the stub, and ground it into the dirt. "Don't give up hope, eh?" He stepped away. "I think that she'll be in oNdini if she's anywhere."

"Yes, sir," Andrew agreed. *I won't give up until I find Mariana or see her dead body.*

CHAPTER 22

"Gentlemen." Wood sounded pleased as he spoke to his assembled officers. "Lord Chelmsford has contacted us with good news. As you know, our southern column is under siege at Eshowe. His Lordship is going to drive through a relief column and wants us to create a diversion to draw off some of the Zulu army."

The officers nodded in satisfaction. They wanted revenge for Moriarty's reverse and the disaster at Isandhlwana. Buller's raids were morale-boosting but barely pinpricks against the forty-thousand-strong Zulu army.

"We know that British arms, properly led, can defeat the Zulus," Wood said, hardening his tone to drive the message home. "Our spies, while failing to locate the unfortunate woman captive, have given us some information that may prove invaluable."

The officers listened, with some lighting pipes and others with long cheroots. Andrew stirred impatiently. In his opinion, generals and brigadiers were very slow and ponderous.

Wood continued. "Our spies have informed us that Cetshwayo has sent an impi in our direction. We don't know whether it intends to launch them at Khambula or cross the border to attack Utrecht. If the former, we will be ready to receive them."

The officers stirred again, with some murmuring approval.

Wood waited until the hum died down. "We also know that a small impi has joined the abaQulusi on the heights of Hlobane." He nodded to the great flat-topped mountain ten miles to the east.

Buller lifted his head. "Maybe we should strike there, sir."

"My thoughts entirely, Buller," Wood said. "If we attack the abaQulusi on Hlobane and capture their cattle, we should draw Cetshwayo's impi toward us and not to Utrecht. So far, Cetshwayo has had things all his own way. His impis have found us unprepared. That will not happen here, gentlemen!"

The officers gave a subdued growl, unlike anything Andrew had heard before. He saw the determination on their faces, the set jaws, and clenched fists and some of his doubts about the outcome of this war dissipated.

"Colonel Russell and Colonel Buller," Wood said. "I leave it to you to prepare a striking force for Hlobane."

"Yes, sir," Buller said with satisfaction as Russell gave a brief nod.

Wood lifted his hand. "Infantry officers, you and I will ensure we adequately defend Khambula. I want the men trained to respond to an alarm within two minutes. Colonel Russell, organise your attack on Hlobane. That is all. Thank you, gentlemen."

Buller gathered his officers outside his tent and spread a map on the ground. "Gentlemen," he said. "You heard the Brigadier. I have drawn this map from my own observations, plus the information from spies and informers."

Andrew studied the map, memorising the main features. He pushed away his memories of the plateau above Isandhlwana as Buller, tall, commanding, and full of confidence, continued.

"I want you all to be familiar with the topography, so nobody gets lost when we're up there."

Hlobane was a high hill rather than a mountain, with a four-mile-long *nek* or pass connecting it to the Zunguin range. Hlobane consisted of two plateaux of different heights and sizes, with the lower plateau, 850 feet high, the smaller and closest to the nek. That plateau rose a rocky two hundred near-vertical feet to a narrow passage called the Devil's Pass, which led to the second and higher plateau. Andrew judged the higher plateau to be over three miles long and a mile and a half in width, with a nek at the east. This eastern nek, Ityentika nek, stretched to the mountain known as Ityentika.

"Now, gentlemen." Buller spoke softly, but nobody could mistake the intensity of his eyes. "You must remember that the abaQulusi is not a normal Zulu clan. Shaka himself sent them here, and they think of themselves as royalty, a cut above the normal Zulus. When they say they are children of heaven, they mean it."

Andrew fretted slightly, not caring what the abaQulusi thought of themselves.

Buller noticed Andrew's reaction. "That means the abaQulusi will be even more determined to defend their homes," he said. "They live in kraals across the area and withdraw to the plateaus when somebody threatens them. According to our spies, the abaQulusi also barricade the paths between each plateau with piles of rocks, so don't expect to gallop from place to place." Buller raised his voice. "This won't be a quiet stroll around Hyde Park, gentlemen. Prepare yourselves for some hard fighting."

Andrew studied the map again. "I see only two tracks up to the plateau." He jabbed down with his finger. "One at the western end and one at the eastern."

"That's correct, Baird," Buller said. "The one at the west is so steep that horses will find it nearly impossible, but we will use both paths. Once we reach the Hlobane plateaux, our informants tell us there are around two thousand cattle and maybe a thousand warriors."

"How will we proceed, sir?" Peterson asked.

"Colonel Wood has drawn up the plan," Buller said. "I will lead a force up the eastern track with the larger force of mounted men, plus a battalion of friendly Zulus and a rocket trough. We shall drive away the cattle. Colonel Russell will use the steeper western track and occupy the lower plateau with the Mounted Infantry, the remainder of the mounted men, a second rocket trough and the rest of the friendly Zulus. Colonel Russell is in overall charge of operations. There is a terrible road known as the Devil's Pass joining both plateaux, but we won't have to use that!" Buller looked up, smiling. "Are there any questions?"

"When do we start, sir?" Andrew asked, and Buller grinned.

THEY LEFT KHAMBULA BEFORE DAWN ON THE 27TH OF MARCH, riding across the country with scouts out and friendly Zulus marching alongside. Buller had given Andrew Second Lieutenant Fletcher, Sergeant Meek and twenty men to command, and he rode in the centre of the column. Most of the men were eager to avenge Moriarty and the dead at Isandhlwana, with others openly nervous.

"Can we trust these Zulus?" one man asked, jerking a thumb at Uhamu's men running beside the column.

"Yes," Andrew replied shortly. "If Cetshwayo or the abaQulusi capture them, God knows what their fate will be."

That first day was uneventful, and Buller set up camp in the early evening five miles southeast of Hlobane, with his tents mushrooming on the rough ground and the hill looming on the horizon. He sent out strong pickets and created a rough barricade in case of a Zulu attack.

"After Intombi," Buller said grimly, "we're taking no chances. If anybody hears or sees anything suspicious, wake me at once. Fire first, boys and ask questions later." He looked back towards Khambula. "And watch for the Border Horse; they seem to have got lost somewhere."

Andrew checked his rifle for the tenth time that day, brushed a speck of dust from the breech and stared across to where Russell's campfires winked through the dark. Russell had taken his force on a different route, heading for the opposite side of Hlobane.

"It's good to know we have company," Peterson said, lighting a thin cheroot.

"If you see their fires go out, sound the alarm," Andrew said. "I wonder how many Zulus are watching us now."

Peterson drew on his cheroot. "How ever many there are, there'll be less when we get among them."

Andrew did not smile. He could still hear the Zulu's triumphant yells as they plunged their assegais into the fugitives of Isandhlwana. "I hope you're right, Peterson." He thought of Elaine, caressed his rifle, and glanced over to Hlobane.

"Grab some sleep," Buller ordered. "We're only here for two hours rest."

Andrew dozed for an hour and then took over as duty officer. He was checking the pickets when Buller loomed out of the dark. "Where the devil is the Border Horse? Where are Weatherley's men?"

"They've not arrived yet, sir," Andrew said. "They must have taken the wrong route."

Buller shook his head. "I thought the colonials were better than that."

Andrew said nothing. *We'd have heard firing if Weatherley ran into trouble.*

"We can't wait for them," Buller decided. "Build up the fires so the Zulus think we're still here."

Leaving the fires blazing, Buller led his column toward the Ityentika Nek. They marched closer to Hlobane, halted for an hour, and moved again. At three in the morning, they reached the foot of the path.

Andrew looked upward at the looming mass of Hlobane to

the left and Ityentika on the right, patted Lancelot and wondered what the day would bring.

"Somebody told me that it was always hot and sunny in Africa, sir," Meek said as the skies opened with heavy rain, punctuated by thunder and lightning.

"Maybe they've never been here," Andrew replied. He pulled his recently adopted broad-brimmed hat down and his collar up. "This weather is as bad as we have in Britain."

"Dismount!" Buller ordered. "Lead the horses up the path. They'll have enough work to do later."

The column filed onto the steep track, with the rain turning the ground into a torrent and the frequent flashes of lightning revealing where they were.

"Keep moving!" Buller ordered as Andrew trudged up with his head bowed.

"Come on, Lance!" Andrew said, with every footstep splashing and the hill rising, dark and ominous, before him. He held his rifle muzzle down to protect it from the rain and moved in utter misery.

Every step brings us nearer the top, and every fight helps us win the war. Keep moving; left, right, left, right, left.

Andrew heard the first crack of a rifle, far different from the deeper grumble of thunder and knew the Zulus had seen them.

"Here we go!" he shouted, suddenly uncomfortable at the thought of being shot at as he climbed a narrow path with a long drop below.

"The Zulus are in caves!" Kerr shouted, and a man screamed as a bullet tore into his chest.

"Fire at the muzzle flashes," Buller ordered, "and keep moving!"

When some of the men responded, a desultory firefight began between the slowly climbing column and the unseen defenders. Andrew peered into the slanting rain, decided he had little chance of hitting anything and plodded on.

The Zulus continued to fire, wounding a few men and more horses, but Buller pushed his column up.

"Don't stop," Buller ordered. "Keep moving. The allocated men will take care of the wounded."

Andrew swore as a bullet thumped the rock beside him. He saw the blue mark on the stone and pushed on, refusing to waste cartridges he might need later. He remembered Isandhlwana when the infantry ran out of ammunition. Twice he stepped over dead bodies on the track and once heard a terrible scream as a horse toppled over the edge.

"Keep moving, men!" Andrew repeated Buller's words and heard officers echo the order the length of the column, diminishing in volume as the command reached the men still near the foot of the path.

Buller forced their passage up step by stubborn step, and by dawn, the British formed up on the higher plateau. Piet Uys, who led the only force of Boers to join the British, spoke to his four sons and nodded to Buller, smiling. As the British formed up, the storm passed, leaving the ground slippery, with grey light reflecting from the wet rocks.

Andrew counted his men, thankful he had lost nobody from his squad, although they all looked bedraggled and downcast.

"Heads up, men," Andrew ordered. "Check your ammunition." He forced a wry smile. "At least we don't have to worry about filling the water bottles."

"Sir, look over there!" Kerr pointed to the right, where a powerful body of abaQulusi was trotting around the plateau's edge with shields held above their heads and the weak sunlight glittering from their spearheads.

Buller rode slowly in front of his men, tall and imperturbable.

"If we move into the plateau, sir, they'll cut us off from the path," Peterson said.

Buller smiled and gave a calm order. "I want a troop of the Frontier Light Horse to skirmish with these fellows. Stop them from blocking our retreat."

"Yes, sir," Lieutenant Carrington of the Frontier Light Horse said happily and led his men toward the abaQulusi. The Light Horse's sand-coloured uniforms, braided with black, bobbed away as their broad hats, sodden from the morning's rain, flopped over their heads.

Within a few minutes, Andrew heard the crackle of musketry as the Light Horse fired on the approaching abaQulusi.

"I want our Zulus and other African infantry to round up the cattle and drive them to the west," Buller said. "The Zulus are expert cattlemen."

Andrew watched the friendly Zulus trot over the plateau, covering the ground at a pace British light infantry would have envied.

"Baird!" Buller said. "You look eager. It's time you proved your nickname, Up-and-At- 'Em. Take your men and support the Frontier Horse."

"Yes, sir." Andrew pulled Lancelot out of the main formation. "Come on, lads! It's time to earn our magnificent pay!" He led his men after the Light Horse.

The tactics were simple. Approach close to the Zulus, keep out of range of the throwing assegais, fire, withdraw, reload, close, and fire again.

The abaQulusi trotted toward the Light Horse, dropping to the ground when the British fired to minimise their casualties, rising, and advancing. They never wavered despite the scattering of dead and wounded, held their shields at an angle and extended their ranks to outflank the British horsemen. Andrew led his men beside the Light Horsemen, firing and withdrawing, breathing in the gun smoke, reloading, and returning to the fight. They skirted the plateau's edge, with the rising sun rapidly drying the ground and the abaQulusi outflanking them and taking minimal casualties.

One of the Light Horsemen swore, pointed downward and shouted, "Look to the southeast!"

When Andrew looked down on the plain, he saw a long

column of Zulu warriors in the far distance, with another further back. Ignoring the abaQulusi, he lifted his field glasses and studied the plain.

"Damnation!" Andrew saw another Zulu column a quarter of a mile to the right of the second and then a fourth and a fifth.

"That's the main Zulu army," Andrew shouted. "They must have left oNdini earlier than expected to get here so quickly."

Oh, dear God in heaven, here we go again.

CHAPTER 23

Andrew felt a chill run up his spine at the size of the Zulu army. Ever since he saw the thousands of Zulus smash into the 24th at Isandhlwana, he had dreaded witnessing such an impi again.

"Warn the Colonel, Fletcher," Andrew ordered and watched as Fletcher spurred across the plateau.

Andrew was aware of how dangerous their position could be. With the abaQulusi on Hlobane and a massive impi only a few miles away on the plain, the Zulus could easily cut off the British and destroy them piecemeal. Without Buller's mounted men and the African infantry, the British position at Khambula would be considerably weaker, and the Zulu impi might overrun the defences. Even worse, the impi could ignore the Khambula position and attack the town of Utrecht with its tiny garrison and civilian population. Andrew shivered, remembering the horror of Inglenook.

"Sir!" Fletcher returned at a gallop with his hat bouncing from his head and his face flushed. "Colonel Buller sends his compliments, sir, and requests that you join him."

"Very well," Andrew replied. "Take over here, Fletcher." He winked. "We're witnessing history, Paul!"

A group of officers surrounded Buller when Andrew arrived. "I saw the impi, Baird," Buller said. He looked along the plateau, assessing the situation. "We'll have to return to Khambula, but the impi is too close for us to chance the eastern track." He thought for a moment. "We'll have to take the Devil's Pass."

"How about the cattle, sir?" Peterson was a farmer from Cape Colony, and cattle were nearly as important to him as to the Zulus. "We can't abandon the herd to the Zulus." He pointed to a thin-faced ensign. "Go and warn the Frontier Light Horse and the Border Horse if you can find them. Tell them to retreat at once by the right."

"Yes, sir," the ensign shouted and galloped off.

"Well, gentlemen," Buller said, "here we are. We have the main Zulu impi advancing across the plain a few miles away and the abaQulusi approaching us with murderous intent." He grinned. "As soon as the last of the cattle is away, I think we should withdraw. Are there any dissenters?"

There were none.

"My men, sir," Andrew reminded. "My men are with the Border Light Horse."

"Fetch them, Baird," Buller replied. "You may withdraw by whichever route seems better."

"Yes, sir." Andrew kicked in his heels and galloped across the plateau.

"Come on, lads!" Andrew gestured from a hundred yards away. "Leave the abaQulusi! We're heading back to Khambula."

Andrew's men galloped across the rocky ground and formed behind him, still exchanging shots with the abaQulusi as Andrew led them towards the Devil's Pass.

"Fletcher," Andrew shouted. "Take the lead. You can see Buller's men ahead; ride for them." He dropped to the rear, where the abaQulusi followed at a steady trot. Encouraged by the British retreat, the Zulus redoubled their efforts and pressed hard on the heels of Andrew's men.

"No, you don't." Andrew saw one young warrior running ahead of the rest with his throwing assegai poised. He reined up, aimed his rifle at the man's midriff and fired. The Martini kicked back into his shoulder, and the bullet threw the shocked warrior backwards.

The short delay had enabled the abaQulusi to close, and three throwing assegais hissed toward Andrew. He pulled Lancelot aside, impressed by the distance the Zulus could throw their spears and gasped as an assegai ripped the arm of his tunic and opened a shallow wound.

That's my second wound in this campaign.

"Come on, sir!" Kerr had pulled back in support, fired at the nearest abaQulusi, and reined up beside Andrew. "You're hurt, sir!"

"Only a scratch," Andrew said, although the wound was stinging abominably. "Come on, Kerr!"

As they pushed on, more assegais whizzed past, some to impale themselves into the ground with the long shafts vibrating. Andrew saw his men ahead, with the most nervous crowding in advance of Fletcher and Buller ushering the mounted men towards the nek to the lower plateau.

"I asked Russell to cover this pass," Buller fumed. "Where the devil is he?"

"I'm damned if I know, sir," Lieutenant Browne, Russell's second-in-command, looked equally annoyed.

"Well, we'll have to do without him," Buller said. "I've sent the men down, Browne. You may command the rear guard."

"Yes, sir." Browne accepted the post of danger without hesitation.

Buller noticed Andrew approaching with his men. "Ready to meet the devil, Baird?" Buller asked, grinning.

"Not yet, sir," Andrew replied, glancing over his shoulder at the rapidly approaching abaQulusi. "I'll live to fight another day."

"That's the spirit," Buller said. He shook his head. "Are you sure we haven't met before? There is something very familiar about you."

"No, sir," Andrew said, ducking as a Zulu bullet whizzed over his head.

"I'm damned if I haven't seen you somewhere." Buller took no notice of the increasing Zulu fire or of the approaching abaQulusi. "We can discuss this later, young Baird." He lifted his revolver and fired at the abaQulusi. "Missed, damn it. The range is far too long. After you, my boy." Buller indicated the steep path, strewn with boulders, down which the raiding party struggled.

Andrew glanced down, seeing an almost perpendicular *kranz*, with boulders and rocks thrusting from the bottom of a path so narrow men would have to descend in single file.

Kerr, the last of Andrew's men, was already twenty yards down, riding his horse with supreme skill. Andrew watched Kerr, seeing horses and men all jammed together, with Piet Uys guiding his Boers down the steep, rock-strewn path.

"After you, my boy," Buller repeated.

"Thank you." Andrew gave a little bow. Buller's calm assurance gave him confidence. Although Andrew did not fear death, he wanted to live to burn down oNdini and rescue Mariana if she were still alive.

Dismounting, Andrew began the descent, leading Lancelot down the path. He holstered his Martini as being too unwieldy, grabbed his revolver instead and negotiated the rocks. The Devil's Pass was an accurate description, Andrew thought, as he braced himself to prevent Lancelot from sliding. He would have hesitated to use this descent even on a quiet day, and with an aggressive impi behind them, the British took appalling risks. Not for the first time, Andrew blessed Lancelot for being a sure-footed Kabul pony rather than a taller, showier thoroughbred that was less able to negotiate the precipitous slope.

A Zulu appeared behind Andrew, with his shield held high to his face and only his eyes and the upper half of his head visible. Feeling remarkably calm, Andrew judged where the warrior's body would be behind the shield and fired a single shot towards his chest. The hide shield was no protection against a pistol bullet, and the force knocked the warrior backwards. Even as he fell, he threw his *iKlwa*, but the weapon was designed for stabbing rather than throwing, and it was clumsy in flight. The *iKlwa* clattered against a smooth boulder and fell to the ground.

There was broken rock on either side of the path, loose scree with baboon paths, far too narrow and steep for horse riders to traverse, but lightly armed Zulus scrambled down to appear alongside the retreating British. They waited for an unwary man and lunged out, stabbed, and withdrew, or killed a horse, knowing the heavily encumbered British would be slow on the plain below.

Andrew stepped on, slid on a loose stone, and ducked as a throwing spear hissed past. He saw a man ahead stumble and fall, with a trooper saving him. The rear guard was firing volleys, the sound reassuring on that hellish pass, and then the firing ceased.

"What the devil?" Buller looked upward, and for the first time since Andrew had met him, his calm façade cracked. "These idiots have stopped firing!"

"Yes, sir," Andrew agreed, ducking as a Zulu stood on top of a rock and threw an assegai, which whirred down and clattered against the rock beside Buller. Andrew fired back and reloaded before negotiating the next section of the pass. He saw a horse fall over the edge, legs kicking, to bounce on rocks and fall again. He saw a Mounted Infantry private crawling down the track, leaving a trail of blood.

This retreat is Isandhlwana all over again!

Scores of Zulus lined the edge of the plateau, throwing assegais or heaving rocks at the retreating column. More men and horses fell; some troopers returned fire, ducked, or tried to hurry down the crowded path.

"Don't rush!" Buller roared. "Everybody, keep calm. Every

second man fire back, try to make the Zulus keep their heads down!"

The rifles and carbines cracked out, with bullets whizzing both ways. Andrew saw one of the Boers fall with old, heavily bearded Piet Uys dashing back to save him. Andrew lifted the wounded Mounted Infantryman and laid him across Lancelot's saddle, saw Piet Uys fall and gasped as a throwing spear sliced the outside of his thigh.

Three wounds, damnit. Andrew clasped a hand to his thigh in a vain attempt to ease the sting. Blood, warm and sticky, flowed over his hand.

"Baird?" Buller was at his side, concern in his eyes.

"I'm all right, sir," Andrew said. "It's only a nick." He felt the blood flowing down his leg, realised his arm was still aching and wondered if he would survive the day.

Things happen in threes, I believe. That's two wounds in this battle so far; maybe the third will be fatal.

Buller nodded and shouted encouragement to his men. "Keep moving, but don't panic. Help the wounded men!"

Andrew saw Buller lift an injured man onto a horse, stop to encourage the despairing, and fire at the Zulus above and on either side.

Does that man ever stop?

"Get down that hill, Baird!" Buller ordered. "You have a woman to rescue, remember!"

"Yes, sir," Andrew agreed. "I haven't forgotten." He was surprised that Buller could remember such a detail in the middle of a pressurised retreat. The Mounted Infantryman was moaning as he lay across Lancelot's saddle, writhing at the pain of a wound in his side. "Lie still, chum," Andrew said. "We'll get you home." He staggered as the pain in his thigh increased, took a deep breath, and continued.

They scrambled down that terrible pass, with Buller always at the rear, encouraging, helping the injured and shouting commands. Andrew guided Lancelot, limping as the wound in his leg throbbed. Every few moments, he heard the scream of a terrified horse or a wounded man. He shot at Zulus, reloaded, and moved on, unaware he was shouting Elaine's name, yet with an image of Mariana in his mind. When Zulus bounded at them from the baboon tracks at the side, Andrew crouched behind a boulder, fired, and reloaded. For a moment, he was unsure where he was, at Isandhlwana or Hlobane, until a heavy hand clamped on his shoulder.

"Don't stop, old boy. It's rather unhealthy here!" Buller grinned at him, as calm as if he were strolling around the parade ground at Aldershot.

"Yes, sir," Andrew said.

As they neared the foot of the pass, Andrew saw men streaming away across the plain, with many riding pillion and others wounded. A litter of dead and dying horses showed the appalling losses, and Andrew felt a twist of remorse that so many animals had died. Living on the Border between Scotland and England as much as the family home in Herefordshire, he had grown up with horses and developed a deep affinity with them.

"Come on, Lance." Andrew limped beside the horse, with his wounds stiffening and the wounded infantryman unconscious across the saddle. He knew it was a long walk back to Khambula, but he had survived the debacle on Hlobane, and tomorrow was a new day.

"Sir!" Fletcher shouted and rode toward him with the remainder of his men in a column of twos. "We thought we lost you in the melee!" He was hatless, with blood trickling down his face from a wound in his scalp. Sergeant Meek shared a horse with Kerr, and two men were injured.

"Not yet," Andrew said. "You did well, Fletcher," Andrew said, pleased his men had retained their discipline amidst such chaos.

"Get your men back to camp, Baird!" Buller ordered.

Andrew nodded, hesitating between obeying orders, and following his instinct to remain behind and help the stragglers.

Buller took him by the shoulders. "Go, Baird! We need good officers, and you're carrying a wound."

"Yes, sir!" Andrew felt his strength draining away as the strain of the retreat told.

"Lead on, Fletcher; I'll take the rear."

He felt pride as his men headed back and lifted his head when he heard the war cry.

"Usuthu! Usuthu!"

"Dear God in heaven!" Andrew saw the small impi explode from a tangle of rocks where they had been waiting. Rather than attack the stragglers, the Zulus charged at a formed body of eight Mounted Infantrymen, spreading out into the horns of the buffalo. Andrew recognised the distinctive white shields with the black fringe and the leopard skin headbands as the Zulus ran with their stabbing assegais held high.

The Abanonya again.

Andrew was out of effective revolver range but fired, hoping to alert the Mounted Infantry of the threat. He did not see the effect of his shot as the Zulus smashed into the British. Assegais stabbed and slashed, the British fired a few rounds, and then the skirmish was over, with five British and three Zulus lying on the ground and riderless horses galloping away. The Abanonya raised a cry of triumph, and the three remaining Mounted Infantry were fleeing for their lives.

With the wounded man draped over Lancelot, Andrew could not ride closer, and he was reluctant to order his men into danger while he remained behind. As he hesitated, the affair ended. He unholstered his rifle as Jama stepped toward him with blood dripping from his *iKlwa.* The two men stared at one another across the plain, and the Zulu lifted his assegai. Andrew did not know if it was a salute, a threat, or a gesture of acknowledgement.

"Shall we attack, sir?" Fletcher asked.

Andrew glanced at his men; tired, with some wounded and riding wearied horses, they were in no condition to fight.

"Not today, Lieutenant," Andrew decided. He saw Jama form up the Abanonya and trot away.

"Come on, lads," Andrew turned Lancelot's head and limped towards Khambula, with his men following behind him.

29TH OF MARCH 1879

"That's another Zulu victory," Andrew said as he stood outside the wagon laager at Khambula, listening to the cattle lowing in the nearby kraal. The dawn was not far off, with the early morning chill keeping him awake. "How many did we lose?"

"Over two hundred, including the native troops," Peterson said. "The Zulus wiped out the Frontier Light Horse and the Border Horse. Both units went the wrong way and ran right smack into the Zulu army. We lost fifteen officers and seventy-nine white men."

Andrew shook his head and stuffed tobacco into the bowl of his pipe. "It seems that the Zulus have got our measure." He took a deep breath and looked around the laager. Everything appeared so ordered here, with a field kitchen making bread, butchers slaughtering cattle, a quartermaster checking the stores and a sergeant drilling an awkward squad of replacements. Andrew listened for a moment as the sergeant screamed, red-faced.

"Left foot, I said, Sanderson! Left foot! That's the one on your left leg, you useless bugger! Good God, when the Queen parted with a shilling for your services, she should have asked for ninepence change! Try again, you ham-footed, useless, ginger-haired bastard!"

Andrew looked away. He had seen the same scenes at Isandhlwana before the Zulus came, and then nothing except carnage. It did not seem possible that the Zulus could destroy so much regulated order in so short a time.

"They'll come here next," Andrew said quietly. He rubbed the wound on his leg. An army surgeon had cleaned and bandaged his wounds, but they still ached abominably.

"You were at Sandlwana, weren't you?" Peterson asked.

"I was," Andrew agreed.

"And now, Hlobane."

"And Hlobane," Andrew confirmed.

"The Zulus won them both. Maybe you're a Jonah," Peterson said pleasantly. "You were here when we learned about the Intombi massacre as well."

Andrew nodded. He did not feel inclined to discuss defeats.

I'm further away than ever from finding Mariana. Maybe I am foolish even to think she is alive. Nobody has heard of her, and the Zulus don't take prisoners.

"You lost your sweetheart as well," Peterson continued.

Andrew lit his pipe, feeling his hands tremble with anger. "Don't you have some duty to perform, Peterson?"

Peterson stepped back. "I'm keeping away from you, Baird," he said, only half joking. "You're bad luck."

"Thanks," Andrew said dryly. "Keep your distance if you wish; it's all one to me." He watched as Peterson walked away and joined a group of subalterns. As Peterson spoke to them, the subalterns glanced backwards, and Andrew knew he was the subject of their conversation. He shrugged. It did not matter. Once this war was over, he planned to hand in his papers and leave the army.

"What are you doing, Baird?" Buller strode over to him, frowning.

"Checking the men, sir." Andrew lowered his pipe and saluted, feeling untidy under the gaze of the imperturbable Redvers Buller.

Buller pulled at his moustache. "That won't do, Lieutenant Baird. That won't do at all. I don't like to see officers idling their time away when there's work to be done."

"Yes, sir." Andrew felt the colour rush to his face.

"You realise the Zulus could attack here any time," Buller said. "Or they could head for Utrecht." He held Andrew's eyes in a ferocious glare. "Which would you prefer, Baird?"

Andrew knew Buller was testing him. "It would be better if the Zulus attacked here, sir."

Buller lit a cigarette. "I didn't ask which would be better. I asked which you would prefer."

Andrew lifted his chin. "Yes, sir. I'd prefer them to attack here."

Buller puffed out smoke and nodded. "Why?"

"We are better prepared to meet them, sir," Andrew said. "It's time we faced the Zulus on our terms rather than theirs."

Buller moved away, then abruptly turned. "Are you not nervous about fighting them again after your experiences on Hlobane and Isandhlwana?"

Andrew stiffened, reading Buller's words to be an implication of cowardice. "No, sir."

"Are you sure?" Buller's eyes were like granite, unyielding as they bored into Andrew's head.

"Quite sure, sir," Andrew said.

"Good." Buller's expression softened. "I'd hate to have recommended a Victoria Cross to a man who would be too nervous about accepting it. Find another horse; yours will be done up and join Raaf's Transvaal Rangers; he's going out to find the impi."

"Yes, sir." Andrew saluted and stepped towards the horse lines. A few seconds later, Buller's words sank in, and he turned around. "The Victoria Cross, sir? Why?"

"For saving a wounded man under fire." Buller had not moved. "Now get out there and stop thinking about that blasted woman."

"Yes, sir."

Lancelot looked over when Andrew entered the horse lines, and Andrew fed him a handful of mealies. He selected a lively pony, introduced himself, mounted with difficulty as his wounded leg troubled him, and rode out to join the Transvaal Rangers.

Pieter Raaf looked younger than Andrew expected. He nodded when Andrew joined his force, grunted what could be a welcome and trotted out of the laager to search for the Zulu impi.

"Try to keep up, *rooineck*," Raaf said, speaking English with a thick accent.

"I'll do my best," Andrew told him. He had seen Raaf performing heroics on Hlobane and knew he was an excellent fighting man.

"I saw you at Hlobane," Raaf said. "You know how the Zulus fight."

"Yes," Andrew replied shortly.

Raaf nodded. "So do we," he said and spurred forward.

As they rode away from Khambula, Andrew noticed a couple of companies of the 13th Foot moving out to collect firewood for the field bakeries. Zulus or no Zulus, the daily routine of the camp had to continue. He also saw Uys's burghers ride away, disheartened after the death of Piet Uys at Hlobane.

We'll miss the experience and skill of the Boers.

"Come on, *rooineck*," Raaf shouted.

Raaf's Transvaal Rangers spread out, with Raaf at the head and the men in an extended formation. They moved quickly, allowing their horses to find the best route as they covered the ground with a minimum of fuss. Andrew had long known that colonials rode differently from the British, with longer stirrups, leaning back in their saddles and looking more relaxed, as if they and the horses were a single unit. He had learned from them and copied their stance, with his borrowed pony seemingly happy to carry him.

Within a couple of hours, Raaf lifted his hand. Andrew saw a lone man running across the stark countryside, raising a thin trail of dust. Set against the vast background, the runner seemed timeless, as if he could represent the spirit of Africa, jogging effortlessly and holding a shield and handful of assegais. The runner saw Raaf's patrol and altered direction towards them, neither increasing nor decreasing his speed.

Raaf kicked in his spurs and met the man, spoke for a few moments, and returned to the patrol.

"This man is one of Uhamu's warriors," Raaf announced. "The main Zulu impi is going to attack the camp at Khambula in about four hours. We had better warn Brigadier Wood."

The Rangers headed back, with the Zulu trotting at their side with the graceful ease that Andrew always admired. They arrived at Khambula at eleven, passing the pickets with a casual wave, and Raaf reported to Wood as men gathered to listen.

"According to Uhamu's man," Wood informed the officers, "Ntshingwayo commands the impi that is heading this way." He pushed back his hat. "To remind you, Ntshingwayo masterminded the attack on Isandhlwana when he split Lord Chelmsford's army."

Some of the officers stirred uncomfortably.

"How many men does Ntshingwayo have, sir?" Buller asked.

"Judging by what Uhamu's man told us, Ntshingwayo has around twenty-four thousand men."

"That's a fair number," Buller said.

Wood scratched his head. "Most of them are the regiments that fought at Isandhlwana; some were at Intombi, and the abaQulusi from yesterday's fight at Hlobane." He paused. "The Zulus will be high on confidence and expect to defeat us again."

Peterson looked at Andrew as if he were to blame for every Zulu victory.

Wood continued. "Some have rifles they took from the 24th at Isandhlwana, and some rifles from our dead at Intombi, so we are not only facing spears. The enemy has weapons as good as our own."

"Dust, sir!" One of the mounted patrols galloped in. "Dust approaching from the east."

"Go and check, Baird," Buller ordered. "No, hang it all," he said with a grin, "I'll come as well."

They rode to a ridge of high ground and focussed their field glasses. "Over there, sir." Andrew pointed. "Five columns." He tried to keep the tension from his voice. "I'd say about five miles away."

"Slightly closer than five miles, I'd guess." Buller gave his opinion. "We'd better warn the Brigadier."

CHAPTER 24

Wood nodded when Buller gave his report. "Shall we say the Zulus are four miles distant, gentlemen? They should arrive in about thirty minutes, by my reckoning. Well, we've trained the men so they can man the defences within ninety seconds of us sounding the alarm, so there's no rush." He smiled. "I don't like to fight on an empty stomach, and I see no reason to starve the men. Order them to have their dinner, drive the cattle into the kraal and call in the wood-gathering party."

The bugles trilled out across the laager; men hurried to and fro, frantic parties herded the cattle into the kraal, and sergeants bellowed the firewood parties from the plain outside.

Buller nodded to Andrew. "Baird, you have the twenty men you commanded at Hlobane. Act as a mobile reserve and support wherever you are most needed."

"Yes, sir," Andrew replied.

"Strike the tents!" Wood ordered and practised hands folded away the long ranks of weather-stained white canvas within half a minute.

"Bring out reserve ammunition!" Ever since Isandhlwana, officers had debated if a lack of ammunition had helped create the disaster, so NCOs removed the brass restraining bands and unscrewed the lids on the ammunition boxes. Sweating soldiers carried the heavy boxes around the laager and distributed them behind the men at the barricades.

Less-than-eager privates hauled more ammunition boxes to the redoubt, where a company of the 90th Perthshire and another of the 13th Foot waited, reinforced by two seven-pounder guns. Another company of the 13th shared the kraal with the draught oxen while the remainder of the infantry were in the main laager.

"Let them come," Sergeant Meek murmured. "They'll not face infantry in company strength this time, by God."

Andrew agreed. He knew that despite the mobility of the mounted men and the artillery's firepower, the infantry was the backbone of the army. Underpaid, often unglamorous, hard-drinking, hard-swearing and hard-used, the sweating men in scarlet tunics had the final say wherever the Union flag flew. Queen Victoria and all her government ministers may make the decisions and formulate policy, but it was the often-undersized men from the slums and the sodden country lanes who enforced British rule. Andrew looked at them now, the young, acid-eyed, jesting men who knew they might be dead within an hour and wondered from where they had come and what their futures might be.

The 90th Foot took up their stations at the north and west sides of the redoubt, with the 13th on the south and east. Andrew saw the lines of scarlet tunics and stained sun helmets, with the sun gleaming from rifle barrels. A sergeant stopped his shouting for a moment to encourage a nervous young soldier with a wink and then checked his platoon's rifles one by one.

"Make sure you fill your canteens from the regimental water butts," a long-faced corporal said. "Fighting is thirsty work. If you think I'm lying, just ask the missus; she always runs to the pub after she fights with me." He waited for the nervous laughter. "Not me, though; I get the drinks in before the fight to get me courage up to face her, see?"

Andrew could nearly taste the tension in the air. These men knew all about Isandhlwana; they had heard of the disaster at the Intombi and had seen the wounded survivors return from Hlobane. Now it was their turn, and twenty-four thousand highly trained warriors were about to attack them, ready to plunge their assegais into cringing bodies.

Augmenting the infantry, the Royal Artillery manned another four seven-pounders, standing between the laager and the redoubt. The guns were *en barbette*, sited on raised ground and therefore able to fire over the parapet at the Zulus. With a hundred and ninety yards between the guns and the laager, Andrew did not envy the gunners their position. Wood shared Andrew's thoughts as, with no infantry support or cover, he ordered the artillerymen to leave the guns and take refuge in the laager if the Zulus approached within throwing-spear distance.

"Throwing spear distance?" one of the 90th scoffed. "If these bastards came within two hundred yards of me and I hadn't got a bundook, [1] I'd be off like a bloody shot, so I would."

Andrew shared the private's concerns. He had seen Zulu warriors keeping pace with a cantering horse and knew the artillerymen were not trained in fast running.

The horse lines were in the centre of the laager with the irregular horsemen, mostly colonials who had long feared the Zulus and were eager to finally see the professional infantry destroying the impis with steady volleys.

"How many men do we have, sir?" Peterson asked Buller.

Buller did not hesitate. "Twelve hundred and thirty-eight infantrymen, a hundred and twenty-one artillerymen and nearly six hundred and forty mounted men, with ninety sick in the hospital tents."

"Just under two thousand men," Peterson said. "And the Zulus have twenty-four thousand veteran and blooded warriors."

He glanced at Andrew. "Let's hope nothing goes wrong this time, sir. Let's hope we don't have a Jonah in the laager."

Wood frowned. "That's a strange thing to say, Peterson."

"Yes, sir. I wondered if there was a connection between our reverses at Isandhlwana and Hlobane, sir. Maybe one officer who was present on both occasions."

"The British Army does not believe in superstition, Lieutenant Peterson," Wood said coldly. "I'd thank you to attend to your duty."

Peterson coloured, saluted, and marched away, glowering at Andrew as he passed.

Andrew tried to control his nerves, fighting the worry that Peterson might be correct. He had returned the borrowed pony and reclaimed Lancelot, for he preferred to fight on a horse he knew.

Andrew checked his men had ammunition and water, torn between a terrible desire to grab Lancelot and flee or a thirst for vengeance. Strangely, he had no dislike of the Zulus for the dead at Isandhlwana or Hlobane, for that had been straightforward warfare. He even accepted the Zulus' custom of slicing open the bodies, but the murder and possible rape of Elaine and kidnapping of Mariana infuriated him. He disagreed with making war on women, especially when they were friends and more than friends.

Andrew sat upright on Lancelot, lifted his field glasses to his eyes and scanned the terrain outside the British position. The Zulus were close now, easily seen by the naked eye, and Andrew saw the two columns on the right altering direction to the north, just out of range of the seven-pounders as they circled the British position.

"Ntshingwayo knows his stuff," Buller murmured. "Not many savages could calculate the range of artillery like that. Give that fellow a frock coat and a top hat, and he'd pass top of his class in Sandhurst."

"He could probably lecture at Sandhurst, sir," Andrew said

without irony. "Most of the lecturers are passed over officers and duffers."

"What makes you say that, Baird?" Buller asked. He gave Andrew a curious look. "Have you been to Sandhurst?"

Andrew swore silently, knowing his loose mouth had again betrayed more about himself than he liked.

"They're getting closer," Andrew tried to divert attention away from himself. Two Zulu columns had halted on the north-west, while the remaining three had positioned themselves south of Khambula Hill.

"They are no closer now than they were five minutes ago," Buller contradicted. "I don't think we should allow them to settle. Even Zulus must be weary after their marching." He smiled. "I think it's time to disrupt them before they're properly rested."

"Yes, sir," Andrew said, glad that Buller did not pursue his enquiries.

"Are you ready for some fresh air and exercise?" Buller asked, suddenly grinning.

"Yes, sir," Andrew said. He always felt it was better to act than to sit waiting for something to happen.

"Let's see if Brigadier Wood agrees with you," Buller said, wheeled his horse and approached the Brigadier.

Andrew surveyed the defences, with the waggon wheels chained together and the booms tied across the brief intervals between each vehicle.

"Come on, Baird!" Buller shouted as he called up the mounted men. "Let's goad these Zulus into attacking us! Bring your men!"

The mounted men followed Buller towards the Zulu force in the north. Andrew remained close to Buller with his men at his back. He noticed the colonial horsemen carried carbines, shorter and more manageable than the longer rifle he had.

"Here we go again." Sergeant Meek sounded tired. "Let's hope for a better outcome than we had yesterday!"

Yesterday? Was it only yesterday they had scrambled down the Devil's Pass from Hlobane?

They trotted out, with the horses' hooves drumming on the ground and the infantry watching from under tilted helmets.

"Good luck, lads!" a hard Perthshire accent called after them.

Buller led the mounted force around the laager and, within half a mile of the Zulus, lifted his hand and ordered them to dismount.

"Every fourth man, you are the horse holders!" Buller shouted.

Andrew patted Lancelot and stepped forward. After the previous day's debacle, he felt vulnerable as he saw the closest Zulu impi, maybe five thousand strong, with the regiments holding their long shields and the sun glittering from the points of thousands of spears. Yet he knew this day was very different, with hundreds of British regular infantry waiting in support only a short ride away.

All the same, Andrew knew that whatever else happened in his life, however long he lived, he would never forget the sight of a Zulu impi in full battle array.

Buller led by example, striding forward, and firing at extreme range. "We won't weaken them much," he said, ejecting the spent cartridge, "but we might irritate them into charging to clear us away, and the 90th can decimate them with volley fire."

Andrew agreed. He aimed toward the Zulu mass that spread across the landscape, tried to focus on an individual warrior and squeezed the trigger. The Martini-Henry kicked back into his shoulder, and he grunted. The mounted men had fired the first shots in the battle of Khambula.

This could be the decisive battle when the main Zulu impi meets a dug-in British force. We always fight best on the defensive, as at Waterloo or like Campbell's Highlanders at Balaclava.

"Keep firing," Buller ordered. "Move closer. Horse handlers, don't get too far behind." The dismounted men stepped closer, firing carefully. Those Zulus who had rifles tried to retaliate, with their shots whistling high.

Andrew saw the Zulu lines quiver as the shooting caused casualties, for the colonial troopers were nearly all excellent marksmen. The line inched forward, with some warriors shaking their spears in impotent rage.

"The UmBonambi don't like that," Kerr said casually. "I wonder which regiment will charge first."

"Which regiments are there?" Andrew looked for the Abanonya's familiar white shields with the black fringe.

Kerr fired, ejected his cartridge, and reloaded. "The UmBonambi, UNokhenke and uMcijo," he said, indicating each *amabutho* as he spoke. "I believe they were all at Isandhlwana, sir."

Andrew aimed and fired, worked the under-lever, aimed, and fired again. The Zulu line edged forward, drumming their spears on their shields.

"Back on horseback, gentlemen," Buller ordered, and the men thankfully remounted. Andrew felt safer knowing he might outrun the Zulus if they charged. "Now close with the enemy!"

The mounted men trotted closer until Andrew could make out the features of the individual warriors and see the pattern of the cow-hide shields. Buller spurred another ten yards, taunting the Zulus, so some warriors left their line and hurled their throwing spears. One spear thudded into the ground a few feet from Andrew, with the shaft nearly erect and the head deeply embedded.

"Fire!" Buller shouted and waited until his men obeyed before wheeling his horse and trotting away. That volley was one too many for the uNokhenke *amabutho*, which broke ranks and ran forward in pursuit. Andrew saw the sun glitter on hundreds of assegais and an array of cow-hide shields and bobbing plumes.

"*Uzitulele, kagali muntu*!" they sang. "He is quiet; he doesn't start the attack."

"Here they come!" Buller remained closest to the Zulus,

holding his Martini one-handed. "Give them another volley, boys!"

The horsemen responded, then galloped back towards the laager with the uNokhenke in noisy pursuit. After four hundred yards, Buller halted again, ordered another volley, and repeated the manoeuvre.

"They're all coming now," Kerr said as he thumbed a cartridge into his carbine. He aimed and fired in a single movement and reloaded with a fluidity that told of long practice.

Other *amabuthos* had followed the uNokhenke, with the UmBonambi and uMcijo also charging toward the thin, galling line of horsemen.

"That's enough, lads," Buller shouted. "We've given them pepper; now let the infantry put salt on their tails! Head back to the laager!"

The mounted men turned and spurred for the sanctuary of the laager, except for the Natal Native Horse, who chose a different route.

"Where are the Native Horse going?" a deep voice asked.

"They're buggering off!"

Rather than ride into the wagon laager, the Native Horse galloped right past.

"They've had enough!" Fletcher shouted in disbelief. "Come back, you cowards!"

Andrew watched them flee with mixed feelings. He knew the defenders would miss the Native Horse's rifles but also knew they had fought at Isandhlwana. They had seen the business end of a Zulu impi and had no desire to repeat the experience.

I understand.

"Godspeed, lads," Andrew said.

A sergeant of the 90th roared orders to shift aside one of the wagons, and the riders galloped in. When the last of Buller's horsemen were safe, the sergeant supervised the privates to roll the defences back in place.

"Get these thornbushes back under the body, lads, and watch

there's no gaps. I don't want an angry Zulu sticking a dirty great spear up my jacksie!"

"Yes, Sergeant!"

Andrew studied the terrain. To the north of the British defences, a gentle slope ran downward, forcing any attacker to run uphill to the waiting rifles of professional soldiers. On the south, the terrain favoured the Zulus as the British had a killing zone of only between a hundred and two hundred yards. Beyond that, a cliff descended into the ravine of the White Umfolozi River.

"If I were Ntshingwayo," Kerr said. "I'd mass my men in the Umfolozi Valley. They've only a couple of hundred yards to cover, and at the speed the Zulus move, our lads will only get in a couple of volleys before they're at the barricades."

Andrew nodded in agreement as his men gathered around him, breathing heavily from their exertions. Andrew's grasp of the Martini-Henry was greasy with sweat as he thought of the ferocity of the Zulu attacks. He heard the Zulus chant and saw the regiments advance, the line of long spears and glittering, deadly assegais and knew the decisive battle was about to begin.

"This is the first time a full Zulu impi has faced a British army in its chosen position, sir," Fletcher said. "If we lose here, we may as well pack up and go home."

"If we lose here," Andrew said, "you and I will be dead. I'm not retreating again."

How about Mariana? Will I condemn her to a lifetime of slavery in Zulu hands? I can't afford for us to lose. We must win here.

"Here they come!" Fletcher shouted. "God help us all."

CHAPTER 25

The 90th Foot was already firing volleys, the heavy crashes joined by the deep barks of the four seven-pounders. Jack saw the front rank of the Zulus ripple as hundreds of .45 bullets smashed into them, with shell bursts rising in columns of grey-white smoke. Unsure what the artillery fire was, some warriors paused in their charge and stabbed at the smoke, believing guns were firing soldiers at them.

"They're taking casualties and still coming on well," Fletcher said, focusing his field glasses.

"There's no doubting their bravery," Andrew said. He watched Lieutenant Arthur Bigge manage the seven-pounders, changing from common shell to case shot as the Zulus came closer. Each blast of case sliced a bloody swathe through the advancing warriors, slowing them without halting the charge. The artillerymen loaded, aimed, and fired, with Bigge giving crisp orders.

"The gunners are from garrison companies." Fletcher revealed a surprising depth of knowledge. "Not the top drawer, yet they're working like heroes."

"They are," Andrew agreed.

The gunners stood in the open, exposed to Zulu musketry,

but fortunately, the warriors had not mastered modern rifles, and most shots whizzed overhead.

Despite their losses, the Zulus kept coming, shouting their war cry, "*Usuthu! Usuthu*!" that Andrew knew would haunt his dreams for years, provided he survived the day.

"Come on, lads, join the 90th!" Andrew ordered, hating being an impotent witness. "Fire when they reach three hundred yards."

"Yes, sir!" Fletcher replied as the men readied their carbines.

By now, the infantry in the redoubt had joined in, pouring in an enfilading fire that smashed into the Zulu flank. An induna charged in advance of his *amabutho,* holding his shield high and escaping the torrent of bullets.

Andrew sighed, lifted his Martini, and aimed at the *induna*, aware of the importance of good leadership. Sad to shoot a brave man, he fired and saw the *induna* spin as the heavy bullet smashed into his leg.

"That's you out, my man," Andrew said, feeling satisfaction he had hit his mark. "Fire, men!" He aimed into the mass, shooting, reloading, and shooting again, with little feeling except a desire to survive. The crash of infantry volley fire and the bark of orders, the yelling of the Zulus and the swearing and joking of the 90th all combined in such a cacophony that no single sound predominated.

Kerr was loading and firing slowly, aiming each shot, while Fletcher was racing.

"Slow down, Fletcher," Andrew advised. "Aim first and lower your sights; you're firing high."

"Yes, sir." Fletcher looked round, wild-eyed. "They're getting close."

"Look at the 90th," Andrew said. "Do you think they'll let the Zulus through?"

The 90th Foot was firing in disciplined volleys, waiting for the word of command, and exchanging dark humour.

"No, sir," Fletcher said, gasping for breath.

"Nor do I. Take a deep breath, mark your man, aim low, and you'll be fine."

Andrew moved on, giving encouragement and advice.

By the time the Zulus reached two hundred yards of the 90th, the heat had gone from the charge. Andrew saw two warriors helping the tall *induna,* and then the infantry fired another volley, and all three fell. A few warriors advanced to the British barricade, and some even leapt into the laager, but the 90th chased them out with the bayonet.

"Get back to Cetshwayo, you bastards!" the 90th jeered as the final Zulus retreated. "Or come back and try again!"

The NCOs shut the men up. "Enough! Save your energy! They'll be back!"

Andrew found he was gasping for breath, with his fresh wounds aching. He leaned against the timber wood of a wagon and counted his cartridges before checking on his men.

"Take the artillery horses back inside the laager," Wood ordered. "We're losing too many of them!"

Andrew realised the Zulus' plunging shot was landing among the horses, with half a dozen already dead or wounded. He ordered half a dozen of his men to help round them up. In South Africa, animal transport was vital. Without horses, mules and oxen, the British Army would be immobile.

As the attack on the 90th's position ended, Ntshingwayo ordered his men to charge the British right, advancing on the front and rear simultaneously.

"I told you they'd use that damned ditch, sir!" Kerr said.

The Zulus had crept along the ravine, safe from British musketry, emerged and threw themselves at the British positions. The defenders had expected this manoeuvre and retaliated with a blast of fire from both the south side of the laager and the men in the cattle kraal. The initial crossfire disposed of the initial assault, but the Zulus poured increasing numbers of men into the attack, forcing their way into the space between the cattle kraal and the main laager.

"Ntshingwayo knows his stuff," Buller said quietly. "He's buying space with his men's lives." He looked sideways at Andrew. "Even although he wasn't at Sandhurst." He nodded to the Zulus. "You'd better give the 13th a hand, Baird."

"Yes, sir."

Andrew led his men to the northeast side of the laager and fired into the mass of warriors attacking the cattle kraal. The company of the 13th fought the Zulus hand to hand, bayonets and rifle butts against assegais and shields, while British curses mingled with the more resounding chants of the warriors. They fought among the lowing cattle, with men leaning across the shaggy backs of oxen to strike at their enemies, but as more Zulu reinforcements poured in, the outnumbered 13th Foot withdrew. They backed away, step by step, to the redoubt that some called Fort Khambula.

"The Zulus won that round," Andrew said as Zulu riflemen lined up inside the cattle kraal to snipe at the British manning the defences.

A dozen *indunas* rose from the ravine and stood on the ridge, encouraging the inGobamakhosi *amabutho* to leave the shelter and charge the laager. Andrew noticed one *induna* carrying a red flag and wondered if that was Ntshingwayo. He aimed his Martini and fired to see the *induna* walking behind his men unharmed.

"Is that Ntshingwayo?" Andrew asked.

"I don't know, sir," Kerr replied. "I've never knowingly met him."

Wood countered Ntshingwayo by ordering Major Hacket to take two companies of the 90th Foot to support the 13th.

Andrew watched the move and counter move, seeing the warriors and infantrymen as pawns on the Khambula chess-board, with death and horrendous injuries the price for a failed manoeuvre.

It must be easier to command an army if one thinks of the soldiers as chess pieces rather than living men.

As the Zulus left the ravine, the warriors on the north side attacked again, this time in a screaming charge towards the exposed artillerymen and the east front of the laager.

"They're attacking both sides at once!" Fletcher shouted. "This Zulu general is no fool!"

"He's a master of manoeuvre," Andrew agreed, firing and reloading. He tasted the acrid gun smoke, blinked at the sting, and fired again. He grunted as the stitches in his arm parted, and the wound reopened.

Major Hacket marched his men out of the laager at the double and, rather than launch them immediately at the enemy surging from the ravine, ordered them to form a double line.

"Fix bayonets!" Hacket shouted.

Andrew heard the distinct click as the men fitted the long bayonets into place, and then Hacket led them forward. Lieutenant Strong, smiling, drew his sword and stepped to the front of his company. They advanced gradually, then broke into a charge that matched the Zulus in intensity and courage. Not many European regiments would stand against a British bayonet charge, but the Zulus held for a while until the Perthshire men won the battle and forced them back over the rim into the ravine.

"Fire on them!" Hacket ordered, and his two companies of the Ninetieth stood on the rim and fired volleys at the inGobamakhosi. Their bullets caused considerable casualties, but standing in the open, the British were also vulnerable. Ntshingwayo ordered his riflemen to crawl through the long grass of the British refuse tip and fire into the 90th's ranks.

Andrew heard the 90th's bugle sound the retire as Hacket and a few other men fell before the Zulu fire. Andrew wiped the sweat from his forehead, swore as his Martini jammed and worked furiously with the ramrod to clear the swollen cartridge. He saw Brigadier Wood fire and hit the induna with the red flag.

"Good shot, sir!" Captain Maude of the 90th shouted. "Was that Ntshingwayo?"

"No," Wood replied. "It was another brave Zulu *induna*." He grunted as he saw one of Hacket's men crumple, clutching his thigh. "Look at that poor fellow!" He darted towards the edge of the laager, shouting to the man to hold on.

Captain Maude of the 90th lunged forward and took the brigadier's arm. "Really, sir," he said. "It's not your place to pick up single men," and ran forward with Lieutenants Lyons and Smith of the 90th. They rescued the wounded man, but Smith returned with a Zulu bullet in the arm.

When Hacket's men withdrew, the Zulus in the ravine emerged again to find the 13th Foot waiting behind the wagons, with rifles loaded and ready. However courageous the Zulus were, they could not avail against the disciplined firepower of British regulars.

"Here they come, boys," the officers roared. "Aim low, never mind the shine and volley fire on my word!"

The infantry waited, cursing, joking, some with pipes in their mouths, and many hiding their fear. They sighted along the thirty-three-inch-long barrels of their Martinis, nursed bruised shoulders from the brutal recoil and blew on the fingertips of their left hands, blistered from the barrel's heat.

With memories of Isandhlwana fresh, the British officers were nervous about running out of ammunition and kept the men under a tight leash. They forbade independent firing, so the men only fired volleys. As the 13th Foot repulsed the latest Zulu charge, Brigadier Wood moved from the main laager into the open ground between the laager and the strongpoint of Fort Khambula. He watched the course of the battle from every angle, taking notes, issuing orders to his staff, and occasionally firing at the enemy.

On the left front of the laager, the Zulus continued to attack, wave after wave of determined men charging into massed musketry that killed them by the score and the hundred.

"Don't these lads ever learn?" Andrew asked as he led his men to the areas that seemed most hard-pressed.

"They're too stubborn," Buller said. "Keep firing, Baird. The more of the enemy we kill today, the less there is to kill us tomorrow."

"Yes, sir," Andrew said, watching his men take positions behind the wagons and fire into the enemy. They had learned not to waste ammunition and aimed before they fired, taking a terrible toll on the advancing Zulu warriors.

"Keep it up, lads!" Andrew encouraged. "Sergeant Meek, find us some ammunition. Ensure every man has at least seventy rounds."

"Yes, sir," Meek replied.

Gunsmoke lay heavy over the laager, reducing visibility so the Zulus were indistinct even under the glaring sun.

Brigadier Wood slipped back into the main laager and sent for Buller.

"You wanted me, sir?" Buller asked.

Wood smiled. "Yes, Colonel, because I think you are just going to have a rough and tumble."

"Do you want us to sally out, sir?" Buller asked hopefully.

"Soon," Wood replied. "Ensure your men are ready when I give the word."

"Yes, sir," Buller replied.

Wood raised his voice, ordering two companies of the 13th to remove the Zulus from the cattle kraal and another company to push the Zulus back from the right front of the laager. He watched as the infantry filed from cover with the sun glinting from their bayonets and their ammunition boots crunching on the hard ground.

Andrew spoke to his men as the 13th pushed back the Zulus.

"Only fire if you have a clear target," Andrew warned. "I don't want us to shoot any of the infantry; that's the men in scarlet tunics. They're on our side."

Andrew's men laughed. They seemed relaxed as Wood organised the defence, and the British quelled each successive Zulu attack. Andrew glanced at his watch and started when he saw how late it was. The battle had lasted over four hours, yet it seemed only minutes since the mounted men had fired the opening shots.

After charging into relentless musketry time after time, the Zulu attacks at last faltered. Andrew did not know whether they could not take any more or whether Ntshingwayo realised he could not win and ordered them to stop. Either way, the impis began to withdraw.

"Baird!" Buller shouted. "The Zulus are falling back, Baird. Stop fooling around and join us!"

Andrew lifted a hand in acknowledgement and raised his voice. "You heard the colonel, lads! Mount up!"

He ran to Lancelot in the horse lines, waited for his men to saddle and mount, and followed Buller as he led the mounted men in pursuit of the now retreating impi.

TROTTING OUT OF THE LAAGER TO CHASE DEFEATED ZULUS WAS a different proposition from running with a thousand warriors on his heels. Andrew looked around, seeing the eagerness of his companions. They had lived in awe of Zulu power for the last few months, and after the massacre of Isandhlwana, they wanted revenge. The Natal colonists had lived on the lion's lip all their lives, while the Frontier Light Horse were hungry to destroy the abaQulusi for the killing of so many of their colleagues the previous day.

Was that only yesterday? It seemed like a different world.

Andrew felt as if he had spent his entire life fighting Zulus. If he closed his eyes, he could see screaming Zulu faces and raised assegais, and the sound of Zulu war cries rattled through his mind.

The Zulus had altered quickly from attack to rapid retreat, with few attempting to delay the pursuing horsemen. Buller's men pursued them, killing without mercy, shooting them from the saddle or picking up assegais from dead warriors and using them like lances. Andrew had little stomach for slaughter but joined the pursuit, if only because his duty was to kill.

I'm no soldier. I should be killing our enemy rather than making loud noises and galloping Lancelot across the plain. The Zulus would not hesitate to kill me if the position was reversed.

Andrew heard the whoops of delight as the horsemen hunted their quarry.

"That's another for the game bag!"

"Got you, you devil!"

"Shot him right through the head, by God! Good work, Carruthers!"

Andrew saw one slender Zulu trying to hide beneath a thorn bush and readied his rifle to fire. The man saw him, lifted his Abanonya shield and adopted a pose of defence, although he stood little chance against a mounted man with a rifle and revolver.

Andrew aimed, then hesitated when he realised how young the warrior was.

Good God, he's only a boy! He can't be more than twelve years old! The words of his father returned to Andrew.

"*We are soldiers, and soldiers fight soldiers or warriors. We should always be merciful to women and children, whatever their station in life.*"

"Put your assegai down," Andrew said in Xhosa. "I will take you prisoner."

The Zulu raised his shield higher. "You will torture me."

"No." Knowing he was taking a chance; Andrew lowered his rifle. "I won't torture you, and neither will anybody else. I will ask you some questions, and that's all."

"What questions?" The Zulu had a deep voice for a boy and a handsome, intelligent face that viewed Andrew with suspicion.

"Come back to the camp with me," Andrew said. "We can talk there. It's not safe here with all the soldiers."

The Zulu glanced around, where the horsemen were laughing, killing, and riding hard, chasing the fleeing Zulus as far as Hlobane. "I am your prisoner," he said, raising his shield above his head. "My name is Jabulani."

"Keep your spears, Jabulani," Andrew said.

They sat outside Andrew's tent with a small fire between them and the stars glittering in the black abyss above. Andrew passed a hunk of beef to Jabulani and bit into another.

"You are a brave people," Andrew said.

"We are the Zulus," Jabulani said as if that were a sufficient explanation.

"You attacked with great courage."

Jabulani smiled. "When we saw the soldiers take your tents down, we thought you were about to flee. We were dismayed when you began firing at us."

"I am looking for a white woman," Andrew said. "Some Zulus crossed the border into Natal, killed all the people on a farm and kidnapped the woman. Have you heard of such a thing happening?"

Jabulani chewed his beef for a few moments before he replied. "No," he said.

"Are you sure?" Andrew asked. "Think carefully, Jabulani."

"Cetshwayo ordered that no Zulu was to cross the border into Natal," Jabulani said. "Disobeying the king's command would mean death, and maybe death for the whole family."

Andrew frowned. "I saw the house," he said, frustrated. "I buried the people myself, and the younger girl was missing."

"The Zulus did not kill them or steal the woman," Jabulani repeated.

"There are renegade clans in the north who raid into the Transvaal," Andrew said. "Perhaps one of them moved south."

"If they crossed this land, the abaQulusi would have seen them," Jabulani told him. "They are loyal to Cetshwayo."

"What would the abaQulusi have done?" Andrew asked.

"Killed them," Jabulani replied with disarming simplicity.

"Ah." Andrew did not doubt Jabulani's sincerity. "You are of the Abanonya, I think?"

"I am." Jabulani lifted his head in pride.

"Thank you, Jabulani. If Cetshwayo had ordered a woman kidnapped, where would he keep her?"

Jabulani screwed up his face. "The ways of kings are not like the ways of other men," he said solemnly. "I cannot say what is in Cetshwayo's mind."

Andrew nodded. "I understand that," he said. "I have little understanding of what happens in our royal palaces as well. However, you are a Zulu and know the ways of your people better than I do. Tell me what you think."

Jabulani smiled. "If I had a woman prisoner, I would keep her close, or another man would steal her away."

"Do you mean she could be in oNdini?" Andrew asked.

"If she exists, and if the king ordered her captured," Jabulani said. "She will be in oNdini."

Andrew dug his heel into the ground and sighed. "That's what I thought, Jabulani. Then I'll go to oNdini."

Jabulani smiled. "Cetshwayo will welcome you," he said cryptically.

Andrew heard rapid hoofbeats and stood up hurriedly when he saw Buller approaching.

"Well, young Baird, I see you have a new friend." Buller dismounted and stepped beside Andrew.

"This is Jabulani, sir," Andrew said.

"Of Ntshingwayo's Zulus?" Buller asked.

"No, sir, he's of the Abanonya," Andrew said.

When Buller opened his mouth wide and reached for his pistol, Jabulani grabbed at the assegais at his feet.

"No, sir." Greatly daring, Andrew placed a hand on Buller's arm. "He's my prisoner, sir, and he won't attack us."

"Good God, Baird! The Abanonya are one of our most dangerous enemies!"

"I know, sir, but Jabulani and I jog along pretty well." Andrew put his free hand on Jabulani's shoulder.

Buller frowned, releasing his grip on the pistol butt. "I only knew one man with an attitude like that, Baird."

Andrew smiled. "I thought I was unique, sir."

"No. I have said I knew you, but I don't." Buller stepped back, still watching Jabulani. "You reminded me of somebody."

"Who is that, sir?" Andrew already guessed the answer.

"A man old enough to be your father, Baird. Fighting Jack Windrush."

Andrew could not help the blood rushing to his face. "Indeed, sir?"

"Indeed, sir," Buller said. "I know Fighting Jack well; we served together through the Ashanti campaign. I met his wife there as well, a handsome, charming lady."

"I am sure she is, sir," Andrew wished Buller would change the subject.

"Mrs Windrush had an Indian mother and a Scottish father." Buller was dragging the information from his mind. "Her father shared your name. He was Baird." The colonel stared at Andrew. "She spoke of her son, Andrew David Windrush."

Andrew looked away.

"By God, man, you're Jack Windrush's pup!"

CHAPTER 26

Andrew lifted his chin. "Yes, sir. Major Jack Windrush is my father."

"Well, my boy, why the devil didn't you say so?" Buller held out his hand. "Why hide who you are?"

"I want to make my own way in the world, sir," Andrew explained. "I don't want to live in my father's shadow."

"Good God, man, with a background like yours, you could have your pick of any regiment in the army and not be footling around in some ragamuffin colonial unit!" Buller pumped Andrew's arm as he was dragging water from far underground. "My God, Fighting Jack's pup out here in Zululand."

"That's just it, sir." Andrew rescued his hand and felt to see if any bones were broken, for Buller had a grip like an Irish navvy. "I want to rise on my own merits, not because of my father's achievements."

Buller eyed him. "I see. Well, we'll talk about this later, young Windrush."

"Baird, sir."

"Baird," Buller corrected himself. "In the meantime, what will you do with this Abanonya fellow? You can't leave him running loose around the camp. He might forget himself and start slaughtering people, and we can't have that, can we?"

Andrew smiled. "No, sir. I suppose not."

"Old Jack, I mean your respected pater, has a close friend among the Pathans, I recall. Is that your intention with this Zulu chap?" Buller nodded at Jabulani.

"I hadn't thought that far ahead, sir," Andrew admitted.

"Have you pumped him for information?" Buller asked.

"I've asked him about Miss Baxter, sir," Andrew replied.

"Ah, yes, the missing girl." Buller looked uncomfortable for a moment. "I'd forget about her if I were you, Baird. As your father would tell you, these savages aren't kind to their women. The Zulus probably killed her weeks ago, and she's better dead than a Zulu prisoner."

Andrew thought it best not to argue. "Yes, sir, but I'll keep searching until I know for sure."

"As you wish, Baird." Buller stepped back to his horse. "Well, if you've finished with this Zulu chap, either kill him or set him free, eh?" He faced Jabulani and spoke in a mixture of Xhosa and Zulu. "Before the fight at Isandhlwana, we had Zulu patients in our hospital, and when the Zulus invaded the camp, the patients rose and helped kill those who had been attending them."

Jabulani nodded without comment.

"Is there any reason we should not kill you?"

"Yes," Jabulani replied. "There is a very good reason you should not kill me. We kill you because it is the custom of the black men, but it isn't the white men's custom."

Buller grinned. "You are a plausible young rogue; I'll give you that." He faced Andrew. "What do you want to do with him, Baird? He's your prisoner."

"I'll set him free, sir."

"Very magnanimous of you. Kick his backside back to Hlobane, eh, so he can tell his little friends how powerful the white man is." Buller mounted and lifted a hand. "Fighting Jack's pup, eh? I should have guessed it." He frowned and pointed to Andrew's sleeve, stiff with dried blood. "Is that another wound?"

"No, sir," Andrew said. "The one I got yesterday opened up again."

"Get rid of young Shaka here and let the surgeon see it," Buller ordered.

"Yes, sir," Andrew said and watched as Buller rode away, shaking his head. "Come on then, Jabulani, let's get you back home."

THE CAMP EXPERIENCED ONE ALARM AT THREE IN THE morning of the 30th when an outpost fired a few shots at a lone Zulu, and the colonials within the laager immediately opened fire.

"Cease fire!" Wood jumped from his wagon as the colonials' bullets ripped through the canopy above his head. "What the hell do you think you're doing?"

A company of the 13th Foot echoed the Brigadier's sentiments with stronger language as the colonial's bullets zipped and whined past them.

"We're on the same side, you stupid bastards!"

As the colonials stopped firing, the alarm passed, and normality returned to the camp. When burial patrols found over seven hundred Zulu bodies within a few hundred yards of the laager, Wood ordered the men to shift location.

"There will be other bodies we can't see," Wood explained. "That will spread disease."

"What were our losses at Khambula?" Andrew asked.

"Twenty-nine killed and about seventy wounded," Buller replied, puffing at his cigarette. "We lost some good men, including Hacket, who had led the 90th advance."

"Did the Zulus kill him, sir?" Andrew asked.

"No, Baird. He is blinded," Buller told him. "He's an

Irishmen and was a dedicated regimental officer, rather like your father."

Andrew did not reply.

"Hacket bought his promotion in the days when such things were normal." Buller watched Andrew closely for a reaction. "He was a good man."

Buller's use of the past tense was chillingly final. One day Hacket was a good officer, and the next, he was finished. Andrew nodded; only a fool thought that war was glorious. "Yes, sir."

"I hope his family look after him," Buller said. "At least they know who he is."

"I understand, sir," Andrew said.

Buller nodded. "Good. Did you hear about the white prisoner at Ulundi?"

Andrew lifted his head as his heart rate increased. "What white prisoner?"

Buller smiled. "I thought that might interest you. The Frenchman, Baird."

Andrew's hopes died. "Tell me more, sir."

"The Zulus captured a French fellow from the Border Horse at Hlobane, Baird. They took him to Ulundi and sent him somewhere else, but he killed his guard and escaped."

"Thank you, sir," Andrew said. "Is he in the camp now?"

"Try the hospital tent, Baird." Buller looked sympathetic. "Don't raise your hopes too high."

"I won't, sir. Thank you."

Ernest Grandier, late trooper of the Border Horse, was lying on a cot in the hospital tent, staring at the canvas ceiling, when Andrew stepped across to him.

"I didn't know there were Frenchmen fighting with us," Andrew said and introduced himself. "I am Lieutenant Andrew Baird. I believe the Zulus held you in Ulundi?"

"There are a few Frenchmen in Zululand," Grandier looked surprisingly healthy as he replied. "Some of us fought the Prussians and through the Commune."

Andrew showed polite interest. "What happened to you?"

"The Zulus captured me during the retreat from Hlobane," Grandier said. "They stripped me naked, lashed me to a pole and carried me to Ulundi."

Andrew listened, curbing his impatience.

"In Ulundi, women spat at me, and Cetshwayo interrogated me and sent me to Mbilini so that he could torture me to death. I killed one of the guards with an assegai and escaped during the first march."

"And you made your way here," Andrew said.

"Yes, sir," Grandier agreed.

"That was some adventure." Andrew doubted most of Grandier's story. "When you were in Ulundi," he said. "Did you see any other white captives?"

Grandier looked annoyed at the question. "I was the only prisoner of war the Zulus captured."

"Did you hear of any other captives?" Andrew persisted. "A woman? I am looking for Miss Maxwell, a woman the Zulus might have captured in the early days of the war."

"No," Grandier said. "I did not hear of any other prisoners."

"Thank you." Andrew left the hospital tent. Although he was no better informed, he felt that Grandier had confirmed Jabulani's story. The Zulus may not have captured Mariana, but if they had, she might still be alive. If Cetshwayo had not executed a prisoner-of-war, he was unlikely to kill a woman, who might be a useful hostage if the war turned against him.

Andrew held onto that tiny flicker of hope as Wood waited for Lord Chelmsford's orders to advance towards oNdini.

"DID YOU HEAR THE NEWS, GINGER?" PRIVATE JULIAN SAID AS he passed Andrew's tent.

"What news?" Sanderson asked suspiciously.

"His lordship smashed the Zulus at a place called

Gingindlovu," Julian told him. "Imagine that, a battle named after you."

"What do you mean, named after me?" Sanderson asked.

Julian smiled, knowing he had trapped Sanderson. "You're called Ginger, so the lads are calling the battle Ginger, I love you." He repeated the phrase. "Oh, Ginger, I love you!"

"If you say that again, Julian, I'll smash your teeth through the back of your head." Sanderson could imagine his peers tormenting him. "Anyway, you've got it wrong. It's not Ginger I love you; it's gin, gin, I love you!"

As their voices faded away, Andrew left the tent to confirm the rumour. Buller greeted him with a smile.

"It's true, Baird. We smashed the Zulus at Khambula, and Lord Chelmsford did the same at Gingindlovu," Buller said with satisfaction. We've turned the tide, and now all we need to do is capture Ulundi, and we'll break the Zulu power forever."

Andrew agreed. By winning his twenty-minute battle at Gingindlovu on the 2nd of April, Chelmsford had redeemed himself and lifted the siege of Eshowe. The Zulus tide had ebbed from the high-water mark at Isandlwana, Britain had endured the expected initial disasters, and retribution had begun.

Thousands of reinforcements left a Britain filled with nationalistic fervour. Bands played patriotic airs, and crowds of civilians cheered from the safety of the quayside as the scarlet-uniformed soldiers sailed to war. Union flags fluttered in the breeze, newspapers published glowing accounts of British valour, and politicians expended much rhetoric in praising or damning Britain's war effort, depending on their party allegiance. Meanwhile, in Zululand, Wood's garrison became part of the scenery as the horsemen mounted patrols that extended further afield.

"When are we going to advance, sir?" Andrew asked.

"When his Lordship decides we have sufficient manpower," Buller told him. "You know as well as I do, young Up-and-at-'em, that Chelmsford wants a smashing victory before the government replaces him. He can't afford another reverse."

"Yes, sir. It seems that we've already broken the Zulus spirit if they only fought for twenty minutes at Gingindlovu. Khambula lasted over four hours."

"Cetshwayo still has over twenty-thousand men in his army," Buller reminded gently. "Lord Chelmsford will only move when he is confident he can defeat the Zulus in an open battle. Now take out another patrol and see what you can find."

"Yes, sir," Andrew said, saluted and left, hiding his frustration.

THE DAYS CRAWLED PAST, WITH ANDREW THINKING HIS patrols were without purpose and Lord Chelmsford slowly building up his army. As always, Andrew enquired about Mariana at every kraal, with the same replies. Nobody knew about a white woman held in Zululand.

Maybe Mariana is dead, but I won't give up. I may have to visit every imuzi in Zululand before I find the truth.

As the British eroded Cetshwayo's power, small groups of renegades began to raid the Boer lands and along the frontiers while rumours spread among the soldiers.

"Did you hear about the treasure in Ulundi, sir?" Fletcher asked.

"I've heard the shaves," Andrew replied cautiously.

"Cetshwayo's been storing gold and ivory for years," Fletcher said excitedly. "He's got thousands of pounds worth in his kraal."

"I doubt that, Fletcher." Andrew shook his head.

Fletcher continued as if Andrew had not spoken. "I heard a shave that Chelmsford's going to distribute the treasure among all the officers."

"How about the men?" Andrew asked, smiling. "They do as much fighting as we do."

"What would the men do with money?" Fletcher asked. "They'd only drink it away."

"The Zulus don't value gold and ivory," Andrew reminded. "Their wealth is in cattle."

Fletcher laughed. "Maybe Cetshwayo has a thousand prime breeding stock squirrelled away in a secret kraal, sir."

"That's more like it," Andrew said. "His Lordship will give two cattle to each officer. You can take them home to your parents."

Fletcher shook his head. "My parents would prefer the gold, sir. Cattle are not much good in a rectory in Wandsworth."

"Probably not, Fletcher," Andrew agreed.

Perhaps rumours of the treasure had spread, but Andrew noticed a steady influx of the more disreputable elements of colonial society and some from even further afield. Such men had made up the bulk of the NCOs in the NNC, but most left after the early disasters of the war. Now they eased back, some in rowdy bands on foot and others in groups of horsemen settling on the fringes of the British camp.

"Who are these people?" Wood asked as one group of wild riders made their camp close to his headquarters.

"I'm sure I don't know," Buller replied.

"Nor do I," Wood said. "Move them away in case they unsettle the men."

"With pleasure, sir," Buller said. "Come along, Baird." He glanced at Andrew and grinned. "Have you heard about the Natal Dragoons?"

Andrew frowned. "The Natal Dragoons? No, sir."

"I've noticed the same group follow you, Baird, and I decided to make you an official regiment of irregular horse. Congratulations, Lieutenant. You now lead the Natal Dragoons."

"Sir?" Andrew asked.

"Take over the Natal Dragoons, Lieutenant!" Buller said. "Join me outside the laager in an hour."

"Yes, sir." Andrew saluted, unable to hide his astonishment.

"You can create a uniform or not, as you wish," Buller told him.

The Natal Dragoons formed up before Andrew. Twenty strong, they were a mixture of hard-bitten colonials and a couple of newly arrived immigrants or New Chums as the colonials termed them, with a few strays from the Mounted Infantry. They viewed Andrew through suspicious eyes as he gathered them around him.

"Right, gentlemen." Andrew decided to make his speech short. "Colonel Buller has seen fit to make us a unit of irregular horsemen called the Natal Dragoons. You lads from the Mounted Infantry still belong to your parent units, but you'll be riding with me for the duration of this war or until you choose to leave."

The men did not comment. They were accustomed to military life with its long periods of routine followed by a sudden change.

"Everybody will retain their present rank and rate of pay."

That answered any immediate questions.

"Our first task together is to join Colonel Buller and remove these unruly civilians from their camp. Come on, Natal Dragoons!"

Andrew turned Lancelot without another word and headed away from the laager. He heard the rumble of hooves behind him and smiled. He was on his second campaign, a commissioned officer and had his own command, and then Andrew thought of Elaine and Mariana, and his good humour seeped away.

The civilians' camp was untidy, with no latrine discipline and a ragged collection of tents and wagons placed wherever the owner thought best.

Buller stood his horse on a slight incline, waiting until his officers gathered around him. "Let's clean this mess up, gentlemen!" He commanded a hundred and fifty men, divided equally between Mounted Infantry and irregular colonial units, and extended them in a line outside the civilians' camp.

"I am going to see who runs this shambles," Buller told the

officers. "In fifteen minutes, ride slowly forward, taking down the tents and ordering the men back to Natal. If a Zulu impi finds them, there will be another massacre."

The officers nodded and returned to their units. Andrew checked his watch, counting the minutes.

"Are you ready, boys?"

One by one, the men nodded assent.

Andrew watched the minute hand of his watch slowly move, waited until the fifteen minutes passed and snapped the cover shut. "In we go, Natal Dragoons!"

He heard officers give similar orders along the line of horsemen, and they stepped forward into the civilians' camp, ordering the inhabitants to leave and tearing down tents.

"What are you doing?" a bearded man asked indignantly as Fletcher and Kerr cut the guy ropes from his much-patched tent.

"Saving your life," Andrew snarled. "If an impi comes, you won't last five minutes."

"They won't attack as long as the soldiers are near," the man said smugly.

"Pack up your belongings and get back to Natal," Andrew ordered. "I'm wasting time dealing with you when I could be defeating Cetshwayo."

All around the camp, Andrew saw similar conversations as the soldiers pushed out the civilians. He frowned when he heard a familiar voice.

"You've no bloody right to order us away!" the man said. "We've as much right in Zululand as you have."

"Hitchings!" Andrew remembered the man who had deserted from the Cape Mounted Rifles at the beginning of the war. He pulled Lancelot toward the voice.

"Hitchings! What the hell are you doing here?"

"Lieutenant Baird!" Hitchings gave a greasy grin and lifted his carbine in a threatening gesture. "I heard the Zulus killed you at Isandlwana."

"They didn't," Andrew said. "Nor at Hlobane. You're a deserting hound, Hitchings!"

Hitchings' grin broadened as his finger curled around the trigger. "I decided to seek alternative employment," he said. "Something that paid better without the risks."

Andrew realised two of his men had followed him. "Why are you here, Hitchings? Have you come to help fight the Zulus?"

Hitchings sneered. "Fight them? Chelmsford's got sufficient men to fight the bloody Prussians, let alone the Zulus!"

"Why are you here, Hitchings?" Andrew repeated.

"We're after the treasure," Hitchings grinned, holding his carbine, and glancing around. "Everybody knows that Cetshwayo has thousands of pounds of gold and ivory in Ulundi, and we want our share."

"You've got two minutes!" Buller shouted. "Then we'll set fire to your tents, impound your wagons, and arrest the lot of you. Two minutes!"

Hitchings lifted his carbine, realised that most of the Natal Dragoons had arrived to back up Andrew, and moved away, mouthing threats.

Should I arrest him? Andrew wondered.

"Sir?" Fletcher arrived at Andrew's side. "Orders, sir?"

"Kick them out," Andrew ordered and raised his voice. "And Hitchings, if I see you again on this side of the Buffalo, I'll arrest you for the deserting, cowardly swine you are."

CHAPTER 27

20TH OF MAY 1879

Jama looked over his Abanonya. They had taken many casualties at Hlobane and Khambula, and some of the survivors carried wounds. Ndleleni was still there, as staunch as ever, with his steady eyes and ready assegai. Bangizwe was wounded, with the long scar of a British bullet across his ribs, while Bhekizizwe had a bloody rag tied around his left arm.

"The British are winning this war," Jama told them bluntly. "They have defeated us in two battles and killed many of our warriors. Our people are losing heart."

The Abanonya listened without comment. They had all faced the massed rifles of British infantry and knew Jama was correct.

"We cannot get close enough in sufficient numbers to defeat them," Jama said.

The Abanonya stirred slightly, wondering where Jama was heading.

Jama allowed them to ponder for a moment. "The British are building up their forces to capture Cetshwayo and destroy oNdini. We will hunt for any British party we can destroy."

The Abanonya agreed. They had promised to fight and die for Cetshwayo, and they were Zulu warriors.

"We need rifles like the British," Jama told them. "Find some."

The Abanonya nodded, knowing the old ways were slipping away and unsure if they were ready to face the new.

NDLELENI ROSE FROM THE LONG GRASS AND WATCHED THE small British patrol ride towards them. He saw a Zulu guide, two officers and six men, well mounted and confident, nodded when he realised there was not a stronger escort and withdrew to inform Jama.

When the British patrol stopped on some high ground, the two officers scanned the country around the Tshotshosi River, and the younger of the two took a pad from his satchel and made a few sketches. Ndleleni noted that the younger officer wore a dark blue uniform rather than the normal scarlet. His trousers looked too tight, and his white cork helmet was slightly large above a smooth face. His companion wore a dark blue patrol jacket, while his thick moustache and mutton-chop whiskers appeared old-fashioned compared to other officers. The escort wore buff corduroy jackets and broad-brimmed hats and carried short Martini-Henry carbines.

Ndleleni noted all the details in case Jama found them important.

Jama gathered his men around him and told them what Ndleleni had observed.

"The six-man escort is well armed and moved like professionals, while the younger officer is fresh-faced and eager," Jama said. "The guide carries an assegai and may fight."

The Abanonya listened, rubbing hard hands along the shafts of their assegais.

"We will take them," Jama decided as he watched the British.

"See how the older officer defers to the younger? The older man is of higher rank, a more experienced soldier, but the younger gives the orders."

"What does that mean, Jama?" Ndleleni asked.

"I think the young man is royal," Jama said. "Maybe if we kill him, the British queen will remove her army."

Ndleleni touched his *umzimbeet* necklace, tapped the blade of his *iKlwa* and smiled. They watched as the two officers led their escort from the high ground towards a deserted *imuzi* on the north bank of the Tshotshosi River.

"That's Sobhuza's *imuzi*," a local man who had joined them said.

"Come, Abanonya," Jama said and ran forward with his men at his back. When news of Jama's intended attack spread, remnants of other *amabuthos* joined them, men from the iNgobamakhosi, uMbonambi and uNokhenke. Mnukwa, a seasoned induna, shared the leadership of the combined force with Jama.

Tall fields of mealies surrounded three sides of the *imuzi*, descending to the river in a swaying, golden promise. Jama frowned to think that the harvest was going to waste since the British invasion had forced the villagers to flee. On the north side of the *imuzi*, the ground was open for two hundred paces before descending steeply into a dry donga deeper than a tall man.

Jama watched as the British escort warily approached the *imuzi*, dismounted and inspected each *indlu*, prodding their carbines into every corner and thatched roof. Three snarling dogs cowered away and ran as the troopers kicked at them with heavy boots.

"It's safe," the troopers said, and the officers joined them, with the younger smiling as he entered the *imuzi*.

The British knee-haltered their horses and allowed them to graze on the open ground to the north.

"They'll post a guard," Jama said, but the officers neglected even that simple precaution and the escort made a small fire and began to brew coffee. The smell made Jama's nostrils twitch.

The two officers began to talk while the guide wandered away on some mission of his own devising.

"What are they doing?" Bangizwe asked.

"I don't know," Jama replied. "Where has their guide gone?"

"There!" Bangizwe pointed to the Zulu guide, who stood on a small knoll, staring at them. "He'll warn the British."

"Follow," Jama said and led his mixed force into the tall mealies south of the *imuzi,* finding the British saddling their horses without urgency.

"Fire at them," Jama ordered his riflemen. The Zulus aimed and fired in a ragged volley.

The sudden sound panicked the British horses, which reared and plunged, but not a single shot hit its mark.

"Attack!" Mnukwa shouted.

"Attack!" Jama echoed and charged.

"*Usuthu!*" The Zulus shouted their war cry as they powered forward. "Usuthu!"

Caught unawares, the British fled, with the older officer the first to leave the *imuzi*. The other men ran towards the horses, some staring stupidly over their shoulders at the charging Zulus.

Jama was first into the *imuzi* and saw one gasping British soldier trying to run on foot. The man turned, lowered his carbine, and fired. Jama did not know where the bullet went. When the trooper turned to flee, Jama thrust his assegai into the man's back. "*Ngadla*!" he shouted, twisted the blade, and withdrew.

The Zulu guide and two of the British remained in Sobhuza's *imuzi*. Jama saw one drop his carbine and dismount to retrieve it, then throw himself awkwardly, face down, across his saddle. The young officer had not mounted and ran beside his panicking horse with one hand gripping the stirrup leather.

Ignoring the remaining men, Jama ran towards the young officer, with Ndleleni close behind and a mixture of warriors roaring at the back. The officer's grip slipped, and he fell, with the horse trampling him without stopping. Jama shouted in triumph, noted the other British riders fleeing towards the donga and chased after the officer.

As Jama closed, the young officer grabbed for his sword to find the belt had snapped, and a Zulu had lifted the weapon. The officer drew his revolver and fired, with the bullet whistling wide. Jama lifted his throwing spear, poised, and threw. The long weapon whizzed through the air to strike his target in the shoulder. The officer staggered, pulled the spear out and fired his revolver, missing again.

When a second spear thudded into him, the officer turned and fled into the donga. Ndleleni threw his spear, shouting in triumph, when it landed in the officer's thigh. The officer pulled it out, stumbled and fell.

A warrior named Xabanga overtook Jama and thrust his *iKlwa* into the officer's chest, with Jama next and others crowding around to stab the stricken man. A few moments later, the Zulus stopped, with the officer dead from a dozen wounds.

Mnukwa looked down at the dead officer. "He was a brave man," he said.

Jama agreed. "His men abandoned him. Their induna should execute them for cowardice."

Prince Louis Napoleon, twenty-three years old, great-nephew of Napoleon Bonaparte and one-time heir to the French imperial throne, lay broken and dead in the Zululand dust. It was another disaster for the British.

Chelmsford's Second Division and Wood's Flying Column met on the second of June, with men waving to one another as they marched slowly towards oNdini.

"What's happening, sir?" Fletcher asked as the two columns

marched side by side in a display of British power South Africa had never seen before.

"Lord Chelmsford is establishing a supply depot here," Andrew replied.

Fletcher nodded. "What will we do, sir?"

"The Natal Dragoons are remaining with Buller, scouting ahead of the Flying Column into the Mahlabathini Plain."

"I thought so, sir," Fletcher nodded sagely.

Buller, as usual, was in the van with a collection of mounted units that included Andrew's Natal Dragoons. They entered the Mahlabathini Plain with a thunder of hooves and jingle of equipment and rode cautiously onward.

Andrew looked around. "This should be ideal hunting country," he said, for the plain was an undulating basin of long waving grass and soft, sandy soil, where small groups of Zulus scattered before them.

"Yes, sir," Fletcher said. "I wonder who is hunting who. Are we hunting the Zulus, or are they hunting us?"

"Hopefully, we are hunting them," Andrew replied.

"Is it true that General Wolseley is going to take over the army, sir?" Fletcher asked.

Andrew nodded. "I believe so, Fletcher." The government in Britain, unhappy with British reverses and the death of the -pPrince -iImperial, sent General Garnet Wolseley to take command of the army in Zululand.

"Is that why His Lordship is finally pushing forward, sir?" Fletcher asked. "He wants to finish the war before his replacement arrives to steal the final glory."

"I am not privy to the mind of His Lordship." Andrew glanced at Fletcher. "You could be correct, or perhaps we're advancing because all the reinforcements have arrived. We'll do our duty as always."

"Yes, sir," Fletcher agreed.

Buller's cavalry probed deeper into Zululand, seeking a route to oNdini and a suitable spot for the decisive battle Chelmsford craved. Andrew's Natal Dragoons were in the van when Buller's force entered an area of long grass and scrubby bush. The men moved slowly, very aware that a Zulu warrior could easily conceal himself in such close country.

Andrew lifted his head. "There are Zulus here," he said.

"Are you sure?" Buller readied his revolver.

"Yes, sir," Andrew said. He was not sure how he knew. The grass was higher than a tall man, with the horsemen peering forward and around them.

Buller lifted his hand and ordered his men to halt. Silence closed around them, broken by the hum of insects and the gentle swish of grass, the pawing of horses' hooves on the ground and the harsh breathing of nervous men. Even though the cavalry knew the war was in its final stages, they were equally aware of how dangerous the Zulus could be.

"What's that?"

Andrew saw a flicker of movement among the grass ahead and heard the whirr of a thrown assegai. Moving instinctively, he pulled Lancelot aside as the spear whizzed past. A second later, hundreds of warriors rose from the grass, with scores of riflemen firing a volley. The sound was deafening after the previous hush while the muzzle flares sparkled amongst the greeny-brown grass.

"Zulus!" Buller shouted and fired his pistol.

Andrew fired without thought and heard shots whine above his head and hoarse screams as some of the Zulus' bullets found their mark. Three men were down, already dead, with others wounded or cursing as their horses lay, kicking and whinnying on the ground.

One Mounted Infantry sergeant lay under his dead horse, yelling, "Somebody get this bloody animal off me!" as the weight of his mount pinned him to the ground.

"Thank God you sensed something, Baird!" Buller shouted. "Another couple of hundred yards, and they'd have surrounded us!"

Exploding from the long grass, thousands of warriors charged towards the British patrol, rattling the butts of their assegais against their shields and shouting.

"Usuthu! Usuthu!"

"Dear God! These men have spirit!" an officer shouted. "We defeat them, and defeat them, and still they come on!"

Chief Zibhebhu led the Zulus, trying to prevent the British from advancing through the Mahlabathini Valley towards oNdini. The warriors charged forward, fighting a cause that was already lost, putting their bodies in the way of bullets with the courage of their race.

"Usuthu!"

The Zulu battle cry rose above the crackle of musketry and hoarse shouts of the surprised British soldiers.

"Shoot the buggers!"

"Bloody hell! Where did they spring from?"

"Let's get out of here, lads!"

"Usuthu!"

Andrew fired towards the rapidly approaching Zulus and saw a British officer dismount beside the trapped sergeant.

"Come on, man," the officer encouraged. Andrew saw it was Captain Lord William Beresford of the 9th Lancers. The sergeant, dazed by the fall, shook his head. He was too heavy for Beresford to lift, so the two stood, vulnerable as Zibhebhu's Zulus charged closer by the second.

"Frontier Light Horse!" Buller roared. "Natal Dragoons! Hold back the Zulus! Let Beresford rescue that trapped man!"

Andrew's men and the Frontier Light Horse turned around, rode towards the Zulus, and fired, knocking down half a dozen in the front rank. They retired, reloaded, and fired again, checking the advance for a few vital moments. In that time, Sergeant Edmund O'Toole rode beside Beresford, and both helped the stunned sergeant onto Beresford's horse.

Checked but not halted, Zibhebhu's Zulus swarmed around Beresford and O'Toole. Beresford thrust his sword into the nearest Zulu and, with O'Toole holding the injured sergeant secure in the saddle, they rode to safety.[1]

"Well now, gentlemen," Buller said, as calm as if he were in Hyde Park on a Sunday morning. "Now we know which direction not to go." He led them back to the vanguard of Chelmsford's army.

THE BRITISH LAAGER WAS NERVOUS THAT NIGHT. ANDREW could taste the fear as the mainly young soldiers tried to sleep in their crowded tents while the moon shone coldly upon them.

"Can you hear something?" Private Julian asked.

Andrew had grabbed a few hours rest and was patrolling the interior of the laager, exchanging a few words with the sentries, and gauging their morale. As he expected, the younger men were apprehensive as the veterans regaled them with stories of the fierce Zulu warriors and the slaughter of Isandhlwana.

"I can't hear nothing," Sanderson replied.

"I can hear the Zulus. Listen, Ginger. I'm telling you, man. It's the Zulus coming for us!"

"They won't frighten me. I'm from Brummagem. We're tough stuff in Brum!"

Andrew stopped and raised his head. Julian was correct. He could also hear something drifting in the breeze. "Music," he said. "We can hear music."

"They're coming to get us!" Julian shouted.

"No, they're not," Andrew soothed the boy. "They're miles away. If they were attacking, they'd come in silence."

The Zulu singing continued, deep-voiced and distant. When the sound increased, a few officers ordered their men to stand to their arms, but then the noise faded.

"The wind is carrying it to us," Andrew said to the Natal Dragoons. He listened for a while, pushed aside the creeping melancholia that he was witnessing the end of a proud kingdom and retired to his tent. His men were either on picket duty or asleep, the horses well cared for, and there was nothing else he could do.

He thought of Elaine, shook his head, and slept to dream of the River Tweed rippling past Berwick Walls and skeins of geese passing overhead.

"Sir." A corporal shook Andrew awake. "Lord Chelmsford's orders, sir, and we've to get up."

"What time is it?"

"Nearly four o'clock, sir," the corporal reported.

"No bugles today," Andrew said, rubbing the sleep from his eyes. He could be up half the night but still hated an abrupt wakening in the morning.

"Lieutenant Baird?" A fresh-faced subaltern thrust his head into Andrew's tent.

"That's me," Andrew confessed.

"His Lordship sends his respects, sir, and could you take the Natal Dragoons to join Buller at the drift over the White Mfolozi."

"My compliments to His Lordship, and we'll be there forthwith," Andrew said, dressing quickly and buckling on his revolver.

As he left the laager, Andrew looked over Chelmsford's army, comparing it to the men who had fallen at Isandhlwana. Lord Chelmsford commanded over four thousand Europeans, mainly regular British infantry, with nearly a thousand African allies, two Gatlings and twelve pieces of artillery. Tall lances thrust upright in the ground marked the tents of the 17th Lancers, and sentries patrolled, watching for any sign of any Zulus.

The Zulus have taught His Lordship respect, Andrew thought.

Andrew had never seen a Gatling in action and viewed this killing machine with curiosity. He knew an American doctor had invented the hand-cranked, ten-barrelled weapon and wondered how it would perform in the arduous conditions of the field.

"It fires faster than ten men," a proud seaman told Andrew.

"But it jams a lot. The extractor yanks the bases off the Boxer cartridges and fouls the barrels." He patted the artillery carriage on which the clumsy Gatling sat. "You're seeing the future of warfare, Lieutenant. In times to come, there will be ten men with Gatlings and no regiments of sweating Tommies." He winked. "Or even better, sir, wars will become so terrible that politicians will ban them and discuss their differences over a conference table."

Andrew raised cynical eyebrows. "I'd like to think you're right, but I doubt politicians have the humanity to stop wars. After all, they don't have to face a thousand screaming Zulu warriors." He shook his head. "And if that thing jams when the Zulus are charging, I'd prefer to be somewhere else."

The seaman laughed and touched the cutlass at his belt. "If all else fails, I've got this."

"So you have," Andrew said, smiling. "Good luck." He walked away, shaking his head.

"We're in the van again, Baird," Buller greeted him. "Where you want to be."

Andrew looked into the gradually lightening distance and wondered what Africa had in store for him next. "I'm not sure about that, sir."

Buller laughed. "I know differently, Baird. Make your father proud." He rode away before Andrew had time to reply.

As the main force marched away from the camp, the garrison they left behind watched through jealous eyes.

"Give them pepper, lads!" the Royal Engineers shouted while the five companies of the 24th Foot growled, wishing they could avenge the comrades they lost at Isandhlwana.

"Is Lord Chelmsford wise leaving the 24th to hold the laager, sir?" Fletcher asked. "The battalion is full of recruits, and they must be shaken."

Andrew nodded. "They'll fight all the harder after Isandhlwana." He rubbed his leg, where his wound was beginning to ache.

His Lordship is keeping the 24th out of trouble, he thought. *The regiment has suffered sufficient casualties.*

Chelmsford's army formed up, ready to march. Bugles trilled, boots thumped on the hard ground, horses neighed, and NCOs checked the men's ammunition and water. Mounted infantry, with bandoliers crossing their chests, rode alongside the infantry while Andrew's Natal Dragoons watched with the air of slight superiority mounted men felt for their foot-slogging companions.

In Andrew's mind, the battle of Khambula had been the decisive encounter of the war when a well-led British Army had repulsed a confident Zulu impi. However, the Zulus could claim the British could only fight behind a barricade and were afraid to fight in the open. By marching across country, Chelmsford was daring Cetshwayo to send his impis to attack and proving his confidence his men could defeat the Zulus in a straight battle.

"Will the Zulus fight, sir?" Fletcher asked, watching the British army form up.

"Cetshwayo doesn't want to fight," Andrew replied. "He's already sent peace envoys to Lord Chelmsford with elephant tusks, the Prince Imperial's sword, and gifts of cattle. He wants peace, but I can't see his warriors surrendering."

"Even after we defeated them at Khambula and Gingindlovu?" Fletcher asked.

"Even then," Andrew said. "They are a proud people."

Chelmsford formed his infantry into a hollow square, with the men four deep along the sides and the artillery and transport in the centre. They moved slowly, a scarlet uniformed fortress bristling with Martini-Henrys, crawling over the grassy plain of Zululand, challenging the amabuthos to attack.

"Come along, Baird, old man," Buller shouted. "Leave the Tommies to their marching. We have to guide them."

Andrew kicked in his heels and led his Natal Dragoons in front of the square. Lord Chelmsford marched his army with all the pomp of Victorian warfare. The regiments displayed their colours, the bands played martial airs, and the morning sun flashed from lance points, bayonets, and rifle barrels. Mounted men rode all around the infantry, ready to report any Zulus and slow their attack.

Come on, Cetshwayo; face us if you dare.

The British forded the White Umfolozi and tramped on; foot, horse and guns as the Zulus watched these invaders, whetted their assegais, and waited.

"Here we are, finally marching to Ulundi," Buller said, "after such a disastrous start to the campaign, we've been months on a journey that should only have taken days."

"Yes, sir," Andrew's thoughts divided between the campaign and Mariana.

Buller eyed him. "We'll have one last battle, Baird, and this war will end. You might find out about your missing girl, then."

"I hope so, sir," Andrew said.

Buller nodded. "Take your Dragoons to the right flank, Baird, and watch for the Zulus."

"Sir!" Glad to have an active task, Andrew called up his men and cantered away, leaving the slow-moving column behind.

The British passed two Zulu military kraals, kwaBulawayo and kwaNodwengu, and marched ponderously onto higher ground. The light was stronger now, and Andrew checked his watch, surprised that it was already half past seven. What had happened to the three and a half hours since the corporal woke him?

"Sir!" Kerr drew Andrew's attention to groups of Zulus in front. He raised his field glasses to study them, wondering which regiments they were. Sunlight flashed from assegais as a faint breeze rippled the decorative feathers each warrior wore.

"Come on then, lads," Andrew muttered. "Let's get this over with."

He swivelled to his right, the direction from where the British expected the Zulus to attack. Zululand's habitual early-morning river mist combined with smoke from Zulu campfires to obscure Andrew's vision.

"Are you down there, lads? Are you mustering to attack us?"

The British marched on, setting kwaBulawayo to the flames. Blue-grey smoke coiled behind them as Chelmsford's army left a trail of destruction through Cetshwayo's kingdom.

Welcome to our civilisation, lads.

Buller had already selected a site for Chelmsford to stand, and his horsemen led the infantry to his proposed battlefield. Andrew joined Buller, with his Dragoons extended across the country, watching for the anticipated Zulu attack.

"We'll fight them here, Baird." Buller lit a cigarette, took out a small telescope and scanned the surrounding plain. "An area of high ground with no cover for any approaching army. The Zulus will have to approach in the open if they approach at all." He grinned, nearly losing his cigarette. "Now we'll find the answers to our questions. Can His Lordship redeem himself with a victory over the main Zulu army? Will Cetshwayo send out his impis to attack us? And most important of all, will our soldiers stand without a laager to shelter behind?"

Andrew tried not to remember the carnage at Isandhlwana. He thought of Mariana, "We must win here, sir."

"Here comes the opposition," Buller said quietly as a Zulu impi emerged through the mist and smoke. The lines of long shields and spears moved steadily forward, gradually becoming clearer as the headdresses bounced in unison. Andrew wondered if anything could upset Buller's equanimity. He studied the left and left front of the square.

"They're advancing in good order," Buller said. "Regiment after regiment. They'll know what they're facing now."

Andrew nodded. "So do we," he said. "Look to the right."

More Zulus streamed from the thorn bushes off to the right, with *amabuthos* flowing around the square, spears held ready, and shields forming a continuous line of coloured cowhide. Andrew wondered if the world would ever see such a sight again, an Iron

Age army preparing to fight; a truly independent African force defending its traditional way of life. He shook away the thoughts and watched the Zulus run around the British, dimly seen as the mist lifted.

"The horns of the buffalo," Buller said quietly. "They're performing their classic attack strategy, and we're in our traditional defensive formation, as we used at Waterloo."

Andrew nodded, remembering the nervous talk the previous night and how a Zulu attack had defeated even the experienced 24th Foot.

Here is the final encounter, Cetshwayo's last throw of the dice against a British army in the open.

CHAPTER 28

"How many are there, do you think, sir?" Fletcher had reined up beside them. He took a swig from his water bottle.

Andrew concentrated on one area, calculated the numbers, and multiplied by the length of the Zulu line. "Maybe twenty thousand," he said.

"That's what I reckoned," Buller agreed. He raised his telescope again, focussing on a hill in the middle distance. "Look over there, Baird. That's the Zulu commanders waiting to direct the battle." He shook his head. "I don't know their names."

"One of my men might, sir," Andrew said and sent Fletcher to bring Kerr across.

Kerr borrowed Andrew's field glasses. "There's Ziwedu, Cetshwayo's favourite son, sir and a clutch of senior indunas." He pointed them out, dim figures in the distance. "That's Ntshingwayo, who won at Isandhlwana; beside him is Zibhebhu, Mnyamana, and the last fellow is Sihayo."

"Sihayo," Baird said, "he was here at the beginning of the war, and he's here at the end."

"Sihayo's one of Cetshwayo's favourites," Kerr murmured.

"The Lancers are busy," Buller observed as a troop of 17th

Lancers set fire to a small *imuzi* and withdrew amidst a pall of grey-brown smoke.

"That's started the ball rolling," Baird said as a group of Zulus left the disciplined ranks and rushed to attack the lancers.

"Tempt them, tease them, break their formation and defeat them piecemeal," Buller said happily. "There go the Basutos!"

Andrew saw the Basutos firing at the advancing Zulus, then withdrawing. Riding their small, shaggy ponies, the Basutos were fierce fighters, and Andrew thought them the only African people not overawed by the Zulu's reputation.

Buller lifted his voice. "Bugler! Sound the alert! Come on, men!"

Buller led his riders in support of the Basutos as the Zulu line menaced the Lancers. Andrew heard the drumming of assegai butts on shields, the stomping of feet on the ground and a constant low murmur, like bees in a flower garden, as the Zulus attacked. The Zulus had returned to their habitual discipline, *amabutho* lined up beside *amabutho*, each with their distinctive regalia, like the small details with which British units identified themselves.

"Fire a couple of rounds and retire," Buller ordered as the horsemen left the security of the infantry square. "Shepherd the Lancers back."

Having fired the *imuzi*, the Lancers were withdrawing, with Zulu skirmishers harassing the more laggard. Andrew looked for the white-and-black shields of the Abanonya, wondered if his old adversary was present, fired into the mass and withdrew. The Lancers rode past the defending screen, content with a job well done as the smoke from the burning *imuzi* spread across the plain. Andrew did not hear the order that saw the front and rear faces of the British square wheel out but rode thankfully past the infantry. He felt himself relax when the square closed again, presenting a solid scarlet wall to the oncoming Zulus.

"Look and remember," Buller murmured, indicating the

Zulus. "For you'll never see the like again. A traditional African army in all its pride and courage."

Andrew nodded, feeling a twinge of sadness, for he realised the Zulus were advancing to a battle they could not win. If the British kept their discipline, mass rifle fire, backed by artillery and Gatling guns, would overcome the bravest of men armed with spears.

"Here they come." Private Sanderson licked dry lips and glanced behind him. "Just like at Isandhlwana!"

"It's nothing like Isandhlwana," Andrew whispered as images of that carnage burst into his mind. He checked his watch. It was two minutes short of nine in the morning.

The Zulu commanders had sent hordes of skirmishers ahead of the main battle lines, brave men who were first to test the British infantry's Martini-Henrys. Behind the skirmishers, the impi advanced four deep, with the morning sun glittering on their assegai blades and their feathers waving in a slight breeze. Andrew saw the white-and-black shields of the Abanonya, with their leopard-skin headbands and the feathers beneath their knees. He saw Jama in front and, strangely, hoped he would survive the battle.

Fight well, my brave enemy, and go home to your wife.

The British artillery fired first. Andrew heard the loud crack of the guns and saw the explosions among the Zulu ranks. Lifting his field glasses, he saw the results, the cloud of smoke, flame and dust and the mangled bodies of the warriors. Some of the men nearest the explosions prodded at the smoke with their assegais and then trotted on, ready to fight.

"It hardly seems fair, blasting them like that," a Geordie voice said.

"Let's hear you say that when they get among you with their assegais." A saturnine corporal snarled. "They won't show any mercy, son, and neither will we. Now face your front and do your duty!"

Andrew knew the corporal was right, although he also agreed

with the Geordie. He hardened his heart, lifted his field glasses, and watched the Zulus advance. He thought they lacked the conviction of the impi at Isandhlwana and Khambula. They were every bit as brave but moved without the confidence of assured victory. Now a seasoned soldier, Andrew could sense the Zulus' hesitation.

"Get ready, lads!" a heavily whiskered officer ordered.

"They're getting awfully close!" Sanderson shouted, high-pitched, glancing over his shoulder until the saturnine corporal snarled at him.

"Face your front, Sanderson! You're here to fight, not squeal like a little girl!"

The two front ranks of infantry were kneeling, the rear ranks standing, and all presenting their rifles towards the advancing Zulus.

"Check your range," the whiskered officer shouted. "Wait for my word!"

The Zulus advanced through the smoke and fury of the shell fire, their shields held before them, and now Andrew could hear their battle cry.

"Usuthu! Usuthu!"

The sound raised the tiny hairs on the back of his neck as he recalled that same cry before the impis crashed into the luckless 24th Foot and as the warriors attacked at Hlobane. They had shown no mercy then, and there was no reason for the British to be merciful now.

"Usuthu!"

"Fire!"

The call echoed along the British ranks as officer after officer judged the distance, had a last glance at their men and issued the order.

"Fire!"

The infantry opened fire, with smoke jetting from the Martini-Henrys and hundreds of large calibre bullets smashing into the Zulu ranks. Andrew saw the warriors fall by the dozen and by the score. Bullets tossed men backwards, tore off arms and splintered skulls, raising a film of blood above the charging warriors so those at the back advanced through the blood and brains of their comrades.

"Fire," the officers ordered, and the remorseless volley fire of British infantry crashed out, rank after rank, section after section, company after company. The Zulus fell in rows, men leaping over the mangled bodies of their companions but still coming on, still chanting, still willing to fight.

"*Usuthu!*" the Zulus roared, deep-throated. "*Usuthu!*"

"They're not stopping!" Sanderson yelled.

"Then make them bloody stop!" the corporal snarled. "Fire!"

The volleys crashed out, jetting smoke in front of the British square, smoke that drifted back so men coughed and blinked. The Martini-Henrys slammed back against tender shoulders; men jerked the underlever and rammed in brass cartridges, firing automatically. Some shouted at the advancing Zulus; others hid their fear in obscenities.

"*Usuthu*!" The warrior's chants rose and fell, mingled with the yells and screams of the wounded.

Andrew recognised the veteran regiments who sprang up from the dead ground a hundred and thirty yards from the right rear corner of the square.

"Look at that!" Kerr marvelled, naming each Zulu *amabutho*. The uVe, uThulwana, iNdluyengwe and iNgobamakhosi rose to the attack, with the Abanonya in the middle. Experienced warriors who knew what British musketry could do, they still charged forward, screaming their war cry.

"Dismount and help the infantry!" Andrew ordered and led his Natal Dragoons to the firing line.

"Fire!" a calm voice ordered, and another volley crashed out.

A score of men fell, but the rest continued, assegais raised, shields held in front of them.

"Fire!" That was a west-coast Scottish voice as the 21st Foot aimed and fired. Although more Zulus crumpled, their advance never faltered. They were nearly within range of the throwing spears, chanting warriors trained to kill.

The 58th and 21st volleyed together, hundreds of rifles firing at thousand of warriors, with men blaspheming, praying, shouting defiance, laughing, or using dark humour to hide their fear.

The Zulus still came on, a hundred yards away, then only eighty, with Chelmsford riding over to encourage the infantry.

"Fire faster, men!"

Andrew thought Chelmsford sounded agitated, as if he envisaged the Zulus breaking through the four-deep ranks in a confused Donnybrook of assegais, bayonets, and rifle butts.

The nearest cannon, a nine-pounder, fired canister, but the range was too close, and the canister would not burst. Andrew raised his rifle and fired, watching the infantry prepare to receive the Zulus. Two or three privates of the 21st, the Royal Scots Fusiliers stepped forward to meet the challenge until outraged NCOs bellowed them back.

"Damn your eagerness, lads! Let them come to us!"

Gunsmoke lay thick in front of the infantry, obscuring their view. Standing in the fourth British rank, Andrew saw the Zulus advancing, closing ranks whenever a volley knocked over a dozen men and continuing to chant.

"Usuthu!"

Andrew fired, worked the underlever, loaded, and fired again. The Zulus were seventy yards away, then sixty, nearly in range of throwing spears, and they faltered. Another British volley crashed out, and the Zulu attack halted.

"We've stopped them!" Davidson yelled, and the 58th gave three cheers, joined by the 21st.

"Cavalry!" Chelmsford shouted. "Mount!"

The bugler sounded the order, and the cavalry sprang onto their horses, ready for the square to open so they could ride out among the Zulus.

"Mount up, lads!" Andrew ordered and clambered onto Lancelot. His Dragoons obeyed, checking reins and saddles, wiping sweat from their eyes, and looking over the infantry at the Zulu impi.

For the first time, Andrew realised that Zulu snipers were firing long-range shots at the square. He saw a man fall a few yards from him and another drop his rifle and swear, clutching at his arm.

"We make good targets, standing like this," Buller said, with a cigarette dangling from his lower lip. "Thank the Lord the Zulus are terrible shots."

Something whined past Andrew's head, and he knew some Zulu sharpshooter was targeting him. It felt strange that some unknown warrior, who he had never met and would never meet, was deliberately trying to kill him. Andrew straightened in the saddle, determined not to quail or show fear.

"Dismount!" Chelmsford shouted, and the bugle trilled out again. "They're coming again!"

"It's like bloody musical chairs," somebody grumbled. "Mount, dismount, mount; I wish his blasted Lordship would make up his mind!"

The Zulus altered their angle of attack, heading for the side of the square where the 21st abutted onto the 94th, the old Scotch Brigade. Simultaneously, the Zulu rifle fire increased, and Andrew saw some of the 94th fall, dead and wounded.

My father used to say that every battle had a crisis point, a hinge. We are at the hinge now.

The 21st and 94th fired steadily, meeting the Zulu charge with controlled volleys until the attack faltered.

"They're breaking!" Buller said and glanced towards Chelmsford.

The general agreed. "Lancers! Mount!" he ordered.

Andrew checked his watch. It was barely half past nine. The Zulus' attack had occupied only half an hour compared to the four-hour ordeal of Khambula, and only a few had come close to the British line.

"Lancers! Ride out!" Chelmsford ordered. "Go round to the left!"

"Stand to your horses," the Lancers officers shouted. "Mount!"

The lancers, the death or glory boys who sported the skull and crossbones as their cap badge, trotted out of the square chanting "Death! Death!" as they hefted their long lances.

Andrew thought the 17th Lancers made a fine show, with Colonel Drury Lowe leading them to the left as the Zulu sharpshooters altered their targets from the scarlet square to the tall horsemen. The Lancers dressed without haste as Drury Lowe led them at the main Zulu impi, with each troop deciding who they should charge. Immediately behind the Lancers, Captain Brewster led a troop of his King's Dragoon Guards out of the square.

"Heavy cavalry against agile infantry," Buller murmured as his colonial horsemen prepared to leave the square. "This could be interesting."

"You men, join the Lancers," Chelmsford ordered. "Buller, take your horsemen out!"

"Come on, lads!" Buller shouted. "Follow me!"

Already mounted, Andrew led his Dragoons as the 58th marched aside to give them passage. He saw the Lancers engaged with the now retreating Zulus, with men pinning the warriors to the ground while the Dragoon Guards wielded heavy swords that sliced through the Zulu shields.

Buller led his men forward, firing at any Zulu they saw and turning the Zulu withdrawal into a rout.

"Extended order, Dragoons!" Andrew shouted. "Work in pairs, guard each other's backs and don't wander off alone."

Very few Zulus turned to fight, preferring to flee once the battle was lost. Andrew shot one running man, saw him fall and stopped to reload. All around him, mounted men were chasing and hunting the retreating Zulus, shooting the wounded without mercy. The Lancers were experts at spearing their quarry, riding past, freeing their lances with a flick of the wrist, and seeking the next victim. Within minutes the lance pennons were scarlet with Zulu blood.

"Enough." Andrew pushed forward his rifle to lift a trooper's carbine as he aimed at a wounded Zulu. "That man's no threat to us."

"He'd kill us if the position were reversed," the trooper objected.

"We're meant to be the civilised ones here," Andrew said. He noticed another group of Zulus watching and saw the familiar shields of the Abanonya.

The retreating Zulus entered an area of broken ground, with bushes and rocks to provide cover. Colonel Drury Lowe and Buller arrived at the same conclusion and halted the cavalry as Zulu sharpshooters opened fire.

"This is not suitable country for mounted men," Drury Lowe said.

"Back to the square, boys," Buller ordered. "We've broken the Zulu army and chased them away. That's enough for the present."

We've won the battle of Ulundi, Andrew realised as he saw the infantry grounding their Martinis, lighting pipes, and chatting with one another. Such a short battle seemed surreal, an anti-climax after the tension and horrors of the previous few months.

Chelmsford greeted the mounted men with a brief nod. He ordered the square to march to a small stream, the Mbilane, and within half an hour, the cooks were busy making lunch.

"Buller," Chelmsford said. "You'd oblige me by taking your men to the royal kraal and burning the place to the ground."

"Very good, sir," Buller, ever restless, said.

"I've heard rumours of treasure in the king's palace," Chelmsford added. "If you find any, place a guard on it, will you? There's a good chap."

"Certainly, sir," Buller said. "Come on, lads! Let's visit Ulundi!"

CHAPTER 29

ONdini was by far the largest *imuzi* Andrew had seen, with a stout wooden palisade extending for what seemed like miles. He pulled Lancelot up a quarter of a mile outside the Zulu capital.

"I've never helped topple a royal dynasty before," Andrew said.

"It's something to tell your grandchildren," Buller told him. "Look long and hard, Baird, for it's something neither you nor anybody else will ever see again. The capital city of the Zulus, one of the last independent kingdoms in Africa."

Andrew knew that if Marina were not in oNdini, he would probably never find her, yet he hesitated before entering.

"I've heard there are over four thousand separate kraals within the palisade," Andrew said, "and Cetshwayo lives in the middle, in the *isigodlo,* in a house built in the European manner, with a thatched roof."

If Mariana is anywhere, she'll be there. The only reason Cetshwayo might have for taking her with her would be as a hostage.

Buller smiled. "You may be correct. We'll see in a few moments." He lit a cigarette and looked sideways at Andrew. "You'll have heard the shave about the treasure."

"I have, sir," Andrew said. "I've heard at least two different versions, one claiming it dated back to Shaka's day and the other saying it was a tax on the ivory hunters and traders."

"All sorts of rumours fly about in wartime," Buller said. "Come on, Baird. Let's get into Ulundi. There are some unsavoury chaps going around, and we don't want them to get there first."

"No, sir," Andrew agreed, thinking of Hitchings. He saw some stray horsemen heading for oNdini and guessed they were after Cetshwayo's alleged treasure.

"Come on, Baird!" Buller said. "Gallop in, man and see if your girl is there!"

At least a dozen horsemen were racing for oNdini, with Andrew and Buller near the back. All Andrew's competitive streak came to the fore in a horserace, and he urged Lancelot on, pushing for the open gate. For once, he wished he had a faster mount, for Kabul ponies were not renowned for speed.

By God, Mariana, I've strived for months to reach oNdini, and you'd better be inside, waiting for me.

oNdini seemed to stretch for miles, a proper city rather than a collection of *izindlu*, and Andrew wondered at the men who had created such a place without any of the accessories modern civilisation considered necessary. *The Zulus have put an immense amount of work into oNdini, and we're about to burn it to the ground.*

Andrew galloped through the gateway and into another world. He knew that Cetshwayo had ordered oNdini evacuated before Chelmsford's army grew close, but he had not expected such complete desertion. oNdini was a ghost city, with each family *imuzi* empty of everything. There were no people, cattle, goats, or possessions. The Zulus had left nothing for the British except memories and the sad ghosts of a defeated kingdom.

"Mariana!" Andrew roared, knowing his voice would be lost in the vastness of oNdini. "Mariana!"

He heard movement and saw other riders roaming around,

some from units he recognised and others he guessed were searching for loot.

"Mariana!" Andrew's voice echoed among the eerily deserted *izindlu* as he made his way towards where he guessed the *isigodlo* should be, with more armed horsemen shouting around him.

"Where's the king's palace?" one London accent demanded.

"How the hell should I know?" a colonial voice replied and then came the crash of breaking glass as somebody threw a bottle on the ground.

"Where's the bloody treasure?" a coarse Liverpool voice sounded. "Where's Cetshwayo?"

Andrew pushed Lancelot on, past an outer row of *imizi* and into a vast inner ring where Cetshwayo had paraded his wealth. He could smell the homely scent of cattle and shouted again. "Mariana!"

"Who the hell's Mariana?" the Liverpudlian voice sounded. "I'll share her with you!" When the man laughed, Andrew loosened the revolver in its holster. He entered an area of small *imizi*, each containing one large and a few smaller *izindlu*. They were all empty.

A group of horsemen passed Andrew, with one man carrying a broken Zulu shield, another a throwing spear.

"Where's the treasure? There's no bloody treasure!"

"Hey, you," a large man with a sunburned face and the skin peeling from his nose shouted at Andrew. "Where's the king's palace?"

"I have no idea," Andrew replied and moved on, getting lost in the intricacies of oNdini. Every *imuzi* looked the same, deserted, sad and empty of life. Andrew knew he would never have the time to search every *indlu* for Mariana.

He smelled smoke and heard the tell-tale crackle of flames.

Somebody's set oNdini on fire.

"Mariana!" Andrew pushed Lancelot harder, poking into *imizi*, desperate to find Mariana. If she was a captive, she might be lying, bound, and gagged in any of these *izindlu*, or the Zulus could have taken her with them or killed her as an unnecessary burden. When a group of horsemen cantered past, Andrew looked around. They were mixed, Africans riding beside Europeans, but for a moment, Andrew thought he recognised the leading rider.

That was like Ashanti Smith. No, it couldn't be him. Andrew rode on until he saw the larger *indlu* above the pall of smoke and immediately knew it belonged to the king. If Cetshwayo held Mariana captive, she would be either in or near the royal home. He would have to try, however slim the chance of finding her.

The royal *indlu* was huge. Tethering Lancelot outside the door, Andrew pushed in, shouting Mariana's name.

"What the hell are you doing here?"

Andrew whirled around, recognising the voice. "Hitchings? You bastard! What the devil are you doing here?"

Hitchings was as untrustworthy as Andrew remembered, failing to meet Andrew's gaze as he gave a greasy smile. "The same as you, police boy."

"Soldier now, Hitchings, and with little time for a deserter such as you."

"Don't get all holier-than-thou with me, Baird," Hitchings sneered. "We're both after the same thing."

"What?" Andrew asked.

"Cetshwayo's treasure," Hitchings said. "Me and Ashanti and the boys are searching for it. We'll find it and divide it between us."

That was Ashanti Smith I saw!

Andrew coughed as smoke wafted into the *indlu*. He glanced behind him and saw an orange glow of flames. "I'm not interested in the treasure," he said. "You're welcome to any gold or ivory you find."

"Everybody's interested in gold," Hitchings contradicted him.

"I'm not," Andrew said. About to mention Mariana, he saw

the firelight reflect on something on Hitchings' little finger. "What's that ring, Hitchings?"

"What?" Hitchings stepped away, tucking his left hand behind his back.

"Show me your hand!" Andrew unholstered his pistol. "Show me your hand, Hitchings, or I'll blow your bloody head off!"

Hitchings snarled, glaring at Andrew. "What's the matter, Bairdie? I'm not a Zulu!"

The crackle of flames increased, and smoke gushed into the *indlu* from outside. Andrew swore as Hitchings ducked and kicked upwards, aiming for Andrew's revolver. His boot cracked onto Andrew's wrist, causing him to gasp, but rather than drop the weapon, he involuntarily squeezed the trigger.

The bullet flew wide, puncturing a hole in the thatched roof.

"You fired at me!" Hitchings accused, bringing his rifle round. "You dirty bastard, Baird!"

Andrew fired again, with the bullet smashing into Hitchings' arm. Hitchings screamed shrilly, dropped his rifle, and grabbed for the wound. "What did you do that for?"

"Show me that ring, Hitchings, or by God, I'll put the next one between your eyes!"

"You wouldn't dare," Hitchings said, cradling his arm. He whimpered like a frightened puppy. "Come on, Bairdie, you and me are chums!"

"Are we?" Kicking Hitchings rifle into a corner of the *indlu*, Andrew thrust his revolver against the cowering man's forehead. "Let's see your hand, Hitchings."

When Hitchings held up his hand, Andrew saw the ring, now smeared with blood.

"Where did you get that?" He yanked the ring from Hitchings' finger. It was the signet ring his mother had given him, and which he had passed on to Elaine. Andrew pushed the muzzle of the revolver harder into Hitchings' forehead. "Tell me, you bastard!"

"Off a woman!" Hitchings screamed. "I got it off a woman!"

Andrew felt nausea rising in his throat. "Which woman?" he asked. "Where?" He relaxed the revolver, stepped back, and smiled. "Tell me, Hitchings."

The ring seemed to burn in Andrew's hand as he remembered Elaine's smile when he slipped the ring on her finger.

"Your woman," Hitchings whispered. "She gave it to me."

"When and why?" Andrew kept his voice mild, although the fear and worry tore him apart. "When did Miss Maxwell give you this ring, Hitchings?"

More smoke blew into the king's *indlu* as the sound of fire increased. Andrew looked outside, where an orange flicker revealed the *imuzi* was alight.

"At her house," Hitchings said as Andrew pressed the revolver muzzle against his forehead.

"How was she when you left her?"

"Very well," Hitchings gasped. "She was very well, I tell you."

"Who else was there?" The crackle became a roar as the thatch caught fire, with flames bright above their heads and sparks raining down.

"It was Ashanti's idea!" Hitchings said. "He heard you and the woman talking, and he wanted to visit her." He looked up. "We'll have to get out of here, or we'll get burned alive!"

"We'll get out when you tell me who else was there," Andrew promised.

"Ashanti Smith, Simmy and the boys," Hitchings nearly screamed. "Let me out!"

"Did you see the younger sister?" Andrew asked quietly, although he felt sick at the thought of Smith, Simpson, and Hitchings alone with Elaine.

A section of the roof collapsed, landing in a mass of flaming thatch three feet away. Andrew ignored it. "Did you see Mariana, the younger sister?"

"Yes!" Hitchings yelled, staring at the burning roof. "We took her with us!"

"What?" Andrew stepped back. "Took her where? Where is she, Hitchings?"

"Let me out!" Hitchings screamed as another section of the roof collapsed. Some of the thatch landed on top of him, and he pushed it off, yelling. A few sparks remained, quickly spreading on his dry clothes. He tried to beat out the flames.

"Took her where?" Andrew persisted. "Where is she now? Tell me!"

"Help me!" Hitchings screamed.

"Took her where?" Andrew asked. "Where?" He leaned closer until another section of the roof collapsed. Andrew jumped back, cursing, as the flaming thatch landed on top of Hitchings. The man's screams increased.

"Tell me!" Andrew began to haul the burning thatch from Hitchings.

"In the mountains!" Hitchings screamed. "Help me!"

As he spoke, one of the supports for the roof collapsed, bringing down half the thatch. Hitchings' screams intensified, then died away in the roar of flames. When the screaming stopped, Andrew left the royal *indlu*.

CHAPTER 30

Lancelot was outside, shivering with fear as the smoke and flames surrounded him. "Come on, Lance," Andrew said. He looked around oNdini, seeing nothing but dense smoke and burning buildings.

Have I left it too late? Am I trapped in here? No, damn it! There's always a way out!

Andrew tried to remember oNdini's layout, waved a hand in front of him in a futile attempt to clear away the smoke, chose a direction at random and pushed on. Smoke and sparks surrounded him, with the crackle of burning thatch and the whoosh of collapsing buildings loud in his ears.

After five minutes in Cetshwayo's burning capital, Andrew tried shouting, hoping that somebody could hear him, but the sound of the fire drowned his words.

Damn it! There must be a way out of here!

Andrew heard a distinct rattle above the other noises, and a shadowy shape appeared to his left.

"Halloa!" Andrew shouted. "Who are you?"

When the figure did not reply, Andrew saw it was a woman, covered in bones and furs, with a snakeskin around her neck. "Are you the witch doctor I've met before?"

In reply, the woman rattled her knuckle-bone necklace and stepped into the smoke.

Instinctively, Andrew knew the woman wanted him to follow her. He pushed Lancelot into the smoke, forcing the horse forward. "Where are you?"

Again, Andrew heard the rattle of bones. He headed for the sound, unable to see for the dense smoke while the sound of burning thatch filled the air.

"I hope you're not leading me astray!" Andrew croaked, coughing as the acrid smoke caught in his throat.

The bones rattled again, and Andrew saw the woman standing in a small clearing, watching him through familiar deep, dark eyes.

"I'm coming!" Andrew said, fighting to control Lancelot, who was nearly panicking in the heat and smoke. He kicked in his heels. "Come on, Lance! One more effort, and we are through!"

Lancelot whinnied, rolling his eyes backwards. Andrew patted the horse's head, leaned forward, whispered in Lancelot's ear, and pushed on. The witch backed off from him, and Andrew emerged into the clearing, with the palisade before him and oNdini burning at his back.

"Nearly there, Lancelot!" Andrew croaked. "A final effort, and we're out!" He looked around for the witch, but she had vanished.

Lancelot sensed fresh air, took as much of a run as he could and leapt over the barrier to land in a shower of dust outside. For a thoroughbred, the jump would have been easy, but a Kabul pony was not suited for such endeavours, and Lancelot staggered as he landed.

"Good boy!" Andrew patted him. "You got us out of there."

Riding a few hundred yards away, Andrew looked back. oNdini was a mass of orange, with the flames leaping to the sky beneath a pall of dark smoke.

What a sight. Camelot no more. A dynastic capital dying in a funeral pyre as a kingdom crashes to its end.

Andrew sighed. He lifted his water canteen, shook it to test the contents and lifted it to his lips.

"Here's to you, Cetshwayo, and the brave warriors of Zululand who are no more." He took a single sip, dismounted, and poured the remainder into Lancelot's mouth. "We'll find you a decent drink soon, boy."

Turning his back, Andrew walked away, leading Lancelot as a feeling of deep melancholia fell on him. He knew Britain had won the war but somehow felt dirty at the outcome.

JAMA VIEWED WHAT WAS LEFT OF THE ABANONYA AS THEY stood in the smoke of oNdini. Jabulani stood among them, a boy in years but a man who had faced the rifles of the British soldiers and survived. Jama allowed his gaze to linger on him for a moment, and then he returned to his duty.

"You fought like men," Jama told them. "You fought like Zulu warriors, but you could not prevail against the bullets and shellfire of the British."

The Abanonya agreed. About half carried wounds, and all were spent. They had fought in four major battles since the war began and a few more minor but still bloody skirmishes. All the warriors had charged into the wall of flames and lead that was a British position, and many had washed their spears in British blood. The Abanonya had done all that humans could do, fighting impossible odds with bare chests and spears against Gatling guns and case shot.

"It is enough," Jama said. "No man can expect more of you."

The Abanonya listened, leaning on their assegais.

"I am going to hunt for the men who murdered my wife and burned my *imuzi*," Jama said. "I do not expect any of you to follow me. Go home to your wives and whatever the white men have left for you."

Ndleleni fondled his necklace, looked at the ground and took a pinch of snuff. "The British killed my wives," he said. "The man with the green feathers in his hat is as much my enemy as yours, Jama."

Bangizwe stamped his feet. "We are the Abanonya," he said. "We will not leave you." He raised his voice in the song they sang before the war began, Chaka's favourite.

"Thou hast finished off the tribes.
Where wilt thou wage war?
Yes, where wilt thou wage war?
Thou hast conquered the kings.
Where wilt thou wage war?
Thou hast finished off the tribes.
Where wilt thou wage war?
Yes, yes, yes! Where wilt thou wage war?
Jama fought to keep his pride from showing.
"Very well. You are all fools to follow me."

Ndleleni grinned at him. "That is another matter, Jama. Where are you taking us?"

ONLY WHEN HE WAS CLEAR OF ONDINI DID ANDREW consider Hitchings' words.

I've been wrong all this time, blaming the Zulus for murdering Elaine and taking Mariana. If Hitchings was telling the truth, it was Ashanti Smith and his band of renegades that kidnapped her.

As Andrew rode towards the British camp, a score of images entered his mind. He saw Smith and his marauders advancing on Inglenook, laughing. He saw them passing under Elaine's mopane tree, surrounding the farmhouse, and breaking in. He saw them kicking in the door to Elaine's bedroom as she tried to fight back.

No. Andrew shook his head, forcing the images away.

Picturing such scenes is the path to madness. I must find Mariana if she is still alive. I can't leave her with these filthy creatures.

Andrew stiffened as he remembered Elaine taking him to the Bushman's paintings on that terrible, magical wagon road. He had seen a flash of blue then. *That was a police uniform. Somebody was watching us, Smith, Simpson, or Hitchings, without a doubt. They planned this raid all along.*

Smoke from oNdini had drifted across the entire Mahlabathini Plain, hazing the landscape and polluting the sky. Andrew saw Lord Chelmsford and his staff officers standing on a small knoll, watching oNdini burn. They seemed satisfied with their days' work, examining the destruction through field glasses, and exchanging congratulations.

"Why the long face, fellow soldier?" Buller asked. "We won the battle, smashed the Zulus, and won the war. You look as though you found a sixpence and lost a guinea."

"I found out about Mariana Maxwell, sir," Andrew said.

"Tell me more, Baird." Buller's voice altered from joviality to sincerity.

Andrew explained, with Buller listening carefully. When Andrew finished, Buller nodded. "There is a chance she is still alive," he said and rode away.

Andrew worked mechanically for the remainder of that day, performing his duty, and speaking to his peers while his mind was elsewhere. He listened as Chelmsford paraded his army and congratulated them on their good conduct but said nothing. In the middle of the afternoon, Chelmsford marched his men back to the Mfolozi River, with the band of the 13th Foot playing *God Save the Queen* and *Rule Britannia*. When the band stopped, some of the men parodied themselves.

"Oh, the grand old Duke of York,
He had ten thousand men,
He marched them up to the top of the hill,
And he marched them down again."

Kerr grinned at Andrew as they rode on the infantry's left

flank. "Cheer up, old Cock; sorry, sir. We'll be going home soon, wherever home is."

"I won't be coming," Andrew said.

"Whyever not, sir? Have you fallen in love with Zululand?" Kerr probed, with his eyes sharp. "Or are you still searching after that girl of yours?"

"Yes," Andrew said. "I'm still searching." He kicked Lancelot further ahead, desperate to torture himself with his dark thoughts.

The British infantry marched past, many laden with the assegais, shields, and knobkerries they had taken from the Zulu dead. Andrew wondered how many of these trophies would decorate walls the length and breadth of Britain in the years to come. He imagined the men boasting of their deeds, with the tales growing in the telling as the years dragged on.

"Well, Baird." Buller rode beside Andrew. "You'll be worried about Miss Maxwell," he said.

"Yes, sir."

Buller watched the marching army. "We don't know where Cetshwayo is," he said abruptly. "He's vanished completely."

"Yes, sir," Andrew said.

"I'm going to send patrols out to search for him." Buller seemed to be thinking as he spoke. "You speak Zulu, don't you?"

"I speak some Xhosa, sir. It's not the same, but I can generally make myself understood."

"That's good enough for me," Buller said. "I want you to take your ruffians to search for Cetshwayo. Try the hill country at the northern fringes of Zululand." He leaned across from his horse. "When you're out there, I have heard there is a renegade band who may have a woman prisoner. If you find them, Baird, do whatever is needful."

Andrew felt relief surge through him.

"Thank you, sir. When shall I leave?"

"As soon as you're ready, Baird. I don't expect to see you back until you either have Miss Maxwell or until you have definite news of her." Buller pulled Andrew's horse away from the column. "There will still be roaming Zulu bands out there, Baird, so be careful. Take as much ammunition, food, and water as you can carry."

"Thank you, sir."

"And, Baird." Buller extended his hand. "The best of luck. Your father is an expert with small mobile forces, and I can see he has passed his skills to you." He held Andrew's gaze for a long moment. "Now get out there."

TWO HOURS BEFORE DAWN THE FOLLOWING DAY, ANDREW LED his Natal Dragoons away from the British camp on the Mfolozi. He had ensured all his men carried extra ammunition, food and water and borrowed twenty spare horses for the hard riding he expected.

"We're going to Ulundi first," Andrew told them.

"Why is that, sir?" Sergeant Meek asked.

"We have two missions," Andrew explained. "The first is to find Cetshwayo, and the second is to trace a certain band of desperados who have been attacking homes and native homesteads, murdering civilians."

"Is that the same bunch who kidnapped Miss Maxwell, sir?"

"The same bunch," Andrew confirmed.

Sergeant Meek nodded. "If I were you, sir, I'd make them my priority. Cetshwayo can do nothing without his impis, and this band of renegades sound unpleasant." He tapped the row of medal ribbons across his chest. "I don't like deserters, sir."

"I see." Andrew nodded. "How many others think like you?"

"We all know the story, sir. Nobody likes the idea of recreants kidnapping women, and some of our local lads," Meek jerked a thumb at the Dragoons, "have got families near the border."

Andrew nodded. "We all have our reasons to catch these men. Let's look at Ulundi."

The passage of thousands of feet had beaten the ground around oNdini stone-hard, but Andrew cast his men in a wide circle.

"Ashanti Smith's men were all mounted," he said. "They did not come with the British Army, so we are looking for a group of horsemen arriving from a different direction. They'd arrive after Cetshwayo evacuated Ulundi, so we know the prints will be fresh."

The Dragoons nodded. "We'll search for spoor," Kerr said. "It's unfortunate that there's been so much movement."

"Search," Andrew ordered. "We're not looking for Zulus or regular British cavalry. These men will be mounted and probably without any formation."

"Yes, sir," Kerr said.

Andrew split his men into pairs, one to check for any traces of Smith's renegades' trail and the other to watch for resentful Zulus. They started close to the smouldering remains of oNdini, worked in a circle, and gradually extended their search outwards. On three occasions, a man thought he had found traces of a band of irregular horsemen, only for the spoor to lead towards the British camp.

By evening Andrew was tired and downhearted yet determined to continue. They camped a mile from oNdini; Andrew set out sentries and started as soon as there was sufficient light the following morning.

"Sir!" Kerr shouted. "What's this?"

Andrew cantered across, more in hope than expectation.

"A body of horsemen have been here," Kerr said, crouching on the ground. "Around thirty men, coming and leaving the same way."

Andrew dismounted and joined Kerr. "When?"

Kerr pursed his lips. "They arrived and left about six hours apart. Yesterday."

Andrew felt his spark of hope grow to a miniature flame.

"Do you want us to follow them, sir?" Kerr asked.

Andrew considered. "Yes, damn it," he decided. "This is the best trail we've found."

The riders had not tried to hide their trail, so the Dragoons had no difficulty following them. Knowing how skilful Smith was, Andrew sent Kerr in front to watch for ambushes and followed with the remainder of his men.

"Where the hell are the Zulus?" Meek asked as they rode through a deserted countryside. "It feels as if somebody has taken a broom and swept the country clean."

"They'll be here," Andrew said. "They'll know exactly where we are, even if we can't see them."

They rode on, following the trail, ignoring the occasional deer that broke cover around them and the chattering of the birds. The trail was clear, as if the renegades had no fear of pursuit, or even dared anybody to follow them.

Is Ashanti luring us into a trap? Has he placed an ambush ahead of us? Andrew slowed his pace, checking ahead with his field glasses.

"Sir," Meek said quietly. "Kerr's returning."

Both men looked up as Kerr hurried towards them. "Zulus!" Kerr cantered towards Andrew. "There's a small impi three miles ahead, sir."

"How small?" Andrew asked, reaching for his Martini.

"Maybe thirty or forty men," Kerr said. "Large enough to be dangerous."

"Damn," Andrew swore as he made a rapid decision, glancing around. "We'll stay on that ridge," he nodded to an area of high ground on their left, "and you and I will have a closer look at the impi. If we're lucky, they'll pass on without stopping."

"They're Zulus," Kerr said. "And they're hurting after we've burned oNdini and defeated them in battle. They'll attack any small British column they come across."

Andrew knew Kerr was correct. "We'll have a look," he decided, "and more very circumspectly."

"With respect, sir," Kerr said. "I might be better than you at watching them unseen."

"I'm sure you are, Kerr," Andrew agreed. "You can ensure I don't stick my head above the skyline or blow a trumpet or anything. Come on!"

JAMA LED THE ABANONYA AT A FAST TROT THAT EFFORTLESSLY covered the ground. He heard the rhythmic tread of his men's feet and knew they could keep up the pace for hours. Yet he felt that something was wrong.

"Do you feel it too, Ndleleni?" he asked.

"I can." Ndleleni carried a wound from the battle outside oNdini but still ran with the others. Blood had dried down his side where a British bullet had grazed him.

"What is it?" Jama asked.

"White men," Ndleleni replied at once. "I can smell them."

Jama agreed, still running. "There's a man on a horse ahead."

"Over beside that pile of rocks," Ndleleni agreed. "He's watching us."

"He won't be alone," Jama decided. "He'll be scouting for a mounted patrol, probably searching for Cetshwayo."

"I can kill him." Ndleleni lifted a throwing assegai.

"No. Let the scout see us, and he'll return to the others. We'll follow." Jama ordered. "We'll attack them when they camp for the night." He grinned. "Remember the Intombi River?"

Ndleleni smiled, running a thumb along the edge of his *iKlwa*. "That was a good day."

"We'll have another," Jama said. He altered his direction to pass in the sight of the lone scout, passing through an area of long grass onto open ground. He saw the horseman watching, allowed him a few moments to count his men and led the Abanonya into a patch of rocks.

"Stop!" Jama ordered. "Wait here. Ndleleni and I will follow the scout."

Jama waited until the horseman left his position to canter away, then followed, keeping out of sight and a quarter of a mile to his left. The horseman rendezvoused with a larger force of mounted men.

"You were right, Jama," Ndleleni said.

They watched as the scout made his report, and most of the mounted men rode to a rocky ridge.

"They'll camp there for the night," Jama said.

Ndleleni agreed. "The scout is leading another man towards us."

Jama took a deep breath. "That's their induna," he said. "He was at Sihayo's *imuzi* when they first invaded and at Isandhlwana and Hlobane."

Ndleleni knew that Jama was hiding his emotions. "Your son died at Sihayo's *imuzi*," he said.

"He did." Jama agreed. He watched the two mounted men.

"We could kill these two now," Ndleleni suggested.

"If we do, the others might take fright and run," Jama said. "I want to kill them all, like at Intombi Drift."

Ndleleni touched the blade of his *iKlwa*. "That is what we shall do," he said.

CHAPTER 31

"They've gone." Kerr swept the horizon with his field glasses. "I can't see any Zulus anywhere."

"That may be a good thing," Andrew said, "although I don't like to think of an impi, even a small one, ranging near us."

"Do you want me to scout around, sir?" Kerr asked.

Andrew shook his head. "No. If we leave them alone, hopefully, they'll leave us alone, too." He patted Lancelot. "Come on, Kerr. Let's get back to the others. We'll pick up the trail again tomorrow." He nodded to the hills ahead. "Hitchings said the renegades were in the hills, and these lads are heading that direction."

"Yes, sir," Kerr said and stopped. "Something's wrong."

"What?" After two years in the bush, Andrew knew not to distrust a frontiersman's instincts. "What's the to-do, Kerr?"

"Did you hear that bark just now, sir?" Kerr did not move, but his eyes swivelled from side to side, searching for something.

"I did," Andrew said. "A wild dog, I think."

"No, sir. It sounded like a wild dog, but it was a nyala deer, sir, an antelope. That's their warning call."

"I've never seen a nyala deer." Andrew loosened the pistol in his holster and glanced down at his Martini-Henry. "Are they dangerous?"

"No, sir. They've very shy and well-camouflaged. They seldom come out of the forest and never in daylight, which is why something's the matter. We passed a patch of woodland half an hour ago, and if the nyala were anywhere, it would be there. Something must have alarmed it."

"A leopard, perhaps?"

"Maybe, sir, but leopards are night hunters. I'd say humans disturbed the nyala."

"Us?"

"We weren't close enough to the forest, sir."

"Zulus?"

"I'd say so, sir. I'd guess the impi I saw is following us."

Andrew felt a thrill of apprehension, knowing that a party of Zulus might be hunting him. After their defeat at Ulundi, the remnants of any impi would be resentful and desperate for revenge. A stray pair of British soldiers would be a perfect salve for wounded Zulu pride.

"Don't head for the others," Andrew said quietly. "Ride past the ridge without stopping."

"Yes, sir," Kerr said. "The lads will know something's up."

They increased their speed, never riding in a straight line in case the Zulus carried rifles, listened for any unusual sounds, and readied themselves to fight.

"Stop here," Andrew said when they reached a rise topped by a prominent tree. He thought of Elaine's mopane and took a deep breath. "We've no time to fight with Zulus," he said. "Finding Mariana and these renegades is more important."

"We have to be alive to do that, sir," Kerr pointed out.

"Zulu warrior!" Andrew shouted, speaking in Xhosa. "We know you are there. Show yourself so we can talk like men." He heard his voice echo across the undulating countryside as a flock of birds exploded from a nearby tree. "Can you hear me?"

"Why are you in Zululand?" the voice sounded from nearby.

"I am searching for the man who murdered my woman!" Andrew replied. "The war is over." He waited for a response.

"Do you seek Cetshwayo?" The voice seemed to come from right underneath them.

"No!" Andrew replied. "I seek the men who murdered my woman."

"Were they Zulus?" Those three words carried as much menace as any cry of "*Usuthu!*"

"No," Andrew replied, although shouting to an empty landscape was trying on the throat and the nerves. "White men." He saw the fast-closing dust coming towards him and wondered if that was a Zulu impi or his mounted men. "I am looking for a band of renegades that burned my woman's house and murdered her and her family. A white man with two green feathers in his hat led them."

"*Ingwenya!*" the Zulu replied. "The crocodile. A white man with two green feathers in his hat burned my *imuzi* and killed my wives."

"Are you looking for him?" Andrew asked. The dust cloud was closing fast.

"I will kill him," the Zulu replied.

"Then we are not enemies," Andrew said. "That man is Ashanti Smith, and he is my enemy. The enemy of my enemy is my friend."

"I am Jama." The Zulu appeared from three yards away. "This warrior is Ndleleni." Both men were lithe and muscular, with the *isicoco* of maturity. They carried spears and lifted shields from the ground.

"I am Lieutenant Andrew Baird," Andrew said. "This soldier is Mark Kerr."

The fighting men sized each other up warily.

"We fought each other at Isandhlwana," Andrew said. "And Hlobane and Khambula."

Jama nodded. "You killed my sons Kgabu and Funani."

"You killed forty of my men at Isandhlwana," Andrew

countered.

Jama took a pinch of snuff. "We were enemies," he said. "I should kill you."

"That war is over. Now we're searching for the men who killed my woman."

Ndleleni was eyeing Kerr, holding his stabbing assegai underhanded as if ready to strike. "We're all searching for the same man," he said. "We could kill you here or join together to find him."

"Father." Jabulani ran to Jama's side. "This is the man who spared me."

Jama lifted his chin and looked at Andrew. "Why?" he asked curtly.

"He was too young to be a warrior," Andrew replied. "And the fighting was over."

Jama looked from Jabulani's open face to Andrew and nodded.

"Would you trust us to fight at your side?" Andrew asked. "We invaded your country and killed thousands of your people."

Jama smiled without humour. "If you betray us, we will kill you."

"That's fair enough," Andrew said. "But we might kill you first." He nodded to the mounted men who had arrived with rifles held ready.

Jama did not look surprised. "Look again, Lieutenant Baird."

As the horsemen reined up, thirty Zulu warriors trotted behind them, each with his assegai poised.

"Peace or war, Jama?" Andrew asked. "If it is war, we will both lose."

Jama felt Jabulani's hand on his shoulder. "It is peace until we find this man with the green feather in his hat."

Andrew nodded, realising how tense he had been. "Lower your rifles, boys. We have no quarrel with these Abanonya warriors."

Some of his men obeyed, while more were reluctant. Andrew

lifted his revolver, reversed it, and handed it to Jama as a sign of trust. The Zulu accepted the weapon, studied it for a moment and returned it.

"We are at peace with these men," Jama said, and the Abanonya lowered their assegais.

Kerr breathed a long sigh of relief. "What now?"

"Now we find Ashanti Smith, rescue Mariana and get out of Zululand with a whole skin," Andrew said.

"If we can," Kerr said. "Our truce with Jama only lasts until we've dealt with Smith."

"We'll cross that bridge when we reach the river," Andrew said.

JAMA WAS A BETTER TRACKER EVEN THAN KERR AND FOUND Smith's tracks without difficulty.

"This way, Lieutenant Baird." Jama set off at a trot, with his men at his heels and Andrew following. Twice they came to stony ground, and Jama cast around, searching.

"He's lost the spoor," Kerr said.

"Can you see it?" Andrew asked.

"Not a thing."

They watched the Zulus move back and forward, studying the ground, until Ndleleni pointed to a single blade of bent grass and summoned Jama.

"This way," Jama said and cantered away without another word.

"This way," Andrew repeated and followed, with his Dragoons at his heels.

I have lost command of this expedition, and we are in Jama's hands.

"How far ahead are they?" Andrew asked as the evening drew in.

Jama frowned at the question. "Maybe tomorrow," he replied. "We might catch them tomorrow."

"Then what?" Kerr asked.

"Then we kill them," Jama replied.

"I want the man with the green feathers," Andrew said.

"He is mine to kill," Jama told him.

Andrew felt the eyes of Jama's impi on him and knew if he argued, he'd precipitate a full-scale battle between his men and the Zulus.

"We'll have to find him first," Andrew said. *And when we do, Smith is mine.*

Jama eyed Andrew. "We'll find them," he promised.

"I don't know how much we can trust these people," Kerr murmured. "Remember what happened to the 80th Foot at the Intombi."

"I haven't forgotten," Andrew said. He raised a hand to Jama.

"We should camp for the night soon," Andrew said.

"There is sweet water ahead," Jama replied. "You camp on one side of the river and us on the other."

Andrew agreed. "You and I may trust each other, Jama, but our followers may be less controlled."

"How can we trust a nation that invaded our country?" Jama asked quickly.

Kerr stepped forward, gripping his rifle. "The Zulus invaded all their neighbours," he said until Andrew frowned at him.

"We're trying to establish friendly relations, Kerr," Andrew reminded. "You're not helping. Stand back!"

"You didn't grow up on the Zulu frontier, sir," Kerr said.

"No," Andrew said. "I lived on the Scottish-English frontier where we had a thousand years of warfare and slaughter. We managed to make peace, and so will Natal with the Zulus."

When Kerr opened his mouth to object, Andrew pushed him back. "Stand clear, Kerr!"

"Yes, sir," Kerr growled.

Jama watched the interaction, turned aside, and crossed the river with his Zulus at his back.

"Sergeant Meek," Andrew said. "Post three sentries tonight.

One colonial and two British."

Meek had seen Kerr's reaction. "I'll take the first stag, sir."

"I'll take the second," Andrew decided.

Meek nodded. "Yes, sir." He lowered his voice, "We have to forgive the colonials for being a trifle volatile, sir. They've lived in fear of the Zulus all their lives."

"I understand, Sergeant," Andrew said quietly. "Things are changing rapidly."

"Yes, sir," Meek said diplomatically.

They camped for the night, with both parties keeping sentries in mutual distrust and keeping a fire alive. Kerr kept his rifle by his side, with his revolver under the saddle he used as a pillow.

Twice during the night, Andrew heard a lion roar and rose to grab his rifle. Each time he looked across the river, he saw Jama standing with his knobkerrie in his hand, watching him. When Andrew raised a hand in acknowledgement, Jama responded, unsmiling. Ndleleni sat under the shade of a tree, nursing his *iKlwa* and watching over Jama.

Jama's protecting his men, as I am looking after mine. We are not much different, he and I.

"WELL, WE SURVIVED THE NIGHT," ANDREW SAID AS THE MEN woke, yawned, scratched themselves and looked around. The Zulus squatted silently on their side of the river, waiting for the Natal Dragoons.

The combined party moved on, steadily heading north into the north and west of the country, an area disputed between the Boers and Zulus.

"Be careful here, Lieutenant Baird," Jama warned. "The Swazis infest this land, as well as European renegades. The Swazis are not warriors but can be treacherous."

"Thank you, Jama," Andrew replied. "We'll be careful."

They moved on, with the terrain becoming rougher and less cultivated with every mile. The hills were low but well-wooded, and they saw more wildlife, with leopard's harsh barks common and the terrifying roar of lions breaking the sultry heat.

"Here!" Jama pointed to the ground. He knelt with Ndleleni standing at his side, watching the Dragoons.

Andrew nodded to Kerr. "Take a look, Kerr."

"Yes, sir." Kerr dismounted and joined the Zulus while keeping one hand on his rifle.

"The renegades changed direction here," Kerr explained a moment later. "They're heading towards that mountain over there." He indicated a long, densely wooded hill ahead.

"That may be their lair." Andrew consulted his map. "From there, they can strike into Zululand, Swaziland or attack the Boer farms of the Transvaal."

Jama stood up, consulted with Ndleleni, and set off for the mountain. His men followed, showing no signs of weariness although they had been on the move for days.

"The trail is fresh," Kerr said. "It's not more than a couple of hours old. We are getting very close."

"Ride ahead and warn Jama to be careful, Kerr," Andrew ordered. "Smith is a wily man." *Kerr's the only Zulu speaker we have, but can I trust him not to restart the war?*

"Yes, sir," Kerr said and looked up as a rifle shot sounded sharp and clear, silencing the bird life. One of the Zulus staggered and crumpled, dead before he hit the ground.

"I think Smith knows we are here," Andrew said.

He stopped suddenly as the witch's words returned to him.

"Beware of a foe who is a friend and take care of the friend who is a foe." Jama was the foe who was now a friend, and Smith, the friend who had become a foe. *The witch was correct. "Expect grief and loss."* He had lost Elaine and Abernethy. *"You have much blood in your future and a woman who will wait for you."*

All the witch's prophesies have come true. Mariana must be waiting for me. Oh, please, God, let that be true.

CHAPTER 32

Andrew did not have to give an order as his men spread out and dismounted with their rifles held ready. Jama's Zulus had also scattered, with the warriors crouching behind trees or rocks, facing the direction from where the shot had come.

I should have known Ashanti would have guards posted. My carelessness cost that warrior his life.

"Can anybody see him?" Andrew peered forward, searching for tell-tale gun smoke.

"No," Kerr replied.

"Stevens, look after the horses," Andrew said. "Meek, take the right flank; I'll take the left. Now, ease forward and find that guard."

Andrew heard Jama talking to his men, with the Zulus creeping silently through the undergrowth.

After the cacophony of bird song, the silence was eerie. Andrew crouched, moving from cover to cover, hoping not to stand on a snake or scorpion. He ducked as the rifle sounded again, followed by a long scream. A deep voice rose, "*ngadla!* I have eaten!"

Ndleleni rose from behind a mopane tree, with blood dripping from his *iKlwa*. "A Swazi dog," he said casually and wiped the blade clean.

"Those shots will have alerted the others." Andrew fought the doubt that they had followed the wrong group.

"That is true, Lieutenant Baird," Jama said. "I'll send some scouts ahead."

Andrew nodded. "Your men are best for the job," he agreed. He wondered if he, as a British officer, should allow a Zulu induna to take command, then shrugged. Jama knew the local conditions better than he did, and his men moved faster and quieter in the bush.

"How did we ever beat these lads, sir?" Kerr asked as two Abanonya warriors seemed to disappear among the undergrowth.

"We nearly didn't," Andrew said dryly. "Move forward, boys, but be careful." He checked behind him and saw Stevens had knee-haltered the horses to prevent them from straying.

"We're on foot from now on," Andrew ordered. He knew he was losing the better view on horseback, but he was also less of a target.

The trail divided a hundred yards further on, with individual horsemen choosing different routes, so even Jama's men found it harder to follow the main force. The joint force moved slower, jinking left and right, although always heading towards the mountain.

When one of the Zulus hissed a warning, Andrew gestured to his men to halt. He crouched behind a tree, watching a procession of ants march across the trunk, lost in their world. When he heard a rustle ahead, Andrew eased his finger around the trigger of his rifle. Leaves shivered around him, a shadow moved, and Ndleleni appeared behind Kerr with his *iKlwa* in his right hand.

Andrew turned, rifle ready, but Ndleleni gestured ahead, where Jama slid from the shade of a mountain aloe.

"There was one sentry, Lieutenant Baird," Jama said. "Ndleleni dealt with him. There are more ahead."

Jama gave a quiet order, Andrew signalled to his Dragoons, and they moved forward, step by slow step. Andrew held his Martini ready, ignoring the insects that whined and buzzed around his head. He could no longer see a single Zulu or any of the enemy. Andrew felt as if he was alone in the dense undergrowth, a lone human among the insects.

He glanced up, where a pair of vultures circled, with others joining them, watching the ground below in the hope of fresh meat.

These birds know humans are predators, and where we go, death follows. They clean up our mess.

Andrew moved again, sliding towards a man-sized rock, half seen amidst a tangle of vegetation. He heard a shout from ahead and threw himself down.

"*Ngadla*!" a Zulu shouted and then came a fusillade of shots. Andrew stood, glaring ahead as a dozen men broke cover in front of him.

Kerr was only three feet away, although Andrew had not known he was close.

"What's happening?" Trooper Grey asked and fell, choking, as a bullet smashed into his throat.

"Grey!" Andrew shouted. He saw the rising smoke where the shooter was, aimed and fired, with Kerr a fraction faster. They moved forward together, with the other Dragoons following.

As the Dragoons and Abanonya advanced, the defenders melted away, sometimes after firing a final, defiant shot.

What are these people guarding?

Andrew heard a long scream, followed by Jama's voice, rising in triumph. "*Ngadla*!"

He shivered, knowing that sound would haunt him for years.

"Come, Lieutenant Baird," Jama shouted. "The way is clear."

As Andrew moved forward, with the Dragoons at his back,

the Zulus appeared from cover, having removed any threat in their path.

"The horns of the buffalo," Kerr said with a wry smile. "We were the chest moving forward, and the Zulus went around the flanks, surrounded the enemy, and then bang! The end."

Andrew nodded. "I know," he said. "I've seen them in action before." He remembered Abernethy's death at Isandhlwana and that young drummer boy hanging upside down.

No, we're allies now. Think of Mariana and forget the past.

They moved on with Jama's Zulus scouting in front and on the flanks. The hill rose above, nameless on the rough map, rugged, with dense forest covering the lower slopes. Above them, half a dozen vultures circled, waiting for the men to provide them with a kill.

"There," Jama said, crouching behind a tree with his Abanonya spread out on either side. "Can you smell it?"

Andrew twitched his nose.

Kerr nodded. "People and cooking," he said. "People have a distinct smell."

Andrew lifted his field glasses and scanned the mountain. He looked for anything that should not be there, such as a drift of smoke or a flicker of an unusual colour. He stopped, frowned, and handed the glasses to Kerr.

"Under that spur; see what you think."

Kerr looked and slowly nodded while Jama watched.

"I see something," Kerr said. "The ground is worn away halfway up."

"Like a path," Andrew said. He told Jama and handed over the field glasses. Jama looked at them in suspicion and passed them back. He shouted for one of his men, pointed to the hill and ordered him to check.

"Thank you, Jama," Andrew said. He formed his Dragoons into a defensive circle, knowing that Smith was a very wily campaigner.

The Zulu scout returned within the hour, giving Jama a lengthy report.

"What's happening?" Andrew asked.

"The enemy has a camp at the base of the mountain," Jama reported. "Many men, Zulu, Swazi, Basuto and white."

Andrew listened, thinking of such a force of renegades invading Inglenook. He thought about how terrified Elaine and Mariana must have been and what they must have suffered.

"Did your scout see a white woman?" Andrew asked. "A white captive?"

"He did not," Jama replied.

Am I wasting my time and the lives of my men? Did Smith murder Mariana and dispose of her somewhere?

Andrew shook away his doubts. "We'll attack them," he said. "We'll use the horns of the buffalo again."

The Zulu tactics are similar to Wellington's at Badajoz. Put in a frontal attack as a diversion and hit them from the rear,

Jama considered for a moment. "Your men attack from the front, and we'll act as the horns."

"That's what I thought," Andrew said. He respected this tall Zulu with the haunted dark eyes and knew he could grow to like him. "Good luck, Jama."

"Fight well, Lieutenant Baird," Jama responded.

When Andrew held out his hand, Jama looked at him curiously until Andrew explained it was a gesture of trust and friendship.

Jama smiled uncertainly and took the hand, and then they parted.

"We're the chest of the buffalo," Andrew explained to his men. "Jama and his Zulus are the horns. We don't know how many of the enemy there are or what defences they have, but Ashanti Smith is a seasoned campaigner, and his men are desperados, outlaws, and they'll fight like fury."

The Dragoons nodded.

"I don't expect they will grant quarter," Andrew said. "Whatever the outcome, don't leave any wounded behind."

When Jama divided his Abanonya in two and set off through the bush, Andrew waited a few moments.

"We're going in fast and hard, boys," Andrew said. "Shoot first, aim low and guard your backs."

The Dragoons nodded, with some looking understandably nervous.

Andrew checked his watch, closed the cover, and tucked it away inside his tunic. He touched the signet ring he had replaced on his right hand, wondered why his twice wounded leg was beginning to trouble him again and forced a smile. "Right, men. I'll take point. Keep your heads down, shoot to kill and follow me."

Andrew moved forward, crouched low, dodging from cover to cover. He knew Smith would have sentries out and expected the challenge from a man perched high in a tree.

"Halt! Who are you?"

Andrew fired on the sentry's final word, with his bullet knocking the man back from his perch. The sentry hung perilously from the branch for a moment, then plunged, screaming to the ground.

"They'll know we're coming now," Kerr said laconically.

"Increase the speed, boys!" Andrew ordered, reloaded, and pushed on. He heard the crackle of musketry ahead and saw muzzle flares among the trees, with the hideous zip of bullets clipping the branches above. Andrew's men responded, firing at the flashes, and dodging between the trees as they moved on.

Andrew heard a yell behind him and knew the renegades had hit one of his men.

A ragged volley sounded from their front, with the bullets crashing past the Dragoons and thumping into trunks.

"God!" somebody said. "There's thousands of them!"

"Sergeant Meek!" Andrew shouted. "Your section will give covering fire! My section will advance!" It was a drill he had copied from the Mounted Infantry. They moved forward in short rushes, running from cover to cover and firing whenever they saw a target.

Another of his men fell, crumpling without a sound, and Andrew instinctively knew he was dead. A bullet screamed past Andrew's head, smashed into the tree behind him and sprayed him with wood splinters. He ducked and fired, reloading before he saw the result of his shot.

"Halt!" Andrew ordered. "Meek! Advance your section!"

Sergeant Meek moved forward as Andrew's men opened rapid fire ahead. Meek's men moved quickly, ducking behind cover, firing, reloading, and zigzagging forward until they were ahead of Andrew.

"My section!" Andrew yelled and moved again, gradually closing with the renegades' camp.

When a bullet ripped past Andrew's head to burrow into the ground beside his right foot, he flinched and looked upward. Smith had positioned men in the trees, from where they could shoot down at the attackers.

"Damn, but he's good," Andrew said and swarmed up the nearest tree. He heard another crack and saw a bullet slice a long splinter of bark from the trunk an inch from his face.

If they kill me now, who will rescue Mariana?

Andrew positioned himself on the fork of a branch, shuddered when he saw a snake coiling away and concentrated on the renegades. He lifted his Martini to his shoulder, aimed at an enemy sharpshooter and fired. He immediately knew he had hit his target, reloaded rapidly, and searched for more of the enemy.

Two further renegades crouched in the trees, one pointing a Snider towards Andrew. He slid further up the tree to put the man off his aim, brought the Martini to his shoulder and fired.

Andrew immediately knew he had rushed the shot, and splinters flew above the renegade. The man, heavily bearded and with the brim of his hat turned back, grinned, and deliberately aimed as Andrew frantically loaded.

Andrew winced as he heard the sharp crack, and then the renegade stiffened and fell to hang with his left foot trapped in the fork of the tree.

"There's another one, sir," Kerr shouted from below.

"I see him," Andrew replied and aimed at the same time.

The final sharpshooter was a Basuto and was already trying to descend when Andrew fired. The bullet caught him in the shoulder, tossing him backwards. He yelled, dropped his Snider, and began to whimper. Kerr finished him with a shot to the head.

"Come on, men," Fletcher shouted and ran forward. Andrew slid down from his tree, loaded rapidly and joined his men as Meek's section provided covering fire.

With their outer defences breached, the renegades clustered behind a thorn-tipped palisade, waiting for Andrew's men to show themselves in the open space before their camp.

"Wait!" Andrew said. "Keep under cover." The men crouched behind trees and rocks, firing at any defender bold enough to show himself. Smith had cleared the ground for two hundred yards in front of the palisade, making any frontal attack nearly suicidal for a small party of men.

"Keep their heads down," Andrew ordered, thankful his men carried spare ammunition in their bandoliers. He peered at the dense bush around the clearing, hoping Jama was ready to attack.

The defenders met fire with fire, laying down a barrage of shots that ripped through the trees around Andrew's position.

"How many are there, for God's sake?" Meek asked, firing, and ducking down as a bullet tore through the bushes at his side. "They outnumber us, that's for sure!"

"Too many," Kerr said. He lay prone, took careful aim, and fired. "That's one less."

Andrew grunted. *Can I trust the Zulus not to let us down? Jama is probably thinking the same thing about us.*

"I want half the men to lay down fire," Andrew said. "Sergeant Meek, you remain here and cover me. I only want volunteers to follow me."

He took a deep breath, knowing nobody would volunteer. *Sorry, Mariana. I might not live to save you.* "I'll count to five and charge forward."

Up-and-at- 'em Andy indeed. I wonder what my father would have done.

He loaded his Martini, checked his revolver was loaded and loose in its holster and shouted. "Elaine!"

CHAPTER 33

The first shot lifted a fountain of grass and dirt a foot from Andrew's leg. The second shot ripped through his tunic, unsettling him, so he swayed to the side, which caused the third bullet to whine past his ear. At that instant, the wound in Andrew's thigh opened and he staggered, gasping.

"Sir!" Kerr shouted. "Are you all right, sir?"

Fighting the sudden weakness, Andrew nodded and ran on, limping heavily as bullets kicked up the dirt at his feet. His erratic progress might have helped as he saw heads bob up behind the palisade, barrels of rifles and the bright muzzle flares as men fired at him. He jinked from side to side, surprised he was still alive.

That wound might have saved my life.

"Nearly there, sir!" Kerr shouted, and then they were clambering up rising ground towards the base of the stockade. Bullets hissed past Andrew's head to knock splinters from the barrier. He felt blood flowing from his thigh, glanced down and saw his trousers already wet with blood.

I'll have to finish this quickly or I'll be too weak to stand, let alone fight.

"Meek is keeping their heads down," Kerr encouraged.

Andrew nodded, slammed against the palisade, gasping, saw half a dozen men had joined him and thought it miraculous they had crossed the open ground safely.

The stockade was composed of roughly hewn stakes, between eight and ten feet tall and topped with a barrier of thorns. Andrew knew that delay was fatal and threw himself up. Ignoring the thorns that ripped into his hand, he dragged his body over and vaulted to the interior, yelling as pain sliced through his leg. He lay dazed for a second, hearing other men thumping beside him.

A lithe Swazi gaped at him, pointing and shouting. Andrew shot him without compassion, ducked and reloaded, ramming in a cartridge with shaking fingers.

"Mariana!"

Inside the stockade was like any other *imuzi* in southern Africa, with a collection of grass *izindlu* and a couple of more solid-looking European-style buildings. Half a dozen renegades faced Andrew, some armed with assegais and two with rifles.

"Come on then, you bastards!" Andrew roared. "Where's Mariana?" He lifted his Martini, feeling a wave of dizziness wash over him. He staggered, recovered, and forced himself to concentrate as the world seemed to sway.

"*Usuthu*!" Jama yelled and appeared over the barrier at the left, with Ndleleni on the opposite side. The Abanonya cascaded into the encampment, shouting.

Thank God, Andrew breathed with relief, heard a thump behind him and then the sharp crack of a Martini.

"With you, sir," Kerr snarled, reloading.

Other Dragoons joined them, firing at the retreating renegades as the Zulus pushed in from the sides.

"Come on, Dragoons!" Andrew shouted. In such a confined space, his rifle was too cumbersome, so he dropped it, drew his revolver, and staggered forward, gasping at the pain in his thigh.

With the Zulus closing in on the flanks of the camp and the

Dragoons in front, the renegades could either fight or run out the back.

"Fight them!" Ashanti Smith emerged from one of the European-style houses with a Martini-Henry in his hands and two holstered pistols at his waist. Two green feathers adorned his broad-brimmed hat. "Send the bastards to hell!"

"Ashanti!" Andrew roared, limping forward as his vision cleared. "Where's Mariana?"

Even above the cacophony of shots and yells, Smith heard Andrew's shout. He swivelled to face him, lifting his rifle. "It's you, is it? What are you doing here, young Baird?"

"Where's Mariana?" Andrew repeated, pointing his revolver. He saw Ndleleni disposing of a fleeing Basuto with a single thrust of his *iKlwa*, and then Simpson appeared from the door of an *indlu*, staring open-mouthed at Andrew. Simpson hesitated for a moment as a Swazi woman grabbed his arm, then pushed her to the ground and tried to run.

"Simpson!" Andrew shouted, aimed, and fired. He felt the kick of the revolver in his hand and saw the bullet strike Simpson high in the right thigh.

"Don't kill him!" Andrew said as Jama saw the writhing man. "I want to talk to him." Jama ignored the order and plunged his *iKlwa* into Simpson's stomach, ripped it sideways and moved on.

"Where's Mariana?" Andrew stood twenty yards from Smith, swaying as the blood drained from his leg.

"You've changed," Smith said, holding his rifle at hip level. "You were as green as a lettuce when I met you. Now you're a soldier." He ignored the fighting as the Dragoons and Zulus wiped out his renegades.

"Where's Mariana?" Andrew repeated his question, walking slowly towards Smith with the blood squelching in his boot. "You murdered my girl."

Smith smiled. "She fought back," he said. "You flaunted her, Bairdie. You shouldn't have done that. I'll make a bargain with you; let me ride away, and I'll tell you where the sister is."

Andrew felt hatred surge over him as he thought of Elaine and the Maxwell household. About to refuse, an image of Mariana came to him. She was laughing and talking to Lancelot, discussing Tennyson and King Arthur.

"Where is she?" Andrew asked, and lurched to his left as his leg gave way beneath him.

Andrew was a fraction too late to see the triumph in Smith's eyes. Smith raised his Martini and fired at the same instant. Andrew saw the muzzle flare the exact second as Jama's thrown assegai landed in Smith's shoulder, jerking him back so the bullet rose high in the air.

Andrew ducked instinctively as Jama strode forward. Wordless, Jama smashed Smith over the head with his knobkerrie, stunning him.

"You saved my life, Jama," Andrew said. "Don't kill that man. I want to ask him about the missing woman."

Jama plucked his throwing assegai from Smith's shoulder and cleaned the blade. "No, Lieutenant Baird. He murdered my wives and stole my cattle."

Ndleleni stood beside Jama, with the other Zulus gathering, some with blood dripping from the blades of their *iKlwas.*

"I think the strange truce is about to end." Kerr aimed his Martini at Jama as Sergeant Meek and the Dragoons lined up, ready to fight.

"Wait," a hoarse female voice sounded from the nearest *indlu*, and the witch appeared. "Stand back, Jama and the Abanonya!"

Andrew was shocked to see the sudden fear on the proud warrior's faces as all three witches stepped in front of them.

"Put your rifles up, boys," Andrew ordered.

"Sir?" Sergeant Meek sounded worried.

"Do as I say." Andrew holstered his pistol.

The three witches faced Jama.

"Go, Jama," the leading witch said, flicking her gnu-tail wand at him. "Take the cattle from the kraal and go to Cetshwayo. Your job here is complete."

"That man murdered my family." Jama pointed to Smith.

The witch flicked her gnu-tail wand at Smith. "I want him for his bones," she said. "I've been waiting for you, Jama. Go now."

Jama turned, with his Abanonya at his back, and trotted from the camp without another word.

"Witch," Andrew said. "I am looking for a white woman."

The leading witch faced him with her eyes full of age and wisdom. She touched Andrew's wound with her gnu's tail, then pointed at the *indlu* from where she had come.

"The woman has been waiting for you," the witch said. "You take the woman and I take him." She lashed Smith with her gnu-tail. "He has an *abaThakathis* within him and his bones will make strong medicine."

"I want to kill him," Andrew said, as Smith began to stir.

"I need him alive," the witch replied. "We will take his bones while he lives. Take the woman."

"Sergeant Meek," Andrew said. "Take over. Search the huts for renegades and stray Zulus."

"Sir," Meek said, glanced at the witch, saluted, and stepped away.

Ducking under the low door, Andrew entered the *indlu*. The interior was dark, with a small fire giving minimal light, and he heard shuffling in the corner.

"Halloa!" Andrew drew his revolver. "Who's there?"

"Andrew? Is that you?" Mariana crouched in a corner with a bloody bandage over her left hand and her eyes huge.

"It's me," Andrew confirmed, feeling a mixture of relief and worry. "I've been searching for you all over Africa." He holstered his pistol and held out a hand.

"I know," Mariana said.

"How do you know?"

"The witch told me. She told me to have patience and wait, and you would arrive."

Andrew had not heard the witch return, but she crouched in

one corner of the *indlu*. She touched first Andrew and then Mariana with her gnu's tail.

"We won't meet again," the witch said.

"That woman looked after me," Mariana said. "She said my man saved her life, so she would save me for him. All the Africans are petrified of the witches and didn't allow Ashanti Smith to touch me."

"What happened to your hand?" Andrew pointed to the bandage.

Mariana lifted her hand. "I had to pay a price," she said quietly. "I paid one finger, which the witches use for their spells."

Mariana's words were so casual that Andrew knew she was hiding her true feelings.

"Come on, Mariana." Andrew put an arm around her. "You're safe now. You can tell me your story later."

Tears filled Mariana's eyes as she clung to Andrew. "Come friends," she whispered. "It's not too late to seek a newer world."[1]

Andrew held her tight. He had not quoted Tennyson since he had buried Elaine. *We are in a new world now, Mariana and me.* He looked at her fondly as she repeated the phrase while they walked out of the kraal.

"It's not too late to seek a newer world."

What was the newer world he was entering? And was Mariana a part of it? He looked into her dazed, vacant eyes and knew he would be there if she wanted him. He had tried to escape his father's influence, yet his father's advice had kept the witches alive, and they had held Mariana for him. Fighting Jack Windrush was still with him, whether he liked it or not. *One can't escape one's past.*

"Come on, Mariana, let's create our own Camelot."

Mariana looked at him as they limped into the sunlight.

"WHERE ARE YOUR WARRIORS, JAMA?" CETSHWAYO ASKED. "Where are the men of the Abanonya?"

Jama indicated the thirty men at his back. "We are the Abanonya, my king."

Cetshwayo eyed the Abanonya. All carried at least one wound. Their eyes sunk into tired faces, and they were gaunt from lack of food and rest, but all carried their weapons. They were still warriors. "Where are the others, Jama?"

"They lie on the field of Isandhlwana, at Hlobane and Khambula, Intombi and oNdini," Jama said, remembering the raw courage of his Abanonya charging into the smoke. He could name each man and how he fell.

"The witches will cleanse you, Jama, and then go home," Cetshwayo said. "You have given enough. Find a wife and build a new life for yourself. I free you from any obligation to me."

Jama stood up. "*Bayete,* Cetshwayo, *inkosi*. *Bayete*."

As Jama left the king, with Jabulani at his side, Cetshwayo signalled for a woman at the back of the *indlu* to follow him. Thadie smiled and obeyed.

GLOSSARY

abaThakathis - spirits that infest animate or inanimate things.
Amabutho –Zulu regiment
Amaqhawe – young warrior
Amadlozi- ancestral guardian spirits
Amasi – meal of milk curds, a staple Zulu food
Ashantis – tribe and nation in what is now Ghana, West Africa.
Assegai – spear
Bayete – a royal salute
Boer – Dutch speaking settler in South Africa. The name means farmer.
Bundook – rifle, British army slang
Donga – wide ditch, often dry except during heavy rain
IKlwa – Zulu stabbing spear
Imuzi – African homestead, often wrongly termed a kraal
Imizi – plural of African homestead
Indlu – African house, built of locally sourced materials
IniKozikasi- Zulu great wife, often chosen for dynastic or family reasons.
Inkosi – chief or king.
Isicoco - a band of fibre sewn into the hair, coated with gum, polished, and worn as a mark of a married man
IsiDawane - a werewolf or vampire
Isigodlo – king's or chief's private enclosure
isiHlangu – Zulu war shield
Izindlu- plural of African house
Kaffir – nonbeliever; an Arabic word
Kloof – deep ravine
Knobkerrie – Zulu fighting stick with heavy knob at one end
Kop – prominent hill
Koppie – small hill
Kraal – enclosure for cattle
Kranz/Krantz – cliff face or crag
Laager – defensive formation of wagons, perfected by the Boers.
Mealie – maize
Muckle Cheviot – hill on the Scottish – English border
Nek – mountain ridge between two hills
Paythan – British pronunciation of the Pashtun people of northern Pakistan and eastern Afghanistan
Pont – flat bottomed ferry boat pulled across river by means of ropes.

Rooineck – redneck, a term of abuse the Boers used against often sunburned British soldiers.

Spruit – riverbed

Stoep - veranda

Ubaba- father

UmuTsha - a cord around a man's waist from which hung lengths of fur or cowhide.

Umzimbeet – native South African tree

Xhosa – group of related Bantu peoples in Southern Africa

ABOUT THE AUTHOR

Born in Edinburgh, Scotland and educated at the University of Dundee, Malcolm Archibald writes in a variety of genres, from academic history to folklore, historical fiction to fantasy. He won the Dundee International Book Prize with 'Whales for the Wizard' in 2005.

Happily married for 35 years, Malcolm has three grown children and lives in darkest Moray in northern Scotland, close by a 13th century abbey and with buzzards and deer more common than people.

To learn more about Malcolm Archibald and discover more Next Chapter authors, visit our website at www.nextchapter.pub.

NOTES

CHAPTER 1

1. Amabutho - Zulu regiments were known as amabutho and formed of men of the same age. After months of training, they were allowed home and usually reformed only to guard their local area in times of war or for national festivals.

CHAPTER 2

1. *The Charge of the Light Brigade,* by Alfred, Lord Tennyson

CHAPTER 4

1. Quote from *The Charge of the Light Brigade,* by Alfred, Lord Tennyson.
2. *Ode on the Duke of Wellington*, by Alfred, Lord Tennyson.
3. Quote from *The Lady of Shalott,* by Alfred, Lord Tennyson.
4. Quote from *The Holy Grail,* by Alfred, Lord Tennyson.

CHAPTER 5

1. Quote from *Ulysses,* Alfred, Lord Tennyson.

CHAPTER 6

1. Isicoco- a band of fibre sewn into the hair, coated with gum, polished, and worn with pride.

CHAPTER 7

1. Quote from *The Lady of Shalott,* by Alfred, Lord Tennyson

CHAPTER 8

1. *Idylls of the King,* by Alfred, Lord Tennyson
2. *The Lady of Shalott,* by Alfred, Lord Tennyson

CHAPTER 9

1. The Byrne Settlers were immigrants to Natal brought out by the company J. C. Byrne between 1849 and 1851.

CHAPTER 10

1. *The Lay of the Last Minstrel,* by Sir Walter Scott.
2. The transformation occurred in 1879, but I pushed it forward a year for the purposes of the story.

CHAPTER 11

1. *Morte d'Arthur,* by Alfred, Lord Tennyson

CHAPTER 12

1. Cameronians- a Scottish Lowland infantry regiment.

CHAPTER 15

1. From *Idylls of the King,* by Alfred, Lord Tennyson.

CHAPTER 16

1. Rorke's Drift

CHAPTER 24

1. Bundook - Rifle

CHAPTER 27

1. Beresford and O'Toole got the Victoria Cross for the rescue. Originally the award was granted only to Beresford, but he refused the honour unless O'Toole was also granted the medal.

CHAPTER 33

1. *Ulysses,* by Alfred, Lord Tennyson

Printed in Great Britain
by Amazon

34137827R00219